CARA & GIAN

THE COMPLETE GUZZI DUET

BETHANY-KRIS

Published by Bethany-Kris

www.bethanykris.com

Print ISBN 13: 978-1-988197-90-6

Cover Art © Mignon Mykel at Oh, So Novel Designs
Editor: Nina S. Gooden

For Gian and Cara, who inspired a whole army of next generation boys that stole my heart a million times over when writing them.

CONTENTS

UNRAVELED

BOOK ONE

ONE

The most devastating emotion was grief.

All-consuming.

Suffocating.

A horrible, monster of an emotion that embedded its very poison into a person's soul, and didn't let go. Instead of eventually freeing its victim from the never-ending torment, to allow them to step back and breathe, the grief continued to spread and infect like a disease.

There was no healing. There was supposed to be. The stages of grief were eventually supposed to move on to a point where a person could go forward, away from the constant struggle, and begin to heal.

Cara Rossi had yet to find that stage.

She didn't think she would ever reach it.

Her grief had gone far beyond the instant devastation, and straight into a hellish non-existence where no one could possible understand how bereft she was, left in her little world.

There were those people who believed that when a person lost someone they loved, a piece of their soul went with them. Cara wasn't sure how she was supposed to take that statement every time someone offered their well-intentioned, yet incredibly hurtful, advice.

She hadn't just *lost* someone she loved.

Her best friend. The identical face she stared at for everyday of her life since birth. Someone she hadn't spent more than a few hours away from at a time for two and a half decades.

It wasn't a piece of her that was missing. It was an entire *half* ripped away. Twenty-five years together and then … *gone*.

Her identical twin was dead.

Just like that.

But, *it's been four months, Cara.* And, *look at the beautiful day outside, sweetheart.* More of, *she would want you to smile, and to be happy.* A few, *can't you try a little more?*

Four months was a long time to be missing something so incredibly important to Cara's everyday life. It was a long time to be walking around out of control of her emotions, incomplete, alone, and lost.

She had a hard time closing her eyes.

She could see that day.

Perfectly.

Clearly.

Painfully.

When gun fire rang out …

When white marble steps turned red with blood …

When her twin died.

How was Cara ever supposed to move on, when every time she closed her eyes, she was standing back on the steps of that mansion, staring at her sister's blood on her hands, and listening to Lea gasp for help?

She couldn't.

She never would.

"You could always come back to Chicago," Tommas said, posing the suggestion quietly. "I could get you a ticket tonight, Cara."

Cara rubbed at the tension headache beginning to form at the base of her skull, and focused on the words her older brother was saying over the phone. She wasn't sure how to answer without hurting his feelings. The siblings had already been separated by countries for years, only occasionally coming together for family events. Tommas, in Chicago. And Cara, in Toronto, studying at the university.

"The break might be good for you," Tommas continued, when Cara stayed silent. "Chicago isn't Toronto. Things might feel familiar here."

"Chicago isn't home," Cara snapped.

Tommas took a sharp inhale. Cara was even surprised at her outburst, colored heavily with anger. Her brother's silent response was answer enough. Cara wished that she could check her temper toward her brother, but she didn't have anything to give him, but for her anger.

Her brother—more than anyone left living that she loved—knew how she felt about Chicago. Or … her parents.

Or rather, the remaining parent she had left.

Addiction, hate, and pain. That was all their childhood had ever been. It was all that was left in Chicago.

"Ma would like to see—"

Cara stopped her brother before he could even attempt to say more. "I don't give a shit about Ma, Tommas."

Tommas cleared his throat. "She lost her husband. Give her a break, Cara."

"A man she hated. A man she only pretended to love and only when she was drunk. A man she beat on. A man she put first before her children. So, her husband is dead, big fucking deal. I doubt she feels even an ounce of the hell that *I've* been living with for *four months*."

"We don't know what goes on inside Ma's head."

"I don't need to know. Her soul is black. Her heart is black. She should be dead like he is. We would *all* be far better off without them both."

"*Cara*."

The truth hurt, but it was better than a blissful lie. Those hurt worse in the end.

Cara and Lea had been eighteen years old when they'd left. Dual Canadian citizenship and the family ties they had in Ontario got them away from their abusive, alcoholic parents. Tommas, however, had been long gone from the house by the time the twins left.

Tommas also had ties to the Chicago Outfit—a criminal organization that had been bred deep into their family's blood and name for decades— like their father. It was all he knew. Leaving Chicago, and the Outfit, had never been a thought in her brother's mind.

Now, seven years later, Cara was twenty-five, their sister was dead, and nothing was going to ever be the same again. Tommas thought going back where she hated the most, to the people of the Outfit that he called family *and* the place that had taken Lea from her, would fix this.

It never would.

"I'm not going back to Chicago," Cara said after a long stretch of silence.

"Ever?" Tommas asked.

There was no judgement in his tone. He'd asked it with very little emotion, as though he already knew exactly what her answer would be.

"Not if I can help it, Tommas."

Cara waited for those words to sink in, hoping that her brother finally got the point. She loved Tommas, even if their relationship was strained from years of separation and the past. She knew that Tommas loved her, too.

"I don't think you understand how difficult it is to get up in the morning. I pass her bedroom and try not to breakdown. I still have *all* of Lea's things. They litter this apartment from top to bottom." Cara couldn't bear the thought of getting rid of any of it. But she could barely stand to look at it all, either. "The apartment—and even Toronto—is basically the same thing. I struggle daily, to even leave the apartment and get done what I need to do. Every place I visit, all the sights I see, are touched by a memory of Lea. And that *hurts*," Cara said quietly.

There was a lot she didn't say, too.

Her college marks were suffering, her dream of becoming a therapist diminishing with missed classes. Frankly, *she* needed to be the one talking to a therapist, but that meant opening the front door and *going outside*.

It felt like her heart was ripping apart at the seams, the second her hand touched the front doorknob. She was leaving behind the only tangible ties to her sister that were not merely memories.

She was so useless like this.

Broken.

Incomplete.

Without.

"Cara," Tommas said.

The softer tone her brother used brought Cara from the black abyss that was her thoughts. Her new constant companion.

"Yeah, Tommy?"

"I know it's hard—"

"Harder, actually," Cara interrupted.

"I'm sorry. I want to do something to help, but I need you to give me some kind of direction here, Cara. Or *how* to help. What do you need me to do?"

Leave me alone, she thought. *Stop making me remember. It hurts.*

Cara would never say those things to her brother, as they would hurt him.

It had been *his* people who had taken her sister away, even if it hadn't been him, directly, who had pulled the trigger. It was still *the Outfit.* Tommas was an Outfit man. Cara didn't know how to separate Tommas from the organization.

It was dirty money, bad blood, stained histories, and pain.

"Cara?" Tommas asked again.

She took a deep breath and rolled from her side to her back on the bed. A comforting place that she rarely left, now. Slinging her arm over her face, she blocked out the light that filtered in through the blinds.

"Just give me some time," Cara settled on saying.

"Is more time actually going to help, Cara?"

"I don't know."

• • •

Cara stumbled from her bed. The persistent knocking—the bitch of a thing that had woken her up in the first place—continued to echo throughout the quiet apartment.

She'd made it perfectly clear to everyone that she wanted to be alone. She wasn't without family in Toronto. She had her aunt and uncle, a couple of cousins, and a few friends from school.

As for the family side, Cara tried to stay away from their business as much as possible. Unless it was for something she couldn't excuse her way out of, Cara tried not to intrude on their lives. And usually, they didn't intrude too much on hers.

Well, before Lea died. She had seen more of her aunt and uncle since Lea's death than she wanted to admit. She wished they would all go back to the polite greetings and occasional meet ups.

For good reason … It didn't seem to matter where Cara lived, Canada or the USA, she couldn't escape her family's legacy.

The Rossi family—from the Canadian side, all the way to the American—was marked by *crime*. The mafia had weaved itself through her family tree from the very distant members, to her closest relatives. Cara needed distance from her family, and all the rest of the shit that they were involved in, as she always had. Now, though, since Lea's murder *because* of the mafia, she needed that distance even more.

"*Cristo*," Cara swore in Italian as she neared the front door to the apartment. The knocking had yet to cease, and that only kicked her irritation up to another level. "I'm fucking coming, relax."

Cara flicked the deadbolt lock, and yanked open the door with more force than was necessary. She didn't even bother to wipe the scowl off her face. She was not expecting who she found waiting.

Bambi Emmi.

For a long while, Cara simply stared at the young woman until Bambi's usual wide smile faded a bit. In a tight, red dress that fell at her mid-thigh, and complimented her ruby lips and dark hair, Bambi was an exceptionally beautiful woman. Cara, with her crazy, red, curly hair and blue eyes, had never quite felt inferior when standing next to Bambi, though.

Their previous meetings had been passing, brief moments when Bambi's friendship with Lea had managed to involve Cara as well, and politeness was expected.

"Hi," Bambi said, shifting the diamond-studded clutch she held from one hand to another.

Cara said nothing.

She didn't know *what* to say, truthfully.

While she would consider Bambi a friend of sorts, the girl had been much closer to Lea. Despite being close, and twins, the girls hadn't always shared the same likes, dislikes, or behaviors.

Lea had been out-going, making friends wherever she went. Cara preferred to stand off in the shadows and watch people interact in all sorts of situation. To her, that was fascinating. To Lea, interacting and growing her circle had been the interesting part of life.

"So …" Bambi said, drawing the word out for much longer than what was necessary.

Awkward.

Finally, Cara's mouth decided to play catch-up with her brain, and work. All she managed to say was a confused, "So."

Bambi didn't look offended over Cara's lack of response to her presence, never mind her lack of enthusiasm at conversing like a normal human being. No, if anything, Bambi looked happier, her smile growing all over again.

And then Cara had to go and open her mouth to ruin it with, "What exactly are you doing here?"

Bambi's smile vanished instantly, replaced by a hurt dancing over her pretty features. "I'm sorry. Am I not allowed to visit a friend?"

First, Bambi had always been more of a friend to Lea than Cara, for the most obvious reason ... being Bambi's lifestyle. *For lack of a better word,* Cara thought.

She could be brutally honest—Bambi liked her *made* men. Mafia men were just her thing. But the second reason why Bambi should not be knocking on Cara's door?

Cara looked at the clock on the wall. "It's eleven-thirty at night."

Jesus. Was it really *that* late already? Hadn't she been talking to her brother that afternoon?

Well, shit.

Cara had literally slept her day away. She'd missed another round of classes. An exam. An assignment that was due. A lecture.

And she needed groceries.

Fuck.

She was a *mess.*

She didn't even know how to go about fixing it. Or even if she wanted to.

Bambi only stared at Cara as though she had suddenly grown a second head in the span of seconds. "What are you talking about?"

Cara pointed at the clock. "It's late."

"Yeah, if you're fifty."

"I have school in the morning."

Bambi cocked an eyebrow. "Tomorrow is Saturday, and I remember Lea saying once that you don't have classes on Saturdays."

Was tomorrow Saturday?

What was happening to her life?

Cara rubbed a hand over her face. "What do you want?"

"I was in the neighborhood. I thought you might like to see a familiar face."

"You thought wrong."

Cara could have softened that blow, but she didn't have the patience to. Bambi didn't seem all that offended. In fact, she looked as though she had expected that.

"Yeah, seems I'm not the first person you've chased off with your nasty attitude lately. People talk, and others tend to take notice and listen. I know we're not the greatest friends, but your sister looked out for me a lot, and I'd like to think that Lea would be super pissed at me if I didn't offer the same to you."

Cara cleared her throat, more uncomfortable than ever. "I'm fine."

"Well, that's a lie."

"Bambi—"

"You look like shit just came over and took *another* shit on your head."

Ouch.

7

"Okay, that's enough," Cara said, grabbing the door to close it in the woman's face. "It's time for you to go."

"Wait." Bambi put her body into the doorway, effectively stopping Cara from closing her out. "One night, Cara. You can take *one* night to get out of this apartment, away from this …" Bambi waved at the darkness behind Cara. "Whatever this mess is, and do something. Maybe it'll be fun. Maybe you won't have to think for a while. Maybe you'll even smile. What would it hurt to *try*?"

It could hurt *a lot*.

"I'm not even dressed or done up," Cara said weakly.

Bambi smiled slyly, gesturing at herself. "That is why you have *me*."

"I can dress and do my own makeup, thanks."

"And I will be right here to make sure you actually do it. A new club opened up three blocks away, last week. I happen to know the owner is a great guy, and throws an awesome fucking party. Give it a chance."

Cara was too mentally tired to argue. Or maybe it was that she *wanted* to feel normal for a minute. Even if that meant using alcohol and deafening music to do it.

That was that.

"All right," Cara said. "Give me fifteen minutes."

Bambi looked her over. "Twenty, at least."

"You could be nicer."

"You could look less dead."

Bitch.

TWO

"You're looking terribly *miaou* tonight."

Gian Guzzi gave his mother a kiss on her head. "*Mamma*, it's not appropriate to catcall your son. Even when you're doing it in French."

"Am I the first woman to tell you that this evening?"

"I came here from the penthouse. Where would I find a *femme* to catcall me?"

"Well, one would think in your *penthouse*, considering."

Gian chose to ignore that jab, if only because Celeste Guzzi meant no harm. She wished for better things for her two sons and one daughter—happier things. At the moment, Gian was the only one of her adult children that she felt was *not* happy, for a multitude of reasons. Especially at his twenty-nine years of life, she wanted to see more from him.

He could only give what he had.

"I have a club opening," Gian explained. "New suit, one of several, since the season is going to change."

"Armani, I think."

His mother knew her brands well.

Gian smiled. "*Oui*, Armani."

"Give me another kiss before you run off to find your father and grandfather," Celeste ordered, pointing to her cheek, but never looking up from her magazine.

He indulged his mother, bending down to kiss her again before straightening to his full six-foot, four-inch height again. Something else he had taken from the male, Italian side of his family, and not the short, pale-skinned genetics of his mother's Acadian *Français* side.

"And show off that new suit!" his mother shouted at his back.

Gian waved a hand over his shoulder, offering nothing else.

He loved his mother dearly. As a child, he had been enamored with her ability to never fail, never falter. She always wore a smile, and she had loved her husband, unwaveringly, through his many faults. If possible, he would prefer to have a woman like that. Silent strength and steadfast love.

Wishes, however, were not for made men whose lifestyle—one governed by the rules of *Mafioso*—was meant to benefit *la famiglia*, not the individual man. Especially not one like Gian.

As it were, he had been given too much privilege being born with his last name. According to some, anyway.

Gian navigated the halls of the mansion, heading up to the second level where he knew he would find his father and grandfather. Usually, he

9

would meet his grandfather—the boss of their Cosa Nostra *famiglia*—at his home across the city, but tonight had been a change in scenery, for whatever reason.

From all the way down the hall, Gian could already hear the Italian murmurings between a father and son in the office. It never failed to amuse him—or confuse the fuck out of people he brought around as a younger man—that depending on which part of the house a person was in, the language could change. From French, to Italian, to English. Some, like he and his siblings, or his parents, could easily navigate between the three languages without issue in both reading, writing, and conversing.

His half Italian, half French, but fully Canadian family was certainly … colorful.

In more ways than one.

Well, considering the men were criminals and the women were wives of those same criminals, he supposed that led a little credence to the color.

Gian's presence was instantly noticed when he stepped foot in the opened doorway of the office. His grandfather—Corrado—sat in one of the many chairs, while Gian's father stood next to the windows, peering out over the darkness that had settled outside on the massive, private property.

"*Il mio ragazzo!*" his grandfather greeted.

"*Ciao*, boss."

Corrado made a face. "No boss nonsense tonight."

Gian nodded. "All right. I interrupted a conversion, didn't I? The Raptors game, I think. Someone thinks they're going to lose the next one."

Corrado passed Frederic a look. "They've been on a streak. Every time that damn team goes on a streak, they choke."

"Oh, they do not, Dad," Frederic argued. "They're the best basketball team in—"

"*Merda!* You only believe that nonsense because you're attached to the team."

Maybe Gian should have left the conversation lie with his arrival. "Argue about sports on a night when I don't have somewhere to be, huh?"

His grandfather's sharp, dark gaze skipped to him in the doorway, but the irritation was quickly replaced with the sort of mirth only an eighty-five-year-old man could have. Perhaps had it been another made man, and had Gian's tone not been so playful when he spoke, his grandfather might have gotten up from his chair, ready to discipline his subordinate as only a Guzzi Don could.

But it was Gian.

And this was his *Grandpapa*.

He often got away with more than he should.

Gian tried not to abuse his grandfather's affections. Corrado only looked old on the outside, as his mind was still as sharp, volatile, and prone to violence as it had ever been. He didn't let Gian get away with very much when *others* were around.

Others not including Frederic, of course. Gian's father was not a made man like he and his grandfather. Those rules of respect did not apply.

"You're late tonight, Gian. You almost missed me, I was going to head home and go to bed. It's been a long day." Corrado pushed up from the large leather chair, wincing a bit as he stood. "My bones are getting too old to be up this late."

"You will not, Dad." Frederic jumped into the conversation from his spot at the windows. "It's late, you don't need to be driving all the way across the city tonight. You can sleep in the room you like upstairs. The one with the terrace overlooking the backyard."

"I like that room in the spring, when the birds are back from wherever the hell they go for the winter."

"You'll stay here," Frederic said firmly, shooting his father a look. Then, he gave his son a smile. "Did you say hello to your mother?"

"Would she recognize me as her son, otherwise?" Gian asked back.

"Point taken." Frederic finished the last of the whiskey in his glass, and set it on the corner of his desk. "I'll leave you two alone, then. Keep it at a dull roar, Dad. The room upstairs will be waiting when you're done."

"Yes, yes." Corrado waited until his son was gone from the office, and the door was shut, before he spoke to Gian again. "The new club is opening tonight, *sì?*"

"Opened a while back, actually. This is the first night I'm going in to see the place in action. It's fashionable to be late, or so I'm told."

His grandfather chuckled. "Only when a boss is not involved, or …?"

Gian smirked. "Or you are the boss. I know, Grandpapa."

"You have to learn, Gian, even the stupid, small things. Someday, I won't be here to repeat this same, old shit to you every day of your life, and then who will? How will you remember when the time is most important?"

"You're going to be here forever," Gian said, "so what in the hell do you mean?"

"Not forever." Corrado sighed, turning to face the window. "I'm as old as dirt, and you know it. There are too many people who continue to remind me of how old I am, Gian, and how it would be better if I stepped down for—"

"Fuck those people."

A dark laugh escaped his grandfather as he turned back around. "Yes, what you said."

Unfortunately, what his grandfather said had a lot of merit. Most Cosa Nostra bosses did not live long enough to see eighty-five. Never mind the fact that Corrado had already held his position for forty-five years. Bosses usually retired their seats before their age started to become too prevalent, as no good made man wanted to be seen as weak or senile to his men.

And now, their *famiglia* had gotten to a point where there were, at times, three generations sitting around the table with a voice wanting to be heard. His grandfather's generation, men of his father's age, and then their sons, too. Younger made men who didn't get much of a voice.

Gian didn't fall entirely into the *young* Capo category, considering he was his grandfather's underboss with his own seat at the table, but he understood and sympathized with their frustrations.

"Well, I'll send you off then, since there's nothing to chat about that can't wait until morning," his grandfather said, passing him by with a clap on the shoulder.

"My evening is never as important as you are. I can wait."

"It's fine, just the usual nonsense with the men. I was thinking maybe we could work to erase some of the lines between the generations if we sat down and talked about it, but it can wait until tomorrow. Enjoy your evening, Gian, and *behave*."

Gian scoffed. "I behave."

"Define that word, and then we'll talk."

Corrado was already leaving the office. Gian followed behind his grandfather, only separating at the stairs, where Corrado went up, and he went down to the bottom level of the wing. He expected to leave, as his visit was over, but he found his father waiting at the front door, and nursing another glass of whiskey.

Frederic didn't see his oldest son approach, and for a moment, Gian was struck at how young his father looked in the dim light of the hallway. It was almost like looking into a mirror, although an older one.

All the men in his family shared the same dominant traits—a strong, squared jaw, brown eyes with gold flecks, a nose with a straight, sharp slope, and lips that, even when not smiling, almost seemed to be pulling into a grin of some sort, just from their shape alone. Even their hair was the same dark brown, from his youngest brother Domenic, to their grandfather. Gian wore his hair slightly longer, leaving a bit at the top to be styled if he wanted, while keeping the sides sheared short.

"He didn't keep you up there long," Frederic noted.

"You know how he is."

"I do."

Something in the lilt of his father's tone caught his attention, and not in a good way.

"What is it?" Gian asked.

"Corrado needs to slow down, Gian."

"I'm aware. Tell him that."

"I have, and so have his doctors."

Gian's brow knotted together. "Pardon? He won't go to his doctors for more than a checkup or a flu shot."

Frederic glanced down the hall, behind Gian, as though he were looking for someone to be standing there. No one was. "He's not going to tell you, if he didn't tonight."

"Tell me what?"

"That he's not well. Some strange results showed up in his bloodwork. He went in a month ago to have another round of tests."

"He didn't tell me about any tests."

His father sighed, tipping his glass higher for another sip. "I think he tells no one. I know because I'm the surviving son, I *need* to know."

Gian didn't like where this was going. "What is it, then? What's wrong?"

"Colon cancer, it seems. Aggressive. He's supposed to start treatment within the week, but you know how he is."

Corrado wouldn't put himself in any situation that would give another made man in the organization a chance to point at him and call him weak— *unable*. This would do that, entirely. But not getting aggressive treatment would mean certain death, wouldn't it? If the cancer was already at an aggressive stage …

"Does it matter if he gets treatment?" Gian asked quietly.

Frederic's gaze dropped to the floor. "It'll give him a bit more time."

"Be specific."

"A year or two, with treatment. Six months, maybe, without."

Fuck.

Fuck.

Gian grimaced as pain shot its way through his whole body all at once.

"I'm sorry, Gian," Frederic murmured.

He loved his family. It was what Italians *did*.

But his grandfather?

It was far more than love. It was respect, and an adoration that had followed Gian since he had been a young boy under his grandfather's feet. His relationship with his grandfather had always been different. Sometimes difficult, always strong, and never wavering.

"I … don't know what to do," Gian said lamely. "Do I bring it up to him or no?"

"It's up to him, either way. He's eighty-five; he's old and wise enough to make this choice. Don't ask him, or tell him you know, if he doesn't bring it up to you first."

"Yeah, I got it."

He didn't like it, but he understood. Apparently, like his grandfather, Gian was supposed to simply pretend nothing was wrong. And in six months, when it all went to shit, where would that leave him?

Gian didn't know.

"Try to forget about it for the night. You're young, Gian, and he knows that, which is probably why he didn't want to upset you tonight. I'm not like him, though, and the longer you were made to wait before being told, the angrier you would be. Enjoy your time, deal with the rest another day."

His father's words seemed simple enough. That didn't mean they would be easy to follow.

• • •

Gian bypassed the line at the front door of the new club—*Danza*—and went in through a back entrance where he had a man standing guard. He nodded a greeting to the enforcer as the man stepped aside, and held the metal door open.

"Busy, Raul?"

"Packed full, boss."

Always respectful.

Always appropriate.

It was the little things, like calling an underboss "boss" whenever the actual boss wasn't around, instead of his name. Made men appreciated those things *and* remembered when it was time to give a man his *in* to the family. Although, Raul had been given his button years ago.

Gian clapped the guy on the shoulder. "Good. I won't be long, and then you're free to do what you want for the rest of the night."

"Thanks, boss."

Gian moved through the back hallways that were used for storage, and then up the spiral staircase that led to the offices. One for the manager, and one for his personal use. He didn't run the club full-time, but it was nice to have a place to hide away if the need arose.

Waiting papers rested on his desk, and Gian quickly flipped through what the manager had left for him. He tossed the papers aside again before moving toward the one-way mirrored windows that covered a whole portion of one office wall. He surveyed the people down below, looking for faces he recognized in the crowd.

Only a couple stood out.

But it was a couple of faces he gave a shit about, too.

Stephan Zito and Constantino Rossi sat in the sectioned off VIP area of the club at a circular booth that allowed their backs to be at the wall, while their fronts faced the crowd. Both were Capos for the Guzzi Cosa Nostra, though Constantino was closer to Gian's age, while Stephan was nearing his mid-thirties.

Gian put up with Stephan for the sake of respect, but otherwise, he didn't have a lot of patience for the guy. Constantino, however, had been one of the few men Gian had grown up with—a friend from childhood. Those were hard to find *and* keep in their world.

It was too damn bad that Constantino enjoyed Stephan's company a lot more than Gian did.

Gian brushed off the irritation at seeing Stephan in his club, his gaze passing over the other people sitting in the booth with the two men. An enforcer for both Capos sat opposite to them at the booth, and a familiar woman sat beside Stephan.

Bambi, Gian thought her name was. Stephan's *goomah*.

The guy was not very quiet about the mistress he had, not that it was exactly required for him to be so. Made men were a lot of things, but faithful didn't have to be one of them. Especially, if their wives didn't make too much of an issue out of it.

Gian's gaze skipped to the woman sitting on the other side of Constantino, her red hair—a fiery ruby shade that was almost shocking under the lights of the club—set in perfectly-managed curls fell halfway down her back. That was all he could see of the woman, but guessing by the way she kept her body angled *away* from Constantino, she was not his date.

Gian wondered who she was, or rather, how she had gotten into his VIP section with made men. He planned to find out.

Five minutes later, the bouncer at the roped-off section of the VIP area stepped back to allow Gian through. On the way, Gian had grabbed a glass of whiskey at the bar, the one drink he would allow himself for the evening. It didn't look good for a man to be drunk and acting foolish, even in a place he owned that was meant for drunken foolishness.

"Gian!"

A smile split Gian's lips at his oldest friend's shout. Constantino was already pushing his way out of the booth, offering little more than a fast apology to the redhead sitting beside him.

"You're late," said his friend.

"The boss called. I sent you a text and said I had to run over to Ma's."

That was all he gave as an explanation.

Constantino didn't ask for more.

"Well, you're here now and—" Constantino's words cut off as his gaze fell on someone in the crowd over Gian's shoulder. His eyes narrowed, and Gian knew then that whoever his friend had recognized was about to wish that Constantino hadn't seen him. "He owes me a grand, that fucking cocksucker."

"All right, try not to break anything while you're in here, huh? Keep any blood spills to a minimum."

Constantino flashed a grin. "For you, always."

"Yeah, yeah. Play nice."

"Whatever you say."

He smacked Constantino hard in the back of the head as the guy walked past him, dark laughter escaping him as he ducked an incoming swing from his friend.

"You're getting slow, *cafone*," Gian taunted, his back now facing the booth that Constantino had come from. "You're supposed to be the young one here."

"Give me fifteen minutes," his friend shot back. "We'll see how slow I am."

Then, Constantino was gone, disappearing from the VIP section and off into the swelling crowd of people.

"I see you finally climbed off your grandfather's dick long enough to show your face around here, Gian," came a voice from behind him.

Gian stiffened, his teeth grinding. Reason number *too-many-to-count* why he hated Stephan Zito.

Turning slowly, Gian faced the grinning Capo at the booth, paying no mind to the other people at the table. "Do you want to try that again, Stephan?"

"No, I think I got it right the first time."

"Do you? Think really hard, now. You've got some time."

"Well—"

"Because I'm pretty fucking sure that to you, his name is *boss*, and nothing else. And if we're going to be talking about climbing on dicks, I'll let you take the lead on that one, since you seem to have quite a grasp on which man likes which dick the best. You're the only one speaking up about it, anyhow."

Stephan's face reddened.

Gian only smiled.

"Stephan, grab me another one of these, would you? They're delicious."

Bambi's high voice broke the staring contest between the two men, making Stephan look to his *goomah's* hand, where she held out an empty martini glass. The girl was smart; Gian had to give her that. It was not the first time she had stepped in to divert her man's attention and kept him from getting his face broken.

Made men didn't fight. It was against every rule Gian knew. He'd break that one for Stephan, if pushed the wrong way.

"Yeah, sure, babe," Stephan said, grabbing the glass. "Pretty sure that's what the fucking servers are for in this place, though."

Stephan was pushing out of the booth and heading past Gian without a look back.

Gian couldn't help himself.

"Grab me another drink, too, Stephan," Gian said at the man's back.

Stephan's steps hesitated, and Gian could almost hear the man's refusal trying to force its way out. The guy wasn't entirely stupid, and kept walking. Underbosses trumped Capos, after all. Stephan didn't have to like Gian when the rules came into play.

"You could try not to antagonize him as much," Bambi said quietly.

Gian turned to face the woman again. "Like he does for me?"

"That's just Stephan's ways."

"And those ways will eventually get him killed."

Bambi frowned, but wisely chose not to respond. Then, she turned and said something to the woman at her side but a couple of seats away in the booth, drawing Gian's attention there.

To the redhead.

A woman he *thought* he hadn't known from Adam. She had been so quiet at the table, her attention on the few people at a booth across the way from theirs, and not making a spectacle of herself as Stephan had done for him and Bambi. It suddenly made sense then why Constantino had not been treating the girl as a disinterested date.

It was his cousin, or rather, one of them.

At first, Gian thought *Lea Rossi*. But his mind quickly corrected that, as Lea Rossi's death—an event that had been widely publicized, due to the nature of the murder—had happened months ago. He only knew *of* the Rossi twins, as their uncle was an older Capo for the Guzzi *famiglia*.

Gian had met Lea Rossi on a scarce few occasions when their paths crossed for different events or whatever, but he had never sat down and had an actual conversation with the girl. He had been told by Constantino—the twins' cousin—that the twins lived in Toronto.

He knew Lea had a twin. He did not realize her twin was *identical*.

That red hair of hers that had been so striking under the club lights from up above, was even more stunning close up. A shade that a woman couldn't buy in a bottle, and couldn't quite be duplicated in a salon.

A black double-wrapped velvet choker rested around her throat, showcasing tanned skin and the delicate line of her neck. A simple bow was tied at the middle, making Gian wonder what she would look like with the choker on, looking up from her knees.

He wasn't quite sure where that idea came from, but it was a good one.

Cara, he thought her name was. Wasn't that what Constantino had said before about his cousins—Lea and Cara.

Gian didn't pay attention to names, unless it served him some purpose to.

Her ice-blue eyes looked him over, and Gian was taken aback by the lack of makeup on her pixie-like features. Most woman put too much makeup on instead of too little, determined to make a man focus on attributes instead of imperfections. But all she wore was just enough to shape her wide eyes, and a red tint on her full lips that matched the color of her hair.

From what he could see, her tight black dress fit to her curves perfectly, and guessing by the way she crossed her legs out to the side, she was not a short woman.

Beautiful.

Natural.

Sexy.

All of that and more came to mind.

"You stare a lot, don't you?" the woman asked.

Gian came out of the daze with a bang. "Am I not allowed to stare?"

Bambi glanced away from the two, hiding her smile. "I think I'll go find Stephan and see what's taking him so long."

Do that, Gian wanted to say.

He said nothing until Bambi was gone. The two men left at the booth, quickly followed her lead, leaving Gian alone with the beautiful redhead. He didn't sit, though, simply stayed where he was.

"It's Cara, right?"

She glanced up, her blue eyes widening further. "How do you know my name?"

Gian smirked. "Family friends."

"Right." Cara flashed him one of her own smiles. "It's Gian, right? Gian *Guzzi*."

He lifted a single brow. "My name is well-known around this place."

"The owner—I know. Constantino told me."

"Oh?"

"And Guzzi isn't exactly a … little name, either."

"Would you like a drink, Cara?"

She didn't even think about it before saying, "No."

"A dance?"

"No."

"Then why are you here?" Gian lifted a hand, waving at the club behind him. "That's sort of what you do in a club, *bella donna*."

"I do speak some Italian."

"Good, then you know what I think of you. A very beautiful woman."

She did manage a smile that was slightly truer than her first. "You're terribly arrogant. Flash a smile, say a few pretty words, and I bet most women eat out of the palm of your hand."

"The men of my family like to say it's a learned talent, actually." He grinned, and didn't miss how for a moment that Cara was silenced by the sight. "And as of right now, I'm not trying any of those things on you."

"How do you hold all that cockiness and those damn grins in then?"

"I don't."

"And everyone melts."

"I'm not looking at everyone. I'm looking at you."

Cara laughed lightly, a sweet sound that helped to light up her pretty features. "Smooth, Gian."

"That was nothing, only the truth. But seriously, if you don't want a drink, you don't want to dance, and you don't have a date ..." Gian left that one hanging for Cara to finish for him.

"No date, either."

"Then what are you doing here?"

"I wanted to feel normal for a night. Not so suffocated, I guess, or out of control. Also, someone showed up at my place and wouldn't take no for an answer."

Had someone else said those words, Gian might have been confused. He thought, considering this woman had recently lost someone important in her life, that her statement made a hell of a lot of sense.

"Your sister—your twin." Her lips turned into a frown, a question in her stare. He quickly added, "Her face was all over the news, and Constantino is a very old, and good friend of mine."

"Huh."

"That's what you meant, though, isn't it?"

Cara shrugged. "I'm supposed to be having fun, not being sad tonight."

Gian knew better than to engage Cara in any more conversation than what he already had done. He certainly didn't have the time to invest to be interested in the woman, never mind struck by her unassuming beauty. It would be different, if he wanted nothing more than a quick ride and little else from a woman, but in that moment, he wasn't looking for that, either.

He *was*, of course, but not right then. Cara was still sitting, staring at him, and waiting. He wouldn't usually bother to talk at all.

"Are you going to sit?" Cara asked.

He knew better.

Gian took a seat in the booth when Cara moved in farther.

Knowing better meant *nothing* to Gian.

THREE

Cara wasn't entirely sure how she had gotten tucked into a booth at a club with a man that she had no business talking to.

It wasn't that Gian Guzzi was off-putting. In fact, he was the exact opposite. Cara was sure the man knew exactly how he came across to those around him, and had no qualms about using it to his advantage.

Charming.

Gorgeous.

Sharp lines, dark eyes, a chiseled jaw, carefully styled hair, and that was only the *surface*. That was what he greeted a person with at first glance. It was the second glance, and then the third, that Cara was sure won a woman over. He brought out the Italian pet names, and then murmured a quick line in French with such perfect precision that it was simply shocking. Tan skinned, a three-piece, fitted suit that showcased his athletic form, a smile that surely made most women weep, and an attitude that begged for attention.

Cocky, even, with his smirks and fast replies that took Cara off guard.

Confident.

As his brown gaze had turned on her, the rest of the club had ceased to exist to Gian. He talked to *her*. He looked at *her*. He interested *her*.

Cara wasn't quite sure what to make of that.

She had been so stuck in her own head for four months, that for the first time when she decided to pop back out of it and say hello to the world, it happened to be Gian Guzzi waiting there to greet her.

Gian with his fucking suit.

Gian with his goddamn grins.

Gian looking at only her in a club full of beautiful women.

Cara wouldn't deny that it was something she liked.

There was something she liked about Gian. She didn't know what to make of it all.

Cara was not stupid. She recognized the surname Gian sported—Guzzi—and knew exactly what it meant, even if she didn't know him personally.

She knew enough, like the fact that having that last name meant Gian was no doubt involved in things she avoided. In her efforts to stay away from the mafia, she could blame her success for the reason why she didn't know anything about Gian.

She didn't know what to blame for her attraction.

"You're staring," Gian said.

Cara's gaze moved up from the slight scruff on Gian's throat to the pleased curve of his lips, and then to his eyes. "So are you, apparently."

His grin only widened. "I'm not trying to hide mine, though."

"Fair enough."

"Still can't interest you in a drink, can I?"

"I try not to drink socially, and only on very special occasions. I do like a good beer or glass of wine, occasionally, but I don't indulge often."

Gian lifted a brow high. "Why's that?"

"Alcoholic parents."

She usually wouldn't offer too much information about her history or childhood under the feet of her drunken, neglectful parents, but she found it easy to say to Gian.

Gian took the information in stride, saying, "That's a good reason, then."

"I thought so."

"I could order something … virgin," Gian suggested.

"Kind of a waste, isn't it?"

Gian laughed, leaning into the booth and tossing an arm over the back, behind Cara. Normally, she would have moved, seeing the gesture for what it was—a move to get closer to her, nothing more—and that would have shut down any further advances.

Cara didn't do that.

She rather liked how relaxed and confident Gian looked at her side, his arm resting behind her, and his gaze never leaving her.

"I'm *not* the only woman in this club, Gian," Cara said.

"I'm aware."

"You keep looking at me like I am."

"Is that a bad thing?"

No. "Unsettling, maybe."

"Unsettling, or gratifying?" he asked. "Because I've come to learn that things we find unsettling can often end up being quite gratifying, too."

Cara wet her lips, and didn't miss how Gian's gaze dropped to watch her do that, either. "How thick are you rolling out the charm right now?"

"Not even a little bit, but I doubt you would believe me on that end."

"I do find it hard to believe."

He learned forward, close enough for Cara to get another whiff of whatever spicy cologne he wore, and his grin disappeared. Seriousness clouded his features, and suddenly, the interest she had thought he hadn't been hiding, bloomed in his eyes. It told her that as much as she thought Gian was showing all his cards, he was keeping a few hidden.

"My charm gets me immediate results, and I use it when that's what I'm looking for." Gian's fingers lightly grazed the bare skin of Cara's shoulder, and she damn near jumped at the touch, shocked at the jolt of heat that flooded her. "I didn't have any intentions of leaving with someone when I came into the club tonight, and I still don't. That doesn't mean I don't want to, especially with you, it just wasn't in my intentions."

Cara sucked in a quiet breath at his candor. "So, I don't get the charm, then?"

"Oh, no, you've got the charm. And then some. I may have lied a bit there. But I'm still sitting here, and so are you, because at the moment, this seems far more interesting than sending you off with a smile. Although, you *are* smiling, and I wonder how long it has been since you did that … considering?"

She glanced away, the dull ache of her lingering grief settling deep into her heart again. Whatever smile she had been wearing quickly fled, and Cara felt the weight of her pain come down to sit on her shoulders again.

Gian's fingers slipped under her chin, and Cara found herself looking back in his eyes. "Sorry, I didn't mean to make you sad."

Cara laughed weakly. "I'm always sad, now."

"Actually, earlier, you said out of control, if I remember correctly."

"That, too."

"I'm sure it feels like that, but trust me when I say, feeling out of control should not leave you sad."

"No?"

"That's not what being out of control is, *bella*. Losing control is … a freedom, something you can't get with any other experience because it's one of a kind, Cara. Grief is a weight that you can't get rid of, not right away. Freedom is weightless."

She liked the way he said her name. His interesting inflection to his words—likely caused by his ability to speak Italian and French—made her name sound far more interesting than it actually was.

Like him, she thought, *one of a kind*.

"One of a kind" fit Gian, given what he seemed like, in those moments with her. A man who was more interested in talking and being near her, than getting her to the closest flat surface simply because he liked the way she looked. She assumed that, if given the chance, he would probably take an offer to fuck, but she didn't think for even a second that it was first on his mind.

Then, he glanced to the side, his gaze narrowing at the sight of a couple returning to the VIP section and heading toward their table.

"That," Gian murmured, "is my goodbye for now, unfortunately."

Cara tried to hide her frown, but failed.

Bambi and Stephan were returning, it seemed.

She didn't know where in the hell Constantino had gone to.

"Here, your drink." Stephan set the whiskey glass down forcefully, spilling a good tablespoon of the spirit on the table. Gian offered Cara another brilliant smile. "I've decided I'm not in the mood for it, now."

"You asked for—"

"Cara," Gian said, "I know that it's a no on the drink, but my other offer is still open, if you're interested. My interest here, however, is fading fast."

It took Cara a minute, long enough for Gian to stand and leave the booth, before she realized what offer he meant. She watched him disappear into the crowd, trying to decide if she wanted to take him up on it.

"What offer was that?" Bambi asked.

Stephan grunted something under his breath as he sat down at the booth again.

Cara ignored them both, and decided to go for it.

What would it hurt?

Maybe Gian had a point.

Maybe being out of control—or even refusing to be swallowed whole by her grief for a short while—was actually meant to be a *good* thing.

"Cara?" Bambi asked. "Are you leaving, or …?"

"A dance," Cara replied, grabbing her coat. Gian had been *far* more interesting than what she was leaving behind. "I think I'd like to dance."

That had been Gian's offer, after all. A drink or a dance. Whatever came of those things—or after—had not been talked about really. She only needed to find him.

Cara figured the rest might be worth it.

The club was far bigger than Cara first realized when she'd come in with Bambi, and she was starting to think, after ten minutes of walking around, that she wouldn't be able to find Gian.

"You look lost, *mon ange*."

Cara had gotten lost in the swell of people in her effort to find Gian. It seemed she hadn't needed to look hard, because he had found her.

"What does that mean?" Cara asked, spinning around to face a grinning Gian. "My French is non-existent, and my Italian can be a bit rusty."

"It sounded good, didn't it?"

Cara cocked a brow. "That isn't what I asked."

"No, but it *is* what matters. Do you want that dance, Cara?"

"I came to find you, didn't I?"

"You did."

And just like that, Cara found herself pulled closer into Gian's body and at the same time the loud, fast music changed to something slower. Not quite slow enough that it required a waltz of any sort, but rather, a grinding, deep bass that vibrated the floors under her heels.

Gian led them into the dance, his hands slipping under Cara's jaw to tilt her head up while her body moved instinctively closer to his. She wasn't much of a dancer, but she knew how to move her body, and it wasn't all that hard to match the rhythm of his dancing. With her face in his hands, she was forced to stare at him, taking in all of those lines and gorgeous features, under flashing lights as he kept watching her.

Cara hadn't drunk a drop, but she still felt light on her feet.

Dazed, even.

It was strange and wonderful at the same time.

She had never been quite so attracted—never so fast or easily—as she found herself to be with Gian, for whatever reason. He made it easy. She forgot about the people.

Cara only saw Gian.

He didn't look away from her, either.

"I want you to leave," Gian said, "and spend the night with me."

He didn't even *ask*.

Cara liked that he was of the type to simply state his desires, not dance around them until the truth spilled out. He clearly didn't play games. Maybe he was the kind of man who always won, no matter what.

"Cara," he pressed.

"I don't usually do that sort of thing."

She had before; she didn't make it a habit, though.

"But will you, Cara? If you really want to know what it feels like to be out of control, you've met the right man to get you there, but you have to say yes."

Let go for a night, her mind demanded.

"Yes," she said before thinking better of it. "I will."

• • •

"Just so we're clear on something, before we get to my place," Gian said from the driver's seat.

Cara hadn't entirely heard him, as she was too busy watching the street pass her by.

"Huh?"

Cara glanced over at Gian as the Lexus slowed for a red light. His gaze caught hers, he flashed a grin, and then he was leaning over before Cara even knew what happened. The kiss came fast, stunning Cara momentarily. Something wicked, sweet, and hot curled in her stomach and shot down between her thighs.

She forgot they were at a red light as Gian's lips moved against hers, slow and languid, yet still rough and demanding at the same time. She wasn't quite sure how he did that, kiss her softly, yet managing to take her breath away with the gentle nip of his teeth to her bottom lip. The slight stubble on his jaw left the best sensation on her softer skin. His tongue warred with hers, a lingering taste of whiskey blooming over her taste buds before it too was gone, and so was his kiss.

The car lurched forward as Gian leaned back into his seat, that grin of his still firmly in place. The light had turned green again. "Pay attention to me now."

Cara swallowed hard. "You're very good at distractions."

"So I've been told."

"What was that you were saying—about knowing something before we got to your place?" Cara glanced out the window, thinking it would help to clear the haze. "Let me guess, don't snoop, and be out before morning. I can do that."

Gian laughed, drawing Cara's attention back in an instant. "Not even close."

"Oh?"

His gloved hand—covered with black leather driving gloves—found her thigh, slipped high enough to disappear under the skirt of her body-con dress, and then grabbed tight. Cara's muscles jumped at the sudden touch, but somehow, she didn't move otherwise. It had grounded her.

Then, his hand moved higher, his pinky stroking over the lace covering her sex.

Cara needed air.

Badly.

"You can leave whenever the hell you want, but while you're with me, there's only one thing that matters. This is mine for the night," Gian said, his pinky stroking along the seam of her lace-covered pussy again. She shuddered under the pressure of the touch, surprised at how her body reacted to such a simple thing. "It's mine. When and how I fuck it, and how many times I make you come tonight—that's all mine. Understood?"

His grin had turned sexier under the dash lights.

"Cara?" he pressed.

God, she really needed that air.

"Understood."

Or, she'd figure it out.

Apparently, Gian intended to start teaching her *right fucking then*. His hand came back out from between her thighs, and he flipped his palm up on her lap. "Unclasp the wrist for me and pull the glove off, would you?"

"Why?"

"You'll see."

Cara did as he wanted, setting the driving glove aside. Once the item was out of his way, Gian's hand was back up under her skirt, his fingers slipping under her panties, while his other hand stayed firmly on the wheel. His gaze stayed on the road, too.

First it was a simple stroke of his fingers—testing and feeling along her folds. Then, it was two of his fingers sliding fast into her pussy, the sound of her wetness sucking his fingers in deeper as her inner walls clenched around the intrusion.

How was she *that* wet already?

"Damn," Gian said, the edges of his lips curling with satisfaction, "you're soft like silk, *Tesoro*. And soaked, too. Tight as fuck." His fingers slipped out of Cara's sex with a slowness that damn near killed her, before the very tips found her clit and started working the nub with quick, rough circles. Cara let out a hard breath at the change in sensation, her legs tightening to his hand. Never once did Gian look away from the road. "Has it been a while?"

She did not want to answer that question.

Her mouth worked before her brain did.

"Too long."

"Has anyone ever made you come in a car, going twenty over the limit, in the dark, on the highway, Cara?"

Were they on the highway, now?

Cara's eyes flew to the windshield, finding, *yes*, they were, and she had somehow missed them turning off onto it. She checked the dash, too, noting the speed—twenty over the limit.

His fingertips pressed harder against her clit, making it throb, and Cara stuttered on her next breath. "Holy fuck."

"I quite like hearing my name on your mouth, so try again." As he spoke, he stopped working her clit, and filled her with two fingers instead, widening the digits as he thrust them in. Those wet sounds echoed as he fucked her with slow, measured strokes, each time widening his fingers, dragging them against her walls. "*Try again, Cara.*"

"You're trying to kill me, Gian."

"No, I'm just taking away what you think is your control."

He flashed her with a wicked smile.

His fingers curled against her G-spot on the next thrust.

She came harder than ever.

• • •

Cara's head tilted back as an orgasm raced through her bloodstream and the elevator dinged, the doors opening. Gian's hand slipped out from the back of her skirt like he hadn't been doing a thing to her the entire ride up to what he said was his penthouse.

Her legs were weak.

Her pussy was wet, sensitive, and *needy*.

Her body was hot as fuck.

She took a couple deep breaths as Gian stepped forward, leaving the elevator with a wink over his shoulder. "You're so wet that you left a spot on the arm of my jacket." He lifted his hand, waving the two fingers he'd had stuffed up her pussy as they rode the elevator up to his penthouse. "Not that I mind. It was kind of my fault."

Jesus.

That was damn dirty.

And he'd said it without even a *grin*.

"Are you coming in?" he asked.

Cara nodded, stepped out of the elevator, and kicked her heels off as she looked up. Vaulted ceilings and a beautiful brass and crystal chandelier stared back at her. It was a stunning sight, as most penthouses didn't have cathedral-style ceilings, never mind a bachelor's place. The place was very white—the floor, the walls, and the decoration. All white, yet it made it bright, open, and inviting.

"Wow," she said to herself.

Gian chuckled, hitting a button on the wall that forced the elevator to close. "Admire in the morning. It's my turn tonight."

"Your turn, huh?"

Gian took his time removing his shoes and suit jacket, putting the items away, along with Cara's things. She toyed with the velvet choker at her throat as he checked his cell phone, then put it away with his other things as well.

Then, his attention was back on her.

Entirely.

Fully.

Unwaveringly.

Cara was frozen in place while Gian moved closer, taking his steps slow until he was close enough to pull her in the rest of the way. His one hand slid under her jaw, tilting her head up to look at him while his other slipped lower. She sucked in a sharp breath when his hand skipped under her skirt for the *third* time, only, instead of fucking her with his fingers until she came, he pulled the panties down around her thighs. The article fell the rest of the way to the floor on its own.

"You don't need these, sweetheart."

The second time he kissed her was nothing like the first had been in the car. It wasn't slow or languid, but rough and demanding. Cara barely registered the zipper on the back of her dress being pulled down, not with how Gian's tongue seemed to tangle with hers in a way that made her wish it was working between her thighs. He had quite a talent with that tongue of his, and she wondered what it would take to get him to put it to use.

He made quick work of pulling her dress down, letting the top half pool around her waist as he exposed more skin. The penthouse was warm, as far as that went, but Cara still shivered.

His fingertips dragged down her flesh. His palms flattered to her toned stomach. He stroked his digits softly over her lines and curves, like he was taking time to commit them to memory. Each time, she *shivered*.

The sensation raced over her skin.

"You can't help that, can you?" Gian asked.

"What?"

His fingertips traced invisible lines over her naked breasts—the dress looked better without a bra underneath. "When I touch you, you can't help what happens."

"I don't know if it's *you*."

Gian smirked. "I do. You wouldn't be so shocked if it wasn't a new thing, Cara."

Goddammit, he was too cocky for his own good.

"I'm going to take you hard in this hallway, fuck you until you feel like you can't breathe, and then I'll take you to my bedroom, strip you down, and do it *again*. I like that little spot you left on my jacket, Cara, but I really want to see what you can leave on my slacks before I have to take them off completely. How does that sound?"

"That sounds filthy."

"Really?" Surprise lit up his rugged features. "I would think filthy would be wearing them tomorrow with a new jacket to hide the stains because it gets me off."

Yeah, that was worse.

"I need you to give me a yes or a no," he urged huskily.

Cara smiled as his thumb stroked over her reddened lips. "You make it hard to say no."

"Still not a yes."

"Yes, Gian."

He tipped his chin up, teasingly. "And …"

"And, what?"

"And that sounds …"

Cara let out a groan. "That sounds fucking great."

"Well, one of us will be sounding very fucking great in a few minutes."

He wasn't lying.

Cara had thought he meant he would bend her over in the hallway, that she might use the table for support as he fucked her from behind.

Instead, he had been the one to lean his backside against the edge of the table, and undo his slacks. He didn't say a word, simply reached for her and drew her in closer as he pulled his cock from his pants and boxer-briefs.

Cara watched him fist his length, before she dropped to her knees, and took his cock deep into her throat for no other reason than she wondered what he felt like. Silky smooth and hot on her tongue, that's what. Gian hadn't even asked, and he only stopped her long enough to tug on her hair, bring her up for a kiss, and then he pulled a condom out of his pocket. He rolled the latex down his length, and pulled her in for another bruising kiss.

"Turn around," he demanded against her mouth.

She did as she was told, her dress was pushed up, and he pulled her into his lap. Cara didn't get much of a warning before she felt his cock at her sex, and then he was pulling her down his length with such strength that it took her breath *and* words away.

His fingers had been good.

So fucking good.

But they were a tease.

She hadn't realized how big he was until he was filling every inch of her pussy, and it took her more than a few seconds to adjust to that new sensation, and his size.

"Breathe," came his voice in her head.

His fingertips glided over her skin, her neck, back, and then one hand tangled into her hair. His fingers tightened, tugging hard on her hair with enough strength to make her scalp tingle.

Cara let out a soft gasp.

"What's mine tonight, Cara?" Gian asked roughly, his hips flexing forward to settle just a bit deeper into her pussy. "Tell me, *bella*."

"My pussy."

"And what does that mean?"

Cara took a second or two too long to respond, as Gian grabbed hold of her wrists, pinned them behind her back, moved her forward and took her with another brutal thrust. "*Cara.* I want to hear you use your words to tell me what it means that your cunt is *mine*."

She had never been fucked quite like this before.

Never been used.

Never been manhandled or roughly treated.

It stunned her how hot she was, how breathless, and weak, and *ready* she was.

"It's yours to fuck when and how you want," she managed to murmur.

"Good girl."

Those words felt like a softer caress than even his hands had been, earlier on her skin. Like an approval, his pleasure and satisfaction, all rolled into one, over her simple response.

He fucked her like that—hard, long and brutal thrusts with her arms pinned at her lower back and her hair tangled up in his fist. He urged her on with dark whispers in her ear, until all she could hear was his cock driving into her body, and his voice in her head.

"Ride that cock, Cara."

"Oh, my God."

Gian didn't hold back in the slightest, pulling Cara even harder onto his cock, making her toe a thin line between pleasure and pain.

"My pretty little slut tonight, aren't you?" he murmured in her ear.

She hadn't heard that before, either. Certainly not in the way he said it, like it was a compliment, as though he *liked* it, and not the slur that most used it for.

It didn't sound bad coming from his mouth at all. It sounded rather beautiful. Or he made it sound that way.

It was only when his finger hooked the back of her choker, tugged hard enough to take her breath away for long enough to make her shudder, that she *really* understood what he had meant.

"Come," Gian ordered in her ear.

She didn't think she had a choice. She came as her choker broke, as the air and the relief crashed through her body at the same time.

He touched.

He demanded.

Her body *reacted*.

• • •

Cara awoke with a *shiver*. She wasn't sure what had caused it, but the sensation had started in her toes and ended in her shoulders. She knew she wasn't at home, given the white walls, white sheets, and fluffy white pillows.

White everywhere.

Then, his voice came. The same as it had been the night before. Dark, heady, commanding, pleased, rough, and sinful.

Like sex made in to a *sound*.

"I'm not going to be able to forget that," Gian murmured.

Cara knew exactly why she shivered when he spoke, because she did it again at the same time his finger traced a soft, slow line from her lower back, up her spine, to the nape of her neck.

He touched her, and she reacted.

Simple as that.

"And there it is again," he said, satisfaction curling his tone with a gruff edge. "It's like you can't help it, *donna*. I touch, you take a breath, and I can watch it race right down your skin."

"Stop touching me, and I will help it."

"I think that defeats the purpose, Cara. Besides, I quite like it."

So did she.

That was part of the problem.

It was morning, the night had ended, and that meant it was time for Cara to get back to life. She had taken the night to do something stupid; something wild, crazy, and reckless.

"No, no," Gian said, his fingers trailing pathways over her neck with gentle strokes. "I'm not sure what exactly turned you stiff, but knock it off. I like you where you are right now. You could at least stay for breakfast or coffee before you run off."

"You are too smart for your own good."

"I like to think of it as that I'm *quick*."

"Whatever." Cara rolled to her back, only to find a very naked and pleased Gian lying beside her, his head propped up on his hand. He didn't hide his wandering gaze for a second, his eyes drifting down over her bare skin, her breasts, and then lower. "I still need to head out, Gian."

He didn't react to her statement.

"You look good in white."

Cara laughed, earning her another one of his grins. "Are you going to keep deflecting what I say if it doesn't fit what you want?"

"Will it get me what I want, *dolcezza?*"

Cara thought, *now or never.* A part of her wanted to stay right where she was. Another part knew it wasn't wise.

"Don't be offended, Gian, but I know enough about your last name and your family to make a quick exit. It's not *you*, not really. But it is, at the same time—you're everything I try to stay away from, that's all."

His brown eyes darkened with something unknown, but he hid it by looking away. "I see."

"But you make it really hard," Cara added after a moment, "and you should know that, too. You make it hard for me to not want to stay, or talk again like we did last night, or even fuck again. You make it *really* hard to say no, Gian."

His laugher came out rumbling and thick. Another one of his sexy sounds. "Do I?"

"Yeah," Cara admitted.

"Could I convince you on breakfast and coffee? Nothing more, I promise."

Cara didn't believe him, but still said, "Maybe."

His hand twisted into her curls, and Cara sighed with a smile before Gian pressed a quick kiss to her temple. Just the heat of his body, and the glimpse of his fit form leaning over hers, was enough to send her spinning right back to memories of the night before. Then, his kiss to her temple moved to the tip of her nose, soft and sweet, before dropping down to her mouth. She could plainly feel the hard length of his erection pressing into her thigh, but as fast as he had rolled onto her to kiss her, he moved away.

"No convincing needed—breakfast and coffee it is, and then you can go, Cara."

She nodded from the sea of white heaven that was his bed. "You really do make it hard."

31

Gian smirked. "Clearly not hard enough, unfortunately."

If only he knew …

"Your clothes are … somewhere," Gian muttered, rolling over and sliding out of the bed with ease. "Sorry about that."

Cara snorted. "Probably the hallway."

"I'll have the coffee ready by the time you find it all and get dressed."

She could manage that.

Surely.

Gian moved easily through his bedroom, picking up a dress shirt and slacks as he went. He didn't even bother to put them on, staying naked like he didn't have a single fuck to give in the world. Not that he had to cover up, Cara mused, as his body was a work of art that needed to be appreciated in the light of day.

Once he was gone, Cara went in search of her clothes. Like she thought, she found most of it in the hallway, but her heels and panties were *very* close to the front door.

God.

It had been worth it, though.

Cara headed for the kitchen once she had made herself decent, only to find Gian wasn't there, and no coffee or food was in the works. But as quickly as she realized Gian was not in the kitchen, she heard his footsteps approach from behind her.

She turned fast on her heel, thinking he was up to his tricks again.

Cara came face to face with *heartache*. Gian looked like heartache.

"Gian?" she asked.

He stared at her for a moment, running a hand through the slightly-longer bit of dark hair at the top of his head. In his other hand, he held a cell phone.

"Rain check on the coffee, at least?" He tried to smile, but he ended up with a frown, anyway. "I know that's not what you agreed to."

"A rain check?" Cara asked faintly.

"I'll call you a cab, if that's all right. I have to head out."

"Is something wrong?"

Cara knew better than to ask.

She should have taken this saving grace for what it was, and run with it. Whatever happened, it would get her out of Gian's penthouse quicker than before, and maybe she could leave her strange feelings behind with it. A part of her didn't really want that, though.

"My grandfather," Gian said, glancing down at the phone in his hand, "was murdered this morning, when he stood in front of the terrace windows of the room he uses at my parents' mansion. Sniper shot to the head—dead before he hit the ground—and he didn't see it coming."

Cara's body grew cold all over. "I'm sorry."

What else could she say?

She knew far too well how this life took and took and took, but rarely ever gave back.

"Rain check," Gian repeated.

Cara nodded. "Rain check."

Someday.

• • •

"A shame, that's what it is. *Dio*. Rest his soul."

Cara tried to brush off the mutterings of her uncle, but given the way her aunt passed her a false smile and rolled her eyes, this clearly wasn't a first-time thing.

"It's good to see you, dear," Daniele said, taking Cara's coat.

Constantino came into the house behind her, not even bothering to say hello. He passed his suit jacket off to his mother before she asked for it, and he disappeared down the hallway, likely heading for his father.

"Don't mind the men this week—they're a bit off," her aunt muttered, shooting a glare in the direction her son had gone.

It had been three days since Cara spent the night with Gian Guzzi, and she had not heard a single word from him, about him, or his family. She had come home from school to find a message on her voice mail from her aunt, asking her over for dinner.

She knew what Daniele wanted, and while it irritated Cara to feed into the whims of others, she went. Her aunt meant no harm, she only wanted to check up on Cara and likely make sure she was still amongst the living.

"Food is nearly ready," her aunt said, "so I hope you're hungry."

Cara almost asked if her aunt was going to report her state back to her mother, or even her brother, but thought better of it. No need to be rude to the only family she had left around, even if she would rather keep a distance, given her uncle and cousin's involvement with the mafia.

"Sure, *Zia*," Cara replied, "I'm starved."

Then, her uncle's voice boomed through the house again, making her aunt sigh heavily.

"But, Dad—"

"No one is saying anything, Constantino," Claud complained. "No one knows who killed the boss, or who would even want to. No matter, Edmond and Gian will figure it out, and make whoever it was answer for what they've done."

Gian.

It was the first time in three days that Cara heard his name.

Like his touch, it still made her shiver.

FOUR

Edmond Portella's calls and demands were not ones that Gian typically put in high priority, given both men's status in the Guzzi Cosa Nostra. Gian, as the underboss, and Edmond, as the consigliere to a now-deceased Corrado put them on an equal playing field. Well, to a point. It also put them on very different scopes, regarding *la famiglia* and what their duties were to both the men, and the boss.

Most, if not all, of Gian's control and duty came down to the men, but more specifically, the Capos of the family. He dealt with their issues, kept an eye on them, and if needed, stepped in to handle any problem that came up when his grandfather hadn't wanted to bother.

Edmond, on the other hand, had been Corrado's left-hand to Gian being his right. What Gian didn't step in to handle, like the more personal side of business, Edmond was there to do whatever was needed.

Gian was the business hand of the boss.

Edmond was the personal.

Therefore, whenever Edmond had an issue or demanded someone's presence, it was rarely ever Gian's. Their respective positions neither depended on, nor required, the other.

And yet, ever since Corrado's murder the week before, Gian found himself on the opposite end of Edmond's calls more often than he liked. Sure, the Guzzi Cosa Nostra was facing an upset of sorts, with their long-reigning boss dead, and no one to immediately take the open seat readily available. A murder that, for all purposes, had been done in cold-blood, and for no apparent reason other than to kill the boss.

It was more than that, too.

More, because Edmond had made demands. More, because he made no qualms about hiding the fact that perhaps it would be him who would best fill the open position in the family.

The *highest* position.

Gian was the messenger for the Capos of the family. Whenever Edmond wanted the men to know something or do something, it was left to Gian to deliver the orders.

It was easy to attribute the murder of his grandfather—Corrado had always been more than *just* the boss to him—as to why Gian didn't immediately step in to take control of the family. It was also not that simple.

Maybe he felt he wasn't ready. His grandfather had never told him that he was, after all. Maybe he felt that at his age—twenty-nine—someone older might fill the position with more experience and a stronger hand than he could. That reasoning, too, was a born and bred respect that had been pounded into Gian over the years where Cosa Nostra and made men were concerned.

It was also a major reason why there was so much unrest in the family. He was not the *only* young Guzzi man, a made man of a generation that was often overlooked or dismissed because of their age, which felt it was time for the older men to step aside.

That particular unrest had been brewing long before Corrado's murder, and Gian didn't think it would lessen anytime soon.

However, it was that born and bred respect of Gian's that got him out of his bed at twelve at night on a fucking Thursday, when Edmond called and asked him to come over. Edmond lived outside of Toronto's city limits, in the outer suburbs of a gated community. The large property cost far more than any Canadian would ever hope to make in their lifetime. It took Gian a good hour and a half to get to Edmond's home, and all the while, he still couldn't figure out what the hell the man wanted.

Edmond hadn't offered any hints.

Gian disliked *that* even more.

It was as if Edmond felt he could simply demand, and Gian should answer, no questions asked.

"Ma called today, going on like she does," Domenic said, his voice echoing through the speakers of the Lexus. Gian had been so caught up in his own thoughts that he'd forgotten about being in mid-conversation with his younger brother. "I think she's overwhelmed with what's coming up next week, and all that shit."

"Probably," Gian agreed.

The massive funeral arrangements had been mostly left up to Gian's father, who had passed the task onto his wife.

"You sound off, man."

Gian kept his eyes on the suburb streets, not wanting to get lost in the catacombs of his mind again. "Thinking."

"I could have come with you tonight, if—"

"No, you couldn't."

"Well, I *could*."

"You're not a made man; you can't attend meetings, Dom."

His brother grunted under his breath. "Not for lack of trying, Gian."

"You'll get the button, eventually. It takes time, but until then, you can't attend this kind of thing. Whatever it is," he tacked on at the end, still irritated at being left out of a very important loop.

Finally, the long driveway leading up to the massive house belonging to Edmond came into view, and Gian turned off the road. "I'll call you when it's over, Dom."

"All right. And hey?"

"What?"

"Be careful," his brother said. "A lot of people you don't get to talk to that *I* get to talk to on the streets aren't happy right now. You only chat with made men, I get the word from the soldiers, too. I think they might get to hear some shit being said from their Capos that you aren't getting to hear at all."

"Go on."

"I told you—people aren't happy, Gian."

"That's not news, Dom."

"No, I don't mean the usual younger guys having rifts with the older guys. I mean they're looking for some kind of stability here, and coming up with nothing. That's not good on the streets. It makes people fight about stupid shit to have something to do."

Gian scowled. "Yeah, I got it."

"So yeah … maybe be careful."

He didn't need his younger brother lecturing him on how Cosa Nostra—or the made men within the family—worked, but he let Domenic have his moment. If nothing else, to let his brother feel like he had done something useful.

"I'll call you when I'm done," Gian repeated.

He hung up the call through the Bluetooth before Domenic could reply. Soon, he had driven the long length of the Portella driveway, and parked his car, cutting the engine as he surveyed the circular entrance.

Gian did not like what he saw.

Cars.

Several cars.

Yet, not enough for it to be a formal family meeting.

Of course, he recognized the vehicles, and could name the men to whom they belonged. A significant portion, if not all, of the older generation of Guzzi made men. Not one younger man, or one closer to Gian's age.

Except for him.

Gian stepped out of his car, not bothering to lock it as he headed for the front entrance of the large home. Edmond's wife let him in with a quiet greeting, and pointed in the direction of the upstairs.

"You'll find him in his office," she told Gian.

"*Grazie*," he thanked her.

Sure enough, Gian walked into an office that wasn't entirely filled with made men, but held a significant number to pull weight. All of them, with their graying hair, slightly rounded bodies, and older features, barely spared him a glance as he entered.

Edmond sat behind his large desk, a glass of scotch in his hand, and a lit cigar in the other. "Took you long enough, Gian."

Gian shrugged, stuffing his hands into the pockets of his suit jacket. "Seems everyone else that you wanted to be here must have gotten a call before me, Edmond."

"Oh, it isn't that, now. I made a call to Matthew and he called a few more."

Matthew, the older Capo in question, tipped his glass at Gian in greeting.

Gian offered nothing in response.

His attention was back on Edmond instead. "We both know that there are a lot of issues right now within the family, between the generations of men, and this isn't going to help, Edmond."

"I'm not sure I get what you mean."

Really?

That was likely half of the damn problem.

"You've called a meet for the men—clearly, look around—but not *all* of them. It's not good for the divide between the generations to add fuel to a fire when half of them already feel dismissed or overlooked in their positions. This will do exactly that, once they hear about it."

Edmond sighed, using two fingers to massage his forehead while his cigar dangled dangerously between his lips. "It won't matter after tonight, anyway. I called in the men who make a difference, the only ones whose voices need to be heard in this case."

Gian didn't like what he was hearing.

Nor what Edmond suggested.

"And what case is this?" Gian asked, not bothering to hide the edge of irritation sharpening his tone.

"It's time to fill the seat, Gian. We've gone a week without a boss, now, and that's not how it works in *la famiglia*. We'll do the nomination tonight, and take a vote. By morning, the Guzzi family will have a new boss, and we can all move forward."

"Except that's not how it works, Edmond."

"Why not?"

"Because *every* made man gets a voice in that vote, not a select few that *you* picked to be here for it."

Edmond smiled, a sight cold enough to make Gian stand a bit straighter. "As I said, once the boss is the boss, there is nothing to argue about. Your grandfather would have understood, given the current atmosphere of the family, that this is the best way to go about stabilizing the ground floor of this *famiglia*."

"Not to the detriment of more possible problems," Gian argued.

"Right now, you're the only one causing a problem, Gian."

"Or is that how you want it to look, Edmond?"

Gian had hit the nail directly on the head, and he knew it in that moment. The old consigliere to his grandfather was not even bothering to hide the sneaky way he intended to go about taking the boss's seat. He was not going to even allow the majority of younger made men in the family to speak.

Perhaps because they wouldn't choose Edmond.

Perhaps because they would pick someone like Gian.

That pissed Gian off.

But what could he do?

Gian was acutely aware of his current situation, and how dangerous it could be for him. In a room full of made men, he would likely be the only one on his side. He could be killed, though, it was technically forbidden without proper reasoning, and no one would speak up and say why. Not when the older men felt as though they were getting what they wanted.

This was not a good situation for Gian.

Suspicion weaved through Gian's bloodstream, and he disliked how it left him feeling. A distasteful sentiment stuck heavily on his tongue as he looked to Edmond, and was forced to wonder … had he found the hand that ordered the gun on his grandfather?

He had no real reason to believe that, and the friendship between Corrado and Edmond was a long one. Far longer than both men's marriages, even.

It could be that Edmond was a fucking upstart, and this had been his chance to take control. Something that was entirely unrelated to Corrado's murder, but rather, a happy by-product.

Gian didn't particularly like either of those ideas.

But here he was.

Fucked.

"I know you're unhappy about this," Edmond started to say.

"That's an understatement."

"But it is for the best, Gian." The older man rested back in his chair, steepling his fingers in front of his face before he spoke again. "And consider that once the men have proper stability again to fall back on, we can begin to work on other things."

"Like what?"

"Corrado's killer, for one."

Gian's jaw ached from clenching so hard. "I see."

"It's time to let the men nominate, and take their vote to fill the seat. Don't you think so?"

No.

Absolutely not.

It would not help the unrest within the family ranks to allow a boss to be chosen without every man's voice being involved.

He still didn't have a choice.

"I guess it is," Gian said quietly.

• • •

"*Any* other day would have been far better than today for this," Gian muttered.

His attempt to complain quietly to his father without his mother overhearing had not been missed, unfortunately. Celeste glared over her shoulder, effectively quieting her son and whatever else he might say.

With his mother's attention back on the speaking lawyer, Gian glanced up at the ceiling.

"A funeral would have been enough, I agree," his father said softly. "But apparently, Corrado wanted his Last Will and Testament read before burial, and this was the only time the lawyer had available this week to do this. It's extensive."

Obviously.

They had already been stuck in the reading for two hours.

Once it finished, they had to be at the church for the ceremony and subsequent entombment of Corrado's casket until the thaw came in the spring. The mid-February ground was still far too frozen to dig.

"To my eldest grandson, Gian …"

Gian's head lifted at his name being called out by the lawyer. It was the only time that Gian had shown any interest in the reading of his grandfather's Will, and not because he didn't care. He simply wished that it could be done one thing at a time. He didn't want to watch the things and legacy his grandfather worked so hard for be handed off and divided up on the same day they had to say goodbye.

The lawyer continued speaking, explaining the details of the things Corrado had left to Gian, including a trust, two antique roadsters that had been stored in the city, and other family heirlooms.

"And the building, including the two-level penthouse, in Ottawa," the lawyer said, looking over the rim of his large glasses to stare at Gian. "You're aware of that property, correct?"

Gian stiffened as the room quieted.

Of course, he knew the property. Everyone in their fucking family knew it. And what his grandfather had used it for, three decades ago.

At his side, Gian's father cleared his throat uncomfortably, spurring him to talk.

"Yeah," Gian answered quickly, "I know it."

"Good," the lawyer said, glancing back down at the papers. "All that's left in regard to you, Gian, is a few words your grandfather wanted you to hear. *Duty, legacy, and only then, love—always in that order. Always.*"

Those words were not new to Gian. He had heard them spoken from his grandfather's very mouth more times than he cared to count. He figured Corrado wanted the chance to say them one last time, to remind Gian.

It wasn't like he could forget.

He certainly couldn't forget what Corrado had left unwritten in his final note, either. *For when a man fails at duty, Gian, his legacy becomes nameless, and his love, hopeless.*

• • •

It seemed for a time, the usually bustling streets of Toronto where Corrado Guzzi had spent his life building an empire suddenly quieted. As if the shopkeepers knew what the gray skies meant, and the constantly moving people felt the need to step aside, away from the grief.

It was the only day, in a string of many days, where the men of the Guzzi Cosa Nostra quieted their grumblings, put aside their misgivings, and settled in to pay respects to a boss unlike any other.

Gian had expected sadness. He'd prepared for it.

He found his grief was different for the funeral than it had been leading up to it. Not lessened, but rather, softened. He had done well to keep his emotions buried when he needed to, but as he traveled behind the hearse in a black town car, the grief was not as striking.

It still ached. It still hurt. It had simply softened for a moment.

Gian surveyed the familiar faces as the vehicles parked in a long line along the church, and then began to empty of people. He stood alongside his mother, father, brother, and sister as the hearse backed up to the entrance of the church, stopping at the steps.

Despite all the people, Gian still felt singular. Above, perhaps, looking down. Not entirely there, as the back of the hearse was opened to showcase the shined, black casket with gold-plated bars and leaf designs along the corners and sides. The casket matched the one his grandmother had been buried in two years before, after her heart had finally given out.

The whole day felt familiar.

Except for the fact that the men who pulled their caps off and bowed their heads, were not doing so for respect of their boss's grief, but rather, the loss of that very same man. He had not been expecting that second of distant familiarity.

"Let's go," Domenic said, his hand landing hard on Gian's shoulder.

Gian stepped forward with his brother as another six men filed in behind them. Six familiar faces to help carry the casket in, before they would help to carry it out, too.

One of those men happened to be Claud Rossi.

Gian had known that Claud would be one of the pallbearers for his grandfather, chosen by Edmond and several others in the family. Still, he looked around for the man's family, only finding Claud's wife and son. His oldest friend, Constantino, nodded at Gian as he passed, but oddly, that wasn't the face of a Rossi he had wanted to see.

He'd wondered if Cara might show up.

She certainly had no reason to, and no connection to his grandfather.

Gian had a million and one other things to let consume his mind lately, but more often than not, his thoughts drifted back to the redheaded Cara, and the coffee she had promised him.

He was going to need a break from his life after today.

Something to let him breathe.

Cara just might do …

Gian simply had to figure out *when*.

• • •

"Whiskey, neat," Gian ordered.

His grin deepened as Cara's head popped up at the sound of his voice. From behind the bar, her eyes widened.

"Gian."

He leaned over the top of the bar, pointing at the specific brand of whiskey he wanted. "That one, please."

Cara didn't make a move to reach for the bottle. "What are you doing here?"

"I could ask you the same thing."

"I asked first."

So she did.

"I have a meeting with your uncle and cousin. I'm a bit early—better that than late, I suppose. I figured I would get a drink while I wait, and here you are."

Under the specialty lights of the restaurant's bar, Cara's red hair seemed darker. Her blue eyes surveyed him with barely-hidden interest, and curiosity. Gian had the strangest urge to reach out and tug on one of the curls, to feel the softness under his fingertips, but he managed to hold back. Somehow.

"My uncle had a server that took sick, and his back up is gone for the week on vacation. I happen to know how to mix drinks," Cara explained. "Plus, my aunt thinks if someone doesn't force me out of the apartment every once in a while, I will likely die in there."

Gian chose not to comment on the second part of her statement, instead focusing on the first. "Yet, you don't drink them."

"A dichotomy, I'm aware."

"In a way," Gian agreed.

Cara reached for the bottle behind the bar, and a clean glass to go along with it. She poured Gian's drink with a smile that he returned.

Soon, her smile faded.

"I'm sorry about your grandfather," she said quietly.

Gian let out a sigh. "Thanks."

"The funeral was a couple of days ago, right?"

"It was. I didn't see you there."

Cara shrugged as she slid the drink across the counter. "Don't take offense, but I try to stay away from family business, you know."

"So you told me in bed."

At the mention of their hookup, Cara's cheeks flooded with a pretty red. It wasn't quite the same shade as her hair, but it was damn close.

Gian chuckled. "How—after that—can you be shy with me?"

She shot him a look, her lips curving with amusement. "A gift, I guess."

"Well, speaking of that night," Gian started to say, reaching for an item he had in his pocket. "I have something for you."

Cara's brow lifted. "Oh?"

"You forgot it. Or I broke it and you probably didn't think much about it after that."

Gian pulled the thin, double-wrapped choker with a small bow from his pocket. He had taken it to a jeweller to have the velvet fixed, and the small piece of the chain that had broken repaired as well.

"Here," he said, holding it out and letting it dangle on two fingers. "Ready for you to wear again." Carefully, Cara plucked the item from his grasp.

"You didn't have to—"

"Of course, I did. I broke it; it's only right that I fix it."

"It's just a cheap necklace, Gian."

"Maybe. I liked the way it looked around your throat. I might like to see it on you another time."

All over again, Cara's cheeks reddened.

"Huh," she said quietly.

"You do still owe me coffee, *mon ange*."

"I figured you would have forgotten about that by now," she admitted, glancing up at him.

"Why?"

Why on earth would he have forgotten about her? She was not easily forgotten, even with the sudden craziness his life had become. Gian fully intended on learning more about Cara Rossi, even if he knew that he had zero business doing so.

"For starters," Cara said, "because we hooked up and that's all it needs to be."

"Tell me that's all it is, though, and then and *only* then, will that be all it needs to be, Cara."

Cara didn't get the chance to answer.

"Gian, you're early!"

He spun on his heel, whiskey in hand, only to come face to face with a stone-faced Claud Rossi. Constantino stood at his father's side, his hands shoved in his pockets.

Claud passed a look between Gian, and Cara. "Busy night, Cara?"

"Busy enough, *Zio*."

"Good, good." Claud turned his gaze back on Gian. "Thanks for agreeing to meet with me. Constantino says he's sure we can work something out about the little problems the guys have been having on the streets, if you're involved."

Gian nodded. "Sure."

He hated to end his conversation with Cara short, but ...

"That coffee," he told her over his shoulder, "is happening soon."

He didn't even leave it open to question.

It was no longer an offer.

Cara nodded, but quickly headed to the other side of the bar.

Then, as Gian turned back to discuss the business at hand with the father and son Capo-duo, Claud was still watching him. It was a pensive sort of stare that put Gian on edge.

"What?" Gian asked.

"Should I be asking you that, Gian?" Claud asked.

Constantino cleared his throat. "Dad—"

"Did I see you give my niece a gift like you're friendly with her?"

Gian resisted the urge to tell Claud to mind his business, though he had every right. "And if I did?"

"What in the hell are you doing, Gian?"

That was the million-dollar question, wasn't it?

Even Gian didn't have the answer.

FIVE

Cara tried to listen to the lecturer at the front of the hall, but her gaze kept drifting back to the time on her laptop. It wasn't that the lecture was boring—the effects of mental health driven on or exacerbated by addiction and the statistics for the children growing up in those situations, was a particular subject Cara had great interest in. If for no other reason, to help better understand her own childhood and parents.

For whatever reason, she couldn't concentrate long enough on the lecturer's words to keep track of where the guy was, or what he was currently discussing. That was probably caused by the fact this was her last thing to get done at school, and then she had the weekend free.

Cara had been doing well.

Two weeks, no missed days.

She hadn't even missed study halls or the specific lectures that were not considered required attendance for her grades.

Given her track record over the last few months of missing more time than she actually attended, Cara was going to take that as a win. It was one lecture—the current one—that she probably could have afforded to give herself off to relax, but she had refused. Seems she should have skipped it and downloaded it later off the university's online portal, because she wasn't getting a damn thing out of it anyway.

While it wasn't good form on a student to leave a closed lecture hall, Cara considered doing just that and grabbing a bite to eat on her way to the bus stop. She ended up pushing through those last ten minutes or so, taking the time to close down her laptop and pack her things away. Some lecturers went far over their time, but thankfully, this one was done the second the clock hit four.

Cara was done, too.

Normalcy, she told herself as she walked out of the lecture hall. *You're trying to get back to some kind of normal here.*

So far, she was succeeding.

Or it seemed so.

She hadn't stayed in bed for hours on end. She went out and did things, grabbed groceries, paid bills, and whatever else needed done. It wasn't like she was a social butterfly, but she made it a point to grab coffee with a couple of friends, and have lunch with her aunt, too. Which was a hell of a lot more than she had been doing before.

Cara hadn't realized how deep her head had been stuck in the sand for all those months. To an extent, she had liked the darkness of being alone, even if the loneliness felt like it might kill her.

She figured, what did it matter?

No one would be able to understand her grief, anyhow.

Cara was right on that end.

No one *did* understand. But they sympathized.

Maybe it was that the hardest part of her grief was finally waning enough to let her breathe. Maybe she had somehow managed to survive the depression that had sank its dirty claws into her mind for so long. Or maybe forcing herself to do normal things and actually see what was happening around her had been enough to wake her the hell up.

Maybe it was none of those things.

She did know that whatever it was, she was grateful. There was nothing to life, if a person wasn't living it. Lea would have understood that better than anyone else.

"Hey, Cara!"

She had opened the main doors to Hall Three to leave, but turned to face the familiar girl running up to her. Lynn had been one of the few mutual friends that Cara and Lea had shared together, who had come from them attending the university.

"What's up, Lynn?"

The girl smiled widely. "Just wondered if maybe you might want to hang out this weekend? We're all thinking of heading to the new club that opened up in Niagara Falls."

"That club is supposed to be crazy popular right now, isn't it?"

"Yep."

"So, four hours of waiting in line to get inside a club that is so full, you can barely see what's happening five feet in front of you?" Cara asked, slightly amused.

Lynn shrugged. "I guess. You interested?"

"Not this weekend, but thanks."

Cara didn't regret refusing the invite. She didn't have shit going on, she had no plans coming up, and she liked that fine. Lynn didn't seem to mind either, giving her friend a hug before heading back in the direction she came.

Normal, Cara found herself repeating.

Like a damn mantra.

She was coming to learn that sometimes, breaks were good, too. A break from the world, from friends, and from life. It didn't mean she was doing worse or whatever, just that she needed a little time out.

That's what she wanted this weekend.

A little time out.

• • •

Of course, *he* would be waiting in front of her apartment building when Cara got off the city bus. Of course, he would be wearing one of those fucking three-piece suits, looking like a goddamn God, as though he had nowhere else better to be in that moment.

And fuck, did he look good.

Cara hated how almost every part of her knew instantly that her attraction to this man was not the least bit containable or innocent.

Gian Guzzi.

Leather driving gloves. Shined, leather shoes, untouched by the dirtiness of the winter in the city. Lazy grin. Confident posture.

Gian.

She didn't have the slightest clue how Gian knew where she lived—she hadn't given him her address that morning weeks ago, and she hadn't even given him her phone number, despite his promise of coffee. She knew that him showing up at the restaurant when she was filling in for a bartender that night a few days back had been nothing more than happenstance, and even then, he *still* hadn't asked for her information.

Almost like he didn't have to.

Like maybe he already knew.

Cara couldn't decide if she liked that, or not.

She stayed back a few paces, as he clearly hadn't seen her get off the bus, and decided to watch him for a moment. He *was* exceptionally beautiful for a man, in a rough, cocky sort of way. When he tugged on the wrists of his leather driving gloves, Cara's cheeks heated with the memory of taking them off, just so he could get his bare hands up her dress in a car.

Nothing innocent about this at all.

Gian both amazed and terrified Cara.

Never had a man had the ability to make Cara so entirely aroused, yet coy at the same time.

She was not shy, yet in a blink, he could make her that way. She was not loud, but he could easily make her scream. She was not controlled by selfish desires, but a *big* part of her still screamed *want, want, want* when it came to Gian Guzzi.

And that was bad all over.

Or was it?

Cara didn't know.

"Are you going to stand there and stare at me all day, or come over and talk to me?" Gian suddenly asked, never once looking away from the opposite direction of where Cara was standing. "Not that I mind your staring, because, well … *Tu as de beaux yeux, ma chérie.* But I already have a big enough ego to fill this city, no need to go adding to my complex."

That fucking French of his was going to kill her someday.

And she wasn't even sure she understood what he said.

"Did you say I have beautiful eyes?" Cara asked.

Gian's grin turned even sexier as his gaze finally landed on her. "I did—well done, Cara. *Brava.*"

And there went his Italian.

Cara sighed. "You're Catholic, right?"

Sure, he was.

He was French and Italian.

He was a damned Catholic.

"Of course," Gian said, turning to face her more. "Why?"

"Then you're familiar with the Bible and sin. Tell me, is there any place in the good book that explains how much of a sin it has got to be that you can manage to be *that* attractive and charming in three languages?"

Gian laughed loud and hard.

Cara's stomach tightened into a dozen more knots.

Fuck.

Yes, that's what she was.

Fucked.

"There is no such thing in the Bible," Gian assured.

"There should be," Cara mumbled to herself. "It's not fair to all us unsuspecting women walking around, you know."

Gian lifted a shoulder. "There's really only one woman who needs to be worrying about it, at the moment."

"Oh?"

His brown eyes lifted to meet hers unabashed, his grin still firmly in place. "You, Cara. Just you."

She didn't know what game this man was playing, but he was damn good at it.

"What are you doing here, Gian?"

"You owe me a coffee. It also happens to be dinnertime, so I thought you might like food, too."

Cara came a little closer to the back of his Lexus. "And you knew where I lived, how?"

"Constantino is chatty when he drinks," Gian admitted. "I tend to use that to my advantage at times."

"My cousin?"

"Surprised he knows things about you?"

"A little," Cara replied. "We're not really close."

"You don't have to be," Gian said, not elaborating further. "He also mentioned you might have your weekends free, which is why your uncle often calls on you, if he needs an extra hand at the bar like he did the other night."

Cara eyed him curiously. "So, you've been asking about me?"

"*Oui*. Is that a problem?"

"Maybe."

"Funny, *bella*, you don't sound like it's a problem."

Cara barely held back her smile.

Damn him.

"Is your weekend free?" Gian asked quieter.

"My *whole* weekend?" Cara shrugged. "That's a hell of a lot more than coffee or dinner, Gian."

"It is, but shit, go big or go home, Cara. I'm interested in you—*very* interested, love. I'm not about to hide my intentions in that regard. It won't get me what I want, if I do. So if your weekend is free, and you might like a bit more than dinner with me, you should get your pretty ass inside my car as soon as you possibly can, so we can get out of here."

Cara sucked in a sharp breath, stunned and aroused at the same time. With only a few words, he'd provoked her into a reaction, and this time, he hadn't even needed to touch her to do it. He demanded, she reacted.

Damn him, indeed.

"And what would this weekend include?" Cara asked.

Gian waved a hand, smiling. "I've come into some real estate in Ottawa, and I greatly need a break from my life. I'll get to leave this city for a bit—breathe outside of this familiar hell. It's not been a fun couple of weeks. I'd like to see the real estate, *and* enjoy myself while I do it."

Cara wet her lips. "With me."

He nodded, that piercing gaze of his pinning her in place. "With you, Cara."

Well, then …

"I have to grab a bag," she said.

Gian gestured at her building. "I'll be here when you get out."

• • •

"This was not at all what I expected when you said real estate," Cara admitted, taking in the old oak floors and outdated—yet beautiful—pieces of furniture in the two-level penthouse. There was nothing modern about the decoration of the penthouse, and even the light fixtures threw back to yesteryears, when Cara hadn't even been alive. It was beautiful, to be sure, but *old*. "It's like we jumped back in time about fifty years."

Gian hummed under his breath, running his finger along the curved wooden arm of a chaise. Not a speck of dust was anywhere to be seen, yet the place looked like it hadn't been lived in for years. "As far as I know, that was about the time he bought it."

"He?"

"My grandfather."

"Oh," Cara said softly.

"Mr. Guzzi!"

Cara damn near jumped out of her skin at the new voice, though Gian barely moved a muscle except to smile at the newcomer. An older gentleman, and a slightly younger woman, came walking down a spiral staircase. The woman stayed behind the man, her uniform suggesting she was a maid of sorts, while the gentleman's suit said something entirely different.

"We've been looking forward to seeing you, and taking you on a tour," the man said, coming to stop in front of Gian with his hand extended.

Gian shook politely. "Yes, well, the tour won't be needed, Derek, but *merci*."

"But—"

"I think Cara and I can handle the exploring on our own for the weekend." Gian gave her a wink over his shoulder. "Right, *mon ange*?"

"Sure, we can."

She didn't think he had any exploring in mind, to be honest.

"If you're sure," Derek started to say.

"Perfectly sure."

"Penelope comes in to clean and dust Mondays, Wednesdays, and Fridays," Derek explained. "She is done for the day, and all the beds have been stripped and changed."

Something odd took over Gian's features. Cara didn't recognize it.

He cleared his throat, glancing upward at the ceiling. "And which room did he prefer? Or, which one did they use, so I can avoid that?"

"Well, Corrado hasn't been here in more than a decade, Gian. And those items are long gone."

Gian didn't appear to care. "Which one?"

"The only one without a balcony," Derek replied quickly. "Louise didn't like heights."

"Great. I have your phone number if we need anything, so ..."

Derek and the maid seemed to catch on to Gian's unspoken words quickly enough, and made themselves scarce. Cara only heard the quiet click of the front door closing before she turned back to Gian.

He had walked forward, further into the penthouse, toward a row of windows that still had wooden frames, and could be opened from the inside. He crossed his arms, staring out the windows at the old buildings across the way.

"Your grandfather hasn't been here in ten years, but kept a maid on a three-day-a-week schedule?" Cara asked, confused.

"And Derek is on call, too, as he's the building's ... well, like a consigliere, of sorts. This is one of the only suites in this building that hasn't been renovated or updated in some way over the years. They would greatly like me to keep it that way, as it increases the value of the building as a whole, to say the original owner's penthouse is in mint condition from when it was built fifty years ago."

"But you don't want to," Cara assumed.

She hadn't realized it was more than the penthouse that he owned.

"I didn't want this place," Gian muttered heavily. Sighing, he turned to face her again. "Would you mind exploring on your own for a bit? I have a call to make, and I'll order us some food, too."

"Sure," Cara said.

She could tell something else was on his mind.

Gian was good at hiding it, but she saw it.

Whatever it was.

Cara figured it wasn't her place to push. She hadn't come with him for the weekend to pry into his personal life. She had come because, like him, a break from life was just what she needed.

And who the hell said she couldn't have fun while she did it?

• • •

"Is this your grandmother?" Cara held out a black and white glamor shot of a beautiful woman, as Gian walked into the bedroom without a balcony.

"No, that isn't Aurora. And my grandmother died two years ago. Heart attack."

Cara's brow furrowed, as she took in the dozen and one other framed photos on the old armoire. Most held the woman, but a few had children, and some, an older gentleman that looked a hell of a lot like Gian, if he were in his forties or fifties.

"Then who is it? Oh, Louise, right?"

Gian stared at Cara, not saying anything.

"What?"

It took her far too long to realize what he *wasn't* saying. A woman named Louise had lived here, and she *was not* his grandmother. A woman who, guessing by the photos and the statements made about the bedroom, had been involved in a romantic relationship with Corrado Guzzi for years.

The photos of the children caught her attention again.

Decades, actually.

"Oh," Cara said quietly, carefully putting the photo back. "Well, then."

Gian shrugged one shoulder, but didn't move further into the room to join her. "Louise died a decade ago, about the time my grandfather stopped coming for his weekend visits. Apparently, he didn't want much to do with the place when she wasn't here, but he also didn't want to sell it."

Cara glanced back at the old photos of the children. "What about their kids?"

"Louise had kids—they weren't my grandfather's."

"Huh."

"You sound ... bothered," Gian said.

Cara's brow furrowed. "Weren't you bothered that he had a whole other life, with another woman, in a different city, that *wasn't* his wife?"

"It was a secret that was not really a secret in our family. I was told—like everyone else in my family—that it was not a topic we were to discuss, for obvious reasons. I didn't feel much about it, I suppose it wasn't my place to. That was, until the deed was handed over to me. Now, I have to consider *too* much."

She understood that.

It couldn't be pleasant.

"Let's get out of this room, then," she suggested.

Gian nodded, and stepped back into the doorway, gesturing for her to follow. "Food is here, by the way."

Cara walked on past, but nearly stopped as she felt his hand find her lower back. That all too familiar shiver crawled over her skin at his touch. "And what comes after the food, Gian?"

She felt his smirk grow as he pressed a quick kiss to her cheek. "*Any* other bedroom but that one, Cara."

• • •

Cara crawled onto the foot of the bed, moving up Gian's naked side in nothing but one of his dress shirts. The man woke up at the ass-crack of dawn, and it was disturbing because Cara *liked* to sleep.

She couldn't sleep when Gian wasn't, though.

He wouldn't let her.

Gian had tossed the beige sheets across his lower midsection and groin, but that still left the rest of his body free for Cara to admire. It was quite a sight, especially in the morning with light coming in through the opened windows. For every defined cut of muscle on his body, Cara's attention was caught and spun. He was lean like a runner, yet built enough like a fighter. It was easy to tell over his suits that he was fit, but it was when he was naked that Cara couldn't stop staring.

A *beautiful* man.

Cara laid along Gian's side, though lower than he was, so that her top half ended at his waist. He peered over the book he was reading, those brown eyes of his raking over her form and the shirt she wore.

"Shame you can't go out like that all the time," he said under his breath.

"I could say the same."

"Yes, and then where would all those unsuspecting women be, huh? Falling all over themselves, I imagine. It would be hazardous for me to do that to the world."

"Arrogant ass."

"Complex," he corrected with a grin.

Then, he went back to his book.

His free hand came down to tangle in her hair as he continued reading, his fingers stroking through the strands carefully. He didn't tug or pull, not like he did when he was fucking her, but rather, stroked her hair gently as if to relax her.

And it did.

Before Cara had realized what was happening, her face rested in Gian's palm, and his thumb stroked her cheekbone.

It was intimate.

But not the kind of intimate like the night before, when he fucked her until she couldn't breathe or see properly.

It was sweet.

But not like his pet names, not like his French or Italian nothings in her ear.

Cara was pretty sure this was not how hookups were supposed to go, and she certainly shouldn't be considering feelings for Gian, but he made it difficult not to. This was only supposed to be a weekend away—a break, nothing more. And yet, it felt strangely domestic. Something familiar and comforting, with someone she didn't know all that well.

She decided to get her mind off of that nonsense.

"Are you going to read all morning?" she asked.

"It's good for the brain, Cara."

"So is food. Or coffee. Television. A shower. *Sex.*"

Gian's right eyebrow lifted and his lips curved salaciously. "Those are all good things, too."

"Not good for the brain?"

"Some of them," he said.

Before she could think better of it, Cara snatched his book away and tossed it to the floor. As it landed with a thump on the hardwood, Gian's narrowed gaze turned on her. That one look threatened fun and bad and sinful, all at once. Cara simply smiled back in the face of his unspoken threat.

"Oops," she whispered.

"That was not nice. I was at a good part."

Cara shrugged. "Oh, well."

"That was terribly bratty, too."

"Yes, but—"

Gian lurched toward her before Cara could even get her words out properly. She didn't even have the chance to try and get away from his hands grabbing hard to her waist and pulling her higher up the bed. Her laughter bounced off the walls as his fingers danced over her skin, tickling with killer precision and making her sides ache.

Somehow, though she wasn't quite sure how, Cara managed to get up on her knees, and then stand. Gian followed right behind her, still holding tight and refusing to let her go. She grabbed for a pillow, but he knocked it back down, and she fell with it.

Gian went with her.

That was how Cara found herself pinned under a grinning Gian and how she knew her plan to at least get him out of the bed before noon was *screwed*.

But she was probably going to like it.

"Word to the wise," he murmured an inch away from her lips.

"What's that?"

"Compliance will get you everywhere with me, but brattiness will get you something, too. You like the one, so you'll probably like this as well."

Then, his fingers pressed harder, sliding lower down her sides, and his body followed the same path. Sliding down her body, Gian pushed the dress shirt she wore higher, his lips coming down to kiss against her heated skin every so often. And his tongue ... it lapped at her flesh, taking small tastes of her body before darting back into that wicked fucking mouth of his. Her legs widened for him, and she couldn't even find it in herself to be ashamed that she hadn't pulled on a pair of panties after showering that morning.

"Now, be a good girl," Gian said as he hovered over her pubic bone, "and let me eat in peace, Cara. On your knees, please."

She blinked. "What?"

Gian only tipped his chin up, and that was it. He didn't repeat himself; he didn't like to, she had learned.

Cara's brain finally caught up to the rest of her body and she scrambled to get on all fours like he wanted. She had thought watching him between her thighs would be a nice sight first thing in the morning, but he apparently had other plans.

If there was a torturous, sinful hell, Gian's mouth was it.

It was his tongue lapping against her sex as he spread her ass cheeks wide and grabbed hard enough to leave his fingerprints behind. It was the way he groaned at the first taste of her pussy, so deep and rough that it traveled over her spine before it even reached her ears. It was the curving flicks of his tongue that beat against the underside of her clit over and over again until her legs shook, and she was pushing back into his mouth to *get more*.

And then he was pulling away, those fucking chuckles of his filling her senses with his satisfaction and her growing orgasm that was now lost.

"The taste of you could kill me, Cara. I'd eat you, morning, noon, and night, and I wouldn't even *think* about anything else. It would *kill me*."

She let out a shaky breath, unable to say anything.

She needed a second to think again.

"Do you remember what I told you?" he asked a second before his palm swatted gently against her wet sex. His fingers slid along her clenching opening a second before another soft slap landed against her ass. The sound echoed in the bedroom, making Cara suck in a sharp breath. His fingers—three of them—slid into her pussy, stretching her open and making her back arch from the sudden intrusion.

"About this—your cunt and me, love. What did I say?"

Cara didn't even have to think about it.

Even when she thought they might not see each other again—and certainly not for sex—she still heard those words of his.

"It's yours, when we're together," she mumbled against her arm.

Gian's pleased hum answered her back before he said, "Exactly that, Cara."

She felt him move on the bed, reaching for something. Cara looked, only to see him pull his cell phone from the bedside table. Gian's eyes turned back on her with a wicked gleam.

"Your pussy is so pink and wet, especially when you want to come. I want you to see what it looks like when you're bratty and greedy, Cara. Let me."

"You'll delete it—"

"Not a chance," he interrupted fast, "but no one else will ever see it."

Just the cadence his tone took on told Cara he was telling the truth. She nodded and his hand slipped over her body with the softest touch again—something she was learning was a sign of his approval, his happiness. He was rough in bed, not that she minded, and the softness only came when he wanted to gift her something back.

Cara heard the phone's camera ding with a familiar shutter-like sound. She looked over her shoulder, only to see Gian's attention was on her body again, and his fingers were pressing deep into her hot sex. Every single nerve ending she had seemed to be attached to her pussy as his fingers slid in and out with a slow assuredness that drove her fucking *mad*.

"I want to come," Cara mumbled.

Her body ached for it.

Her mind screamed for it.

Gian only smirked, his gaze never once leaving his work. She felt his thumb drive upward, spreading her sex open before sliding over her clit with small circles.

"*Gian, let me come.*"

He didn't.

Not right away.

In fact, he pulled away from her again, only long enough to find a condom from a pack he'd tossed aside the night before. Never once did that damn phone of his leave his hand, but Cara found that she didn't give a shit. She wanted *one* thing from him right then.

Just the one. To come.

He filled her full all over again, his cock much thicker and longer than his three fingers had been a minute before. And yet, there was no hesitation in the way her body took him entirely, and she could *hear* how fucking wet she was as his groin fit tight to the curve of her ass.

"I want to—"

Gian's hand landed where the curve of Cara's ass met her thigh, and it fucking *stung*. But that quick bloom of heat quickly melted into something delicious as he rubbed the same spot. "I'm aware, but you can wait."

"*Why?*"

And why was she so damn whiney?

"Because I like how you sound when you're like this, and you deserve it after what you did to my book." His fingertips danced up her spine before tangling in the hair at the nape of her neck with a firm tug, pulling her head higher. "Just feel me for a bit, Cara. Christ, all I can feel is you."

It was the dip in his tone, the way it roughened and edged, that made Cara shiver. She knew he liked that—enjoyed seeing it—and so she didn't even try to hide it.

His thrusts came deep, but slow, at first. Measured with every flex, and quick on the pull, like he wanted to dive right back in again. Each one brought her higher, right back to the peak of bliss where he'd stop, tease her with his hands and his words, and then start all over again.

And then his thrusts came harder, faster, and even *deeper*. He tossed his phone to the pillows, so he had another hand free. Cara's gaze caught sight of the video playing on the screen of the device, her senses caught between *watching* and feeling. His fingertips dug into her ass, pulling her back with every flex of his hips. The trembling in her legs had spread to every other part of her fucking body, and she couldn't breathe again, not when all she could think about was release, and when she could finally get it.

Gian's hand slid from her hair to her throat, his fingers curving around the delicate line there as he pulled her up from the bed. Her back fitted against his chest as his fingers tightened, and there it was … enough pressure on her throat to make her impending orgasm continue on for what felt like forever.

That little trick of his made her crazy.

"Now you can come," she heard him say, his words a husky murmur in her ear. "And then you can beg me for another and another, Cara."

She would.

He was a drug to her system.

And she did beg for him to tease her and fuck her all over again—*again and again and again.*

· · ·

Gian had moved the chaise in the sitting room to the old windows that could be opened. Despite the time of year, a warm breeze came in from the windows. Cara found it was a nice place to sit, with her feet propped up in on the windowsill, and her head tucked against Gian's chest.

"So, a therapist, huh?" he asked above her.

She shrugged. "That's the goal. I want to have a main focus, though. Addiction. Recovery. Maybe some child-work."

"Is that because you feel you owe something for your raising, or because it's something you want to personally do?"

"A bit of both."

"As long as you know," he murmured. "When you do something because you feel you owe it, or you have to, you'll never be as satisfied as you want to be."

Gian's fingers roved through her hair as they chatted.

"I know you wanted a break from … everything that happened," Cara started to say.

"I did, yes."

"But you can't only talk about me, Gian. It's not fair."

He laughed, rocking them both on the chaise. "Fair enough. What do you want to know?"

"Well, anything."

"Like what?"

"Your grandfather, maybe. You seemed like you were close, especially if you needed to take a break after burying him. That sounds like someone who needed to get away from their feelings."

Gian cleared his throat. "Interesting way to put it."

"Am I wrong?"

"No. You're very right, actually." He sighed, shifting beneath her a bit. "I don't have time to grieve, in a way, because there's much more happening, now that he's gone. And that feels terribly shitty of me, that my focus can't be on a man who practically raised me for a bit, because responsibility and duty wait on no one."

Cara frowned. "I'm sorry."

"Don't be. Believe it or not, but this *break*, is not entirely a break. I've thought a lot more about my grandfather this weekend than I would have been able to, had I stayed in Toronto. Less bullshit—less noise in my head and from other people."

"I get that."

"Now, your turn," he said.

"For what?"

"A question that isn't entirely safe."

Cara stiffened. "Depends on what it is."

"Too bad—I answered yours." His hand landed on her bare hip under the afghan blanket, holding firm as if to keep her there. "Tell me about your sister. Not the kinds of things you tell other people. How you're feeling. Certainly, not something to placate me. I'll know if you do, *bella donna*. I am not a dumb man."

No, he certainly wasn't.

Cara barely had to think about her response, though. "She was not like me. Lea was the complete opposite of me. And maybe, sometimes, that left me feeling a bit left out when she could so easily fit in and I couldn't, but I always had her, regardless. It took me a bit to realize after she had died that I depended on her for a lot more than being my sister and roommate. I didn't know how to be Cara without Lea."

"Oh?"

"I'm still not sure that I know."

Gian's lips pressed to the top of her head. "I only know you—what you let me know, of course—and I think you do *Cara* very well."

She smiled. "I think you would have liked Lea, though."

"I *like* you, love. And that's the important bit."

"Is it?"

"Sure."

Cara fell silent, lost in the sensations of Gian stroking her skin under the blanket and the comfortable breeze coming in through the window. She hadn't known how much she needed the quiet and a break from life and a city that never stopped moving. Sure, below them, another city was moving like the end was near, but she barely heard a thing.

It was only Gian's speaking again that broke her from the daze.

"We should do this again soon," he said.

"That might make it seem like we're dating, Gian. We hooked up, ran away for the weekend, and now you're planning the next one. I don't get involved with your type of man—I told you that once."

"It's a little late for that, isn't it?"

Cara bit her bottom lip. "Maybe."

"We're doing this again."

It wasn't even a suggestion that time.

"Are we?"

"Oh, yes."

SIX

"Gian."

He almost missed the call of his name by the familiar voice, as he started his ascent of the church steps. It was unusual for his closest enforcer—Chris—to call him by his name, as it was usually "boss" only to the man, but Gian understood why the sudden change.

Edmond clapped Gian on the shoulder as he continued climbing the church steps to a waiting Mass. When the boss was around, Gian could not be "boss" to his own men, as anyone in a higher position than him took precedence.

It hadn't much mattered with his grandfather, but Edmond was not Corrado.

That was obvious to everyone.

"I messaged you this morning," Gian said, turning to face the enforcer standing on the bottom step. "It's not like you to be late, Chris."

The barrel-chested man shrugged his wide shoulders. "Sundays are my off day—that's what you always say, anyway. No business on Sundays. I put the phone away."

"All right, I'll take that."

Only because it was true.

"You needed me for something?" Chris asked.

Gian ignored the passing people—many he recognized—as he reached for the velvet case inside his jacket pocket. Pulling the item out, he rested it on his palm. It was as long as his hand, and about as wide. "I need you to run this across town for me."

"Seriously?"

"Yes. I don't make you run errands very fucking often, so don't start complaining now."

Chris held his hands up, a silent apology. "No worries. Where's it going to?"

Gian didn't answer right away, instead, opening the velvet case to check the item inside for a fifth time since he had picked it up earlier in the week. He'd wanted to give it to Cara himself. He hadn't seen her since the weekend before, but it looked like it was going to be another couple of days before he could drag himself away from the nonsense that had become his life. He figured the gift would be a nice way to tell her to look forward to a visit, and that he hadn't forgotten about her.

In a way …

Inside the case, a black lace, Victorian-styled choker rested on crushed velvet. A small, oval diamond hung from the middle, giving it a bit of regal beauty to go along with the classic. He'd found the item by chance, when he had gone into his jeweller's to pick up one of his Rolexes that needed to be fixed.

There was something about the choker—and the way he thought it might look on a delicate throat—that made him purchase the item without even hesitating.

"A woman, then," Chris assumed as he glanced down at the choker.

Gian quickly snapped the case shut. "A woman."

"You don't usually give gifts to women."

He didn't.

It wasn't appropriate, really.

"She's worth the step out from my usual," Gian replied vaguely. He handed the case over, and rattled off Cara's address. "Redhead, tall, beautiful. You won't miss her, and you might even recognize her. You're not to leave until this is in her hands, and you're not to allow her to refuse it. Understood?"

Chris nodded. "Got it."

"Tell her to text me if she wants someone to argue with about it," Gian added with a chuckle.

He'd plugged his number into Cara's phone the weekend before, and occasionally sent her messages throughout the week, but no actual phone call. He wondered how she would react to the gift, but he would have to settle with the aftermath.

"Go," Gian ordered, pointing in the direction Chris had come.

"Later, boss."

Gian didn't correct Chris's slip that time, but only because the steps had mostly cleared of people. No one was close enough to hear the man's casual use of a title that technically didn't belong to Gian.

Not wanting to be late for Mass, Gian headed inside the church, taking the steps two at a time. He'd missed it last weekend, and two in a row would never be overlooked by his devout Catholic mother.

Not to mention, Gian wanted to be seen.

Especially by the men of *la famiglia*.

With so many younger Capos and foot soldiers upset by the change in power—a change that Edmond had made without their input—Gian wanted to bring some sense of peace. Before any fighting within the ranks could begin, he wanted to stop it. He hoped, though he didn't know how well it would work, that his presence alongside the new boss might keep those men closer to his own age under control of sorts.

Even if Gian didn't entirely trust the new boss.

Gian found his usual seat in the third pew from the front of the church. He rested into the pew beside his younger brother. Domenic—

though Dom to his family and friends—passed Gian a curious look.

"What?" he asked.

"You're having Chris run gifts around for you now?"

Gian stiffened a bit in the pew. "Saw that, did you?"

"A few people did. You know, they're talking too, right? You disappeared last weekend, but *someone* knew where you went, and didn't keep it quiet. Add the gift thing to it, and the gossip will fly, Gian. You're not the kind to stir the pot. So, Cara Rossi, is it?"

Fuck nosy people.

And those that couldn't keep their mouths shut.

"Mind your business," Gian told his brother.

Dom rolled his eyes upward. "Not on this, man."

"There's nothing to talk about, so leave it. What I do privately is my own concern, and not for you or anyone else to worry about."

"But you took her away for a weekend."

"So?"

"And you bought her a gift—I saw it, too, it's not a little trinket, Gian," his brother added quieter.

"Again, *so?*" Gian asked, his irritation rising.

"According to Dad, it's one thing for you to hook-up with somebody and go your way. It's quite another for you to be … getting cozy. It makes a statement that you might not want, or the family, if you get what I mean."

"And Dad should mind his own business, too," Gian said.

"Ma—"

"You know, out of everyone, I bet she'll be the least likely to open her mouth and bitch about all of this. And do you know why? Because she knows I haven't been happy on that side of my life in a long fucking time. You know that, too, Dom."

Dom met Gian's gaze, nodding once. "Yeah, I do know."

"Then fuck off about it."

"I don't give a shit how it makes us look, as far as that goes," Dom said, "but I worry about *you*, man. And how it might make a target out of you, given some of the rumblings and the recent changes."

With that statement made, Dom nodded toward the *new* boss, an aisle over and two pews ahead of theirs. As he looked at the boss, Gian wondered how many eyes were watching him and his brother in that moment.

"Might he make a show out of you, to control those who favor you?" Dom asked.

"He's got bigger worries," Gian replied, "like keeping his older sheep happy and compliant. He's not even looking at the younger men right now."

Dom scoffed. "All he's done is piss off a lot of made men."

Yeah, that too.

Still …

"Don't worry about me, or this, or my business, all right?"

Dom shrugged. "You say that like it's easy, Gian. Grandpapa is dead—nobody's looking out for you like he would have done, so I'm trying to. That's all."

"You're not a made man yet, Dom. There isn't a whole lot of looking out you can do at the moment."

"I do what I can."

That, too, was true.

Gian appreciated it.

But still … "Stop talking about all of this in church. No business on Sundays, Dom. It's a rule."

"But—"

"You'll never get your button until you learn to listen more than you talk."

Dom finally shut up.

Gian was grateful for that, too.

• • •

I got your gift, read the text message.

Gian smiled, typing back, *Oh? Did you like it?*

He knew what her answer would be—yes, Cara liked the choker. It wasn't the choker itself that she probably struggled with, but the idea of accepting a gift from him. After all, it had been a whole *day* since Chris delivered the choker, and Gian got nothing but radio silence in return. He hadn't been particularly surprised about that, either.

When Cara didn't immediately reply, Gian hit dial on his phone's screen, and put it up to his ear as he headed into the restaurant. A business he owned, liked to use as an office of sorts, and had a meeting at later with Constantino and the asshole, Stephan.

They wanted to talk about what had happened with Edmond.

Gian wanted to placate the younger Capos for a bit.

"I was replying," Cara said as soon as she picked up Gian's call.

"You were taking too long. Probably overthinking. As I suspect you've been doing for the last day, *bella*. It's a necklace, one that suits your style, and I wanted to see you wear it, nothing more."

"Gian."

"Hmm?"

"You're being …"

"What, charming, again?" he suggested.

Cara sighed. "I'm agreeable to casual here with you—"

Yes, because apparently casual did not mean dating to Cara Rossi.

Gian didn't give a shit.

"And that means if I want to buy you something, I can and will. You should expect it," Gian interrupted before Cara could say more.

He swore she muttered, "You're fucking impossible."

"Drop the casual bit, and you'll see how impossible I can get," Gian urged with a smirk.

"That doesn't exactly make me want to jump in with both feet, Gian."

"Liar. You know it does."

Cara didn't reply.

Gian didn't need her to.

She'd already told him once ...

You make it hard to say no.

"I do like the choker ... a lot," Cara finally said, softly.

"Send me a picture with it on, show me."

"You're serious?"

"Would you like to see some of the pictures I already have of you, Cara?"

He didn't even need to see her face to know it was red, like her hair.

Gian laughed darkly, weaving through the restaurant and ignoring the patrons as he headed to his back office. "They're *beautiful*, by the way."

Cara made a noise under her breath. "Pretty sure that was *videos*."

"I took some stills of them. I have an app."

"Oh, my God. I have an app, he says. Like it's not a big fucking deal or something."

"Send me a picture," he demanded again. "Show me how much you like it, sweetheart."

Gian said a quick goodbye, as he had to get some work done before the guys showed up for dinner and the meet. He hated doing it to Cara, as he didn't get to talk to her much as it were, but he didn't have a choice.

To make up for it, as soon as he hung up the phone, he scrolled through the gallery images and videos. He hadn't lied—the video he had took, and the subsequent stills, *were* beautiful. Hot, sexy, and *sin*.

Pure fucking sin.

Porn, at the very least to some.

Art, to him.

He'd gotten a shot of his fingers buried deep into her pussy while she was on her knees, her sex pink and wet, her arousal smeared across his hand. Another of his cock stretching her open, and a quick peek at the handprint he'd left on her thigh. Then, later in the day, he'd pulled the phone out again to catch the way his cum looked, painted down Cara's toned stomach in white, ropey streams.

Gian was terribly careful with his phone. No one touched it but him, and not one single person knew his passcodes to get inside. He wouldn't share the images or videos with a soul, because that wasn't why he'd taken them.

He took them for *him.*

Because it made him hot and it got him off.

Because he liked reliving those moments.

Because his memory didn't do Cara Rossi any sort of justice.

He shot off a couple of the images, and one of the videos he'd shortened to a few seconds. All had been changed to a black and white, and he'd stripped the sound from the short clip, too.

He really liked that app.

Not a minute later, his phone buzzed on the desk as he were going over orders for the restaurant. Gian picked it up, gave the message a look, and laughed hard.

Are those even me?!

Every single one of them, he typed back.

He'd cropped some of the images, zoomed in to keep Cara's body and face from being entirely identifiable. But he wanted her to see what he saw, too.

Beauty.

Sex.

Lust.

The sweetest temptation that had ever crossed his path.

She would certainly be the cause of his eventual unraveling.

Gian didn't think he would mind.

That's porn, Gian, Cara's next message said.

Beautiful porn, he corrected. Then, he sent another right after. *I can do it again, oui?*

Cara's reply had him grinning. *Hell yes.*

He stuffed his phone away, and went back to work.

His mind was definitely not on the orders, though.

• • •

"They don't see it like you're *just* doing what you're supposed to do, though, Gian," Constantino argued. "The younger Capos—guys like us—see it like you're standing on Edmond's side of things, here. That you approve of what he did and how he did it."

Gian's jaw clenched, his one and only show of irritation at his best friend's statement. "You, of all people, know I don't approve. But what exactly could I do? I was put in a position where I couldn't do or say anything. He called the vote without telling me that's what it was, and he made the calls on who would be there for it. There's nothing I can do now."

"Not saying anything now certainly isn't helping your fucking case, either."

"Don't forget, it's my grandfather's legacy here, too. And I have to consider—"

"Your last name won't mean shit, with Edmond as the current boss," Constantino cut in fast.

Stephan nodded his agreement. "Everybody—especially the younger guys—knew it was going to be you next in that seat, Gian. It's what Corrado was working towards for years, slowly getting everybody ready for a change. He'd sped it up a bit recently, because obviously, there were some issues between the generational lines, and he probably thought putting you in the seat would help smooth that over."

"Corrado didn't talk about those things with me."

"He didn't *have* to," Constantino pointed out quietly. "It was expected. Edmond took advantage of a situation you weren't ready for and it makes you look weak as shit."

Gian bristled at that comment. "Say that again, *cafone*."

Constantino scowled. "I'm only saying it now for your benefit."

"You weren't ready for it because of Corrado's death," Stephan jumped in again. "Because someone—probably fucking Edmond—put a bullet between his eyes, or ordered it done."

"We don't know that he did it," Gian said quietly.

But he certainly had reason to suspect the new boss.

Every goddamn reason.

"And they were old friends," Gian added. "He's given me reason to think it was him, but that's circumstance, and nothing more. It's not likely that he *did* kill my grandfather."

Gian absolutely planned on finding out, though.

God save Edmond's soul.

"Friendships mean shit in Cosa Nostra," Stephan muttered. "Not when power is right there in front of you, ready for the taking."

Gian passed Constantino a look, not ready to agree to that statement. He'd known Constantino since he was ten years old—unless he had to, unless given no other option, Gian couldn't imagine putting a bullet in his oldest and best friend. They had too much history, too much time watching each other's backs.

Friendship *did* mean something. At least, to Gian.

"You need to, at the very least, make a statement against what Edmond did to put your own image and respect back in place for the younger Capos," Constantino said. "Don't bite the fucking hand that feeds you, Gian, not with this. Those men would have wanted you, and every time they see you running for the boss, or standing at his side, is another day that they feel like it was you that betrayed them, not him."

Gian considered those words carefully. "And then what if I do, what after that? Then I have a pissed off boss to contend with, and an older generation of men who wouldn't think twice about killing me to get me out of the way. I'm walking a very thin line here."

Constantino shrugged. "So, do it *carefully*."

"Easy for you to say. You're not the one sticking the target on your own back."

"You sure about that, man? Because the way I see it, anyone on your side is not on theirs. And that's a pretty big fucking target, Gian."

Fair enough.

• • •

Gian headed out the back entrance of the restaurant, entering into the alley where he had parked his Lexus. After the meeting he'd had with Constantino and Stephan, Gian needed five minutes to himself. He needed to get his thoughts together and figure out whether or not the Capos' warnings had any real merit for him to consider.

Then, his phone buzzed. Gian pulled the device out of his pocket, ignoring the chill in the air. Cara's name popped up on the screen, but the message surprised him the most. An image file, it seemed. He didn't even hesitate in opening it, his grin growing the very second it loaded.

Tanned skin.

Black thigh-high stockings with lace trim at the top.

Red curls framing delicate shoulders and naked breasts.

And that fucking choker …

She had taken the image in front of a mirror, from her painted-red smile down, but it was perfect. He was instantly hard and no longer giving any shits about his problems.

Took you long enough, he texted back instantly. Then adding, *But so worth the wait.*

He got a wink in response, but that wasn't enough for Gian.

I'm coming over, he messaged, *don't take any of that off.*

Gian didn't even wait for Cara's response before he grabbed the key fob from his pocket, and pointed it at his car thirty feet away. He hit the unlock button, felt his phone buzz, and then the blast came.

Hot.

Loud.

Dead.

Gian was sure he was dead.

Except, dead people couldn't feel pain, and he was in a hell of a lot of pain.

SEVEN

I'm coming over, don't take any of that off.

Cara stared at Gian's final text message, and then the one she had sent to him right after. *I'm not home right now, at dinner with my aunt.*

The reason it had taken her so long to send him the picture that he wanted—as he was quick to point out when she had finally sent it—was because she was in a rush. Her aunt had called last minute to invite her over for dinner, and as much as she wanted to say no, Cara wasn't very good at doing it.

She'd taken the picture for Gian before she'd thrown on a suitable black dress to match the stockings and heels. Then, she forgot to actually *send* it until the taxi dropped her off at her aunt's home.

Nonetheless, Gian hadn't answered her reply back.

That wasn't like him.

Cara didn't actually spend a lot of time on the phone with him, as far as that went, but when she did, Gian never wasted time on replying. His texts were always an instant response to hers, never leaving her waiting.

It left her with an odd feeling.

Cara shot off another text when her aunt's back was turned, asking Gian what in the hell was up. She stuffed the phone into her clutch before her aunt could see her with it when she turned back around.

Daniele gave Cara another once-over, her gaze lingering on the very short length of the black dress. It fell high on her thighs, enough so that the lace at the top of the thigh-high stockings were visible.

"Were you going out tonight?" her aunt asked.

Cara shrugged. "Nope."

It wasn't a total lie.

She hadn't expected to be leaving a bed, after all.

"You wear outfits like that on regular nights at home?"

"I grabbed the first black dress I saw—it was a bit short. It still worked."

"A bit short," her aunt echoed.

Cara held back the urge to roll her eyes. At twenty-five, she was not about to go explaining her attire, or the reasons for it, to anyone. And certainly not her aunt. "Anyway, what's for supper?"

Maybe if she got the hell out of there as soon as possible, she could salvage some of her night. With Gian, preferably. *If* she could get a hold of him.

"Food," her aunt replied with a wink. "Food you will eat and enjoy."

66

Well, that was that.

Thirty minutes later, a rigatoni dish soaked in thick, rich sauce was shoved in front of Cara's face. Across the table, her uncle stuffed a cloth napkin into the collar of his shirt as he waited for Daniele to give him a plate, too.

"It's good to see you around more," Claud said.

Cara wasn't quite sure how to respond to that. "It's been a rough few months."

"Yes, but it's better not to wallow. When things can't be changed, you move on. *Capisce?*"

"Yeah, I got it."

She didn't agree.

But that was an argument for another day.

It was only after Daniele had served her husband, and then herself, did she sit down at the other end of the long table. Her aunt said the usual dinner prayer, giving thanks and asking for a blessing from above, before they could even touch the food. It was one of the few things Cara had a hard time with—the blessing, not the actual act of praying. Even through her parents' drunken stupors when she was younger, they never forgot to go to church, make Cara and Lea, and Tommas say their prayers at night, or ask for a blessing when her mother managed to remember to cook food.

Maybe that was it; maybe it was that God had been the thing her parents chose to hold onto, even through their years of addiction, and not the three people they had brought into the world.

Cara really didn't like to think about it.

"All right, let's eat," her uncle demanded.

His booming voice brought Cara from her depressing thoughts. For once, she was grateful for Claud's loud demeanor.

Cara was a quarter of the way through her aunt's pasta dish when the home's landline started ringing. Claud waved at his wife to go pick it up, clearly not wanting to be taken away from his food. Daniele shot him a dirty look as she tossed her napkin to the table and headed for the sound of the ringing phone.

Thirty seconds later, Daniele shouted. "Claud!"

Cara stood from the table at the same time her uncle did. Panic had laced her aunt's yell. She quickly followed behind her uncle, watching as Daniele passed the phone over with wide eyes and worry setting her lips into a hard frown.

"What is it?" Cara asked her aunt.

Daniele acted as though she hadn't heard the question.

Claud spoke fast—and in Italian—into the phone. As it were, Cara's Italian was a bit too rough around the edges, and she had an even harder time keeping up when someone was speaking quickly.

But she did manage to catch a few words she knew mixed in.

Gian.

Autobomba.

Ospedale.

The name of the hospital was repeated, too.

Claud hung up the phone before Cara had even realized what happened. He waved a hand wildly at his wife. "My keys, get me my damn keys, *donna*."

Cara didn't move as her aunt rushed by her. "Gian is at a hospital?"

"What?" Claud's gaze snapped to Cara, but just as quickly, he dropped the stare and headed for the front of the house. Cara followed right behind. "It's none of your concern, Cara. Enjoy dinner with Daniele; keep her company for tonight."

No.

She refused to relent, her heart beating hard in her chest. "Is that why he didn't message me back earlier? A car bomb, that's what I heard you say."

Claud froze as he tried to put on his jacket. "Why are you even conversing with Gian Guzzi?"

"Because I'm a grown woman and I want to. Why won't you answer my questions?"

"Because I'm not required to," her uncle growled.

Cara straightened like a rod had been shoved up her spine, the familiar sense of being a woman in a man's world creeping into her mind again. This was how it always was for the women in this life—told to turn cheek, shut up, and behave when it counted. She hated that the very most.

"Let me give you a piece of advice, Cara," Claud said, finally slipping his jacket on properly. "You're right, it isn't my place to tell you who you can and can't be running around with, now that your father is dead and your brother has the say over you, but that doesn't mean you shouldn't still *listen* when you are told. My brother—your father—would tell you the same damn thing. Stay the hell away from Gian Guzzi, before you end up in a world of trouble that you don't want and can't handle."

"Aren't *you* a part of that world, too?" Cara shot back.

"You have no idea, do you?" Claud's eyes blazed. "Stay the hell away from the man, Cara."

"I want to go to the hospital."

"No. Not with me, anyhow."

Her uncle didn't even give her a second look before he went in search of his wife *and* his keys. Cara had already called a cab before Claud slammed the front door on his way out.

Fuck him.

She would do what she wanted.

• • •

Cara stepped out of the taxi after getting her credit card back from the driver, and stared up at the bright lights of the emergency room of one of Toronto's largest hospitals. She tried to stay away from hospitals—and this one in particular—as it reminded her a lot of Lea. Her twin had wanted to be a general surgeon, and had been a year away from starting her residency, when she died. Another dream cut far too short.

Letting out a slow breath, Cara shook off the unease and headed toward the emergency entrance. Her uncle had about ten minutes on her, so she assumed Claud would already be inside and doing his own thing by the time she figured out exactly where Gian was situated. Maybe he would even be gone by then, and that would be even better for her. Claud would be less likely to make a scene with others around, if he happened upon Cara.

She didn't even make it inside.

"Cara?"

Constantino stepped out of the shadows, a lit cigarette dangling from his fingertips. The cherry-red tip glowed as he came closer. "What are you doing here?"

Why couldn't anything be easy for her?

"Did your dad get here already?" she asked her cousin.

"Five minutes, or so, ago. He left right after. Now, answer me."

Cara tightened the belt on her tweed coat, willing away the cold. "Take a guess."

Constantino cocked a brow. "You probably shouldn't be here."

"Someone already tried to tell me that tonight. Try something new."

"How did you hear about the bomb?"

So it *was* a bomb.

Cara tried not to let that word frighten her too much, but it was *hard.* "I overheard Claud's phone call. Gian was supposed to come over, but I was already heading out. He hadn't answered my message, telling him I was already gone."

Constantino blew out a hard breath. "Don't go around saying that too loud."

"Saying what?"

"Nothing," her cousin muttered. "It's been a long night. Gian's already discharged, anyway. He's not even here, and he's chilling out where he can't be bothered."

Cara stood firm. "I want to see him."

"Yeah—"

"And why isn't he answering his phone?"

69

"Kinda got smashed on the way down to the pavement, and yeah," Constantino said. "Why don't you head home, and I'll let him know you were here."

Nope.

"I want to see him," she repeated.

Constantino scowled. "Since when did you become so fucking irritating and stubborn? Weren't you supposed to be the quiet twin?"

Cara couldn't quite let those comments roll off her shoulders. "You don't know shit about me. Don't pretend like you do, Constantino."

"Clearly."

"Take me to Gian."

Her cousin shook his head. "Fine. Whatever."

• • •

The very moment Cara laid eyes on Gian from across the club's floor, a swift relief coursed through her system. It was a feeling she hadn't quite experienced before, and she didn't know what to do about it. She hadn't realized that from the second she heard *bomb* uttered alongside Gian's name, fear had put her back in robot mode.

She'd gone back to that black space in her mind. Things moved around her, she did what was needed, and went through the motions of life amongst the living, but Cara wasn't *really* there. Not entirely. Not like she should be.

You're catching feelings for someone you shouldn't, her mind taunted. *And for no good fucking reason.*

Cara ignored her inner voice, her attention snagged entirely by the man across the floor. His gaze caught hers, and time stopped as he smiled. Even surrounded by a group full of men, all chatting with drinks in front of them, Gian looked at her and *smiled.*

A reddish discoloration marred his right cheek, up to his temple, but other than that, Cara couldn't see any visible issues that should be a cause for concern. Then again, she wasn't close enough to tell.

"Wait here," Constantino demanded.

She glared at her cousin's back as he crossed the club floor to the sectioned-off table where Gian was currently seated with the other men. Constantino bent down, said something, and then nodded quickly. That was it, and her cousin took the seat that Gian vacated not a blink in time later.

The club was hot as hell, so Cara pulled off her coat as Gian crossed the space between them, and hung it over her arm. She tried to shake off the lingering anxiety, and seem like everything was fine, but she couldn't quite do it as he came to a stop in front of her.

"You're not who I expected to see showing up here tonight," Gian said.

Cara shifted from one foot to the other. "You didn't answer me back."

"Something happened to my phone."

"Something like a bomb?"

Gian shrugged one shoulder. "I mean, we can do details, but it won't help all that much."

Cara sighed, trying hard not to meet his gaze. If she did, he would surely see all the crazy worry swimming in her mind, and he would know that she actually *cared*. Cara didn't know if she wanted to go down that road with Gian, quite yet.

"Shouldn't you be in the hospital?" she asked quietly.

Gian lifted his arms, and turned slowly as if to let her look him over. "Mild concussion, which means no sleep tonight. I can't hear all that great out of my right ear, but there's no lasting damage. I've got a bruised kidney, but I only need one, anyway."

Cara shook her head in disbelief. "Lucky."

"Some people do say the Guzzi blood is made of nothing but gold, luck, and dirt."

"Who are these people?"

He only grinned.

Cara finally met his gaze then, holding firm. "So, a club is where you decided to come after you get released from the hospital then? Not ... home, or—"

"To you."

His voice turned lower, cool and curious at the same time.

"You don't have to come to me. That's not what I meant or what I said."

"But would you have liked me to?" Gian asked.

Cara reached up to ghost her fingertips along the discoloration on his cheek and temple. "That looks like it hurts."

"Not a lot. Answer my question."

"Why a club?" she asked instead.

"*Dio*, you are difficult when you want to be. Do you know that?"

Cara smiled. "I've been told. Why a club?"

Gian gestured over his shoulder. "Someone thought I needed a drink, I couldn't refuse, given a lot of the shit that's happened over the past few weeks with the family. I've got enough problems, without making a certain group feel like I'm shunning them."

"I don't understand a word you said."

"Yeah, I know, but I like that you're not all that interested in those semantics of my life, anyway."

Cara let out a shaky exhale, and dropped his gaze. "This—tonight—

freaked me out a little bit."

"I can tell. You didn't have to come running, though. I was fine, as far as that goes."

"I was gone before I even knew what was happening, so …"

Gian chuckled.

That was all Cara got—one of his husky laughs—before he grabbed her waist, pulled her in close, and kissed her fast. The bruising force of his mouth crashing against hers took her breath away, and all that remaining fear and worry stopped, *just like that*. His hands slid up her sides and cupped under her jaw while his tongue darted into her mouth and gave her a taste of the bourbon he'd been drinking.

Cara felt dazed-like, when Gian finally pulled away.

Breathless.

Stupid.

Spun.

"I knew this would look good," he said.

"Huh?"

His thumbs slid down over her throat, hooking under the delicate lace of the black choker he had sent to her the day before. "This here, it looks perfect, *mon ange*."

"It does have a certain appeal," she admitted.

"There was a white one—"

"*Gian.*"

"But this one matches those stockings you're wearing, anyway," he said, never missing a beat.

Cara rolled her eyes. "So, hey, if you're good here with … your friends, then I'll head out. I don't need to be here, and you've got my number."

"I am good," he said, "and so are they, so how about—"

"Lea?"

Cara froze in Gian's warm hands like ice water had been poured down her spine. Gian, too, stiffened, his hands tightening to her neck at the quiet call of a name Cara rarely heard spoken anymore. She didn't think it was random, not with the way the man posed the question over Gian's shoulder, or the way Gian's gaze turned cold and hard in an instant.

A beat of time passed, and then another.

Cara's breath felt painful in those moments.

Gian moved to her side, his arm snaking around her waist. Cara faced the well-dressed man, who looked to be around the same age as Gian. Clean-cut, fresh-faced, and good-looking. He certainly wasn't anything to scoff at, and whoever he was, he looked like he *recognized* her.

"Frankie," Gian said, his smile belying the coolness in his voice. "I don't think you've met Cara Rossi, have you?"

The man—Frankie—suddenly appeared as though he had taken a

punch to the gut.

"My bad," Frankie said, offering Cara a fleeting smile. "Constantino wanted to know if you were going to head out, Gian."

"*Sì*, I think I am."

Frankie nodded. "All right, have a good—"

"Why did you call me Lea?" Cara asked.

"You're mistaken," Frankie murmured. Then, he gave another nod to Gian. "Later, boss."

He was gone before Cara could question him again, but *Gian* wasn't.

"Come on, let's go," Gian said, turning them both and directing them toward the front of the club. "My place is closer, if that's okay."

"Whatever," Cara replied. "Why did he call me Lea?"

"I don't know."

Gian was lying.

Cara could hear it in his voice.

"*Gian.*"

"Some people in my circles knew Lea from being around ... so maybe—"

"No, he sounded like he was in pain when he said it," Cara argued. "That's not a passing friend, Gian."

"Just drop it, *bella*. It's not important."

She didn't think so.

"Why are you lying?"

"I'm not," Gian said.

"I think you—"

Cara suddenly found herself yanked down a hallway behind Gian, and pulled into what looked to be a storage room of some sort. She didn't even have time to ask him what in the hell he was doing, before his lips were on hers again, taking away her words, thoughts, and breath.

"I didn't tell you how much I liked this dress, did I?" Gian asked.

Cara's head fell back against the closed door. "No."

"I do, I like it a lot."

"Who was that guy, Gian?"

"Nobody important."

"Gian."

He either wasn't listening, or he wasn't hearing Cara. As his hands slid up under the short skirt of her dress, and he lowered to his knees, Cara couldn't decide if she really gave a shit in that moment.

"Yes, I really like it. And the length is perfect, because it takes nothing to get it up," Gian muttered.

Hot.

Sinful.

Teasing.

That damn mouth of his was all of those things. And it was the only thing Cara focused on, as Gian dragged her panties down her thighs and his mouth was on her pussy. He had a wicked tongue with more talent than most men had in their entire bodies. He sucked on her clit, his tongue drove fast into the little nub right after, and she couldn't see straight.

"Holy shit," Cara gasped.

Distractions, she thought.

That's what he was doing.

Distracting her.

Fuck.

It was a good distraction.

• • •

Sleepy-eyed, Cara leaned in the doorway of the small gym, and tried to get some of the sleep out of her head. Gian didn't seem to notice her presence as his speed on the treadmill picked up from a jog to a thirty-second sprint before it shut off. He didn't even give himself time to breathe before he moved off the machine, and headed to the bar for a set of a dozen chin-ups.

Cara had no idea where this man got his energy.

But shit, it was a beautiful thing to watch.

The power, his body's lines, and the way he focused in on his task … it was all rather beautiful.

Gian dropped to the floor once his chin-ups were finished, and reached for a waiting water bottle and hand towel. Cara let him relax before she cleared her throat to make her presence known to him.

He flashed her one of his signature grins as he came close enough to press a kiss to the top of her head. "Morning."

"How long have you been awake?"

"Most of the night," he answered.

"The concussion, I forgot."

"You didn't need to be staying up with me, anyway. Beauty sleep."

Cara scoffed. "You do *see* me, right? Because nothing about this screams beauty at the moment."

Her hair was wild. Her eyes were sleepy. She had shoved on his forgotten dress shirt instead of her clothes because it was easier. She needed coffee, food, and a shower, and *then* she might be half presentable to the public.

Gian's hand tangled into her messy hair as he brought her closer for a kiss to her cheek. "Shut up and take the compliment, Cara."

Well, then …

"Fine, but I'm all fucked-out, so don't think you're getting laid for that one this morning."

His laughter came out dark and heady, waking Cara up even more. "Fucked-out, that's a new one."

"I need more time being awake to properly converse like a real human."

"Well, let's get some food in you and then see how you feel," Gian said.

Cara followed behind him as he headed toward his penthouse's kitchen. "Now is probably the best time to ask this, then, huh?"

"Ask what, Cara?"

"Who that guy—Frankie—was last night, and why he called me Lea."

Gian's steps came to a full stop.

Cara damn near ran into his back.

Slowly, he turned to face her, his amusement from earlier gone entirely. "You're not going to drop that, are you?"

"As much as I like you on your knees, eating my pussy like it's the last thing you're ever going to taste, no, that's not going to work today. If that's what you meant to say."

Gian's lips pressed into a thin, unimpressed line. "Cara—"

"I dealt with the distraction last night. Try the truth today, please."

"I don't know a lot about it."

"Tell me what you do know, Gian."

He crossed his arms, and Cara matched his posture in the hallway. She wasn't moving a damn inch until he started talking. Simple as that.

"Sometimes, Frankie runs in the same circles as me, but we're not friends, not like Constantino and I are. But like I said, sometimes we run into one another. As far as I know, from passing mentions or seeing them out, Frankie went out with Lea for a while a year back or so. Those were the few times I actually saw her or came in contact with her."

"Like a few dates, or …?"

"I think it was more than that," Gian admitted, "but I can't say for sure, and there's certain things men don't ask each other in this business, when women are brought around."

Cara's brow furrowed. "I don't understand. Lea didn't have a boyfriend before she died, and even before that, there was no one she talked about."

Sure, her sister went out and did her own thing. Lea had a social life that didn't include Cara a lot of the time, because she wasn't into that sort of thing. But a man? A boyfriend, for *months*? Cara didn't think so.

"As far as I know, it ended a couple of months before Lea died," Gian said with a shrug. "I only know that because … well, because I do."

"Because *why*?"

Gian scowled. "Because Frankie got married to the broad that ended up pregnant with his kid; he married her, and it was the right thing to do. That's what a man is expected to do when he knocks a woman up—marry her as soon as possible. I don't know the *personal* details because that shit is private. I know what was presented to me like it was to everyone else."

Cara suddenly felt like someone had sucked all the air out of her chest. "What?"

"Sometimes, it's better to drop things, Cara."

"Did Lea know he was running around with someone else?"

Gian barely blinked. "Maybe it didn't make a difference to her at the time."

It did to Cara.

It was all the same to her.

She thought her twin would have felt the same.

"I think I want to go home," Cara muttered.

Gian didn't even try to convince her to stay.

Cara needed to *think*.

She couldn't do that with Gian around.

EIGHT

"Johnnie was pulled out of the lake this morning," Constantino said. "All limbs attached, though, so clearly they wanted us to know."

Gian rubbed a hand over his jaw, feeling the stubble he hadn't bothered to shave that morning. "Fuck."

"Edmond is making a point."

"Or the older generation did it," Gian pointed out.

"It's still *for* the boss, Gian."

"Yeah, I know. I'm saying—"

"Johnnie had a verbal disagreement with one of Edmond's favorites the night after your car went boom last week, and all of the sudden, he shows up dead." Constantino scoffed, quickly adding, "Not to mention, he's the second body this week, but he could have been the third in *two* weeks, had the bomb on your car been successful."

Constantino was making all kinds of sense, even though Gian wished it didn't have to be this way. The sudden surge of violence on the streets between the younger and older generation of made men in the Guzzi Cosa Nostra was disconcerting, but not entirely a surprise.

The younger men had taken the bomb on Gian's vehicle as a personal affront, as though it was the boss's one way of removing the last person the men thought might give them a voice. Any verbal or physical action that disagreed with the boss was suddenly met with severe punishment—to make a point, to make the men sit down, and shut the hell up.

"I've been shut out for a week," Gian admitted.

"Completely?"

"No calls from Edmond or his new consigliere. No calls from the older Capos, and any attempts I've made to see them or check in, have been fucked over in some way. He's shutting me out."

Constantino swore under his breath. "This isn't good."

"No."

"What are you planning on doing now, Gian? Reconciliation was fine *before* someone tried to knock you off, but what now?"

Gian didn't have a simple or easy answer for that. "I need to find out who tried to kill me first, and then I'll figure out the rest."

Somehow, he held back from adding.

"Look to Edmond, or one of his minions."

"I'm aware, asshole," Gian said, "but I want a name behind the bomb and a reason first."

Gian still wasn't entirely sure what was going on within his own *famiglia*. Violence, yes. Discontent, sure. Lines had been drawn in the sand, and Gian had attempted not to put himself on either side of it, but managed to get put on one anyway.

"These issues—the problems between the generations—have been ongoing for a decade," Gian said. "Why now, has it suddenly gotten so out of hand?"

"You should already know the answer to that, but the fact that you admit these problems have been ongoing says you have chosen to be blind to the complaints for a long time, Gian."

He let that insult brush off his shoulders.

Sort of.

"It was manageable when Corrado was alive," Gian replied. "That's all I'm saying."

"It was manageable because one side knew that when Corrado was dead, they would finally have what they wanted—a younger boss they respected and had common ground with in *la famiglia*. You, Gian. And they didn't get you. They got another ancient fool in Edmond, who doesn't understand that it's not the forties and fifties anymore, and the rules need to change with the world we live in."

"You're starting to piss me off again; Corrado wasn't—"

"He chose to be blind or placate, too. Don't make that mistake, man."

"He's shutting me out," Gian reminded his friend. "That means he's not going to let me get close enough to put this to an end."

"And the bomb," Constantino said. "Don't forget the bomb."

How could he?

"I have too many things to deal with, all at once. Corrado, Edmond, the men, the fucking bomb. All of it."

"What if it's all the same man behind those things, though?"

"That's too simple," Gian said. "It's too easy. This life isn't easy. Nothing about it ever is."

Constantino didn't bother to argue that point.

"One thing at a time," Gian added, "and whether you want to admit it or not, there are a lot of men who would benefit from putting me in the boss's seat."

"Your point?"

"It's easy to point the finger at Edmond; easier, even, to make me look at him. No one said these men were fucking dumb, Constantino. I'm not going to treat them like they are, it could have been *anyone*."

"I still think Edmond—"

"Yes, because you would also benefit from me, not him, holding the highest position," Gian interrupted. His friend stayed quiet for a long minute. "Do you see my point, now?"

"To an extent," Constantino said quietly.

"Then give me time to think and work this out. I need to talk to people, look them in the face and see if they lie to me. I know these men, I've spent my whole life with these men. It has to be one thing at a time, man. That's how a smart man does it. I won't tear a whole organization apart, in an attempt to rid myself of only a couple of bad seeds. My grandfather *built* this fucking family into what it is, and I won't ruin it."

"Don't take too much time." Constantino laughed, though it came out strained and dry. "You were lucky with the bomb, but that luck won't last forever."

"Yeah, I know. Thanks."

"Just saying."

"I'll call you later," Gian muttered.

He didn't even bother giving a proper goodbye before he hung up the phone.

The elevator door opened, and Gian stepped out to a waiting consigliere for the building. The man smiled, and held out a key fob.

"Your new Mercedes is waiting at the front, Mr. Guzzi."

Gian took the device. "Thank you, Gene."

"Have a good day, sir."

He looked over the key fob for the new Mercedes as he exited the building. The car he'd wanted had to be shipped in from Quebec, leaving him without a vehicle for most of the week. He'd simply used his enforcer as a driver, but he was glad to have his own wheels again. The sleek, black two-door parked in front of the building was running, warming up in the cold March air.

Gian unlocked the car, but he didn't even get the chance to slip inside the driver's seat. Another black car, a four-door Mercedes with dark windows, pulled up beside his on the street. He recognized that damn car, and it took all he had not to ignore it and get inside his Mercedes.

The back window of the car rolled down.

Gian gave the man sitting in the back a look. "Edmond."

"I think you mean 'boss,' Gian," Edmond replied coolly.

"I said what I meant."

Let the fool make of that what he wanted.

Edmond's jaw tightened. "Get in the car. Let's take a drive."

Gian's hand twitched with the urge to reach for the gun at his back, but he knew better. It was broad daylight, in the middle of a very busy street and city, that was filled with cameras for the city *and* the police.

"I'm not sure that's a good idea. I'm not interested in taking a swim in the lake today," Gian said, turning back to his waiting vehicle. "I'm sure you understand."

"Get inside now, or Nathan will paint the side of your new car with your brain matter, Gian."

Well, then.

Gian chose not to question Edmond on whether or not the man's driver *did* have a gun pointed at him in that moment. The windows were tinted too dark for Gian to truly see inside and know for sure.

"Front seat, passenger side," Edmond ordered.

Fuck.

Gian slammed the door of his Mercedes shut, locked the car, and jumped inside Edmond's vehicle as he had been told. Sure enough, the driver and enforcer had a gun out, pointed, and ready to blow. Gian stared down the barrel of the weapon, both irritated and cold inside.

"You know where to drive," Edmond told Nathan. "Take it slow, though, as I'd like to have a chat with my underboss on the way."

"Got it, boss."

Not for a single second, did Nathan drop the weapon as he pulled back onto the road. Gian's gaze didn't move away from the gun, either.

"Unsettling, isn't it?" Edmond asked.

"Be specific. This whole show feels rather fucking unsettling."

"The gun."

"It's not even half as unsettling as a bomb blowing up thirty feet away from you," Gian replied. "Or having your boss shut you out from at least half of your organization. Or getting a sniper shot to the head while you drink your morning coffee and stare out the window. At least with a gun in your face, where you can see it, you know what is waiting for you. It's not trying to sneak up on you when you least expect it."

Edmond chuckled. "Someone's prickly."

"You did ask."

"I did." The older man sighed heavily from the back seat. "Seems we have a problem happening on the streets, don't we?"

"Seems so."

"One would think, given the attention we've received from the officials lately, what with Corrado's murder, amongst other things, that we wouldn't need or want more eyes on our organization," Edmond said.

"I would agree with that."

"Except you don't."

Gian shrugged. "Some things can't be helped. What's happening between the men, the rising discontent, is not *new*. It's an ongoing problem, only now they feel like they can be heard if they shout a little louder, or make a few more problems."

"You see those men through very rose-tinted glasses, Gian."

"I think I take them for their word, and see what they give me," he replied easily. "It's you who doesn't think the younger Capos deserve a voice in this organization. You told them that again and again—you made it even more apparent, when you placed yourself into the boss's seat without allowing them a vote in it."

"Be that as it may—"

"That *is* what it is," Gian interrupted. "There's no other way to look at it, Edmond."

"But there is," the boss replied quietly. "There is, because there is *you*, Gian."

"I beg your pardon?"

"I believe things have gotten out of hand these last couple of weeks, and I place the blame for that squarely on you."

Gian barked out a laugh, and for the first time, glanced away from the gun to stare at Edmond. "*Me?*"

"Yes, you. Had you not given half of my men a reason to believe they could dissent and rebel, then I wouldn't have these problems at the moment. They genuinely assume that by supporting you, they will eventually get what they want. And so, this is what we're going to do about it."

"Do tell."

"You're going to walk yourself back over to my side of things—act as the proper underboss your grandfather trained you to be for the last few years, and shut your mouth about the rest. Because, you see, when the men see *you* getting in line, they'll begin to move back into their proper places as well."

"You honestly believe it's that simple?" Gian asked, amused.

"I believe it's what needs to happen. They're all sheep, they will follow the wolf, as sheep tend to do."

"I wasn't standing on either side of any lines until a *bomb* was set on my car, Edmond." Gian smirked. "And even now, I haven't properly taken a side. I didn't think there was a side to take."

"Then you are stupid and naive. There is always a side, even when there isn't a war to be won."

"A good boss would want harmony in his family, for the sake of business."

"I don't give a shit about harmony, I want compliant *men*."

"I don't think I can help you with that," Gian said honestly. "They have their own mind. The fact you believe they'll follow along with me, simply because I am me, speaks to *your* naivety, Edmond. And considering someone recently tried to blow me up—I haven't put you out of the running for that one quite yet—you can't expect me to jump at the chance to help you, now."

"Well, that's too bad, isn't it?"

The car began to slow, and then pulled off the road altogether. It was only then that Gian realized where they were, and he barely contained his surprise at the apartment building staring back at him.

Cara's apartment building.

"Consider this your final warning, Gian," Edmond said. "Get in line, and help the rest of the men follow along, or I will remove you altogether. It might cause me a bit of trouble after I remove you, a few years' worth of feuding or nonsense, but those dissenters too will learn to shut up, fall in line, or dig their own grave."

Edmond smiled. "I don't mind doing it like that, though I would rather do it the easier way and make it quick. And then, you also get to live and keep your place. It's very simple."

Gian didn't care.

He was still staring at Cara's apartment building.

Why would the boss bring him here?

What point was there to be made with this?

"Do we understand one another, Gian?" Edmond asked.

Gian forced his features to remain cool and calm. "I certainly hear you."

"Consider my words, but I won't give you much time." Edmond waved at the building. "I hear you've been spending a lot of time with a young woman who lives here, so I figured this would be a good place to end our little chat. Have a good day, Gian."

"She's not even home."

It was mid-week.

Cara was at school.

Edmond shrugged. "Walk back, I suppose. The fresh air will do you good, and the time alone will allow you to think. You need both, clearly."

Nathan leaned over, opened the door, and jerked the gun from Gian to the outside.

Fucking great.

• • •

Gian waited patiently as the town car's back door was opened by the driver, and Cara was helped from the vehicle. His grin grew at the sight of her wild, red curls and the annoyed expression she sported. His gaze traveled down the maroon dress she wore beneath her opened trench coat; a tight number that stopped a few inches above her knees, made her legs look fucking fantastic, not to mention the heels.

God, the *heels.*

Gian loved heels.

Cara's stare landed on him, and she shook her head. "Do you often send cars to pick people up without any warning and with no indication of what they are going to be doing?"

"Chris told you to wear something nice, didn't he?"

"You're missing the point *and* the question."

"You would be surprised at how many people I call on to do whatever fits my fancy." Gian winked. "But not women, if that's what you meant."

Her iciness bled away a little. "I'll have to take your word for it."

"A man is only as good as his word."

Cara surveyed the restaurant behind him. "Dinner?"

"You're simplifying it, *Tesoro*. It's a date. You and I, *having* a date."

"Why?"

Because he thought she might like it.

Because he didn't want to only *fuck* Cara.

He wanted to know her, too. He wanted to do normal things with her, like taking her to dinner, listening to her talk, and whatever else she wanted to do. He knew very well this woman was worth far more than how well she could take his cock, and he needed her to know it, too.

Gian stepped up to Cara, close enough that he could smell the hauntingly-sweet perfume lingering on her skin. Only a few inches shorter than him, she stared up at him, waiting for what he would do next.

A simple, quick kiss was all he offered before he straightened again with a smile. But it wasn't so quick that he didn't feel the gentle grin of hers form against his kiss before he had pulled away.

"Because it's been a week since I last saw you, and it didn't end well," Gian settled on saying.

Cara looked away. "Well—"

"And you haven't contacted me, either, so don't try to say it's fine. I don't fall for that bullshit."

"I wasn't going to."

Gian was pleased about that. "Dinner, then?"

"I thought it was a date?"

"Dinner is one part of the date, Cara."

Her painted-red lips curved at the edges. "All right, then. Most men actually think to *ask* for a date, though."

"Seems when I ask for things, we end up in a bed, and we don't do much else." Gian chuckled at the sight of Cara's cheeks turning pink at his words. "Not that I mind, but change is always good, too. I tried a different approach this time, let's see how it works out for us."

"Let's be honest here, probably still in a bed."

"At least we'll do something first."

Cara nodded. "Good enough."

Gian's hand found Cara's lower back as they walked into the restaurant. There was no waiting for a table, as he owned the restaurant, and had the private dining area reserved for the evening until his dinner was finished. Once he had Cara seated at the table, the server made his way in with a smile and menus in hand.

"I don't know what I want to order," Cara admitted after the server had offered the specials and what he would recommend. She looked to Gian. "Surprise me?"

"Believe it or not, but if I order for us, it won't be something fancy and pretty."

Cara laughed, gesturing at the silk table cloths and then to the extravagant crystal lighting above their heads. "Even in a place like this?"

"They know what I like," Gian replied with a shrug. "And it's not always spectacular, but something to enjoy. Sometimes, the chef likes to make something that isn't an affair in his kitchen, too."

"I stand by what I said, then."

Surprise her.

Gian only had to nod at the server, and the man was gone from the private dining space. He didn't even need to tell the man what he did or didn't want—the employees knew the owner well enough, and Gian made a point to dine often at this particular restaurant. He *did* like the food, after all.

"How was your week?" Gian asked.

It was a safe topic of conversation. Something he could move into what he really wanted to ask.

Cara made a face. "Busy at school. Quiet all the rest of the time. *Dull.*"

"Why dull?"

Her blue eyes sparkled with mischief. "I get bored when I'm alone."

"You sound surprised at that."

"I never used to mind being alone."

"I'm not very good company for myself, either."

Cara stared beyond Gian, at the artwork behind him. "I find it hard to believe that you spend much time alone."

"Cara."

She didn't look at him.

"*Cara.*"

"Yes?"

Gian reached across the table, and slid his fingers under her chin so that he could *make* her look at him. "If you have something to ask, then do so."

"We're casual, not exclusive. I said that, Gian. I don't *need* to know anything."

"You can still ask, *donna.*"

Cara's lips pursed. "That would suggest more than—"

"My God, *ask.*"

"I don't *need* to, Gian. That's the point. I was thinking too much this week—overthinking like I do—because of my sister and that guy. She had online journals she used to keep, you know? I went through some because I have her passwords and her laptop. I never did that before. And her phone, too. I still have that. I charged it and read the messages she hadn't deleted."

Gian frowned. "And what did you learn?"

"That it didn't end between them when everyone thought it did. She still saw him occasionally, after he was married. She knew, too, about the other girl before the pregnancy thing came up. Why didn't she ever say anything to me? Why didn't she tell me? I'm her twin."

Cara sighed, her manicured nails rapping against the table cloth as she added, "But then, I know why she didn't say anything, because she knows me, too. She knows I wouldn't have been happy—that I would not have agreed with what she was doing. So, I'm stuck in this headspace of being angry that she left me out of a private thing, and being grateful that she did at the same time. I feel like I didn't know her, or this part of her. It's messed up."

"And this made you overthink because …?"

"Because I don't want to be one of several woman, Gian. I want to be one woman to one man. Except that wasn't what I told you before, so—"

"You are one woman to one man," he interrupted smoothly. "I'm not with anyone else, and I haven't been for a long time. I didn't even do a *casual* thing with women, I did the random thing for an evening and that was it. Things are simpler in my life that way. I have … well, expectations of me, and it's easier when I don't have to bring others into that mess, too."

Cara's fingers stopped their dancing instantly. "Yet, you're bringing me into it."

"Not really. You've made it clear that I am not your type of man because of the business side of my life, Cara. You have no interest in being there. It makes it easy to keep you the hell out of it, when you don't want to be a part of it at all."

"Oh."

"It's an unnecessary fucking complication," Gian said, knowing damn well he sounded cross and harsh. "And I like that we have this way of just enjoying each other, our time together, talking in bed, you thinking you're sneaking up on me in the mornings when I know damn well you are there. Me reading in bed and you wearing my shirts. I *like* those things. They are uncomplicated, easy things for me to do, Cara. You don't ask for more, so I don't offer. But if you did ask, if you did want more, then I would try to give you that, too."

"And you're not doing that with someone else," she said.

"No."

"Or anything else, either."

Gian chuckled lowly. "No, again."

"Okay." Cara gave him one of her brilliant smiles that lit up her pretty, delicate features. "I was also kind of irrationally pissed off at you this week, too."

"For what?"

"Knowing something about my twin that I didn't."

Gian scowled. "That's unfair."

"I told you it was irrational."

True.

"Fair enough," he uttered. "Are you still angry about that? Even irrationally."

Cara laughed a tinkling, musical sound. "Lucky for you, no. I'm not mad, or I wouldn't have come tonight."

"You would have come."

"You don't know that."

Gian's grin deepened. "You came tonight, not even knowing what this was. You came with a tight-as-hell dress on, even though I know my man only told you to dress appropriately for an upscale evening. You came with fuck-me-heels on and your hair loose and wild the way I like. You put the red lipstick on that I like to see stained on my sheets. You would have come, Cara, whether you were pissed off or not."

Her cheeks reddened. "So you're a good fuck—I never denied that, Gian."

"Try again."

She blew out a slow breath. "God, you're insufferable."

"Try again, *mon ange*."

"I know that means you're calling me your angel. I know how to use the internet, Gian."

"Try again."

"Could you try to be a little less arrogant?" she asked.

"I don't give an inch, because everyone thinks they can take a mile. Try again."

Cara's eyes blazed as she turned them on him. "I came because I like you, and you make it hard to say no, even when you're not asking."

He'd take that.

Fucking right he would.

"Except right now, you're making me want to—"

"Make a trip to the closet private space to get me between your legs?" he asked with a smirk. "Because I only actually need to move my chair closer, Cara, to get that job done with one hand. The tablecloth hides what goes on beneath."

"You are—"

"Are we ready for drinks?"

The sudden appearance of the server made Cara sit straight in her chair while Gian only winked at his companion. "Red wine, and bring it with the food, please."

"Five minutes, Sir."

"Wonderful."

Gian didn't take his gaze off Cara, but he listened to the footsteps of the receding server.

"What did you order us, anyway?" she asked.

"Poutine."

Cara repeated the word, and butchered it the way most Americans and Western Canadians did whenever they said it.

"No, not poo-teen," Gian said with a laugh. "Pou-tin. Or, *pu-tsin* if you're French."

"Isn't that, like, fries and gravy?"

"It's a delicacy, invented by the French. Homemade fries, cheese curds, and a dark gravy, piled into one giant mess on a plate. Everybody has their own way of making it, some add different nonsense to it, which frankly, ruins what it's supposed to be in the end. It's not pretty, but it is delicious."

"And what about *after* the food and wine?"

Gian shrugged one shoulder. "Whatever you want, Cara. I can take you home, and drop you off. I know you probably have classes tomorrow. Or we can go see a movie, maybe a show if you want. It's up to you."

"So, a *real* date, huh?"

"One that ends however and wherever you want it to, *bella*."

She smiled a wicked sight.

Gian knew *exactly* where their date was going to end.

He didn't mind a bit.

NINE

"More," Cara demanded, her voice thick with sleep and content.

Gian chuckled, rocking her body that was tucked tight against his. "You were supposed to be up an hour ago."

"Just read."

"Cara."

"*Gian.*"

He made the sexiest noise under his breath. "You know I can't refuse you when you say my name like that, Cara. That's unfair."

"More reading, less nagging."

"You have terrible morning habits."

"I also have a gorgeous man in my bed and a study group, first thing, that I can afford to miss. Shut up and read, Gian."

In French, actually.

He was reading in French, and Cara *loved* it. She didn't understand a damn word he was saying, for the most part. There was something about his voice that soothed her *and* provoked her at the same time.

With a half-hearted sigh, Gian continued reading. *Les Misérables*, to be exact. She didn't know what to do with this conundrum of a man. He wasn't entirely good, but he wasn't entirely bad, either. He wore shoes and suits that cost more than what most people made in a month, yet ate comfort food and liked cheap beer. He had set a gun on her nightstand the night before, but brought a classic novel in from his car like he needed it just as badly, too. He was educated, high-class, and Toronto elite, but rough, dirty, and full of sin, too.

Cara didn't know what to do with all the pieces of Gian Guzzi.

Not a clue.

The cadence of Gian's tenor changed before his French turned to English as he asked, "You don't even understand what I'm reading, do you?"

Cara shrugged, snuggling in closer to Gian and soft sheets. "Don't have to."

"That's sort of the point of being read to, right?"

"Not right now."

"I don't understand."

"You wouldn't." Cara hummed a happy sort of sound, grinning up at the dark-eyed man staring down at her. "It's your voice. It's an all the time thing, Gian. The way you sound, you probably don't even hear it, but I do."

"And how do I sound?"

She could have said many things.

Sexy.

Lovely.

Comforting.

Arousing.

Deep.

Provoking.

The truth was, Gian's voice—and him, really—was a mix of *all* of those things. Settling on one was not enough. It did not do him justice.

"Dangerous," Cara whispered. "You sound dangerous, Gian."

For a long while, Gian stared at Cara, never blinking or moving a muscle. It was as though he didn't quite know what to make of her statement. "I've never been told that before."

"That's kind of sad."

"Is it?"

"You should know the way you can affect people, Gian. It's more than wearing a suit and a sly smile, with a gun hidden at your back. It's knowing that you only need to speak and people listen. A man with a dangerous voice has far more command than anyone could possibly understand, he needs to know how to use it." Cara rolled over to her back and reached for her phone on the nightstand. She checked the time, and scowled at it. "I do need to get up soon. The study group was okay to miss, but I have a paper I need to hand in for the class after that."

Gian didn't reply, which made Cara look over at him. She found that he was still looking at her, but the intensity she saw in his eyes made her heart stop for a split second.

An appreciation, churned with lust and mixed heavily in his admiration and hunger. As though she was the sweetest, most precious thing to have ever spoken in his presence, and he wanted nothing more than to be right there with her forever. She had seen his many stares before—when he wanted to fuck, his irritation, or his indifference.

This was not the same.

It scared her for a moment.

Something else to add to her rapidly growing pile of confusion.

"I don't know what to do with you," Gian finally said, breaking the silence.

"The same thing you have been doing, I guess."

"It's not enough. It's not nearly enough, *bella*."

She tossed her phone back to the nightstand, and then turned back to Gian, taking her sweet time to crawl on top of his naked body, under the sheets, until she straddled him. One of his hands landed on her waist, his fingers gripping tight to keep her still, while the other slid from her stomach, up between her breasts, and stopped on her throat.

Cara only smiled at the sensation of her heartbeat thrumming under his hand. "I like that, you know. I don't really say it, because I figure I don't have to. But I like that a lot."

Gian's fingers drummed against her throat. "This?"

"Yes. Especially when you squeeze hard enough to take my breath away, like I'm floating for a few seconds, all the control is gone, and it's only a *feeling*. Nothing else. Just the way I feel."

"What else?"

She shifted her weight on top of him, attempting to ignore the length of his erection resting between her legs. It didn't help, really. She only ended up grinding against his cock more, soaking in the silky feeling of his length sliding along her pussy. She used her hands as support against his lower abdominal muscles to keep her steady as she reveled in that simple pleasure.

"Cara," Gian murmured.

That voice of his would kill her someday.

She was sure of it.

Her attention was back on him in an instant, and she remembered what he had asked. "And I like the way you talk when you're fucking me, how you always take and demand, and you rarely ever ask. You don't push, either, but you don't have to. It's raw and it's filthy and I like it that way."

"Why?"

His question seemed simple enough.

Except his voice was laced with huskiness and heat.

"Because there's something about you that's different," Cara admitted quietly. "You use me in bed like a toy, like I'm yours to ruin and fuck however you want to; like your own personal little slut. And then you open my doors, you hold my hand, and you tell me I'm beautiful."

"Of course I do, Cara."

"Yes, *because* you're different. Because there's more to a woman than how she behaves in a bedroom, but most forget not to bring it beyond the bed, too. You don't, and I like that."

She leaned down, close enough that her lips were a breath away from Gian's as she said, "And nobody's ever fucked me quite like you do, Gian."

"That's a damn good thing, then."

That was all Gian said before his lips slammed into Cara's with a bruising, demanding kiss that silenced her mind and made her heart race. His tongue found hers in a familiar dance that came like a comfort, and a battle at the same time. It was only when he pulled away enough to bite into her lower lip that she realized how badly she needed air, but couldn't get in a good breath.

His hips had started moving with the gentle beat of hers, too. Rocking, grinding—putting pressure in the right spot and then taking it away before she could get more.

Cara was sure her juices had soaked his cock already.

She couldn't even find it in herself to be ashamed.

"Why?" Cara managed to ask while his teasing mouth traveled over her throat.

"Why, what?"

"Why is it a good thing that no one has ever fucked me like you?"

His arms encircled her then, one curling around her back and neck so that his hand could grab onto her hair. His other arm went between her legs and up over her ass so his palm laid flat to her lower spine. He held her there, forcing her head back so he could look her in the eyes while her body fucking *shivered*.

"Does it matter?" he asked.

"I answered your questions. Answer mine."

"Because I like that it's only been mine this way," he told her. "The way I fuck you, how you let me have you. Your pussy, your ass, that fucking mouth, and the rest of your body. How you say my name and the sounds you make when you're about to come but you know you need to wait. You're greedy as hell when I'm eating your cunt and then sweet as hell in the morning, demanding that I read to you. When you want to get on your knees like you're about to pray, but all you do is open up that goddamn mouth of yours and suck me dry instead. It's ... it's insane, but it's fucking beautiful, Cara. And it's only been mine like that. Someone else might have gotten something else, but I get *this*, and that's addicting. You're addictive."

She took a shaky breath. "And you don't think you're addictive, too?"

His arms tightened to her body and her hair. "As long as it's mine, sweetheart."

She was ruined for anyone else, anyway.

Didn't he already know that?

Well, how could he know, when she was now realizing it, too?

"Who the hell else could make me fucking crazy like you do, Gian?"

He only grinned—sexy, cocky, and pleased.

"You know what I was most pissed off about, the morning after my car got bombed?" he asked.

"What was that?"

"I ruined my damn phone and—"

"Lost your filthy porn."

Gian laughed. "Well, yeah."

"You'll get more."

"Of you? I'd say so."

Cara's gaze snapped to his fast. "Only me."

Gian's grin melted into a smile before he kissed her mouth once more, softer than before. "Who the fuck else?"

Exactly.

"You do have to get up and get ready," he reminded her.

She was more interested in his mouth, hands, and cock.

They were far more interesting.

"In a minute," Cara said absently.

He let her go then, his arms releasing her from that snake-like hold so he could grab her face and kiss her mouth over and over.

Cara rotated her hips on Gian's hard cock once more, determined to get back in her happy place, but he had other things in mind. *Better things.* His hand dove between their bodies, and the next time Cara ground along his length, he filled her full with one hard flex of his hips, driving upwards against her pussy.

She hadn't been expecting the move, if only because he was always so careful to grab a condom first, though she had told him before that she was on the pill. But she liked him this way, too—bare and natural, filling and stretching her full, making her ache with nothing but him.

"Shit," Gian groaned, holding Cara tight to his body so that she couldn't move. "Fuck, I love your pussy."

"Because it's yours."

His nod answered her back, and his eyes closed as she felt his cock jerk inside the tight walls of her sex. She was wet as fuck as her hand snuck between their bodies to feel the base of his bare cock fitted snug to her cunt. Hot, too, she realized.

Cara's fingers slid over her clit with gentle strokes, making her inner muscles tighten and release with each touch.

"Could you come like that?" Gian asked, never opening his eyes. "Just stretched full of my cock and playing with your cunt, could you?"

"Yes, but not as fast as I would like."

"And how would you like it, Cara?"

"You already know."

Gian's eyes opened, making Cara still on top of him entirely. "Yeah, I do."

She hadn't even blinked before one of his hands tangled into her hair and the other found her throat. The second his fingers tightened, choking and pulling at the same time, his hips thrust upward, driving into her again. Cara let him pull her forward, enough to lift her hips and let him pound into her pussy, deep and hard enough to make the rest of the room disappear. It was only the sound of them—his cock slamming into her, her pussy taking him in, all wet and tight, her whines and his whispers—and nothing else.

"Ride me or take it," Gian muttered through his clenched teeth. "Fuck me how you want to, or take my cock the way I know you can, Cara."

"I want both."

She was greedy that way, too. Greedy enough for him to back her ass into his every thrust, but still needy enough to make him pound into her hard enough to make her fucking crazy.

His fingers tightened around her throat, taking away air and making her fly. She knew what was coming. She fucking vibrated for it, anticipated it, wanting his words to make it sweeter, and better.

"Just fucking come and give it to me, then," he demanded. "Show me what's mine, Cara. *Show me.*"

Shit.

She could do that.

All he had to do was *say so.*

• • •

Cara stepped out of the shower to find Gian leaning in the doorway. "I know, I'm late."

He held his hands up, grinning in that way of his. "I'm saying nothing about that again. I warned you earlier, you wanted to listen to me read, love."

"Well, it sounded good."

"And then fuck after," he added.

Cara shot him a look. "I didn't hear you refusing."

"Why would I?"

She didn't dignify that with a response, instead drying off with a towel and making quick work of rubbing it through her wet hair. She was going to have to rush to get to school and hand in her paper on time, but she couldn't find it in herself to give a shit.

Gian had jumped in the shower with her long enough to clean himself up before he jumped right back out. Cara was both jealous and irritated to see him standing there with his suit on *and* his hair dry.

It wasn't fair that all he had to do was basically roll over and be ready for the day.

"What do you want, if you're not standing there to remind me that I'm late again?" Cara asked.

She headed past Gian in the doorway, going toward her bedroom for clothes. It was what he said next that stopped Cara in her tracks.

"Your brother called."

Cara turned slowly on her heel. "I'm sorry?"

"Tommas—that's your brother, right?"

"Yes."

"He called when you were in the shower. He wanted me to ask you to call your mother."

Nope.

Cara turned back around and went straight into her room without a word. She dug through her closet, while Gian came to stand in the doorway of the bedroom, watching her in that silent way of his.

"Could you give me a ride to the university?"

"You don't even have to ask," he replied.

"Great. Saves me time."

"I take it you're not going to talk about your brother, huh?"

Cara shrugged. "Tommas is fine. Not my mother, though."

Gian nodded as she passed him in the door. "Fair enough."

"And I'm not calling the bitch, either."

"Ouch," he muttered behind her.

Cara kept walking, picking up her bag and the other things she needed on the way. Her hair would have to dry like it was, but it wouldn't be the first time. "It sounds cold because I mean for it to. I have nothing to say to that woman that will be nice, and everybody knows it. Just because Tommas can muster up an ounce of care for the woman means fuck all to me in the end. I've looked for something, Gian."

"And?"

She turned to look at him, unaffected as she said, "It's not there. Nothing is there. Maybe when Lea was alive, or even shortly after she died, when I was so alone here by myself—maybe then I might have found something. But, now? Now, when I'm almost fully okay and I don't need somebody holding me up, it's gone again. I'm not calling my mother. I have nothing to say to Serena Rossi. She can keep drinking away the shit she did to us kids until she drinks herself into a grave. And even then, I don't care."

Gian's face remained passive and calm throughout her tirade. "I'm sorry, *mon ange.*"

"You don't have to apologize. If anything, you're one of the things that woke me the hell up again. I was missing something for a long time after my twin died, and now I don't feel so lost or empty. But you know what does makes me feel that way?"

"What?"

"My mother. Even thinking about her makes me revert back into that shell of a child that played a little quieter than normal, as to not enrage the drunks sleeping upstairs, or waited for her brother to get home so she could eat. That lost, lonely child. So fuck her and fuck Tommas for asking me to care, too."

Gian cleared his throat. "All right. You going to be okay today or—"

Cara opened her apartment door with force. "I'll be fine."

"Really? Because you used more fucks in this conversation than the entire time we've been messing around, Cara."

She locked her apartment up once Gian was out in the hallway with her.

"I'll be fine," she repeated. "I always am."

"Or do you *have* to be?" he asked as she started down the hallway.

Cara tensed, but kept walking. "Does it matter?"

Gian caught up with her quickly enough, his arm curving her waist as he pulled her in tight and kissed the top of her head. It was that simple action—his unspoken concern and care—that slowed Cara's rage.

"It matters to me," he murmured against the top of her head.

Cara sighed. "I'm good."

Gian made a discontented sound under his breath.

"I am," she promised. "Sometimes it spills out, though."

"That's a lot of anger to bottle up, Cara."

They strolled out of the apartment building into cool March air, and Cara breathed it in deep.

"A lot of deserved anger," she pointed out.

Gian nodded as he directed her toward the apartment's parking lot, where he had left his car the evening before. "Sure, except you don't direct it at the person most deserving of it."

"My mother is the type that feeds off attention, negative or otherwise. She uses any time and attention you give her to manipulate you for her emotional games. It's not worth it."

"I'm suddenly feeling like I need to give my mother a visit soon."

Cara frowned. "I didn't mean—"

Gian shrugged as he unlocked his car and then held the passenger door open for Cara to slide inside. Once she was seated, he offered her one of his charming smiles. "You reminded me that despite the fact I am a twenty-nine year old man, I have a mother who still loves me as though I'm her baby. She's always concerned for my happiness, even though she doesn't have to be. I can't even remember her yelling when I was a boy. I have a wonderful mother, and sometimes I don't appreciate her enough. That's all."

Oh.

"I'm sure *she* would like to hear that, too, Gian."

He laughed. "No worries there. I'll be sure to tell her. I think she would like you, Cara."

"Do you?"

"Of course, because I do, *amore*. Maybe you'll be able to meet her soon."

"When?"

Gian winked. "Soon."

Then, he closed the door.

In a blink, he had rounded the car and was inside the vehicle, too. He hummed a sexy sound as the car lit up under his handling, the gears shifting into place as the engine turned over.

"I love this car," he said, "but I do miss the Lexus."

"I can't justify buying a car in a city like Toronto. Everything is a walk away. It would be pointless."

Gian glanced over at her, and then pulled out of the parking spot, heading toward the road. "I travel too much from one side of this city to the other to not have a car."

"Point taken." Cara stared down the road while Gian maneuvered the Mercedes into traffic. Something caught her eye down the way, something familiar. "Is that …?" She trailed off, leaving the sentence hanging as she stared over her shoulder.

Gian followed her gaze, although he was careful not to ram the front of his Mercedes into the back of the car in front of them. "What?"

"There, parked behind that white Toyota."

His teeth clenched.

Cara didn't miss it. "That is my uncle's car."

"Looks like it."

"Why would he be outside my apartment?"

Gian turned back in the seat, his show of irritation all but gone. "Hard to say. Let's get you to classes, Cara."

"But—"

"Hey," he interrupted smoothly, "your birthday is coming up, right? Constantino might have mentioned it, since his is not far off from yours."

Cara's brow furrowed while she tried to decide whether to push him on her uncle's presence outside her place, or call him on his distraction. She settled for answering his question, for now. "Two weeks from Saturday."

"Would a private flight to Quebec be a proper present? We would leave Saturday morning, and be back Sunday evening."

"What's in Quebec, Gian?"

"French. A whole lot of French, *mon ange*. And old buildings, brick roads, shitty drivers, some of the best restaurants, tickets to a ballet, and a fantastic suite booked for a birthday girl."

Cara couldn't help but smile. "A trip to Quebec it is."

• • •

Cara nearly tripped over the waiting bags at her apartment door as she rushed to answer the persistent knocking. With only a towel wrapped around her waist, and her wet hair hanging freely around her shoulders, she figured whoever it was could deal with being made to wait, considering it was them who got her out of the shower.

She pulled open the door with a huff, flipping wet curls out of her eyes at the same time. "What?"

A man she recognized—Chris was his name—stood on the other side, waiting with a smile and a large white box with two smaller white boxes on top of them. Pretty, shimmering pink bows had been tied to each box.

Cara's irritation instantly melted away.

"Gian?" she asked.

Chris nodded. "You know it."

This was the second time Gian had sent Chris to her door with a gift—although this looked to be *gifts*. The first had been the black choker she loved so much. The barrel-chested man had politely explained to Cara that should she continue to refuse the gift, he didn't mind escorting Cara to Gian to accept the gift directly, if she was so insistent on not allowing him to do his job. Given that first meeting, Cara knew better than to refuse Chris, when he was only there to do what he had been told.

And it *was* her birthday, after all.

"He could have waited for tonight," Cara mused as she stepped back to let Chris in.

Her birthday had come much faster than she expected, the end of March skipping into her life before she had blinked.

There was no way she could take the boxes and maintain her modesty by holding up her towel. Chris kept his eyes above her chest as he maneuvered through her apartment to set the boxes down on the kitchen table.

"Early gifts, he said," Chris told her. "Something he thought you might like to have for the trip, and the ballet tonight."

"Oh?"

"That's what was told to me. I'll be waiting outside to drive you to the private air strip when you're ready, miss. Do you want me to take the bags at the door down for you?"

Cara gave the guy a smile. "You *can* call me Cara."

Chris shrugged. "I could, but I won't. At least, not yet. The bags?"

"They're only small. I can do—"

"I'll take them, no worries. Finish getting ready."

Chris gave a two-finger wave as his goodbye, and exited the apartment with Cara's small, overnight bags slung over his shoulder. Once the front door was shut, she turned back to the waiting boxes with their pink bows on the table.

"What did you do now, Gian?" Cara wondered out loud.

She thought it was time to find out. She set each of the three boxes side by side, and started with the middle one first, carefully untying the box and pulling off the top. Patent leather, pristine, white pumps rested inside white tissue paper. Pointed toes and six-inch stiletto heels. Vibrant red soles painted the bottom of each shoe.

Cara knew that signature red sole without even having to look inside the heels to check.

Every girl did.

Louboutin.

A small note rested alongside the shoes, and Cara picked it up to read.

Because beautiful legs deserve to be shown off, birthday girl. —Gian

She reached for the largest box, then, wondering what on earth he had stuffed inside that thing, too. It was a good two feet in length and width. She wasted no time getting the bow and top off, only to find more tissue paper this time covering the item inside.

Her hands shook as she removed the tissue paper to pull the white and silver dress out from within the box. White silk, and silver lace and fringe, covered the form-fitting, sleeveless, knee-high dress. There was no flair to the skirt; it was pencil thin, with the same silver lace fringe along the bottom that decorated the sides and bodice. Sparkling beadwork and crystals had been carefully sewn in to the fringe.

A matching clutch also sat inside the box, waiting to be appreciated.

There was no note in this box, but Cara wondered if that was because Gian intended to let the tag on the dress speak for him.

Dolce & Gabbana.

Already, there was a small fortune sitting on her table in a single pair of shoes and a dress. She was reaching for the third, final, and smallest box of the bunch before she even realized it.

Inside, she found a thin, white lace choker. Maybe an inch wide, the delicate lace was soft against her fingertips, and clasped at the back with a small chain with a single, dangling white pearl.

A note rested underneath the choker.

All white, as angels should wear, mon ange. *You're only missing the wings, now. Happy birthday, Cara. —Gian*

Gian had forewarned her during the lead up to her birthday that she would need something appropriate to wear for the ballet in Quebec, but that she wasn't to worry about it. Cara *had* packed something in her overnight bags, which was why she needed two instead of only one, just in case.

Apparently, she wouldn't be needing it after all.

She looked over the items spread across her table, overwhelmed and happy, all at the same time. Gian was smart, though. He had sent the gifts over late, when he likely knew she would be rushing to finish getting ready, and couldn't overthink the gifts or call him on them. It wasn't that she didn't like them—*oh*, she loved them—but she knew what these items cost, too.

She couldn't help but wonder why a man like Gian had no problem with spending this kind of money on a woman like her.

And for her birthday, no less.

These were the kinds of gifts that were meant for the queens of men—women they loved and adored, whom they cherished enough to treat as the royalty in their lives that they truly were.

Was Cara becoming that to Gian?

Maybe that scared her a little.

And Cara didn't have time to think on it.

Which she was sure Gian had known, sending the items over at this time.

Cara backed away from the gifts and headed for the bathroom. She spent the next half hour getting her hair dried into manageable, free curls and putting on a quick bit of makeup to color her eyes and lips. She had managed to clasp the choker on after slipping into the dress and pumps, when a knock beat on her door, and Chris's voice filtered in.

"We do have to leave soon, miss."

"Coming," Cara shouted back.

She grabbed the white tweed coat she had pulled from Lea's closet when she couldn't find something suitable in her own to wear over the white and silver dress. Her sister had owned far too many clothes, and while Cara had slowly started to go through Lea's things to get rid of what she didn't want to keep, she had barely touched the clothes.

Cara pulled the door open to find Chris waiting on the other side.

His gaze fell down over the dress to the shoes and then back up just as fast. He hadn't lingered, and his expression remained neutral. "Gian will be pleased. You look wonderful, miss."

Cara smiled. "Thank you."

"Let's head out."

She followed behind the man, letting him lead her through the apartment hall, down one flight of stairs, and outside to where a black town car sat running in front of the building. It was only a short stroll away. Chris held the back door open for Cara to walk the remainder of the way and get inside, but something caught her eye as she made it to the vehicle.

Another car—bright yellow, which was what caught her attention first—came speeding far too fast down the city road. Black tinted windows made it impossible to see inside.

By the time the car reached them, the driver's window rolled down a few inches. Cara didn't understand the item that was shoved out the window, not until the color burst from the barrel, and the sound sliced through the air. Rapid gunfire. Bullets.

Pain bloomed in Cara's shoulder as she was dragged to the ground. She was frozen, stuck in a strange nightmarish state of reality and memories. She hadn't heard gunfire like that since the day Lea was murdered. It was as though she had been shoved right back into that day all over again in a split second.

She couldn't bring herself out of it, no matter how hard she tried.

TEN

Automatic doors opened in front of Gian, but they weren't spreading fast enough for his brisk pace or patience. His hands slammed against the doors, pushing against the pressure of the mechanical arm to force them open faster.

His heart was in his fucking throat.

His stomach had fallen to his feet.

Time had become unimportant for the moment.

Gian couldn't remember the last time he felt this way—so fucked up in the head, an anxious mess, but still damn cold and calm on the outside.

Corrado used to tell him that *this* was when Gian was most dangerous. That Gian's emotions often ruled him in his choices and behaviors, but it was only when he didn't allow others the gift of seeing his emotions to gauge their transgressions, that it became dangerous. Because he became unstable, and unpredictable.

His grandfather had never said it was bad thing, though.

Another set of doors didn't open fast enough for Gian's satisfaction, and he shoved that set apart, too. A nurse on the other side barely moved out of the way, and she dropped her bags with a squeak. On any other day, Gian would have stopped and helped the woman, but his mind was somewhere else entirely.

A half of a dozen men stood gathered in a semi-circle outside of the hospital room across from the busy nurse station. Gian recognized their faces—friends of his man, younger Capos that had likely heard something happened and come down for support. He appreciated the effort and their concern, but he was neither in the mood to talk, nor interested in playing to the mafia politics.

His car being bombed was one thing.

He always had a fucking target on him.

Cara, though?

Cara was a whole other matter.

"Gian."

"Shit, nice suit, man. Where were you heading, tonight?"

Gian ignored the greetings and questions that were thrown at him as he passed through the group of men. He strolled into the opened hospital room to find Chris cussing a blue streak under his breath as a nurse stitched a three-inch, clean slice on the enforcer's neck.

"Well, if you hadn't moved so much," the nurse muttered under her breath.

"I rolled over in the bed, *cazzo*. Maybe they should have got it closed up better the first damn time."

Gian cleared his throat to gain the attention of both people. When the nurse looked to him, he jerked his head toward the door. "Get out."

The nurse's eyes narrowed. "But—"

"Two minutes, that's all I need. Get out, now."

Thankfully, the woman went without much argument. She did finish the last couple of stitches before she left, though. Once Gian was alone with Chris, he turned and closed the door to keep his next words from being overheard.

"Well, talk," Gian demanded.

Chris resituated himself on the bed to properly face his underboss. "Nothing too bad, a few scrapes from the pavement. A bullet nicked me on the throat. It's fine."

"*Sì*, I can see how fine you are. That's the only reason I came to this room first, instead of Cara's, because I hoped to calm down a bit more before I see her. What the fuck happened?"

"She's fine, too, boss."

Gian grinded his teeth. "That's a matter of opinion at the moment."

"She is. I got her down in time."

"You have one job when she is in your care."

Chris nodded. "And I did that job, Gian. That's why she's getting released tonight and I still have to be monitored until morning before I get my walking papers."

That was true enough.

For the most part, Gian liked Chris because the man was straightforward and took no bullshit, yet he also understood the weight of respect in their world. So, while he would give Gian the truth in a blunt manner that someone else may not, he did it with the respect of a man who knew he was talking to his superior.

Gian's posture softened, but barely. He was still walking on a very thin line of control. He had never been quite so worried, or so pissed off, as he was right then. "What did you see before the shooting started?"

"Very little. I was turned for Cara, I had the door opened for her. I wasn't watching the street—I didn't have any reason to think I should. The bullets started flying, and I was focused on getting her out of the way, that was it. By the time I got back up, my throat was bleeding all over the damn place and the car was gone. She couldn't tell me anything when I asked, it was like she wasn't even on the same planet, all of the sudden. Shock, maybe."

Maybe.

Or maybe it was something else, too.

"So, basically, you've got nothing to help me?"

Chris shrugged, though the action looked painful. "It happened fast. I did my job. There's nothing else to say."

Gian nodded once. "*Merci*."

"You're welcome."

"I'll see you when you're not in a hospital bed," Gian said before he slipped out of the room.

Outside in the hallway, Gian found the group of men had moved farther down from the door and away from the nurse station. Their conversation, however, was still being held at a level that he could plainly hear.

And it did *not* please him.

"So he was what, picking up the Rossi chick when it happened?" one of the Capos asked.

A solider nodded. "Guess so. Maybe that's where Gian's head has been lately—on her, you know."

The men didn't notice that Gian had left the room, nor that he was standing there listening to their conversation a few feet away. He didn't let them in on his presence, either.

"I heard some whispers about that," another Capo said. "He's found himself a distraction, not that I blame him … considering everything."

"Just call her what she is," Constantino said. "Don't dance around it like stupid fucks."

When had Constantino showed up?

He hadn't been there before Gian entered the enforcer's room.

"Is that what you would call her, then?"

Constantino—Gian's oldest and closest friend—nodded. "Sure, I would. What does it matter? It's better that everyone else knows. Those type come second, anyway. Even Gian knows it, too. Why do you think he's running around with her on the low, not shouting it from the rooftops like someone else might? Cara's a fucking catch, don't get me wrong. She's an awesome girl—my cousin, too, so I can say that and know it's true. But to Gian?"

Gian took the few steps that separated him and the group of men, shouldering one aside as he came face to face and toe to toe with Constantino. His friend didn't even look surprised to see him standing there all of the sudden.

"Say it," Gian dared his friend. "Say what you were going to say, *cafone*."

Constantino didn't blink. "We don't have time right now to be running around after your flavor of the month, man, worrying about who might be coming after her next. It's not an important detail, and somebody probably did this shit today to get your attention, since you're too busy to pay attention to what actually needs it right now. She's just a go—"

He didn't even get to finish his statement.

Gian's fist slammed into Constantino's jaw, shutting the man up, making him bleed, and sending him to the floor instantly.

Made men didn't fight. They sure as hell didn't hit other made men. It was a rule. Gian was learning there were some rules that needed to fucking go.

That was one of them.

Gian looked down at Constantino, not bothering to offer his hand to help his friend back up off the floor. "Don't you ever fucking disrespect Cara Rossi again. Not to my face, or behind my back. Don't shout it, and don't even whisper it. If it happens again, Constantino, I will sew your eyes together, burn your fucking ears off, and cut your tongue out. Maybe then, everyone else will understand what see no evil, hear no evil, and speak no evil really means to men like me. Maybe then, they might understand that a woman is worth far more than the title a man puts on her status. Test me, and watch what happens. Speak ill of her again, and I will slaughter you, friend or not."

He didn't bother to wait around and hear what was going to be said next. He had far more important things to do.

Like a woman in the unit upstairs waiting on him.

Cara needed a ride home. Happy fucking birthday to her, he thought miserably. This was not how the weekend was supposed to be. They should have been in Quebec already—hours ago, actually—watching a ballet together.

An apology was not going to make this better.

Of that, Gian was most sure.

• • •

Cara said nothing, her gaze lowered to the tiled floor of her bathroom as Gian carefully removed her white tweed coat and set it aside. The front of the beautiful dress that had been one of her birthday gifts was stained a reddish brown—Chris's blood, likely.

She had suffered no open injuries, thankfully.

When Cara did finally speak, her dull tone took Gian off guard. Other than her soft greeting at the hospital when he walked into her room, she had said nothing the entire time it'd taken to get her out, and get her home.

He was not accustomed to this steel-spine, sharp-tongued woman being so ... quiet.

"Please don't say you'll buy a new dress to replace this one," Cara said.

Gian shrugged, pulling the zipper down on the garment to expose Cara's back to his hands. He let his palms linger over the warm, soft skin of her shoulders as he pushed the shoulders of the dress down.

"I have a pretty decent drycleaner, actually. He's got a knack for getting blood out as long as it's not too old. A secret trick, or so he says. I think I'll take it to him."

Gian was lying through his teeth.

Blood didn't come out of fabric.

He *would* get a new dress for Cara, he simply wouldn't tell her that was what he had done.

"You don't have to do that," Cara said.

She still wasn't looking at him.

Gian hated that.

"Hey."

Cara let out a soft sigh. "Hmm, what?"

"*Bella mia*, look at me." Gian carefully pulled the dress over Cara's head, and then turned her to face him. Her emotionless expression only hurt him more. "I'm sorry for today, Cara."

"It's not your fault."

Technically, it probably was.

He didn't have to pull the trigger.

"The cops were in questioning me," Cara said, running a hand through her messy curls. "They only got more annoyed when I couldn't give them what they wanted. In case you're worried, I didn't say—"

"I'm not worried about that at all, *mon ange*," he interrupted quickly. "I was worried about you, nothing else."

"Still. I didn't have much to tell either way."

"Chris mentioned you … blanked a bit after the gunfire stopped and whatnot. Like you were frozen on the ground."

Cara shrugged. "It could have been that day in Chicago all over again, because that was all I saw. I could hear Lea asking me to help her, not Chris. My mind is broken that way, I think."

"Or you've got a touch of PTSD. An event like that is difficult to get over, Cara."

"I just …" She trailed off, frowning.

"What, love?"

"I feel like something important happened—or I saw something important—but I can't remember it because all I see is Chicago."

"Whatever it was, it'll come back, if it's important enough. Otherwise, don't stress on it. Certainly not tonight, anyway."

Gian's gaze was drawn to the bruises on the joint of her shoulder, and he had all he could do to quell the rage that suddenly boiled like hot lava inside his gut. With gentle strokes, he let his fingertips ghost over the marks. Chris's attempt to get Cara out of the way as fast as possible had left her with a dislocated shoulder from the force of hitting the ground, and awful bruising around the joint.

"It's not as bad as it looks," Cara said.

"That's a matter of opinion."

It seemed he was saying that a lot tonight.

"You look pissed."

Gian chuckled dryly. "Because it pisses me off that you have any marks. The only marks that should ever be on your body are ones I put there when I fuck you. Nothing more, nothing less."

Cara smiled, but it didn't come off as entirely true. "You don't have to stay tonight. I'm sure you have other—"

"I have nothing to do but sit here with you."

And that was just what he did.

The bathtub practically overflowed with lavender-scented bubbles by the time Gian decided it was filled enough. Steam was already starting to rise in the room as he helped Cara step into the hot, soapy water. He waited for her to get settled in before he pulled a chair from the kitchen into the bathroom, set it beside the tub, and pulled his book out to read.

Out loud, of course.

She liked it.

Cara leaned over and rested her head against his thigh, and Gian sifted his fingers through her silky hair as he read along.

"Other than the whole drive-by thing," Cara started to say.

"Keep going."

"This is mostly an okay birthday."

"I will save the Quebec trip for another time, I promise." Gian bent down to kiss the top of Cara's head. "But it still managed to be okay for you somehow?"

"I didn't realize it until I was in the hospital, but it's my first birthday without Lea. I didn't think about it leading up to today or as I was getting ready this morning. Tommas didn't mention her when he called this morning to wish me a happy birthday. It wasn't on my mind. She was the oldest twin by four and a half minutes."

"You never told me that before."

"Details," Cara said flippantly. "She used to joke and say it was the best four and a half minutes of her life. I'm now six months older than she lived to be."

"Things you don't really consider, huh?"

"I suppose. I was going to say I think she had to be lying about those four and a half minutes, because these past six months have been the worst of my life."

Gian stroked her cheek softly. "You have a good reason for that, though."

"It wouldn't be entirely true." Cara smiled up at him, happier and more honest than before. "The last couple haven't been so bad, really."

Well, then …

He could understand that, too.

"But with the shooting and all," Cara continued, "it brought me back down to reality."

"And what does that mean?" Gian asked.

He wasn't sure he was going to like her answer.

"I don't know right now, Gian."

Yeah, he didn't like that at all.

• • •

The cemetery had a quiet, almost peaceful, quality about it. The usual sadness clung in the air, but it wasn't as thick as Gian expected it would be. He stepped out of his car, and looked down the way, noting no vehicles but one that happened to be parked there. Checking his watch, he figured that gave him a bit of time before the men showed up.

Quickly, he strolled through the graveyard, passing by shined headstones and cleaned graves. Fresh flowers—some of the winter kind, but most for spring—rested upon the tops of a great many of the headstones.

All too soon, he came up to the one gravestone he was looking for. His grandfather's. When his grandmother, Aurora, had died, Corrado made sure that the headstone placed on her grave also included his name, birthdate, and a blank spot waiting for his death date to be added. Now, that spot was no longer blank, but rather, carved in identical font and style to the rest of the numbering with his grandfather's date of death.

His father waited on a nearby bench, a paper in his hands.

"Do you come here often?" Frederic asked.

Gian shook his head. "This is the first time, actually."

"How does it feel?"

"Odd."

"Oh?"

Gian bent down to place a handful of fresh flowers along the ledge of his grandparents' stone. "I thought it wouldn't feel like he was here, but it does, in a way."

"Even though he isn't buried yet."

"Like I said, it's odd."

Corrado's body was still waiting to be buried because of the frost in the ground. Another month, and the ground would be soft enough to dig. Gian didn't plan to attend that event, but he figured that he didn't need to.

"Do *you* come here often?" Gian asked his father.

Frederic set his newspaper aside. "Once a week to say hello to Ma. She used to threaten me that if I didn't come to chat with her—even when she

106

was dead—that she would haunt me for it. Turns out, this is like a haunting of sorts, anyway."

"What about for Corrado?"

His father pointed to his temple. "That's all in here. I hear him all the time there, Gian."

Strange ...

"I don't hear him there. Or rarely."

Frederic lifted his brow and said, "Perhaps you're not listening close enough, son."

"Or maybe he thinks he told me enough when he was alive that he shouldn't need to be repeating it now."

"Or that," his father agreed, chuckling. "What did you want me here for today?"

Gian stood straight again, and crossed the path to sit with his father on the bench. "There have been some ongoing problems lately."

"You must think I'm completely out of the loop because I'm not a made man."

"I assume nothing about no one, Dad."

Frederic looked over at his son. "And why is that?"

"Assumptions make for dead men."

His father tapped the side of his head. "See, Corrado is in there, Gian. He simply doesn't manifest to you the same way he does to me."

"And how is that?"

"I often hear him voicing my failures, or his lack of approval. I never gave him what he wanted—except for you—after all."

"But how do I hear him?" Gian asked.

"You hear yourself, son, because you're too much like your grandfather to find the distinction at the moment."

"We weren't entirely the same."

"It's enough," his father said, vaguely. "I know you're having problems with Edmond and his older men. I figured you would, Corrado probably did, too. I think he hoped to make it longer than Edmond, but knew that wasn't going to happen what with the cancer diagnosis. Nonetheless, here you are. I also hear you've found yourself a ... *friend.*"

Gian's expression blanked, and he was determined to keep his emotions that way on this topic with his father. "I don't need to hear your opinions on that side of things."

"Yes, well—"

"I also don't *want* to hear it, Dad."

"But what exactly are you going to do with the Rossi girl, Gian?" His father scoffed. "It's not like you can have any kind of acceptable future with her."

"Who says?"

"Cosa Nostra, and you know why."

Gian clenched his jaw. "For a man who didn't want to be a part of *la famiglia*, you're well-versed on things you have no business knowing."

"Thank your grandfather for that."

"You can't thank a dead man, Dad."

"Funny, we're always thanking God for something or other. Didn't he die once, too?"

"Move on," Gian demanded with a disinterested flick of his hand.

"Fine. The problems, you said. I already know."

"Good. Stay low, off the streets, you know, the normal when there's issues popping up. Pass the message along to Ma. I'll tell Dom. I want everyone to be safe over the next little while. That's all."

"That implies you plan to make some moves of your own that might agitate an already volatile situation, Gian."

"I'm not implying it," Gian replied quietly.

He looked across the graveyard to see more cars had begun parking along the road. Most, he recognized. Men—the younger side of the family—that he knew would come when he demanded their presence. Even Constantino's car was clearly visible, though Gian expected his friend to still be a little sour over their scuffle a few evenings ago.

"I'm not implying it," Gian repeated, "because I'm outright saying it now."

"Be careful," his father warned. "Things that often seem clear and straightforward in this business rarely ever are, Gian."

"What matters the most is that someone started a war, and I plan on finishing it."

ELEVEN

Spring was finally in the air, despite already being a couple of weeks into it. Unfortunately, the old adage of April showers bringing May flowers held true for the city, even if the only flowers that would grow were in cement pots between benches on the sidewalks. The wetness didn't seem to want to leave, and it had rained almost every day for a week.

Cara was starting to wonder if she should invest in a poncho and rain boots.

It didn't matter how long she lived in Canada, the weather still took her by surprise every single year. It was as though Mother Nature spent three to four months in a bitter rage Canadians liked to call winter, only to then spend two months in the wet, mucky depression of spring.

Cara tightened the coat around her neck to keep the chill of the wind out, while simultaneously keeping the umbrella high to battle the rain. She weaved in and out of the rushing people on the sidewalk, coming nearer to her destination. A small café just a couple of blocks away from her university that she frequented throughout the week.

All the while, she ignored the shadow of a man following behind her.

A bodyguard, according to Gian. Because she needed one of those now. *Just in case.* The guy never came close enough to speak, and Cara didn't even know his name. He'd never introduced himself, and by the time Cara realized she had a new shadow, she was too irritated over the whole thing and didn't want to discuss it at all.

Cara slipped inside the café, mastering the ability to pull in her closing umbrella through a shutting door at the same time. Somehow, her hair and coat still felt wet, despite having the umbrella up the whole time she had walked the two blocks.

Maybe it was time to look into getting a car, after all.

Cara had the money, as far as that went. She didn't live in luxury, her expenses were very little in the grand scheme of things, and her trust fund was still heavily padded with a decent number. She had her long-deceased paternal grandparents—and her brother—to thank for the trust fund that allowed her several years in a university program without needing to work, though. Instead of dividing up their fortune between their children, they included their few grandchildren as well. Had they only left the trusts in the hands of her parents, Cara had zero doubts that her mother and father would have squandered it away.

The trust funds had then been signed over to Tommas when the twins were still under eighteen years of age, so that he could use it for their education, if they wanted. When Lea died, Cara had been giving a letter from a Rossi family lawyer, notifying her that the details and remaining contents of her sister's trust had been consolidated into hers after expenses were paid.

She had money.

Cara was worried about using too much of it, even for an investment like a vehicle or a more permanent home. She liked money better when she could micromanage it, budget every single red cent, and watch her portfolio continue to stay in a comfortable area for her tastes. Maybe when this final year of university was up, and she had steady income from a job, she might feel okay with spending the money, but not now.

She grew up feeling poor, living like she was in poverty, simply because her parents had not cared to look after the state of their children or their home. She had worn clothes until they were ratty and a size or two too small, shoes that didn't work for a Chicago winter, and sweaters, instead of a proper windbreaker in the fall and spring. Tommas had filled in a lot of those things for his sisters when he could, as he had gotten older, buying them what they needed or paying their school expenses and meals.

But she still remembered what it felt like to be dirt poor, even when she actually wasn't.

Neglect came in too many forms to count.

Cara tried to brush off the lingering sadness from her thoughts as she stepped up to the counter and placed an order for coffee and a bagel. Once she had her order in hand, she took a seat at the far end of the café, tucked into a two-seated table with her back to the wall and facing the windows.

She saw him approach the café before she even took her first drink.

Gian didn't come right in, instead stopping to chat with her new *shadow*. He gave the man a handshake, and only then did he enter the café. It was like all of the nerves in Cara's body suddenly zoned in on the one person around her that affected her the most. She didn't even have to see him to feel him nearby.

It scared her.

It calmed her.

Cara didn't know what to do about those strange feelings, but she knew that she wasn't ready to deal with them. Not yet, anyway.

If anything, she needed time away from the way Gian made her feel. Time to figure out what in the hell had happened that'd gotten her into this position with a man that she had no business being involved with. Time to breathe, before Gian called her and she stupidly went running for a feeling and a fuck.

Gian smiled as he crossed the café. Unlike her, he didn't stop for something to eat or drink. Like usual whenever he was near her, she seemed to be the only damn thing on his mind or in his priorities. He dropped a quick kiss to the top of her head before taking the only other available seat at the small table.

"How do you walk around without any sort of umbrella?"

Gian shrugged. "You get used to it, really."

"Seven years here. I'm not used to it yet."

"Too wet for you?" he asked.

Cara scowled at the rain pattering against the café's windows. "It's like we go from snow to weeks of rain without any sort of warning or break."

"The warning is the month of April, *mon ange.*"

Of course it was.

Canadians.

"Summer is right around the corner," he said, the dimple in his cheek making a rare appearance as his smile widened. "It'll go from wet to hot just as fast, as it always does."

"Sure."

Gian's easy smile melted away fast, and he straightened a bit in the chair. "You don't seem happy. It's not the rain, is it?"

Cara looked out the window again, noting the bodyguard standing under a small ledge to keep from getting rained on. "Thanks for meeting up with me today."

"I've been trying to meet up with you all week, Cara."

"I know. I just … needed a break."

"A break for what?"

Cara blew out a hard breath. "To think."

"All right."

"To breathe," she added.

Gian's lips flattened into a grim line, his face betraying nothing. Cara sometimes hated how easily he hid his emotions when he needed to, as though he didn't want anyone to know his pain or irritation, or even his joy. She was sure it was a learned trait, born out of need because of his position—she knew her brother acted in a similar way—but that didn't mean she understood it. Not entirely, anyway.

"I don't have a lot of time today," Gian said quietly, "and I have to head out for a meet across the city soon. Not that I mean to rush you, but I have to, unfortunately."

Cara nodded. "That's okay. I have another class soon, anyway."

"Did your … break … help?"

"Honestly? Not really."

Gian looked away. "I'm not sure what you're trying to help to begin with, Cara."

"This," she said with a wave between them. "A couple of months ago, when we first started whatever the fuck this is, it wasn't supposed to *be* anything, Gian. Fun, quick, dirty, and that was it. That's all I wanted out of it, and here I am, confused again."

"You're confusing me," he said under his breath.

"I didn't want to become integrated in your life—not to the extent that I am. I didn't want to be seen as a target for the people you do business with. I grew up living the sort of life you live, burying people I loved because of their affiliations and business. I was sure that you and I wouldn't … I don't know."

"It's impossible to live separate lives, Cara," Gian pointed out. "I'm not two different men. I am the same man who carries a gun and acts as an underboss for my *famiglia*, and the man you demanded see no one else but you. The idea that I can constantly keep you from being integrated into all of that is ridiculous, and you should already know that."

"Gian—"

"No, listen to me. That's an idea you rationalized to justify your feelings and why you kept coming back for more. That was your fantasy to keep from worrying too much about what might happen or could happen to someone you give a fuck about."

"I never once hid who I was to you," Gian continued, his voice finally heating with anger. "I never once pretended to be anyone, except exactly who I am. It's like Lea, right? It's the same thing, in a way. You thought you both were good, safe away from your family and their business, but you never were, Cara. You can't run forever, and you're always a part of this thing being born to it. A child *della mafia*. This is who you are, and staying away didn't keep Lea alive. So, what in the hell would make you think pretending that I am someone I'm not would keep reality from catching up to you again?"

Cara felt like he had slapped her.

Actually, a slap might have felt better.

"You didn't need to bring my twin into this, Gian," Cara murmured, her voice thick with pain.

"I only told you the truth."

"You said it to hurt me."

Gian shook his head, sadness coloring up his dark gaze. "You're wrong. I never want to hurt you, Cara."

It didn't matter, she decided. Standing from the table, Cara picked up her bag and umbrella. She left her mostly-unfinished bagel and half-full coffee on the table. Gian didn't stand to see her out like he usually would, instead staying firmly seated with his gaze stuck on the wall behind her.

Coldness radiated from him.

Cara knew that feeling well.

She was damn cold, too.

"I didn't want this, not to be a target again, or hurt because I'm too close to you. I don't want to be shot at when I'm leaving my place or to turn around and see some guy shadowing my every move to keep me safe. I didn't want those things, Gian."

"So what do you want?" he asked.

"I need some more time," Cara replied. "Right now, I need time to—"

"Figure out how you got here with me."

"Yeah."

"Take as much time as you need, Cara." With that said, Gian stood from the table in a smooth motion, never crowding Cara as he turned to leave. "But if you want to save some time trying to figure it out, then give me a shout. I know exactly what got us here, *amore*. Honestly, you know it, too. You're one stubborn fucking woman when it comes right down to it."

• • •

"The first non-rainy day in two weeks, and you want to spend it by playing in mud," Cara muttered.

"Not mud, my *flower beds*," her aunt replied with a sweet smile. "I need to get them ready for the seedlings that I'll transplant outside, once I'm sure the frost is going to stay away."

Cara huffed, blowing a stray curl that had fallen in front of her eye out of the way. She resisted the urge to wipe the hair away when it fell right back down again, but that was only because she was wrist-deep in Daniele's flower beds. Or rather, one of several mucky piles of dark soil that was too damp for Cara's liking.

She clearly wasn't a green thumb kind of person.

"Thanks for joining me today," Daniele said.

"No problem." Cara overturned more soil, making sure to pull out any small rocks or dead weeds that had been left over from the year before. "I've been kind of busy lately. Sorry about that, *Zia*."

Daniele shrugged. "Sometimes, that's how life works."

"I suppose."

Cara wasn't going to go into the details of what had been keeping her away and busy, but she figured her aunt probably knew enough to go on without being told. Daniele—considering her husband's affiliations to the Guzzi family—had her own connections to the rumors making the rounds.

However, it wasn't polite conversation to ask about someone almost being shot.

Or who they were fucking.

Daniele was *always* polite.

Always a proper mafia wife.

It was the one thing Cara knew to expect from her aunt.

"So, how have you been?" Daniele asked.

"Busy with school. I thought that since I basically took four months off after Lea died that I would probably be behind, and not graduate on time next year, but I'm on track again now. It took a bit to get there, though."

"Oh?"

"And I got an early spot for a co-op of sorts at a woman's shelter, starting this summer, too. I'll be mentoring the mothers and teen girls, and helping with the outpatient rehab program. Since it's exactly what I want to work in, in a roundabout way, it was a lucky grab."

"That's good," her aunt said absently.

Cara shot a look across the flower bed, only to find Daniele wasn't actually paying her any attention. Her aunt was more focused on dragging the tiny hoe through the soil, overturning it to get the bed ready for planting.

She had been sure her aunt's only reason for asking her over to visit was to pry information out of her, but so far, Daniele hadn't done any of that.

Maybe Cara had been wrong.

Cara went back to helping her aunt clean out the flower beds, before they moved onto the railing pots that were sitting on the back deck. She was half way through filling the hanging pots with a fresh soil and mulch mix when her aunt starting talking again.

"Are you seeing anyone new, Cara?"

Her shoulders grew stiff at the innocuous question.

"Not particularly," Cara answered carefully.

Gian wasn't *new*, after all. And she wasn't exactly seeing him, after their meet at the café the week before. They were a thing, sure, but that meant nothing for now. Or, that's what Cara had been trying to convince herself for a whole fucking week.

"Claud mentioned you were having dinners with a gentleman."

Cara resisted the urge to say her uncle should mind his business. "Did he?"

"Yes, and sleepovers, too."

"Is that what you're calling it, nowadays?" Cara asked, not bothering to hide her sarcasm.

Daniele laughed lightly. "Don't get prickly, I'm only asking to be nice."

"Being nice would be *not* asking, *Zia*. Personal business, okay?"

"I do worry about you, Cara. You weren't your usual self these past few months, and then you seemed to be doing better. I still worry, though, especially if you've gotten yourself caught up in something of a mess."

Cara's brow furrowed as she regarded her aunt. "And what mess would that be?"

Daniele didn't even blink. "Men have a way of causing all sorts of messes that we women are not prepared for. They like to blame the mess on us, of course, but that's only because men fear the fingers pointing back at them when it's all said and done."

"I'm not caught up in any sort of mess, *Zia.*"

"For your sake, I sure hope not, Cara."

• • •

The news program switched to the oncoming weather for the last few days of April, leading into May, and Cara shut the television off. She let out a hard breath, frustrated at herself that she had once again succumbed to her curiosity and checked the news.

She had been checking the news for three damn weeks now.

Every night, she swore that something new popped up dealing with the Guzzi Cosa Nostra family. Something violent—someone else shot, a body found, a drive-by on a restaurant—and another funeral coming up.

Cara never watched the news, if she could help it. But after her own shooting weeks ago, she had turned the television on while she ate her supper to see what was being said. It was then that she learned just how volatile and violent the streets of Toronto were becoming for made men in the city.

She stayed out of family business for a reason.

She didn't ask questions.

She knew better.

This was exactly why ...

Her curiosity once again got the better of her, and Cara watched the news over and over, checking for new stories that might be popping up. She read the Canadian news blogs, because more often than not, reporters hidden behind a screen had more information to offer about crime families and the goings on than what was offered on television programs.

The Guzzi family was in an uproar. They had been that way for a while. Gian had never told Cara about it, not properly. She didn't blame him for that, because she had made it clear on more than one occasion that she simply didn't want to know.

The death toll was piling up. The violence was escalating.

Cara's drive-by shooting had been just *one* event, amongst several attacks. According to sources—though she wasn't sure how trustworthy those could be—the Guzzi family was struggling with an upheaval of power after their long-time boss had died. Gian's grandfather, that was. It appeared as though lines had been drawn between the younger and older generation of men in the family, and it had violently spilled over onto the streets.

It didn't look good.

It sounded all kinds of bad.

Cara worried.

Constantly.

It was every single reason why Cara hadn't wanted to get too involved with Gian in the first damn place. The life he lived was not a right to have in their world. It was nothing more than a privilege that made men and their families fought to keep.

Position. Power. Respect.

That's all the mafia had ever been.

And it scared the hell out of her.

For what felt like the millionth time, Cara forced herself not to grab her cell phone and dial Gian's all-too-familiar number. She had asked for space and time to think, and he had been gracious enough to give it to her without argument. He had not called, not messaged, and he hadn't sent one of his guys to her door with a gift. Even her shadow—the bodyguard that had seemed to come out of thin air—had receded to being simply a faraway annoyance whenever she looked for him. The guy wasn't gone altogether, but she rarely saw him now unless she really searched the crowd hard.

Cara already knew that she was going to fail at staying away from Gian, never mind actually *ending* whatever they were to one another. She was going to fail because she neither wanted to stay away, nor end their fucking mess together.

But she didn't know how to deal with what would also inevitably come with all of that.

The news programs.

The worry.

The violence.

Her fears …

Cara didn't know how to deal with any of that.

Gian had been right—he couldn't and he didn't pretend to be someone that he wasn't. It was *her* who looked the other way. There was going to come a time when Cara wouldn't be able to turn cheek to the sides of Gian that frightened her, and once she did, there would be no way to look away. There would be no more pretending.

Before Cara fully understood her actions, she had grabbed for her phone and dialed a familiar number, but it wasn't Gian's. She listened to the ringing echo through the speakers as she waited for her brother to pick up the call. She didn't entirely expect Tommas to answer, as more often than not, he called her or she left a message.

But on the fourth ring, he did pick up.

"*Ciao.*"

For a whole ten seconds, Cara didn't respond.

All of the sudden, she didn't know what to say.

She heard the speaker crackle with an annoyed huff before Tommas muttered, "Cara, is that you?"

"Yes," she finally said.

"Something wrong?"

Cara glanced at the blank television screen, and considered how to answer that question. "How do you do it, Tommas?"

Her brother cleared his throat, and then she heard him shuffle around as though he were getting out of bed. "You're going to need to make more sense, if you want a proper answer."

She couldn't help but notice how tired he sounded. Not sleep-tired, but a fuck-this-world kind of tired. It was so unlike her brother. He was laidback, cool, calm, and collected. Always.

Cara had never known Tommas to be anything else.

"Are you sure nothing is wrong?" Tommas asked, when Cara stayed silent.

"Nothing serious."

"All right. Ask me your question again, but make more sense this time."

"How do you care and attach yourself to people who feel like their existence in your life is not guaranteed, but more temporary than you're willing to admit. Like tomorrow, someone gets pissed off or offended and suddenly, you're burying your sister … or someone else you love."

Tommas sighed. "That's a heavy question for someone who didn't even thank me for wishing her a happy birthday a month ago."

"Thank you for the birthday wishes, Tommy."

He grunted under his breath. "I don't think about it—that's how I deal. And I protect those people as best I can, I do whatever I need to do so that my choices and my actions don't inadvertently hurt them or take them away from me."

"Huh."

"Sometimes I fail, too," Tommas added, a sadness creeping into his tone. "And that kills me, but it's unavoidable."

"Yeah, but …"

"What, Cara?"

"What about people like me?"

"I do that for you, too. Why do you think you're still in Toronto, huh? Not here, in Chicago, advancing my stupid ass in this fucking family or something?"

"I meant, what about women like me—how do I deal with it? I can't manage it the same way you do, I'm not like you, Tommy."

"That's not an easy answer, Cara."

"Try me. Give me something."

"Why are you even asking this shit?"

"I need to know how to *deal*," she said sharply, offering little else.

"I only know what I see around me," Tommas replied quietly. "Or rather, the women around me. My cousin's wife, or the women in my family. My friends' wives, or *famiglia* daughters that bury their parents with dry faces and shaking hands. They're *strength*, Cara. They are the picture and embodiment of strength all around me. They handle their shit far better than any of us men ever could. They cook dinner, wipe children's faces, do what they have to do, and they smile when faced with their fears. I don't know how they do it, because I am too busy trying to keep allowing them the chance to cook their dinners, love their messy-faced children, and have no fears, all the while. Do you understand?"

"But you're part of the reason they're in that sort of life, Tommas."

"And all we made men do is make the best of what we know, Cara. Nothing more, nothing less."

She took the time to absorb her brother's words. Tommas always gave it to her straight, after all. He didn't pretty shit up.

"Oh, there's something else you need to know," Tommas said tiredly.

"What's that?"

"Serena's body was found this morning by the maid. Suicide, apparently."

Cara wished she was surprised to learn the news of her mother's death. She wasn't.

Something else that was ... inevitable.

"I'm sorry," Cara said softly.

"Are you?"

"For you, Tommy. I'm sorry for you. You've dealt with her your whole life, longer than I ever put up with her. You would only do that—and keep doing it—because somewhere inside, you hold affection for her."

"Not anymore," Tommas murmured. "I can let you know when the funeral is going to be."

"I would rather you didn't."

"That's what I figured."

"Please bury her beside Dad, not on the other side of Lea."

Tommas mumbled his agreement quickly.

"Cara?"

"Yes?" she asked.

"I don't know what's going on, or what made you pick up the phone to ask me all of this tonight, but there's really only one thing that matters in this life of ours, anyway."

"And what's that, Tommas?"

"Do what makes you happy. Be where, or with whom, or do whatever you need to do to be happy. Take that risk—it's worth it. Because this life is fleeting, and tomorrow might be the last time you smile, so it's better to spend today happy."

TWELVE

"Sit, sit!" Gian clapped his hands twice, helping to quiet the men milling around the long dinner table. He waved at the waiting seats, and the men began to fill them. "Dinner is served."

As he said those words, two women, and one man, strolled into the dining room, each holding platters carrying all sorts of foods. Once the food was set down on the table, the help left and then returned with pitchers of drinks.

After they were gone for good, Gian waited to see if any man at the table would reach for food or a drink before he approved it. None did.

Instead, they looked to him, waiting.

As all good made men did for their boss.

It had taken Gian a couple of weeks to really get used to the fact that a great portion of the Guzzi made men saw him as exactly that—their boss.

He thought it appropriate to hold their first unofficial dinner where the last man they respected and followed as a boss had his, too. At Corrado's home, at his dining room table.

Maybe he had done this for a bit of nostalgia, too.

Gian took his own seat, said a quick prayer as had become a custom when sitting down to eat dinner with family, and then he waved again. "*Tutti mangiare.*"

His order for everyone to eat was no faster out of his mouth before the men began to reach for the hot dishes. He wasn't particularly hungry—a shitty by-product of his stress, likely—so he sat back in a chair that had once belonged to his grandfather, and enjoyed the sight of the Capos and enforcers filling their plates.

Conversations filtered around the table between men, some discussing the events and attacks that had escalated rather violently over the past couple of weeks. Gian allowed them those discussions, and only joined in if he was directly asked a question. He found that he learned a lot more, and the men *talked* a lot more, when they had a boss who cared to hear what they had to say.

All but one man at the table was made.

Gian turned to his left, where his brother Dom was stuffing his face with pasta. "Hungry, *fratellino?*"

Dom bristled. "Only little compared to you in age, Gian."

He laughed. "Relax. You're lucky to even be here."

"Yeah, I know."

Being unmade, Dom shouldn't be allowed to share the same

119

experiences with made men until he had earned his seat at the table and his spot within the family. But … Gian remembered times when his grandfather had allowed *him* to sit at the table, and to have a voice. He figured that had been Corrado's way of making his intention clear about giving his grandson his in to the family.

Gian was only doing the same for Dom.

In a way …

"So, do you think—"

Dom's question was interrupted by a ringing phone. Gian recognized the familiar sound instantly, but because he wasn't sure why his grandfather's house line would be ringing, he looked over the table of men to see if it was one of their phones. None reached for their phones. Corrado's mansion had been kept running ever since his death, as the Guzzi family had often used it, and no one was quite ready to put it up on the market officially. Even the cook, maid, and the man who ran errands and greeted guests stayed in the house, with pay.

But they never mentioned the home getting calls.

Eventually, the ringing stopped.

The maid stepped into the dining room, pressing her palm over a cordless phone to keep her voice from being heard on the line. "Mr. Guzzi, there's a call for you."

All eyes turned on Gian. He stood from the table, leaving the men behind with a demand for them to keep eating, and that all was fine. Although to be perfectly honest, he wasn't sure what in the hell was going on.

Just outside the dining room, he took the phone from the maid and put it to his ear. His usual Italian and French greeting slipped out before he could think better of it. "*Ciao, bonjour.*"

"Gian, how are you this evening?"

Gian stiffened in place. "Edmond. Why in the fuck are you calling me at Corrado's home? And better yet, *how* did you know I was here?"

"I know a lot of things."

"Oh? Try me with one."

"Fifteen men sitting around your grandfather's table. Would you like their names? Sixteen, actually, if you include your unmade brother."

"Spying, now?"

"Hardly." Edmond scoffed. "You simply never think to look at any of those young gentleman like you should. They're not all trustworthy, Gian. Each of them has an ultimate goal in mind where this organization is concerned. Sure, it's true enough that some of them tie those goals to you being their boss, but some … some, probably do not."

"You're wasting my time."

As Gian spoke, he had moved through the left wing of the mansion, heading toward the front of the estate. He checked out the windows, to make sure none of the men stationed outside had taken a hit, and that there was no funny business going on. He didn't trust Edmond as far as he could throw the fat bastard.

"It's been a rough couple of weeks, hasn't it?" Edmond asked out of the blue.

Gian let the curtains close, and headed back the way he came toward the dining room. "Depends on who you think it's been rough for. On my end, I think it's been mostly okay. *You* were the one who started this nonsense, remember. I only recently joined in with a few attacks of my own. I can't help it if my attacks are more direct and successful than yours are."

"You assume everything, Gian. Don't you know what they say about assuming?"

"I know you're trying to play some kind of game with me, and my food is getting cold. I'm not in the mood."

"Too bad, it's time to listen. My attacks were pointed, and only done to either calm a situation, or make a point. They didn't have to be direct to be successful. That's what you fail to realize, Gian."

"Are you done?" he asked Edmond.

"Not even close. I know exactly why you're doing this."

"Do tell."

"You think I killed your grandfather," Edmond said simply.

Gian's jaw clenched. "Partly, but it's not the only reason."

"Yes, yes. The younger men, they want a boss they picked, they want to act like spoiled children who have their hands held when they're scared to do what they're told. We've been over this."

"Your bias is showing again, Edmond."

"So be it, they're a dime a dozen. They can be replaced."

"You're wrong again," Gian shot back. "Made men are not commodities to be replaced. Not in this Cosa Nostra."

Edmond laughed. "You have a lot to learn."

"It takes time, or so I was told."

"Be careful not to run out of it before you even get the chance to properly get started." Then, Edmond said quieter, "But you do think I killed Corrado."

"It no longer matters."

"It does, or this would not be happening."

"Wrong again," Gian murmured. "Corrado is only a small part of this. Cosa Nostra is not about the one man on top, but all the men who wait on his direction. It's not *me* who has forgotten that, Edmond. Good luck, but we both already know how this will end. I could ask you to make it easy on me, but we both know you won't."

Gian hung up the phone without a goodbye, handed it to the waiting maid, and joined his men at the dinner table once again.

None of them asked him what was wrong.

Nothing was wrong.

He had this shit under control.

• • •

Gian popped the top off his beer, took a long swig, and glared at the game playing on his flat screen television. "I don't know why you bother to watch this, man. The Leafs haven't done well in decades, and this isn't going to be their year."

Constantino bristled. "Be a proper Canadian, would you? Don't diss the Leafs like that."

"He's more of a Montreal fan," Dom remarked from the Lazy Boy chair. "Depends on who is winning at the time."

"That's a fucking shame," Stephan put in. "Pick a team and stick with it."

Gian had news for them. "Since you three are watching the game on my huge ass television, sitting on my comfy furniture, drinking *my* beer, and you're not at your own places, you can shut the fuck up now or get the hell out."

"Jesus, you're an asshole tonight," Constantino said absently, his attention snagged by the Leafs' player cutting down the middle of the ice. "Why are you so miserable lately?"

Gian took another swig of his beer, refusing to even entertain that goddamn question. His mood had been less than pleasant and for quite a while, it had only been getting worse. He had managed to hide it, for the most part, when he needed to. Lately, especially the last few days, his bad attitude had been showing itself more often, bleeding onto others that happened to be around him.

Like easy fucking targets.

Gian knew better; he was smarter than allowing his emotions to rule him or control how he went about his days and business.

Lately, he couldn't help it.

"It's nothing," Gian muttered, setting his beer down to the coffee table.

He took a seat beside Constantino, and decided to watch the game and get the night over with. It had been a while since he'd actually done something with friends—even if Stephan had showed up with Constantino earlier—so he might as well make the most of it.

Gian had forgiven Constantino for his slip at the hospital, and what he'd said about Cara, but it was a one-time only thing. His forgiveness had come easy once his friend apologized, but that was only because Constantino had been his friend for so damn long that he found it hard to stay pissed at the guy.

"But don't be surprised when the Leafs lose again, like they always do," Gian said. "They are the most boring hockey team to watch—nothing changes, from season to season."

Stephan shot Gian a look. "You should get laid. Maybe that would pull out whatever stick got shoved up your ass."

Constantino chuckled under his breath. "Hey, there's an idea."

Dom wisely chose to stay quiet, but that could have been because he had shoved a half of a slice of pizza in his mouth.

Lucky for him.

"Fuck off, both of you," Gian warned, never taking his gaze off the television.

"So that *is* it?" Constantino asked.

"What?"

"You need to get laid, Gian."

For fuck's sake ...

"I need you to mind your business," Gian said, his irritation rising. *Take the fucking hint.*

"Yeah, that's what it is," Stephan said with a nod. "Cara—the Rossi chick he was running around with—hasn't been seen in a while."

"My cousin," Constantino said, "I don't need a reminder, Stephan. I know who the fuck she is."

Gian's teeth was starting to grind so hard that his molars were aching.

"What I'm saying is, Gian here, wasn't running around with anybody else, so if she's keeping a low profile *without him*, then he isn't getting pussy from anywhere." Stephan laughed under his breath at the glare Gian passed his way. "Yeah, that's exactly what it is. No pussy makes for an irritated mess of a man, doesn't it, Gian?"

"I'm two seconds away from throwing all of you assholes out of my penthouse," Gian replied.

"Hey, I'm just eating pizza," Dom mumbled around a bite in his mouth.

Gian ignored his younger brother.

"Stay the hell out of my business," he told them all. "And that is the last fucking time I am going to say it."

Because mostly, he hated how right the guys were.

He hated how easily they had picked up on his mood and the reason why.

He missed Cara like crazy.

Space, he reminded himself. *You're giving her space.*

And also driving himself insane at the same time.

Gian had hoped Cara would get her shit figured out and all would be fine between them. He hadn't expected ... this. Weeks and weeks of waiting, of wondering, and of being entirely fucking alone.

He almost hated how much control that woman had over him.

Except he couldn't hate that at all.

"If you're lonely or something," Constantino said, "then why don't you go home, Gian?"

Gian raised his brow. "I *am* home. And Cara wanted space. Although, that's not your fucking business, either."

Constantino shook his head. "I didn't mean here, man."

All right.

Fuck this whole night.

Gian didn't even bother to kick the guys out.

He left.

• • •

Gian whipped his car into the parking lot belonging to Cara's apartment building. He checked his phone again, and then triple-checked it *just to be sure.*

Would you pick me up? My place.

That was all Cara's text message had said. Gian had barely gotten his confirmative reply typed out before he had pulled an illegal U-turn on a downtown street and headed his lover's way. He'd only meant to clear his head when he'd left his place earlier, but this was perfectly fine, too.

Gian checked his phone once more, ready to send a message to Cara that he was there, but he didn't need to. Cara appeared outside the passenger side window, Gian unlocked the door, and she slid inside without a word.

He pulled out of the parking lot while Cara was still buckling up her seatbelt.

"Where to?" Gian asked.

Cara stared out the side window, never looking at him. "I don't know. Somewhere ... quiet?"

"We can do quiet, *bella mia.*" Thankful for the lack of traffic, Gian headed toward the bay. It was a bit of a drive, but it would be quiet and private. "Do you want to grab some food or something?"

"Sure."

"Anything specific?"

Cara shrugged. "Anything unhealthy and greasy."

Gian chuckled. "Junk food, then."

"What else?"

It took an hour to grab food, and drive all the way to the bay. Gian pulled the car along the metal fence that kept vehicles from going too far ahead. He had only put the car into park before Cara leaned across the seats, grabbed his jaw in her hands, and pulled him in for a kiss. It was not a sweet, hello kind of kiss. It couldn't be one of those, when her tongue invaded his mouth and she tried to get closer. It was more of an *I want* kind of kiss.

Gian was more than willing to give where Cara was concerned.

"So we're doing this first, then?" he asked against her mouth while pulling his leather jacket off at the same time.

"Yes."

So sure.

No hesitation.

"Whatever you want, Cara."

Gian hooked an arm around Cara's trim waist, and yanked her into the backseat of the Mercedes. He used the space between the front seats to get back there, but it sure as fuck wasn't an easy fit, and Cara fell hard into his lap with a breathless laugh.

He moved so his back was to the door, bringing her along with him. Burying his hands into her hair, he held tight so he could get more of her pretty mouth against his while he had the damn chance. But that only made him want more of her to taste—her cheeks, jaw, and neck. All the spots that he hadn't been able to kiss and bite and taste for *weeks*.

He had time to make up for.

Cara, apparently, had different plans. Her hot mouth started traveling down over his throat, her tongue lapping at his pulse point for a moment before moving on again. Gian decided all he could do was let her do her thing as she lowered even further.

"Jeans, a T-shirt, and a leather jacket," Cara said, working the button and zipper on Gian's jeans. He lifted off the seat enough to let her pull the jeans and his boxer-briefs down, and pull his shoes off. "I think this is the first time I've seen you without a suit."

"You've seen me without one."

"Being naked doesn't count, Gian."

"You've seen me in workout clothes."

"Which is basically a pair of shorts," she pointed out.

"I wasn't planning on leaving the penthouse today," he said in explanation.

Cara pulled his T-shirt up, and for the first time, Gian let go of the hold he had on her hair to allow her to slip the clothing off. "This is a good look, too. Relaxed. I liked the leather jacket."

If she liked it …

"You can take it," he said before pressing another hard kiss to her mouth. "Now, stop talking and start sucking my cock like you were working on doing two minutes ago."

Cara's eyes narrowed playfully. "How do you know that's what I was going to do?"

"Well, if it wasn't, it's sure as fuck what you're going to do now."

She winked and started lowering down his body again. "Lucky for you, that was the plan."

Of course it was.

Cara liked to say that it was him who had a gift with his mouth and tongue, but he didn't think she was aware of her little *talent*. The second her lips encased his cock, and she took him deep into her throat without slowing once, Gian was in fucking heaven. She always knew how to suck him, hard on the swallow, and looser on the way up. Her tongue swirled at the head of his shaft, while her teeth teased along the pulsing vein that matched the beats of his heart.

And *fuck*, she didn't give him a break. She didn't slow.

She sucked and sucked, while her fingers dug into his thighs. She didn't stop when his fingers weaved into her hair so that he could hold her down on his cock, and her throat flexed in the best way around his shaft when his hips bucked upward, wanting more still.

"Shit, shit, shit," he mumbled in a hard groan. "Suck my fucking cock, *Tesoro*. Just like that."

He called Cara a lot of things in bed.

His slut.

An angel.

Sexy. Beautiful. Filthy.

But *treasure*—that one probably fit her best.

Especially when she was sucking him off.

Only something precious and treasured could make him feel as crazy and high as she did when she was fucking him or sucking him dry.

Sex—for Gian—had become something of a nuisance in his life, to deal with when he got the chance. It slowly became a secondary need that took a back seat to his daily responsibilities and the duties that always had to come first.

Not with Cara.

With Cara, sex became a form of his affection. It was yet another way to communicate. It let him *feel*. He was always relaxed—never bothered or worried about outside issues—whether he was on his knees between her legs, or she was above him looking down. He focused in on her, nothing else, and it wasn't such a fucking nuisance to be taken care of.

It was an urge that was constant. Unrelenting.

She was always on the back of his mind now, in one way or another. When he wasn't with her, he was working out a way to be with her. In her effort to have space from him, all she had managed to do was make Gian even more fucking obsessed with her than he had been before. He controlled the urges well enough, but it was like constantly balancing on a very thin string, ready to break. He didn't want her running scared from him again, he wanted her *with* him.

The sound that tore from his throat was almost inhuman, his words jumbling together as the pressure and heat in his spine suddenly grew to the point of no return. He managed to get something out, a mix of "fuck, I'm going to come" and "shit, don't stop." He wasn't really sure what he said, he couldn't hear it. His ears were ringing as his load emptied into Cara's waiting mouth. She kept his cock tight to her lips and deep in her throat as his cum shot out with enough force to make him dizzy.

Like the good girl she was to him, she swallowed every last fucking bit of it down, too. Then she cleaned his cock with her tongue, and kissed her way back up his body until she was sitting sweetly in his lap, straddling him. The pleased curve of her lips told him that she *liked* sucking him off, if only because it gave her some control between them.

She didn't know it, but she had all the control now.

Gian pulled Cara in for a bruising kiss, her lips warm and swollen against his. Despite having just emptied his fucking balls, his cock was still painfully hard, because he wasn't done. It wasn't that simple when it came to Cara.

"Thank you for wearing a dress tonight," he said.

Cara lifted a single brow high. "Why?"

"It makes this easier, and faster."

He'd needed to get undressed entirely, she only needed her skirt lifted up and her panties pushed aside. Then, he could *finally* get back to the heaven and home that came with fucking Cara Rossi.

Gian lifted Cara's skirt and turned her in his lap so that her back pressed to his chest. His hand flew between her thighs to feel what belonged to him there. He buried his face into her sweet-smelling curls as he yanked her panties aside, and brought her down on his length without giving her time to prepare for it. He didn't want to wait, he was so fucking tired of waiting after *weeks* of it.

But *shit* ... it was worth it. Every hot, slick, tight inch of her sucked him in and held him in place like she wasn't going to let him go. Seated deep in her cunt, Gian could breathe again for the moment.

"Oh, fuck," Cara breathed as she squirmed on his cock in the best way.

"Christ, you're wet. How hot do you get sucking me off?"

"It's not normal."

Her words were a mumble. A hot, airless mumble.

"It is," he said with a chuckle, his fingers tangling into her hair. "Now, you got what you fucking wanted—you made me come. Give me what I want, Cara. Give me what's mine, *mon ange*."

Her pussy. Her orgasms. Her sounds. All of that belonged to him when they were like this.

Every bit of it.

"Just give me a sec—"

Gian tugged firmly on her hair, quieting whatever she was going to say. "Fuck me, Cara. *Now.*"

She didn't need to be told again, lifting enough to ride him while he pulled on her hair and kept a hand between her thighs at the same time. He liked the feeling of his cock and her cunt against his fingertips. He could feel everything, from the way she stretched open every time she lowered on to his cock, to the rhythmic pulse of his heart beating in his shaft. All her juices slicked them up, and he wanted to see her clean his fingers off when they were done.

Gian's fingers pressed tighter to her cunt, not quite grabbing it as she fucked him, firm enough for her to feel it. She grinded her clit into his palm at the same time. "All mine, Cara."

"Yours."

Of course, it was.

He hadn't realized how unhurriedly such a thing could build inside him—such a vindictive, needy, greedy, beautiful thing like love. He'd never been in love before, and when he finally understood that he had been slowly falling in love with Cara, he'd been too stupid and too selfish to stop it. He liked the way it felt, after all, even when it hurt.

So yes, all of her belonged to him.

And he wanted her to know it.

• • •

Cara dug through the bag of fast food, pulling out a cheeseburger and fries, and setting her bare feet up on the dashboard. After cleaning up, she'd opted to kick her flats off on the floor of the car.

"Busy couple of weeks?" Gian asked.

She handed him over the bag. "Nothing unusual. Mostly boring."

"That could be considered a good thing."

"It could."

"But?" he pressed.

Cara smiled a bit. "But I missed you, too, so that kind of sucked."

Gian didn't even bother to hide his grin. "Eat, love."

She did, pulling out fries to chew on. Once they were gone, she said, "My mom killed herself, or that's what my brother said."

"Oh."

That felt stupid to say.

Gian didn't know what would be appropriate. An apology felt wrong, considering Cara's feelings regarding her mother. She didn't look entirely sad about it, but she didn't appear to be happy, either.

"Are you going back for the funeral?" he asked.

Cara shook her head.

"Why not?"

"Her death is enough closure for me," Cara admitted under her breath. "I don't need to watch her be buried, too."

"You could have called me."

Gian heard the slight bitterness in his tone, though he wished he could have hidden it better. He didn't want to be angry with Cara for asking that he give her space and time alone. It also wasn't that easy. The longer it had stretched on between them with no word from her, the harder it had become for him to deal with it.

"There was nothing to say," Cara said dryly. "Not about Serena Rossi, anyhow."

"You could have called for—"

Cara glanced over at him, her knowing eyes quieting him instantly. "I wanted to call. Every day. Multiple times a day. Every chance I got. Whenever I looked at my phone. It didn't get easier not to pick it up, but neither did watching the news, seeing shootings and hearing all the problems piling up all over the city. I had choices to make, Gian."

"Like what?"

"Like if I wanted to keep doing this with you. Whether or not I was okay with what that might mean."

He cleared his throat. "And?"

Cara unwrapped her burger. "I'm here, aren't I? I called, didn't I?"

She was.

And she had.

"The only thing that would make this food better is beer," Cara said.

"I could have brought some or picked up a six-pack." Gian set his burger and fries up in his lap. "We couldn't have come out here, though."

Cara shrugged one shoulder. "We'll grab some on the way back to my place."

"Is that the plan?"

"Yep. That's the plan."

"So, we're going to act like everything is good and you didn't run off scared?" he asked.

"We will if you stop bringing it up."

"We *are* going to talk about it, *mon ange*. And other things, too."

She sighed, rolling her pretty blue eyes upward at the same time. "Fine, but we're eating first. Maybe fucking again, too."

"I do love the way you think, Cara."

Her smile was sinful. "I know you do."

"And you."

Cara glanced over at him, her eyes knowing and the silence stretching on. *Now or never,* he thought to himself. If he could feel it, he should be able to verbalize it. How else was she going to know the craziness he constantly felt whenever she was near?

"I love you," he added, quieter.

"I thought we were eating first before all of that."

They would.

Gian nodded at her food. "Eat, but it changes nothing. I said what I said."

She wasn't running this time.

THIRTEEN

"What do you want, red or white?" Gian asked, holding up two bottles of wine for Cara to choose between.

"I thought we were grabbing beer?"

"We are, but you like wine more. Which one?"

Cara eyed the two bottles and said, "Which one do you think I'd prefer?"

"The red for tonight. White for a meal."

"Lucky guess."

"Or I pay attention," Gian replied just as fast, slipping the bottle of white wine back on the shelf. "Red wine is good for rich dishes, too, you know."

Cara crossed her arms as she rounded the corner of the aisle, plucking the red wine from Gian's outstretched grasp. "How can you say you love someone when the only thing you've ever done with them is fuck?"

Gian cleared his throat, glancing at a customer in the next aisle who looked their way. A simple glare from him sent the patron heading in another direction, fast. Then, his gaze was back on hers, the intensity pinning her in place.

"You know that's not true," Gian muttered.

"What—that all we do is fuck? It's *very* true."

"Wrong. We do a hell of a lot more than that. I can't help that all of the things we do happen to get mixed up in the fact we like to fuck a lot, Cara."

"Well—"

"So I'll never read to you in bed again, or in the bath, or anywhere else. We won't stay in bed, talking and talking and fucking *talking*, about everything and anything that comes to your mind. I'll act like you don't enjoy being quiet, and that you smile even when you're sleeping. You don't need to tell me shit about your mother and father, or your brother, and never mind even thinking about saying something when it comes to your dead sister. I'll pretend like I don't know shit about what you like, the things you do, or who you want to be when you graduate in a year. And—"

"I get it," Cara interjected softly. "I shouldn't have said that."

"Be more specific."

"I'm being difficult, Gian."

"Clearly," he responded dryly.

"Say it to me again."

"Say what?"

131

"What you told me in the car earlier."

"That I love you?"

"Yes, that," Cara said.

Gian didn't hesitate. "I love you, Cara."

His inflection didn't change a bit. Neither did his expression. He said those three little words so easily, as though it should be obvious to her, him, and the world that he felt for her in that way. He felt so deeply, so intensely, that he could tell her he loved her privately in a Mercedes, where no one could hear or in a liquor store, where a cashier waited for them to pay and customers milled around.

He said it.

He said it like he meant it.

He said words Cara didn't understand.

Oh, she got the love bit—that she understood well. Too well, probably. She understood that he *did* love her, because she felt that way, too. She felt alone when he wasn't there, she heard his voice in her dreams, and she felt him all around her when he was gone. She missed him constantly, she worried where he was when he wasn't with her, and her best moments had been spent in comfortable silence and sweet whispers with this man.

Of course, she loved him.

It was all the *hows* that made her pause.

It was the *how did this happen* that stopped her from saying it back.

"Why are you staring at me like that?" Gian asked.

"Why don't you ask me to say it back?"

"I don't need you to."

Cara glanced away from the honesty in his gaze. "But you *want* me to."

"That's not what you asked. You asked *why*. I don't need to hear you say something that I already know, Cara. And do you know how I know?"

"I'm listening."

"I know you love me because I can count on one hand the times you've asked me for something, or needed something from me, or wanted *just* me until tonight. I can count on one hand, but I'd only need one finger to do it. Just tonight—that's the only time you've ever taken something from me that you wanted. You called, you wanted me with you, and that says more than anything else you ever say possibly could."

"And why is that?"

She didn't mean to be so goddamn defensive, but it was hard. Her walls were her go-to defense for anything that seemed like it might reach too far inside her emotions or cut her too deeply, when it was all said and done.

Gian was definitely one of those things for Cara.

On both accounts.

"Because you don't need me," Gian said, his tone lowering an octave with the frankness his words took on. "Not in the grand scheme of your life, you really don't. It might fuck you up for a while to send me on my way, but you would come out fine in the end. That's what women like you do, right? You get hurt, brush yourself off, and get on with it—with life. Everybody fails you in one way or another, that's what you've been taught."

"Gian—"

"It's true. Even if they don't mean to, or it's a by-product of someone else's actions, they hurt you. Your parents, your siblings, or friends. And so you prep for the next person you let in to hurt you, too, and when they do, you get to fall, dust it off, and keep going with a few more bruises on your soul."

She almost hated how he saw those things.

She wanted to hate that she had never needed to tell him those things.

"But what's more amazing," Gian continued, "is that you let me in. And that, in some crazy way, you still lower your walls enough to let someone climb over for a time. So here we are, you waiting for me to fuck up, even if I do love you, and even if you do love me, because it always happens, regardless. And you'll be fine when it does—if it does—because that's who you are, Cara Rossi. And we don't get to be anything but exactly who we are."

Cara's exhale felt painful as it rushed out, but with that pain came a sense of relief. "Saves me the trouble of explaining all of that to you."

Gian shrugged. "I never asked for an explanation."

"No, you didn't," she agreed quietly. "Don't you think it's a little sad that you love someone who is just waiting for the other shoe to drop?"

"I think it's sad that the woman I love feels like she has to wait on that at all."

Well, then …

"What about all the shit I don't like?" Cara asked. "The business you do, the things that life has taken from me, and how it hurts me? What if that bitterness I feel and the distrust that's settled deep inside of me never goes away? Doesn't that—in a way—reflect on us? Doesn't that make us doomed?"

"There are a million things that could doom us, Cara," Gian said, stepping forward to stroke her cheek and push a stray curl behind her ear. She smiled at his touch, feeling that familiar shiver race down her spine at his contact. "You know what else could doom us? That instead of taking that risk with me—jumping off the cliff that scares you—you want to debate how and why I love you inside of a liquor store at ten at night. Because that's what you'll keep doing, about everything, on all the little details about us, instead of just *being*."

Cara frowned. "You don't know that."

"I know you worry about details all the time. Right now, you're worried about the details of us, of something like *love*. That should be the easiest, most honest thing you can feel. And your very nature is to question it, Cara, and to question me."

"I don't *want* to."

"But you do. And you know what, that's okay, too. As long as you *be with me*, I don't care about the rest. I don't care about those details and the nonsense. I don't hear the noise of everyone else telling me what I should or shouldn't be doing with you. I don't give a single fuck about any of that, because I love you. Nothing else matters. The rest will figure itself out on its own. I believe that entirely."

"Why would anyone tell you not to be with me, Gian?"

That time, he was the one to look away.

Cara didn't miss it.

"Like I said, it doesn't matter."

She wondered if it *should*, though.

"Say it, again," Cara demanded.

Gian—once more—didn't hesitate. "I love you, Cara."

It became easier to hear each time he said it.

It became easier to believe.

It became easier to understand.

"I want you to say it back," he told her, "but I don't need you to say it because I want you to. I don't need you to say something that scares you enough to send you running away from me for three weeks, only to call me when you can't take it anymore. I don't need you to justify what I already know, *amore*."

"But?"

"But I do need you to be with me, Cara. That's all."

An older gentleman slipped down the aisle, making Cara move closer to Gian to avoid being bumped into by the guy's shoulder. She didn't mind.

She liked it there.

"I do, though," she said.

"Hmm?"

"Love you, Gian."

His smile grew and he kissed her quickly before pulling her into his side. Heading toward the cash with a six-pack under his arm, and a bottle of wine in her hand, Cara felt … settled. For the first time in weeks, she was okay.

"Now do we go back to pretending like we're good and the last few weeks didn't happen?" Cara asked.

"There's no need to pretend. We're perfect, *mon ange*. We always were."

"In a crazy way, maybe."

"In *our* way," Gian murmured before he kissed the top of her head.

So, maybe loving this man wasn't such a bad thing after all.

Maybe.

"Now, we're going to go to your place, put one of those ugly fucking rom-com things on you like, get drunk, and then fuck tomorrow morning away," he told her as he sat the liquor down on the counter.

The cashier's eyes widened, and her cheeks pinked as she reached for the wine first to ring it through. "Usually, I'm supposed to greet customers, but I'm not sure what to say right now, so excuse me for saying nothing."

Gian flashed the girl a smile. "Just tell me what I owe."

"Thirty-five, twenty-two," the girl said faintly.

Cara couldn't even bother to feel embarrassed as she shook her head. "You are awful, Gian."

"Yes, and you love it."

They did exactly as he said they would—shitty movie, liquor, and all. But even when the morning came, and Cara was sure she was going to die from the way Gian's tongue fucked her senseless, she still wanted to hear him say it.

Again and again.

Over and over.

"Say it again," Cara demanded in a whisper.

Gian's chuckles rocked against her inner thigh, and then higher as his lips kissed a path from her pubic bone to below her right breast. "Again?"

"Again."

"*Ti amo. Je t'aime.* I love you. I can say it in three languages, *donna*, what more do you want?"

Cara wasn't sure what she wanted, really.

Not entirely.

More mornings like this, definitely.

Soft sheets. Sunlight on her face. Gian in her bed.

Was that how love was supposed to go? Cara didn't know.

If it was, she had already been doing *this* with Gian for months.

So why did it feel different now?

Why was it *better*?

"Again?" he asked, hovering over her on the bed.

Cara smiled, pushing up on her elbows to kiss his mouth that tasted like her. "I love you."

Gian smirked. "Again?"

"Always."

FOURTEEN

Gian found it was a strange feeling to have so many eyes watching him, waiting on him to speak. Like his words and his direction, was the only thing that mattered. Of course, he'd always been in some sort of position of power, regarding the mafia as an underboss. He always had some sort of control. His direction had always been followed when he had given it.

This didn't feel entirely the same.

This was different, because his word had become law to these men. To them, there was no one above him, no one for them to look at to ensure the direction he was giving, the demands he was making, were the right ones. It was only his word, and his wants, that now mattered.

Before, Gian had not felt the heavy weight of that kind of responsibility on his shoulders where the men of his Cosa Nostra were concerned. He shared that weight between himself, his grandfather, and Edmond. He'd never fully understood how important it was to say the right thing, to make the right choice, the first time.

Maybe he had been spoiled in that way.

"As we expected, Edmond is not backing down," Gian said. "But no one is surprised about that, right?"

None of the men answered, not that he expected them to.

It was their time to listen.

It was his time to talk.

"There's only one thing to do now—push harder, put more pressure on him, on his men, on his territory—where ever the hell we need to, in order to get what we want. None of us should want a street war. As it is, we have too many bodies piling up. We have too much official attention. The police won't leave us alone. The bigger problem is, neither will Edmond. He's not going to back down, and we won't either."

Gian stopped his spiel long enough to take a drink from the server that approached his table. Two fingers of whiskey burned all the way down his throat as he drank it in one fast gulp. He probably should've sipped the drink, as it deserved, but he wasn't in the mood. What he wanted, were quiet streets, compliant men, and Edmond in a grave.

Gian didn't think he was asking for much.

However, if their lives were that simple, then everything would be a hell of a lot cleaner. And as the old saying went, nothing worth having would come easy.

It was his own fault for not being better prepared for this.

Gian only blamed himself for that.

He had spent too much time after Corrado's death, stuck in his own problems, wandering around lost in his own world. Instead of handling the issue that was Edmond from the very beginning, Gian had let it fester. And now what had been a small wound, was a gaping, infected hole, eating away at his *la famiglia*.

"You could always hire someone to finish Edmond, if that's what—"

Gian's gaze cut to the Capo in the corner booth, and the action quieted the man instantly. "Like he did for my grandfather?"

Or, Gian still assumed that had been done by Edmond. He had no reason to believe otherwise, and the fool didn't offer one.

"Well …"

"Say it. That's what you mean."

The Capo gave a single nod. "Fine, *sì*, that's what I mean, boss. Consider what we might gain by ending it quicker."

"In a coward's way," Gian said slowly. "A way that makes *us* the coward."

"No—"

"*Yes*."

"He wouldn't be the first to die by the hands of a hired gun," the Capo muttered under his breath.

"You're right, he certainly wouldn't be."

The Capo also had a good point. Killing Edmond by way of a hired man, someone he didn't know and was not expecting, would end everything. Strangely, Gian did not feel okay with making that call, regardless of the positives that could come out of the situation. He felt—in a way—that it would make him no better than Edmond, killing his rival and not giving the man even a chance to properly defend himself.

Had Corrado been given the chance to see his death coming, might it have ended differently? Would his grandfather have made the choice the Capo was suggesting?

Gian didn't have the answers for those questions.

And he wasn't Corrado Guzzi.

He was only himself.

"But the answer is no," Gian said firmly, "so drop it."

The Capo's confirmative reply was enough for Gian to move on, satisfied his point was made.

"This will all be over soon enough," he assured. "Just keep doing what you've been doing. Clearly, someone wanted a war, and now they've got one. Maybe once they realize that they've gotten what they wanted, it won't be as nice, after all."

Despite wanting to get the hell out of the meeting with the men, and get on with his day, Gian ordered lunch and readied himself for more conversation. As an underboss, he had simply needed to check in on the

Capos and their dealings to make sure everything was on the up and up. His responsibilities kept him on the move, going from one man to the next, without stopping for very long. As a boss, he was learning it was not quite the same.

He had to talk.

A lot.

He had to listen, too.

It almost made him miss the years before he was a made man, when all he had to do was slam his fist into someone's face to get what he wanted.

Life was not that easy, now.

Frankly, it was better he had learned to tamper his temper. Bosses—good ones—didn't need to use violence as a first resort to get business done. That simply wasn't how Cosa Nostra men behaved. Gian had been lucky enough to get all of the roughness out of his system *before* he earned his button, and it made the transition of becoming a made man easier.

To an extent …

His phone buzzed in his pocket as the men droned on around him. He almost didn't pick up the call, as all the people who would usually be calling him at that time of day were sitting around the restaurant, waiting on their meals. Cara, the only one who might call him, should have been at university.

When the buzzing persisted, Gian pulled the cell out and checked the screen. The sexy image of Cara shooting him the peace sign and winking lit up the phone. Gian answered the call instantly. He put the phone to his ear as he stood from the table, turning his back to the men and walking away so his conversation couldn't be overheard.

"*Ciao, bonjour.*"

"I saw it again."

Gian tensed. "Saw what, *mon ange?*"

"The car. The *car*, Gian. I saw it again!"

He didn't have a damn clue what she was talking about, but the frantic pitch her tone took on was enough to make him turn back and head for his table again. He grabbed the jacket hanging off the back of the chair, waved Constantino off when the man stood with questioning eyes, and headed for the front of the restaurant.

"Okay, you saw a car, Cara. What car?"

She made a desperate noise that cut him deep, her panic searing through the phone like she was standing right in front of him. She was across the city, but damn it, Gian swore he could feel her fucking fear radiating all the way to him.

He was already out of the restaurant and moving toward his car and waiting enforcer by the time she gained enough of a breath to answer him.

"The *car*! With Chris—that day, Gian. All the noise and the gunfire.

The fucking car!"

"Are you sure?"

Gian only asked because Cara insisted she remembered nothing about her drive-by attack, except the pain she felt when she hit the ground. She didn't have distinct memories of what happened leading up to it, and discussing it was an emotionally taxing event.

"Yes," Cara hissed. "I saw it and *I knew*."

Now they were getting somewhere.

"Where are you right now?" he asked.

"At the café I like. I wanted a snack before my next class."

"Can you stay there?"

"I'm not leaving!"

Her screech almost made his ear bleed.

"I'm twenty minutes away, Cara. Get something to drink, I'll be there by the time you're done."

"Okay."

Fuck.

He wished she didn't sound so frightened and panicked. He knew she had a lot of baggage regarding the drive-by simply because it reminded her of Lea, and of that event. Her memories of her attack were clouded with the ones she had of Lea's, and even trying to talk about it put Cara in a bad place. That—and only that—was the reason why Gian didn't push.

Gian scrubbed a hand down his face. "It's fine. It'll all be fine, *bella*."

"Hurry," she mumbled.

"Already on my way. Try to relax."

Easier said than done, he knew.

Gian said goodbye, and slipped his phone into his pocket as he took the keys to his car from the enforcer. He did not leave his car unattended after the bomb incident. "Follow me in your own car."

Chris nodded. "Got it, boss."

Gian broke at least a dozen traffic laws, but he cut the twenty-minute drive in half. He couldn't find a place to park, so he simply yanked his car over to the side of the road right in front of the café windows, ignoring the horns honking behind him.

Cara flew out of the café damn near to the second Gian cut the engine, and jumped into the vehicle without even looking over her shoulder once. He pulled the car back onto the road, much to the chagrin of the other drivers he had cut off, and hit the gas hard.

"I thought it was going to happen again," Cara whispered in the passenger seat.

"It's not going to happen again. Tell me what you saw."

"The car."

"Yeah, I got that. I need a bit more info to go on, though."

Cara let out a hard breath and ran her fingers through her hair. "I don't even know how I forgot that was the car—it's so fucking *yellow*."

Immediately, Gian hit the brakes and pulled the car into the nearest parking lot. "Say that again."

"What?"

"The color of the car."

"Yellow?"

Gian nodded. "You're sure that's what it was."

Cara blinked. "It was yellow. I see cars all the damn time, but not one like *that*."

"All right."

Gian cut the engine and got out of his vehicle, rounding the side to open Cara's door. She simply stared up at him, unsure of what she was supposed to do. Chris had pulled up behind them, his car still running and waiting.

"Come on, get out," Gian said, holding his hand for Cara to take.

"Why?"

"I have some business to handle, now."

"Do you know who owns the car?"

"I know who owns a *yellow* car," Gian replied unfazed. It was an odd color to have, especially in their business, when the intention was *not* to draw attention. "And that's not for you to worry about."

Chris had finally exited his own vehicle as Gian managed to convince Cara to get out of his car. He nodded to the man, and urged his lover toward the enforcer with a smile that was entirely forced.

Because inside?

Yeah, there he was *pissed*.

"Chris will take you to my penthouse for the evening," Gian said. "I will be home later."

Cara glanced over her shoulder at him. "Will you?"

"Of course."

After he hurt somebody.

• • •

Louis Portella.

Gian repeated the name as he tugged his driving gloves at the wrists, making sure they were snug against his skin. He watched the twenty-three-year-old solider, Edmond's grandson, stroll out of a strip joint with a grin on his face and not a fucking care in the world.

He figured he ought to let the guy have his happy moment. Shortly, there would be absolutely nothing for the guy to be happy about.

Quickly, Gian stepped out of his car, keeping the engine running. He hit the button on the fob to unlatch the trunk as he pulled his tie free from around his neck at the same time. Crossing the small parking lot without missing a beat, Gian came up behind Louis before the guy even knew what was happening.

Gian had already checked the place out while Louis was inside, enjoying the entertainment. The only camera was located directly in front of the business. None were set off to the side, where the cars were parked. He chose to strike now, because the lot was empty, and he didn't know where Louis was heading next.

Time was always of the essence.

Gian used his tie to wrap around Louis's neck, pulled it tight, and forced the man to the ground. Effectively cutting off the man's airways and his ability to shout for help, Gian pulled the fool back across the lot toward his waiting trunk.

A single, hard kick to Louis's face stopped the man's fighting. Dead weight was a bit harder to pull along, but Gian didn't mind. It was easier to stuff an unconscious man into the trunk of a car, rather than a conscious, fighting one.

Blood trickled out of Louis's nose and mouth, staining the gray interior of the trunk. Gian made a disgusted noise at the sight, knowing he'd have to send his car in to have the interior ripped out and changed, before he slammed the trunk closed.

A half hour later, Gian used the barrel of his gun to poke Louis in the forehead to wake the man up. It took a whole minute for the guy to gain enough bearings to realize he was sitting in a junk yard, inside a beat-up Toyota. Louis yelled for a good two minutes, and Gian let him, knowing no one was coming to help.

It benefitted Gian greatly to know people who knew people.

Like a man who owned a junk yard.

"Didn't your grandfather ever tell you it was a stupid idea to buy a yellow Camaro?" Gian asked.

Louis blinked. "W-what?"

"Your car. The color. It's fucking ostentatious. You can't miss it driving by. It might as well be screaming at you to look at it."

"My c-car."

Gian poked the guy in the forehead with the barrel of the gun again, harder the second time. "That's what I said, dipshit. Pay attention."

Louis tried to move away from Gian, but he didn't get more than a couple of inches in the shitty, worn-down driver's seat. After all, Gian had tied the bastard's hands to the steering wheel, and his legs to the gas and brake pedals.

"What the hell?" Louis asked, yanking on the restraints.

"It's easier when you can't run," Gian explained. "Now, about your car."

"Fuck you."

"Stupid boy."

Gian cocked back the hammer on his gun, aimed, and pulled the trigger. A single shot plugged into Louis's knee, blood splattering over the car and out the door. Gian didn't bother to move when the blood flew, simply stayed like he was and let it stain his suit. It would have to go after tonight, anyway.

Louis's shouts of pain made Gian smile a bit.

"You can keep yelling, but the owner has stepped out for a while to grab some late night snacks," Gian lied.

The truth was, the owner of the junk and crushing yard was waiting in his office for when Gian drove out of the lot. The man would then pick up his payment, left in the usual spot, and junk the Toyota by crushing it with a hundred other vehicles that night without so much as looking inside.

"Now answer me," Gian continued. "Didn't Edmond tell you that color was a bad choice for a car?"

Louis nodded.

"Of course, he did. I remember him bitching about it shortly before Corrado died." Gian chuckled. "Pretty sure he threatened to *junk* it, when you weren't home one weekend."

Louis cleared his throat, water in his gaze.

For the most part, the man hid his pain well.

"When did Edmond order you to do the drive-by on Cara and my enforcer?"

"He didn't—"

"Don't try lying," Gian interrupted swiftly. "It was pure fucking luck that nobody saw your yellow piece of shit that day, and nothing more. The problem is, somebody *did* see it. She only happened to remember it today. Lying makes this last longer, man. See how that works?"

"He told me to use another car," Louis said hoarsely. "I couldn't get my hands on one."

"Stupid."

The man nodded, his silent agreement.

"Why Cara?" Gian asked.

"She was a means to an end."

"The end being what, exactly?"

"He wanted to get you to fall in line," Louis said. "You weren't following the fucking rules, okay? He said taking something away from you might put you back in your place."

Edmond had a lot to learn about Gian, but he saved that lesson for another day.

"Tell me about the bomb, and Corrado," Gian urged.

Louis's brow furrowed. "What?"

"The bomb on my car. The murder of my grandfather. This isn't fucking rocket science."

"I didn't do those things."

"I didn't say *you* did them. I want you to tell me what you know about them."

"Nothing," Louis said quickly. "I know nothing."

"I fucking told you not to lie." Gian sighed, already readying and aiming his gun for Louis's other kneecap. "You had to make this hard—"

"I'm not lying! I swear, I swear I'm not fucking lying!"

Gian barely held back from plugging the asshole with another bullet. "Why in the hell should I believe you?"

"I'm going to die, anyway," Louis mumbled, his gaze never leaving the gun in Gian's hand. "What good does lying do for me now?"

He had a point.

"So you know nothing about those two events," Gian said, wanting to clarify.

"Because my grandfather didn't do them," Louis replied.

"You don't know that for sure."

"I know Edmond said he would have had Corrado shot from behind, so at least the funeral could have been an open casket."

Gian clenched his teeth so hard at that admission that his molars ached. "Did he now?"

"He didn't need to kill Corrado. He was already *dying*."

"How the fuck do you know that?"

"I didn't know—my grandfather did. Edmond told me *after*. Why kill a man that's already got one foot in the grave, huh?"

Gian didn't have the answer for that one.

And he was done with this conversation, now.

Standing, Gian brushed off his pants. Louis looked up at him in enough time to see Gian's gun pointed directly at his head.

Always look at a man when you take his life.

Corrado's words echoed in Gian's mind.

He deserves that respect.

Gian pulled the trigger, and didn't look away.

FIFTEEN

Cara woke with a start, jerking upward on the couch at the sound of a door slamming shut somewhere in the penthouse. She scrubbed her eyes with the back of one hand as she went in search of the cause of the noise. Soon, she had narrowed it down to a bathroom, as the sound of water ran heavily behind the door. She assumed it was Gian, because he should have been back by now, and Chris had not followed her into the penthouse when he'd delivered her there earlier.

"Gian?" she called, rapping her knuckles to the white wood.

"Sorry, *ma chérie*. I didn't mean to wake you. Head into bed, I'll be there in a minute."

She knocked again, instead. "It's like one in the morning, Gian."

"Yes, I'm aware."

"Open the door."

A heavy sigh followed the request, but she heard the latch on the door unlock. Cara opened the door herself, stepping in to find Gian stripped down to his boxer-briefs as he scrubbed a bar of soap up and down his arms with forceful strokes. Bloodstained clothes rested at his feet, forgotten beside a waiting trash bag.

Gian picked up a cigarette from the counter, and took a drag, exhaling thick, white smoke to the ceiling. That was a new thing.

"Since when do you smoke?" Cara asked.

"Not very fucking often, that's when."

Gian continued his work like Cara wasn't even in the room, dragging the bar of soap against his fingernails until he seemed pleased that it had done its job. On the counter beside his burning cigarette, a Berretta sat dismantled, as though it too were waiting to be cleaned.

He was almost mindless in his task, barely paying her any attention. Scrub, wash, dry. Scrub, wash, dry. He scrubbed parts of his body that Cara was sure had nothing on them. Occasionally, he'd glance into the mirror for a moment, or lift up his burning cigarette for another drag, but then he was right back at his task once more.

Cara had a million and one questions to ask. The part of her that hated these sights, and knew good and well what they meant, wanted to demand answers so she could confirm what she already understood.

The bigger part of her that loved Gian, didn't say a thing. It was a choice she had to make. So she made it. Cara found it surprising, how easy it was to make that choice.

"Do you need something?" Cara asked.

"Not at the moment, sweetheart."

"Okay."

Cara turned to leave the bathroom, deciding it was best for them both if she left him alone to do his business. She didn't need to be there to see it, and she didn't think he needed her there, watching him like a bug under a microscope. Plus, the longer she stayed there, the more curious she became and was liable to start asking questions she knew better than to ask.

Neither of them needed that.

"Wait," Gian said quickly, "there is something."

Cara spun around to face him slowly. Gian had rinsed all the soap off his arms again, and was now patting them dry with a towel that he dropped onto the pile of bloody clothes once he finished with it.

"What is it?" Cara asked.

"Remember when I promised you that we would do that trip to Quebec again sometime?"

"Yes."

"I was thinking I could extend it a couple days, if you don't mind taking a couple of days off school. You head out tomorrow, and come back Sunday evening."

Cara's gaze narrowed, as she was not a stupid woman, and she had *not* missed how he posed his words carefully. "*Me.*"

Gian stood firm, his gaze never wavering from hers. "*Only* you, Cara."

"No."

"Chris would be happy to accompany—"

"Gian, that was supposed to be a trip for *us*, not just me. And *no*, I am not taking someone else—especially not another man—on it with me!"

"Technically, it was a trip for your birthday. So *oui*, it was only for you. I was going to tag along."

"You're playing word games to distract me from what you're not saying."

Gian's expression hardened as he replied, "Fine, then I'll say what I mean. It would be best if you got out of the city for the remainder of the week and weekend. It will give me one less thing to worry about, as I do some digging into some people and business that I should have done a long time ago."

"I'm not going anywhere, Gian."

"Cara, now—"

"The answer is no."

"Fuck, you are stubborn when you want to be," Gian grunted under his breath. He turned back to the sink, going back to his task as though that would get him back on track, and Cara's refusals didn't matter. She had news for him. "Don't force my hand here, *bella*."

She stuck her hands to her hips, determined to make him hear her.

"You can't order me around from place to place."

"Can't, *mon ange*? *Can't?*"

"That's what I said."

"That's the wrong word, Cara. I can *do* whatever the hell I please, so long as you are safe and comfortable while I do it. Nobody said you had to be happy about it, though."

"Then what's the right word, your fucking highness?"

Gian's brow dipped in his irritation, his dark gaze flashing over to her in warning. "Won't, Cara. I *won't* do something you ask me not to. See the difference?"

"I see you being an asshole."

Before Cara had even blinked, Gian pushed away from the counter and came for her. His hand caught her around the back of her neck, he pulled her close, and his mouth came crashing down on hers in a fast kiss that seared her from the inside out. It took her fucking breath away, all the languid strokes of his tongue against hers, and the way his fingers tightened to hold her still. He didn't let her move away, even when he stopped kissing her.

"Stop being difficult," he murmured against her lips.

Cara let out a shaky exhale. "I'm not going anywhere that you're not going, Gian."

"I love you, Cara, but you're killing me."

"You don't really want me to go anywhere, either."

"I want you *safe.*"

"With you," she said, kissing him quickly, "I'm sure I will be."

• • •

"Chris," Cara greeted as the man held open the restaurant door for her. "Thank you."

"Very welcome. Have a good dinner, miss."

He still wouldn't call her by her name, no matter how many times she insisted. She figured she could break him of the habit, eventually.

Gian was waiting for Cara beyond the entrance of the restaurant, his sharp, black suit making her gaze travel over his fit form to appreciate the sight of him standing there like he was. With his hands clasped at his back, and his stare focused on something inside the restaurant, he seemed almost relaxed.

Cara knew that he couldn't possibly be as calm as he appeared on the outside. Gian's mind always ran a million miles a minute, and with the problems he had been having lately, she was sure that only made it worse.

Yet, there he stood. Like a fucking rock in a hurricane. Refusing to move or be moved. Unflinchingly calm in the eye of a storm. Always strong.

Cara wondered if this man knew his strength, or the power he wielded because of it. She was positive that if *anything* made Gian a formidable threat to the men in his business, it was this right here.

"Something caught your eye?" Cara dared to ask as she approached.

Gian's head turned, his lips tugging into a sexy grin as his gaze landed on her sapphire-blue, body-con dress. He didn't hide his wandering gaze, making Cara smile and her cheeks heat up. "Something certainly has now, my beautiful girl. How was your day?"

"Long, but I got through it."

"Chris wasn't too pushy when he showed up to bring you to dinner, was he?"

"Chris is always pushy," Cara joked, "but I blame that on his very impatient boss."

Gian winked, his arm curving around her side as his hand laid flat to her lower back, above the swell of her ass. "He's paid very well to put up with me, trust in that."

"I'm sure. Have you ordered?"

"We have, yes."

Cara's brow furrowed. "We?"

As far as she had been told, this was supposed to be a dinner for only her and Gian, no one else. She certainly hadn't expected guests to be included, too.

Gian bent down to kiss her forehead, his fingers pressing lightly to her back to urge her to walk forward. "Seems I wasn't the only one who made reservations here, tonight. They suggested we merge the tables, and I didn't want to be rude."

"Like you give a shit about being rude."

He chuckled. "For some people, I do."

"Well, who is it?"

"Constantino and Stephan, actually."

Cara didn't bother to hide her discontent.

Gian only laughed harder. "We'll be gone before you know it, and I know you were told to pack a bag to stay with me tonight at the penthouse, so stop moping."

"I'm not *moping*."

"What would you call that frown, then?"

Cara eyed him from the side as she said, "A displeased smile."

"Nice try. Don't mope, love. It's not a good look on you."

"I wanted you to myself *all* night. I'm not asking for a lot."

Gian pulled her impossibly closer. "I'll make up for it, but if you insist on that moping of yours, I'll be forced to take whatever action necessary to put an end to it."

"Including having dinner alone?"

"I told you, it would be rude."

"Then, how—"

"I do own this place, and there's a lovely private office in the back. Private in the way that no one can see inside, but they can certainly *hear* a lot."

Cara's body heated instantly. "Stop that."

"I've given you fair warning. Stop the moping. Fix your face, beautiful."

She shot him a playful glare before plastering on a smile that made Gian nod in approval. She had done it just in time, too, as they rounded a half-partition wall to come to a stop at what would be their table.

Constantino and Stephan—a man she hadn't seen since that night months ago, at the club with Bambi—sat chatting together, seemingly unaware that Cara and Gian had arrived. They only took notice when Gian pulled out Cara's chair, and then pushed her in closer to the table.

"Evening, cousin," Constantino greeted.

"Constantino," Cara replied.

Stephan only nodded at Cara before going back to his conversation with Constantino, like she wasn't even at the table. Cara didn't mind, really.

Gian's fingers stoked Cara's thigh under the table after he too had taken his seat, though his hand never wandered higher. No, he simply continued his light, teasing touches, reminding her of his earlier threat to make her smile, if needed.

The *bastard*.

God, she loved this man.

"The food should be here soon, if you want to wash up or anything," Gian told her.

Cara nodded, thinking she should do just that. Chris hadn't given her much time to do anything except throw on something appropriate after she'd arrived home from classes. "I'll be quick."

"Bathrooms are toward the back, *bella*."

A quick kiss later, that was all but ignored by the other men at the table, and Cara headed for the bathrooms. She made fast work of washing up her hands, and did a check of her little bit of makeup in the mirror, finding her lipstick, eyeliner, and mascara had held up remarkably well throughout the day. She fluffed her curls with her fingers, resetting some of the waves, and headed back out to the table.

She nearly rammed into a familiar man as she rounded the hallway corner leading back out onto the restaurant's main floor. For a brief second, as she apologized out of habit for not paying attention, she hoped he wouldn't recognize her.

She knew that was a foolish wish.

Of course, Frankie would recognize her face. Her features were a perfect match to her dead twin's. And from what information she had gathered from Gian and Lea's online, private journals, the two had been involved for quite a while. It still made her a bit uncomfortable, given the circumstances of their relationship, but Cara was now sadder about it, more than anything else.

She wished Lea had told her.

"Cara," Frankie said, taking a wide step back.

"Frankie."

He shifted from foot to foot, shooting a glance over his shoulder before looking back to her. Nervousness wrote heavily all over his actions.

Cara cleared her throat, waving toward the semi-private area. "I should get back to my table."

"Sure, but first, uh … could I apologize?"

"For what?"

Frankie shrugged one shoulder. "A while back—at the club when you showed up. I probably came across as rude, and that wasn't my intention. You shocked me, and your face, it really took me off-guard. I'd seen you from afar before, with Lea, but never up close like that. When she said identical, she meant that quite literally, I guess."

He offered her a tentative smile that Cara returned. "It's okay."

"It's not, Cara. I am sorry."

She nodded quickly. "Thank you."

"How are you?" he asked, posing the question with a careful tone. "Don't feel like you have to tell me, if you don't want to. You certainly don't owe me anything, but in a way, I feel like I might know you. She talked about you often, even though we tried to be casual and keep the personal shit out of it all."

"She's doing well," came a deep voice from behind Frankie.

Cara's gaze flew to Gian, who had clearly come looking for her, and she smiled a bit wider. "I am. I'm doing a lot better now."

Frankie murmured something fast in Italian to Gian, who shrugged in response, as though he hadn't a care in the world.

"All is fine," he assured Frankie. "As long as she says so."

"It is," Cara said. "Thank you again, Frankie."

Gian side-stepped the man as Frankie headed down the hall toward the men's bathroom. "I need to make a call, Cara. Can you find your way back to the table without running into someone else?"

She laughed at his teasing. "I'm sure I can."

"All right, get going. The food is waiting."

He dropped a kiss to her forehead before he headed down the hallway, bypassing the bathrooms altogether and exiting through a back door into what looked like an alleyway.

Cara wasn't all that interested in sharing a table with her cousin and Stephan while Gian was gone, but she sat back down with a smile and surveyed the pasta and salad dish that had been set out for her.

"What the hell took so long?" Constantino asked.

"And where's Gian?" Stephan added.

"I had a conversation with someone," Cara replied, "and Gian is making a phone call."

"Who?"

Cara glanced at her cousin. "Pardon?"

"Who were you talking to?"

Jesus.

Why were people so nosy?

"I ran into Frankie coming out of the back," she said, offering little else. Constantino should know enough to know who Frankie was—or had been—to Lea.

Constantino made a noise that sounded unpleasant under his breath.

Stephan shot his friend a look. "Relax, man."

"These *donnas* make it fucking hard," Constantino muttered. "First the one, now the other. It's a damn shame, like they don't even care how they look or how they're making the rest of us look."

"I beg your pardon?" Cara asked sharply.

Constantino paid her no mind, still going on to Stephan in his way. "You know what I mean, Stephan. You're not quiet about what you do running around with that girl of yours, but at least Lea had the fucking decency to keep out of sight when she was with Frankie, for the most part. This isn't any different, no matter what anybody says."

"*Constantino*," Cara snapped.

Her cousin's gaze cut to hers. "What?"

She wasn't entirely sure what Constantino was going on about, but she certainly didn't fucking like it. She definitely wasn't going to sit back and let him compare her relationship with Gian to the one Lea had been involved with, where Frankie was concerned. She didn't see how the two *could* possibly compare. It was like apples and oranges.

"If you have something to say to me, then say it," she told her cousin. "But keep in mind, your opinion of me, my business, and what or *who* I choose to do are none of your fucking concern."

Constantino rolled his eyes. "That's exactly the fucking problem. You don't care that everyone else is looking at what you're doing, and seeing it for exactly what it is, Cara. Playing a man's whore, nothing else. It's shameful."

Cara felt like he had slapped her. "Why am I playing any man's whore? Because I'm not like every other *principessa della mafia*, getting married the first chance I can, and making sure every little fucking thing I do is

150

approved by a man in my family? Is that why? You know what, don't bother answering."

She stood from the table, already done and wanting to get the hell out of there. She could take a fucking cab home, for all she cared. She wouldn't, however, be sitting there for another second longer.

"Go fuck yourself," she told Constantino before leaving.

SIXTEEN

The first thing Gian noticed when he returned to the table was that Cara was absent. Right off the bat, that put him on edge. Constantino ate his food with heavy forkfuls, as though he didn't have a problem, while Stephan picked at his plate and chatted away on his cell phone.

"Where's Cara?" Gian asked.

He didn't even bother to sit down.

Constantino shrugged. "She left."

"Say that again."

It didn't even come out as a question.

His friend let out a heavy sigh, dropping his fork to his plate with a loud clatter. "I said, she left, Gian."

Gian reached for the cell phone in his suit jacket, but hesitated before pulling it out. "And why the hell would she leave, exactly?"

Constantino made a dismissive noise under his breath, going back to his meal. "She didn't like what she was told, I suppose."

What. The. Fuck.

Gian sincerely hoped this was not another incident like he'd had with Constantino at the hospital, but it was looking worse and worse by the second. "I'm going to give you ten seconds to explain what in the fuck that means before I drag your ass out of this restaurant and beat you fucking senseless."

Made men didn't fight.

It was a rule.

Gian no longer cared for that particular rule.

Especially not when Cara was involved.

Stephan cleared his throat, dragging Gian's attention to him for the moment. The man quickly said goodbye to whoever he was speaking to on his cell phone, hung it up, and put it in his pocket. Standing from the table, Stephan dropped his napkin down and pulled money from his wallet, letting it fall by his glass of water.

"And where are you going?" Gian asked.

Stephan jerked his head in Constantino's direction. "As much as I like this stupid fuck, sometimes he goes too far."

"Hey—"

"You do," Stephan interrupted Constantino. "There are things you need to *not* talk about, or give your opinion, and a guy's girl is one of them."

"Is that where you stand on the line for this?" Constantino asked.

Stephan nodded sharply. "You're damn right it is. Call me when you get yourself straightened out, Constantino. And make sure you *apologize*. Even if it is Gian."

Gian let that barely-hidden insult brush off his shoulders, but only because he had one fucking idiot to deal with for the moment, and he wasn't in the mood to handle two. Besides, Stephan never made an effort to hide his dislike of Gian, in the grand scheme of things. Constantino, on the other hand, had been doing some pretty underhanded shit that left Gian fucking unsettled.

Like whatever *this* was.

"*My* apologies," Stephan said as he passed Gian by to leave.

Gian let him go, never budging an inch, even when Constantino went back to eating his food again. That only irritated the shit out of Gian more.

"Sit, eat," Constantino demanded. "We'll talk this out. I fucked up, big deal. It happens."

Gian didn't sit. "How did you fuck up, though?"

"She mentioned running into Frankie." Constantino waved a hand as if to dismiss what he was about to say next. "I might have mentioned that it doesn't look good on our family to have her running around with you, doing what she's doing, like she is. Just like it didn't look good when Lea was involved with Frankie a while back."

Gian bristled all over. "And you think this is even remotely the same?"

Constantino, stone-faced and dry-toned, said, "It's exactly the same."

"You're wrong."

"No, I'm not, *and* I'm within my rights to say so, if I want to. She's a woman of *my* family, regardless of where her brother is. So, who gives a shit if her father is dead, and her brother is too busy finishing out a war in Chicago to look after his sister's business? I'll speak for them—what you've done with my cousin is a fucking *shame*, Gian."

"You're way out of line," Gian murmured, forcing himself to keep his tone level.

"You know I'm not. Fact is, Cara is now good for what you've used her for, and very little fucking else, man. That's the sad part. Nobody else will ever look at her and think, shit, wife material or anything of the sort. You've ruined that, and I don't even think she *knows*."

"Constantino, I warned you once, didn't I? I warned you—friends or not—I would fucking hurt you, if you spoke badly about Cara again."

Constantino dropped his fork again, standing from the table and moving to stand toe-to-toe with Gian. Neither man moved a muscle, neither looking away from the other. It took every ounce of willpower Gian had left in his body to keep his hands down at his sides, clenched into tight fists he was ready to throw.

"What's worse, Gian, is when you are boss at the end of all this, when it's all said and done, she won't matter. Not for more than what you've already used her for, and maybe even for less. She won't be *allowed* to matter. No whore—"

Gian was pretty fucking sure he broke a knuckle on impact of punching Constantino in his ignorant, disrespectful fucking face. He barely felt the pain, and since he felt like one punch wasn't good enough, he landed another two, back-to-back, sending his friend sprawling to the floor of the restaurant.

Constantino wasn't knocked out, but he was pretty damn close. Gian figured that had been enough to make his point—he didn't need to do more, not when the guy was now bleeding and groaning on his back like an idiot.

Gian checked his knuckle.

Not broken.

Dislocated.

He gritted his teeth, and reset the knuckle as he heard a server approach from behind. With a single wave, the server retreated. One of the many benefits of owning the place, he supposed.

Bending down, Gian turned Constantino's head to make the man look at him. "I warned you, man. I won't be doing it again. We're done. You mean less than shit to me at this point. And unless you pull your head out of your fucking ass and work out a damn good apology for this one, you're going to remain that way. It doesn't matter to me, one way or the other."

Constantino laughed hoarsely. "Just tell her the truth, Gian. See what *she* says."

"There's nothing to tell."

• • •

Gian knocked on Cara's apartment door, ignoring the pain that bloomed in his swollen, bruised knuckle. She hadn't answered his calls as he'd left the restaurant, or the ones that he'd made on the drive over. A quick check with Chris, who had been designated to follow Cara for safety reasons again, had confirmed that she was at home.

Chris didn't have more information to offer, though.

"Cara, open the door," Gian said quietly. "I know you're here, *mon ange.*"

Silence answered him back. He understood why. It still hurt like hell. He'd take ten dislocated knuckles over her rejection. Funny, how love worked that way.

Gian knocked again. "*Cara.*"

"Did you know that in Italian, *cara* means dear?"

Her quiet question filled him with a sense of relief. She hadn't opened the door, but it was a start. Gian would take it.

"Of course, I know," Gian said. "*Mia bella cara, amore.*"

He heard the lock unlatch on the door a second before Cara slowly pulled it open. She stood on the other side, the apartment's darkness shadowing her in the hallway light. She had lost the dress from earlier, and the heels, too. Clean-faced, any makeup had been removed, and she'd tossed her wild hair up into a messy bun. An over-sized T-shirt fell at her mid-thigh, and she looked ready for bed.

"I'm sorry I left without at least waiting for you," she said, crossing her arms under her breasts and staring off to the side. "I got angry and I only wanted to leave. So I did."

"It's fine."

Or, it was now.

Gian understood *why*. He had simply reacted in a different way than Cara had, perhaps a less than proper way, considering his status. Even Cara had walked away when she was offended, Gian had definitely not.

"I'm sorry for whatever it was that Constantino said to you," Gian said. "He has no business putting his opinions in where they're neither wanted, nor warranted. And trust that he absolutely knows that, now."

Cara nodded. "Sure."

"You don't sound sure, sweetheart."

She looked up at him, sadness coloring her blue eyes. "Did he have a point, though?"

"No, absolutely not."

"Really? Because if he feels the need to say that running around with you looks bad on me, and if my uncle felt the need to warn me away from you, then why not think something *is* wrong with it? And what is it that's so wrong? I don't understand. I'm not doing anything wrong, am I?"

"No," Gian rushed to say. "There's nothing wrong with this—with *us*. There never has been. Some people have their opinions because they're stuck in a different time, with different rules. Women should do as they're told, as they're expected to do, and not what they want to do. I'm not of that mindset, Cara."

She frowned.

Her sadness hurt him as badly as her silence.

"And who the fuck cares about those people, anyway?" Gian asked. "I sure as hell don't. I only concern myself with what you think and feel, not them. They get no say in this or us. None at all."

"Then why did I let what someone else thought bother me so fucking much?"

"Because you're allowed to have feelings, Cara. You're allowed to demand respect from other human beings. No one has any right to make you feel less than them, especially when they don't know who you are in your heart. They don't know you. Not like I do."

"You really do know the right things to say."

"I say the truth, love."

Gian stepped forward, opening his arms to test the waters. Cara gave him one of her small, sweet smiles before letting him wrap her in his embrace. Slowly, he walked her backward enough that he could kick the door closed behind him. Tangling his hand into her soft curls, he tilted her head back far enough to steal a kiss from her pretty mouth.

"Anyone who even thinks to breathe a bad word about you in my direction deserves every fucking thing they get," Gian told her, his calm voice belying his inner rage that had finally simmered a bit. "You're mine, Cara. I love you. Nothing else matters."

It was shocking to him in that moment how savage and brutal his love could be. That, without care or consideration, he would willingly and happily hurt someone he thought of as a friend simply because they had hurt *her*. The possessiveness that nearly always filled him whenever Cara was too far away was suddenly settled when she was in his arms, and his restlessness finally drifted away when he could touch her again.

This wasn't wrong.

He wasn't going to let her, or anyone else, say otherwise.

• • •

"Fuck," Gian snarled, pulling his mouth away from Cara's as she laughed. "I'm going to kill whoever that is."

"No, you won't."

The persistent knocking on her apartment door had effectively cock-blocked him in the worst way. He had *just* gotten her out of bed, and ready to sit down and eat something—a feat in itself, where Cara and mornings were concerned. He thought a nice fuck on the kitchen table would be a reward for his good deed before breakfast, but apparently, that wasn't going to be the case.

Cara pushed Gian away, and jumped off the table, pulling the over-sized shirt down her thighs a bit more. "It's probably Chris."

Gian's gaze narrowed. "You don't know that."

"No one else visits me. And I know he's trailing me again. You're not as smooth as you think, Gian."

"Never mind, you." He swatted her ass with a firm pat, sending her flying into the living room with a giggle. "Cover up with something. You're indecent."

"You pulled me out of bed this way!"

"Yes, *for me*. Not for the neighbors."

Cara stuck her tongue out at him, but still pulled an afghan blanket over her lower half as Gian headed for the door. A quick check through the peephole confirmed Cara's theory. Chris waited behind the door, his gaze trained on something down the hall.

Gian pulled it open with a scowl. "Do you not know how to use a fucking phone, or what?"

Chris barely blinked in the face of Gian's rage. "Did I interrupt your morning—"

"Finish that statement."

The enforcer grinned instead.

The fucker.

"What do you want?" Gian demanded.

Chris held up the item in his hands; a brown box, taped across the top, though the tape had been sliced through and it looked as though it had been opened. "This was delivered to me this morning by a friend, of sorts."

Gian eyed the box. "What friend?"

"One of Edmond's enforcers that knew I was more likely to question him first, before shooting. I suspect that's why the old fucker sent him over."

Well, then.

Gian took the box, looking over the cut tape again. "Why did you open it, if you were told it was meant for me?"

"One bomb is quite enough for you, don't you think?" Chris asked quietly. "I didn't go through the contents, only cut and opened to make sure nothing was waiting to go boom."

Gian wasn't the least bit surprised that Chris had chosen to take the risk of opening the box himself before handing it over to his boss. It was that length of loyalty that made Gian appreciate the man even more.

"Thank you," Gian said.

Chris nodded once. "And I am sorry about, you know, interrupting. If I did."

Gian scowled again. "Yeah, you did."

"Sorry, boss."

"Don't worry about it."

With a quick goodbye, Gian closed the door on his man, and headed back for the table. Cara seemed distracted by whatever was on the television, and Gian used that time to his advantage. He pulled open the top of the brown box—no bigger than a shoebox—and emptied out the contents. A small memory card rested on top of a tablet, and photographs fell across the table.

A small, hand-written note fell out last.

A gift, it read. *This has gone on long enough, Gian. Here is what you've been looking for, and it's time to end the rest. —Edmond*

Gian's gaze scoured the photos first.

Constantino.

A man Gian didn't recognize.

He distinguished quickly enough from the images that a trade of sorts was happening—money exchanged hands in the darkness of an alley, and that was it. A few other pictures, taken in the daylight, showed Constantino having multiple meetups with several younger Capos, and even a few of the older ones.

That might not have been such a bad thing, but it unsettled Gian. It bothered him because Constantino had no reason—no business—to be running between Capo to Capo, not when he had his own territory and crew to manage. The dates on the photographs showed Gian that all of those meets had happened *before* Corrado's murder.

Gian glanced over at the couch, seeing Cara was still lost in the television. He plugged the memory card into the side of the tablet and turned it on. He put the volume on low as he scrolled through the images and the one video that loaded from the card. More photos of Constantino showed up, although these showcased him visiting *Edmond*.

Gian tensed all over as he pressed play on the one video the card held.

A video of Claud Rossi lit up the screen, taken off to the side, slightly grainy, but still distinctive enough for Gian to discern who was in the room with Constantino's father. Edmond, and Matthew, the new *boss's* consigliere.

"He's gotten himself mixed up in some kind of shit this time," Claud said.

"Do tell," Edmond urged.

"I think Constantino's found himself over his head. Maybe he overheard me talking to my wife that the boss seemed unwell, or something. He jumped off my radar a lot more often than he usually does, and I took notice."

"Me, too," Edmond said. "Or rather, he was close to Gian. I needed to keep an eye on everyone close to him for a while."

"I didn't want to speculate."

"But you *did*."

"I can't have my son hiding things from me in this business, not in this life of ours," Claud muttered heavily. "It makes for dangerous things. I followed him, sometimes, and noticed he was trailing Gian some days, others he was off on his own. I started looking around, asking some questions to the men in the crew. A few pointed me in the direction of the kind of business Constantino had been asking about."

"What kind of business?"

"A hired man."

Gian's chest tightened painfully at what he was hearing. He didn't want to believe it, but certain things—his old friend's behaviors over the last few months—had left him with a bitter taste in his mouth.

"That's not all, though," Edmond said. "After Corrado, I was having a lot of the men watched, because everybody knew that kill came from the inside. I wanted to know *who*. I owed it to Corrado because, like him, I didn't see it coming until it was too late."

Claud shifted on his chair. "And what did you find, boss?"

"He had the bomb planted on Gian's car. I got photos of the meets and the payment exchanging hands. It speaks for itself."

"Gian is his friend."

"Gian is his way to the top," Edmond corrected with a shrug. "Gian was not making the moves that perhaps Constantino felt he should be after Corrado's murder, and so, I believe he thought to simply *push* Gian in the direction he wanted."

"As in, he didn't mean to kill him, only knock him down for a bit."

"So he would get up swinging." Edmond chuckled. "Frankly, no one knows Gian better than Constantino, if you think about it. Maybe he knew exactly how to push to get what he wanted."

Edmond had a good point, as much as Gian hated to admit it. Constantino had, on more than one occasion, made comments about Gian's habits. Like *always* using his car starter to start his vehicle in the winter, even though it was hard on the engines to do so in the freezing cold weather.

"And if he had fucked up?" Edmond considered out loud. "Well, then I suppose Constantino probably thought of Gian as fodder. He would still get what he wanted, in a way. A war between the younger and older generations that would open up seats all the way across the board."

"What do I do now?" Claud asked. "He's my son."

"He's a made man," Edmond replied just as fast. "And because of that, you'll let him answer as one, no matter who demands their retribution. That's how made men have always done this—it's how we always will."

Gian shut off the tablet.

He had never agreed more with something Edmond said.

He never would again.

SEVENTEEN

"Something smells fantastic," Gian said as he came up behind Cara at the stove.

She leaned into his touch, grinning when his kiss landed softly on the pulse point of her throat. His hand rubbed her back as he peered over her shoulder.

"What are you making?"

"A steak and potato mess," Cara replied, "fit for a king."

"I don't think you've ever cooked for me."

"You always order in."

"Not always, but it is faster."

Cara rolled her eyes. "*You've* never cooked for me."

"I'll rectify that soon."

"Can you even cook, or will you grab a bunch of takeout and set it up on dishes to make it look good?"

Gian swept her hair further behind her ear and nipped playfully on the lobe. "How little you think of me, pretty girl."

Cara tried damn hard to hide her shiver, and failed miserably. "So you *can* cook?"

"I have a French mother who had an Italian mother and a *very* Italian grandmother from my father's side. Yes, I can cook. I learned with bruised knuckles from my grandmama's favorite wooden spoon. My mother, on the other hand, preferred the French dishes, and I found those easier to make, really."

"Why was that?"

"Different teaching methods," Gian said with a chuckle. "Of course, the only reason they thought to teach my brother and I to cook was because my sister absolutely refused to do anything in the kitchen, and they needed to pass something on."

"Ah. Well, then you owe me something Italian *and* French."

"I will see what I can do."

"I'll hold you to it," Cara said sweetly.

She went back to attending her steaks, slathering them in a special homemade sauce that very few people had the recipe to. She preferred to cook her steaks in the oven, rather than on a frying pan. The meat always came out a bit more tender.

Gian moved around her in his penthouse, grabbing items out of the fridge and setting them up on the counter for Cara when she asked. He also pulled out a beer, popping the top off and taking a hearty swig from the amber-colored bottle. Just the way he stared at her, told Cara something was on his mind.

What, exactly, she didn't know.

She could just *see* it.

Their ruined date a few nights earlier had mostly been brushed under the rug. Cara hadn't seen her cousin since, and she didn't plan to seek the asshole out. Gian, on the other hand, kept Cara closer than ever since that evening and the morning after. In fact, he'd packed a bag for her to bring to his penthouse, and he hadn't let her leave since, only for school.

Cara didn't mind, really.

She liked being there with him.

"Everything okay?" Cara asked.

Gian shrugged. "It could be better, but I'll get there."

"Do tell."

"It's not for you to worry about, *bella*. Just nonsense making noise in my head, like it sometimes does. It'll all go away soon."

"If you're sure …"

"Positive." Gian took another drink from his beer as Cara slipped the casserole dish, filled with the marinated steaks, into the oven. "I do have a question for you, though."

"Oh?"

"What do you want in the future?"

Cara straightened quickly as she closed the oven, and leaned against the warm metal to regard Gian as she spoke. "For what?"

"Us, I guess."

"I want you," Cara said simply.

"That's a broad statement, though. I meant … the details, Cara. Of life, you know. The little things. What do you want with me in all of that?"

"What's brought this on?"

Gian smirked in that way of his. "I told you once that if you asked me for something more, I would try my very best to give it to you. I've done that so far, but now I wonder what you want beyond what we have, that's all."

"I want *you*," she repeated firmer.

"Yeah, but—"

"Everything, Gian. I want everything with you."

"Everything," he echoed.

"I mean, yeah. As it comes, you know."

"With me."

"Who the hell else?"

Gian gave her one of his usual smiles, leaned forward, and pressed a kiss to her forehead. "All right, then. That's all I needed to hear."

"And nothing's wrong?"

"No, I needed to hear that. From you."

It was one of the strangest interactions of Cara's life, certainly the oddest she'd ever had with Gian, but who was she to question the things that roamed around in his mind? Sometimes, he was so quiet, she wondered what his mind must be like.

"I have some shit to do, so give me a shout when the food is ready, okay?"

Cara nodded. "Sure."

Something was definitely wrong, she decided as Gian walked away. She still didn't call him on it.

• • •

"Gian?" Cara rapped her knuckles on the opened office door and peered in to find Gian still had his head bent down as he looked over something on his laptop. "Supper is ready."

"Can it wait for a minute?"

"It's set out on the table, but it'll be warm for a bit."

"Good. Come here for a second."

Cara stepped into the office, taking a seat on the couch closest to the window. "What's up?"

"I bought you a ticket. It's for tomorrow afternoon. To Chicago's O'Hare."

She wasn't sure she heard him right.

"I beg your pardon?"

Gian looked over at her, his expression blank as he redelivered the news. "You're going to have to leave for a while. I need you to go, for your own safety, as things are not good here on my end of things. Chicago is the best place to send you, considering everything."

"No."

"Cara—"

She stood fast from the couch. "Absolutely *not*, Gian."

"It doesn't matter how much you argue with me about this, and I know you're going to try, *mon ange*, but it's already been done. The ticket is bought. You'll be in a first-class seat tomorrow afternoon, on your way to Chicago."

"Like hell."

"I already talked to your brother as well. He knows when to expect you. He'll be there to pick you up."

Cara didn't care, and she was no longer listening. "I'm not going *anywhere*."

Gian sighed. "Is that how you want to do this then?"

"I want to stay with you, Gian!"

"If I didn't have to send you away, if I could choose any other option but this one, I would do that, Cara. I can't. This is the only option that completely takes you out of the equation. That way, I can focus on the things I need to for a short while. The faster I get you into a safe zone, the quicker I can get you back *with* me. Don't you understand that?"

"I said—"

Gian held up a single hand, quieting Cara instantly. "It is for your best interests."

"Fuck you."

He barely reacted to her stinging insult. Even *she* was surprised at the venom that her tone held.

"Are you angry that I'm sending you away, or because of *where* I'm sending you, Cara?" he asked.

She refused to give him an answer. Instead, she headed out of the office, going back the way she had come from the kitchen. Gian's footsteps echoed behind hers, albeit slower than her anger induced speed.

"Don't run away from me," Gian called out from behind her.

"Go to hell, Gian."

"Stop swearing at me, Cara."

"Not likely."

She held back from calling him an asshole, but barely.

"Is this what you're going to do, then?" Gian asked, as Cara strolled into the kitchen. "Fucking run because I did something you don't like?"

"I'm not—"

"You *always* run when shit goes south, Cara."

Fuck him again.

She made her way to the plate she had made for herself, and sat down at the table to eat. Gian stood at the other end, in front of his own plate, with his arms crossed as he stared her down.

"What are you doing?" he asked.

"Not running, clearly. I made food. I want to fucking eat it, if you don't mind."

Gian's jaw clenched. "And then what? Because Chicago is non-negotiable, Cara."

She ignored him, grabbing a steak knife to cut into the slab of meat on her plate.

"You're going to be on that flight tomorrow," he said when she stayed quiet.

"Will you shut the fuck up and eat?"

Gian yanked the chair out from the table with more force than was necessary. The two of them ate like that, both irritated and angry with the other, silent and stewing in their frustrations. Cara barely looked at Gian, and she could *feel* his damn eyes burning into her.

She hated that he had been right. She understood shit was bad in Toronto right now for him and the Guzzi family as a whole. He had been going non-stop for days, on the phone, out of the penthouse, and then back at odd hours. She overheard some of his phone calls, though she knew better than to eavesdrop.

Shit was going down.

Or it was about to be going that way *fast*.

Gian was trying to prepare as best he could for it.

Cara was likely one of those things, but he was *so fucking right*. It was not that he was sending her away, but where he was sending her away to. It was Chicago, and all the hell and pain that was about to accompany her on a long trip down a memory lane she didn't want to walk through.

Certainly not alone, anyhow.

And fuck him for knowing it would hurt her, and doing it anyway.

Fuck him for that.

It was only after they had finished the food, after she had cleared the table, that the yelling really got started between them. She had never fought with Gian, certainly not with raised voices and something to actually shout about. Not for something she was truly angry with him over.

This was not the same.

It was the first time Cara yelled in a long fucking time.

She raged.

She was *pissed*.

Gian let her.

She had the distinct feeling he did that because regardless of how much she screamed, fought, swore at him, and said no, she was still going.

And it was going to hurt.

A lot.

EIGHTEEN

Gian closed his laptop the second he heard familiar mumblings coming from down the hall. Cara sounded less annoyed than she had the night before. He took a phone call as he listened to the soft patter of feet down the hall, followed by the click of a closing door. The bathroom, likely.

By the time he was done with his call, Cara stood in the office doorway. She hadn't bothered to put any clothes on; she still wore that frilly, delicate lace that she'd gone to bed in. And that was only the panties, not the bra. She had simply tossed his dress shirt on—unbuttoned—which did very fucking little to cover her breasts.

Never mind what it did for his cock.

Bathed in morning light from the wide office windows. Sleepy-eyed. Mussed hair. Peeks of her soft, smooth skin, from the valley of her tits all the way down to the lace of her panties, demanded his attention. Her lips had turned a faded, stained red from the lipstick she had been wearing the night before.

Gian was sure his maid was sick and tired of trying to clean red lipstick stains out of his white sheets.

Fuck.

He wished he cared.

Cara leaned in the doorway. "Morning."

"You seem more pleasant today," Gian said.

"I was pleasant last night."

"After you yelled at me and then ignored me for hours."

Gian had never imagined a time would come in his life when he found himself controlled by the ways of a woman. At least, he hadn't expected that control to come *because* he loved her.

Cara had no idea of her control over him.

She probably thought Gian pulled the strings.

How wrong she was …

"I know you're not happy about Chicago, Cara."

"It … seems like a bit much," Cara said. "Like an overreaction, maybe. I could go anywhere, but that's where you think I should go."

"Your brother is there. You have family to look after you until I think it's safe to ask you back. It won't be for long. It's only a precaution, *bella*. Sending you to a safe house is one thing, but sending you out of the country is even better."

"Safe." She scoffed. "You do realize that the last time I was in Chicago, I buried Lea."

165

"Yes, but—"

"Because someone *killed* her."

Gian nodded, knowing this was one of Cara's hot-button issues. "I'm aware, but shit is different down there now. Calmer, even. Your brother recently took over as the new boss. It might do you some good to settle a few things while you're down there. And by settle, I mean stuff in your heart—the things that keep causing you pain. Your father died, you didn't go to his funeral. Your mother killed herself not too long ago and you didn't go back for that, either. And even if not for them, then for Lea. You miss her all the time. You say it enough, like you left her behind."

Cara glanced away at that statement. "I hate Chicago."

"You hate how it makes you feel, *mon ange*. That isn't the same thing. Time to face that head-on, and bury it for good."

"Easy for you to say." She blew a stray curl out of her face. "I'm not going to put up more fight about Chicago."

"No?"

"I tried that yesterday."

Gian smirked. "And it didn't work."

"Seems not."

"It won't be for long, like I said." Gian checked his watch. "And you have three hours before you have to be at the airport."

"Breakfast, then? I can cook or we can order in."

Gian took the sight of Cara in again, drinking in her show of skin, the curves of her hips, and her delicate lines. Every inch of her was a giant tease to him. A wonderland to explore, and to use to satisfy the darkest urges beating through his mind and body. Those damn urges only increased whenever she was nearby.

"They won't serve what I'm interested in," he said with a grin.

"Oh, my God. You are insatiable."

Gian shrugged.

This wasn't news.

"Insatiable would imply that I don't give you a break. In case you forgot, you slept alone in my bed last night. *Unfucked*, Cara."

Her cheeks pinked. "Yes, well—"

"By *my* choice, too," Gian interjected quickly.

"I'm surprised you didn't jump at the chance for angry sex, considering the way you go on in bed all the time."

He cocked a brow. "Angry sex is unhealthy. Like anything that's unhealthy, it's usually too enjoyable for its own good. Before you know it, you're causing fights, just to fuck and get that feeling back. Not interested, *bella mia*. We have enough to argue about, without adding nonsense like that in, too. Sorry."

Cara's blue eyes twinkled with her surprise. "That was not a response I expected."

"I'm full of surprises."

Gian crooked a finger at Cara as he leaned back in his large office chair. She didn't question his motives. She walked right over to his side with one of her sly smiles, anticipation burning brightly in her gaze.

Once she was close enough for him to reach out and grab her, Gian did just that. Cara sprawled into his lap, cradled in his arms. Her legs hung over the arm of the chair. The button-down shirt of his that she was wearing had spread open more, exposing the swell of her breasts.

Gian couldn't help but run the tips of his fingers over the peaks of her already-taut nipples. Then, he gave them a pinch, making Cara gasp and arch her back higher, closer to his hands again for more.

Cara gave him a stern stare that only make him chuckle. "How do you live with yourself?"

"Like you," he said, "I've learned to love it."

"You're terribly—"

"Cocky. I know."

"You could at least let me say it."

"You're not saying anything that I don't already know."

"Smartass."

"Yours, though," Gian murmured through a grin.

She preened in that happy, pleased way of hers.

"You always say the right things."

"I do, don't I?" he asked.

"And then you ruin it just as fast," she said with a shake of her head.

"Let me make up for it."

Cara peered up at him through her thick lashes. "And how do you plan to do that?"

"Orgasms. Morning orgasms."

"Well, then."

"They make up for everything, Cara."

"Yours certainly do," she agreed.

"And you wonder why I have a fucking complex, *amore*."

Cara shrugged. "More orgasms, less talking."

"But you like it when I talk and fuck you."

"Yes, but at the same time, Gian."

Fair enough.

"Get those fucking legs open, so I can get to what's mine, Cara," he demanded low.

With a sweet little sigh, she did as he wanted, widening her legs over the arm of the chair. His gaze roamed over the shape of her hips, to the line of the panties keeping her pussy covered with a scrap of lace.

"I love it when you make it easy on me."

Cara's grin turned sinful. "Sometimes, you like to take it, too."

He agreed, but his attention was elsewhere now.

He had a goal.

Get Cara off.

Do it again.

And then fuck her until his brain wasn't such a mess.

Good plan, Gian told himself.

Hopefully, it would be enough to sedate him until he got his stubborn, sexy girl back, but he doubted it. Cara was an obsession for Gian. From the way she talked, to the way she walked. All her smiles, and when she grew quiet. How she felt under his hands and beneath his control. Her desires and fears.

Their *what ifs*.

All of it.

Every single bit.

Gian was so fucking obsessed.

"Will you be my good girl this morning?" He traced the shape of her lips with his fingertips. Cara kissed the digits before sucking the tips into her teasing mouth. "Can you be patient, or will you turn greedy again?"

Cara released his fingers from between her lips to say, "I thought you liked your greedy slut, Gian?"

He grabbed a handful of hair at the back of her head and pulled her up for a bruising kiss. He enjoyed when she melted into the demands of his kiss, but he liked it even better when she fought for control.

Even if she always lost.

Gian pulled away, letting Cara fall back into his lap. "You know I do, but I like it when you listen and behave, too."

"I can listen—I *will*."

"And?"

"And I'll be your good girl, Gian."

"That's all I ask."

Cara licked her lips, squirming under the feel of his hand slipping beneath her panties. Gian's fingers skimmed over the small, trimmed patch of soft hair to get to the heaven between Cara's legs. Her thighs opened wider as he found her hot little clit—something else that was damn greedy, when it came to her body. He wanted her cunt wet, tight, and needy when he filled it with his cock, so he worked her clit until she shuddered and moaned her way through her first release.

All the while, she stayed as still as possible on his lap, never demanding more, and simply taking what he offered. He'd stroked her hair while he teased her clit, and watched the blues of her eyes deepen in color when the bliss raged.

Cara let out a slow stream of air as she calmed in his lap. "I'd demand you give me another, but ..."

"But?"

"Good girls don't demand anything, do they?"

Gian smirked. "No, they say please and thank you, and patiently wait for more."

"This is a lot of work, Gian."

"I always reward you."

"*Thank you.*"

"Good. Now ..." As he'd spoken, he'd been running his fingers with firm strokes over the entrance of her cunt, feeling the heat and juices of her arousal smearing to his digits. "I want you to take off my tie."

Cara radiated curiosity and anticipation as she reached for his throat with careful hands. She loosened and then pulled his tie free. Gian worked her pussy with two fingers, pumping deep and curling into her G-spot with every thrust. He could feel the shake in her legs, hear the way her breath caught, and he knew then that her second orgasm was coming on fast. Cara continued her task until the tie was limp in her hands.

Pleased that she had focused on his demand instead of getting off first, he sped up the rhythm of his fingers until she was crying out with another orgasm.

Cara's back lifted in a beautiful arch. "Oh, my God, Gian." His tie had gotten twisted in her clenching hands. "You know I love you, don't you?"

He chuckled. "Yes, but tell me again."

"I love you, Gian."

Gian pulled Cara into a proper sitting position on his lap. He gave her a kiss—softer and slower than before. "Of course, you love me like this."

"And when you're not like this, too," she promised.

He wondered how long that would last, though.

"Your tie," Cara said softly, offering the item between them like a gift.

"Thank you." The silk slid into his hand, and he shot Cara one of his wicked grins. "Don't panic too much when I take away your sight and make you feel for a bit."

Cara tapped his cheek gently with a shaky hand. "I never panic with you."

Gian took that as her permission.

She barely moved an inch as he blindfolded her with the tie, although her hands gripped tighter around his forearms. He unwound her fingers from his body, and placed them in her lap.

"Be good," he said in her ear.

Gian took a moment to admire Cara like she was—blindfolded, sitting pretty in his lap, and so trusting.

"Hold still," he warned, when Cara squirmed.

He could see her questions getting ready to fall from her lips, but he didn't give her the chance to ask them. Quickly, he lifted them both from the chair, and sat Cara on the edge of his desk. He moved whatever items out of the way that he didn't want knocked over or broken because of what was coming next.

"Tell me how you feel," Gian said as he pulled his own shirt off and dropped his slacks.

"Hot," Cara answered instantly.

"What else?"

He pulled the length of his cock from the confines of his boxer-briefs, and fisted his shaft with firm strokes from the base to the tip. His heartbeat pulsed against his palm.

"Greedy," Cara admitted with a pretty pout.

Gian kissed her lips for that admission. "Good, that's how I wanted you, *mon ange*. My greedy, good girl." He placed her palms to his chest. "Hands on me—it's time to feel for a while. Don't hold back, Cara. I want your cunt squeezing my dick until I can't breathe, and your screams need to be loud enough that I will hear them tomorrow. Understand?"

She nodded, her wild red curls bobbing along with the motion.

"*Perfetto.*"

And he didn't just mean her compliance.

"You might hear the camera on my phone," he said, wanting her to know so that she could refuse. She never did.

"Please fuck me, now."

"Definitely greedy."

"*Very.*"

He dragged his hands over her curves, taking in each soft breath, shiver, and goosebumps that came after his touch. Her responsiveness was his drug. The way she let him love her, use her, *fuck* her, was addicting. She barely moved an inch—only lifted a little—as he dragged her panties down and let them fall to the floor.

"Just feel," he reminded her as he slid the head of his cock through her sex. Her arousal soaked the tip when he flexed forward enough to open her up and let her know that he was a moment away from filling her full. "Don't you fucking move, now."

Cara bit her bottom lip hard. "But—"

"*Cara.*"

She quieted instantly.

Gian left only the head of his cock seated inside the tight heat of Cara's cunt, feeling her sex contracting around him over and over. He reached for his phone. He caught the video of his dick sliding all the way in, the way her thighs widened and her body let him stretch her full. He got the sight of his cock pulling back out, soaked with her cum, and how his shaft throbbed in time with his heartbeat. He lifted the phone enough to catch his thumb sliding over Cara's plump lips and then his hand curving around her throat.

"*Please*," she whispered.

That was all he could take before he tossed the fucking phone to the side, his control gone again. He palmed Cara's ass roughly as he slammed his cock back into her cunt again. There was nothing quite like the contractions of her pussy, flexing around his length, while her fingernails scored hot lines across his chest, and her sweet sounds echoed in his office. He couldn't seem to fuck her fast enough—or hard enough—to satisfy the need beating in his chest. He never could, because as soon as he was done, he knew he would only want more.

Cara's heels dug into his lower back as he pushed her down on the desk, slammed his mouth against hers, and fucked them into a mindless oblivion. Her cunt was so tight that she felt like a hot glove made just for him.

It was only after she had come again, that he pulled his tie from her eyes, and let the pressure building in his spine take over. Her body looked best, spent and sweaty on his desk, his cum spattered up her stomach, and his cock pulsing against her inner thigh.

Then again, she always looked damn good.

It was only hours later, when Gian walked Cara to the waiting car outside of his penthouse, that he finally allowed himself to think of something other than her. He thought about the coming days.

"Message me when you land, Cara."

She kissed his cheek with a smile. "Yes, Gian."

"I'm serious."

"I will."

"I will fly down to Chicago to spank your ass, if you don't."

She grinned. "Don't tempt me now."

Always testing him.

Gian gave Cara a quick kiss and helped her into the waiting car. "It's going to be a busy week, so if I don't pick up your calls, try not to worry. It's just business."

"Got it. I love you."

"*Ti amo*, Cara."

Closing the car door was the last thing Gian wanted to do, but he did it. He watched the vehicle pull out onto the street. It was only when he couldn't see the car anymore, that he turned and headed back for his building.

At the front door, Chris waited. The enforcer said nothing as he followed Gian inside. Once they were in the elevator, Chris turned to him, his expression blank.

"Are you ready for what comes next, boss?"

Gian readjusted his tie. "For duty, always. For the rest … we'll see."

The rest would have to come first.

And then duty would be waiting, too.

• • •

Gian answered the buzzing phone, and continued stirring his stir-fry. "*Ciao, bonjour.*"

"Constantino is on his way up, boss."

"Thank you, Chris."

"Call me if you need me, or when it's done."

Gian agreed, hung up, and went back to cooking his food. Usually, he was too busy to cook, but when he found the time, it was a relaxing process. God knew that he needed to be relaxed today.

Gian lowered the heat on the stove, covered the food, and headed for the elevator entrance of the penthouse when he heard the familiar ding signaling a visitor was headed up. He tossed a dishcloth over his shoulder, using the ends to wipe his hands off as he went to greet Constantino.

His most trusted friend.

Or … that's what Gian had once believed. He now knew that to Constantino—no matter the man's intentions—those words meant nothing. All it had taken was a box, a few careful conversations, and a series of sad realizations, for Gian to understand those words also meant nothing to him as well.

Affection would never cloud his judgement again.

Not after today.

He was not willing to play the blind fool to any man, even if it was to his benefit.

Constantino was half way down the entrance hallway when Gian met up with him. The man wore a big smile, and clapped Gian on the shoulder in greeting as he jokingly looked him over.

It had taken Gian making a phone call to Constantino that included him saying *he* had overreacted, apologizing for hitting his friend, and promising it was all water under the bridge, to get the man at the penthouse. *But* that was all it'd taken, because like Gian in the past, Constantino was predictable where his best friend was concerned, and he didn't want to fight or be on bad terms with Gian.

Gian had only needed to mention Edmond as well, and Constantino was hooked, line and sinker.

It was stupid of him to be, yes.

That was what blind affection did to a man.

"Jeans, shirt, no shoes, *and* a dish towel. Are you playing homemaker today, or what, man?"

Gian laughed, and headed back toward the kitchen while Constantino followed behind. "Taking a break today, that's all."

Constantino sniffed the air. "And cooking, apparently."

"Someone needs to feed me."

"So hire someone."

"It clears my head." Gian gestured at the many chairs around the table. "Take a seat and we'll chat."

Constantino took a seat that faced the kitchen, allowing Gian the chance to watch the man as he finished his stir-fry. He would never turn his back on this man again.

The sad thing was, he hadn't even needed to turn his back the first time. Constantino had simply stabbed Gian in the chest when he wasn't looking. And when Gian did finally notice and asked what happened? Constantino pointed the finger at someone else.

Like any good coward would do.

"Where's the girl?" Constantino asked.

"She has a name. You know it." Gian opened the pan and stirred the contents up. "Cara—use her name."

"Are you still pissed about what I said at the restaurant? I apologized for that, and I only spoke the truth. Like *you* should be doing, man."

He had apologized when Gian called. Although, it had taken some careful prompting on Gian's part to make it seem as though he felt he overreacted that night.

"It's the point of the matter, Constantino."

"Fine. *Cara.* Where is Cara? The other night when you called, you didn't want me coming over because she was here."

Gian checked the clock. "She's probably watching that show she likes. It would be on at this time in Chicago."

Constantino perked. "Chicago?"

"Flew in yesterday."

"She did that herself?"

Gian chose not to answer. He certainly wasn't about to say that *he* had sent Cara away, and raise Constantino's suspicions. He wanted the man thinking that nothing was wrong, like water under the bridge.

Much like the idiot had fooled him.

"That's where she is, anyway," Gian said, pulling the pan from the stove. "I don't know when she'll be back."

That wasn't entirely a lie, either.

Gian didn't know when he would send for Cara. After he had finished business, the smoke had cleared, and it was safe. A week, maybe two. He couldn't let his need to have Cara close cloud his judgement about what was best.

"Better she go," Constantino said.

Gian pulled plates from the cupboard. "Pardon?"

"Cara. It's better she left. She fucks with the way you do things—how you see shit—but you don't seem to notice."

Gian refused to let Constantino push on that nerve. "Maybe she does."

"You know she does."

"Hungry?"

"I could eat," Constantino said.

Gian prepped two plates of food, keeping an eye on the other man at the same time. Constantino seemed entirely unbothered and calm, sitting there, as though he didn't have a thing to worry about.

"I suppose you don't, huh?" Gian asked as he delivered the plate of food.

Gian then took a seat directly across from his old friend.

"Don't what, man?"

"Worry," Gian clarified.

Constantino shrugged, shoving a bite of food into his mouth. "It's a waste of time to worry."

"That, or you feel … privileged. Safe in your spot because of me."

Constantino's brow furrowed. "Is something wrong?"

Gian shook his head. "Should there be?"

"Not that I know of."

"Then, no."

"All right." Constantino went back to his food as though nothing was wrong. Just as Gian expected he would.

"Have you ever heard of blind affection?"

"When a person lets their personal feelings get in the way of what should be obvious?" Constantino asked.

"Exactly that."

"I could see why some people might struggle with it."

"Me, too," Gian agreed.

"So, you said when you called that you're finally ready to finish this out with the boss, then?"

"And more." Gian smirked. "Never call Edmond the boss in my presence again."

Constantino offered an apologetic smile. "My bad."

The man didn't seem to notice that Gian had yet to touch his own plate of food.

"But, that was what you said," Constantino pressed.

"And more," Gian echoed. "Do you want a beer?"

"Sure."

Gian left the table, and grabbed two beers from the fridge. He sat one down at his spot before moving around the table to hand Constantino's bottle over, but he didn't move to return to his seat again.

"I'm not the only one between us that suffers from blind affection," Gian said quietly. "Because if you didn't suffer from it, too, you would have known better than to ever trust me after you betrayed me. All lies come out eventually."

Constantino's head snapped up, his wide—understanding—eyes flying to Gian. It was already too late. Gian hadn't removed the dishtowel from his shoulder until then, and he'd quickly twisted it into a rope of sorts. He had the rope wrapped around his friend's throat before Constantino could even attempt to fight back.

Gian pulled the makeshift rope tight, his emotions bleeding away as a blissful numbness took its place. Constantino fought back against the hold, clawing at Gian's arms and hands, trying to topple over his chair, and even kicking at the table. The plates and bottles jumped with every hit and kick. Gian still held strong.

"I'm not sure if you killed my grandfather for yourself, or because you knew what would happen after his death. I don't know if you meant to put yourself in a higher position because of me, but you clearly intended to use me for something."

Constantino's struggle continued, but Gian paid it no mind. His fighting would end forever soon enough.

"I put it together after Edmond sent me a box with info about the bomb set on my car and who put it there—you. You were stupid enough to try to play *his* side, too, just in case you needed to. I saw the pictures of you heading to Edmond's place, going in and out on all days of the week, when you were trying to get *me* to act against him. That was your mistake. He's a snake, too, like you. And if he thought *I* might get rid of a problem with you, then he was willing to take the risk of telling me."

Gian sighed. "And I thought, *why*. Why would you do that to me, and what else would you do? What else had you done? You knew—despite how fucking ignorant you've been lately—that I would never look to you, Constantino, because you were my friend. And I trusted you. You took advantage of an already-volatile situation, and pushed us all over the edge, because you knew that no matter what, *I* would keep my friend on top."

He pulled the rope tighter still, feeling the man's fight finally begin to leave. "You taught me a lesson that Corrado never did. A lesson he *couldn't* teach me. You have to be ready to kill absolutely anyone that stands at your side, because no one can be trusted."

Gian still didn't feel anything when Constantino's body finally fell limp. He undid the rope, let the corpse fall forward, and then he covered the man's head with the unraveled dish towel.

"Fuck you for being the one to teach me that lesson."

He returned to his seat, popped open his beer, and ate his food.

175

Life went on.

It always did.

• • •

"Last chance to back out," Chris said as Gian handed his gun over.

Outside the restaurant, the street was quiet. As though it—and the shops lining the streets—knew what was about to happen, and that it was better to be out of sight, safely hidden away.

"Why would I back out?" Gian asked.

The enforcer made a show of taking Gian's jacket off, showing to whoever was watching inside the restaurant that he had no hidden weapons to bring to the meeting.

Chris handed Gian's jacket back. "I didn't think you would, I simply said the option is there."

"Would you?"

"No."

"Why?"

"Legacy," Chris said frankly. "The respect of it all."

"Some might think that this is the ultimate *dis*respect," Gian pointed out.

"Those people will never and could never make the choice you are making today."

And that, at the end of it all, was exactly why Gian was doing what he was doing.

"Some men are made for this," Chris added, "and some aren't. Which one are you?"

"I'm tired of my ability being questioned."

"Then good luck, boss. I will be waiting out here when it's over."

Gian gave the man a nod. "Don't miss, Chris."

"I never do."

Gian waited as the enforcer crossed the street, and jumped into his vehicle. Then, he turned and entered the restaurant. This was the most dangerous part, he knew. Simply entering the place with no backup, no protection. It was a hostile environment, and he could easily become a target.

Inside, Gian was surprised to find the place mostly devoid of people. No patrons sat at tables, and no employees served the few men sitting at tables.

"Gian." Edmond stood from his seat at a center table, facing the windows. *Lucky.* "I'm pleased to see you show up today."

Gian crossed the space, ignoring the looks of the men waiting to see what he would do. Only a couple were men that Edmond had asked to come along, others were ones Gian told to be there because of the boss's request. Apparently, Edmond thought having a few men witness their meeting would be better than a larger group.

Let word travel, Edmond had said.

Standing toe to toe with the man, Gian finally spoke. "I took care of the problem on my end, the one you let me know about."

Edmond nodded, seeming pleased. "And come to your senses at the same time about the rest of this fighting and nonsense, I assume?"

No, not really.

He *had* decided enough was enough, though.

"Grudges tend to kill a lot of people in this business," Gian said with a shrug of his shoulders. "I need to learn to let bygones be bygones."

"Good, good."

Then, Edmond held out his hand, the one with a ring that was all too familiar to Gian. It had belonged to his grandfather for years, and while Corrado should have been buried with it, someone had removed it from his home before it could be collected for the funeral home. Constantino might have been the one to pull the trigger where Corrado's death was concerned, but Edmond had not been an honorable man in his intentions after the fact.

Gian could never, and would never, forget that.

He would not forget a shooting intended to *keep him in line* that nearly killed Cara, either.

Things like those were unforgiveable.

The *bygones.*

"Well?" Edmond asked, still holding his hand out for Gian to take. "Are we going to settle this like proper made men and move on as your grandfather would have wanted us to do, Gian?"

The man intended for Gian to bend down, and kiss his ring. Had it been his grandfather, Gian would have done it without question. Because it was Edmond, the significance made him hesitate.

Still, he bent down, grabbing Edmond's hand and bringing it close to his mouth. Gian didn't kiss the ring, though, he simply held it there for a moment.

"You have no idea what Corrado would have wanted," Gian murmured low enough for only Edmond to hear. "But I certainly do."

Gian dropped Edmond's hand, without having kissed the ring, as glass shattered. He straightened to his full height, getting the brief chance to stare Edmond in the eyes for only a second before the man's body began to sway.

A perfect sniper shot had hit Edmond square between his eyes. Blood trickled down from the wound. Death already stared back from his eyes.

This was appropriate, considering ...

Gian let the body fall as one of the men inside the restaurant shouted, a panicked realization starting to take over about what had just happened. He paid the men no mind as he bent down and removed his grandfather's ring from Edmond's slack, lifeless hand, only to slide it down his own finger.

Standing once more, Gian turned to face the men with a smile. Shocked faces stared back at him, unmoving and frozen in time.

Chris was one hell of a shot.

Word would *certainly* be traveling now.

"I'll answer to Don or Boss, only, and anything else will cost you a body part of your choice," Gian said quietly. "Now, I need someone to move this body."

NINETEEN

Cara missed her bed—or better yet, Gian's—the moment she opened her eyes and looked around. The unfamiliar bedroom staring back at her wasn't necessarily off-putting. The big bed, earthy tones, and soft bedding were comforting enough, as far as that went. But it wasn't home.

Her body knew it instantly.

She'd already been back in Chicago for a week, and no matter how many times she woke up in the guest bedroom of the Trentini mansion, it was still startling. It only reinforced her desire to go back to Toronto; the need to be home in familiar spaces thrummed deep.

It was only Gian's demand that she stay away until he called her back—when it would be safe again—that kept her from booking a ticket.

Well, that, and her brother.

Tommas was not letting her go, either. Each time Cara brought up her desire to return home sooner than she was allowed to, her brother was quick to shut that idea down. Things were happening, he would say. She was better, and safer, right where she was for now.

Cara knew better than to argue with difficult, stubborn men. Or rather, she knew which battles to pick.

This was not one.

Cara rolled over in the king-sized bed, ignoring how empty it felt to sleep in such a large space with no one else to help fill it up or keep her company. She had been alone for so long, happy to find occasional fun with a man, but perfectly fine to send him packing before morning even arrived. She couldn't quite say the same, now.

It was only a *week*. The loneliness growing in her heart should not have been taking up so much fucking space, like a weed getting out of control.

Love made things difficult.

Complicated, even.

Cara thought it was kind of lovely, too.

She missed Gian.

Terribly.

Cara found her charging phone on the nightstand, and brought it closer, squinting through tired eyes to see if she had missed any calls or messages throughout the night. There was nothing, and that only hurt a little more. She *had* talked to Gian a few times over the week, but it was never long enough. Their conversations never had enough substance. She couldn't see his face to tell if he was simply hiding something to make her less worried, or if there really was nothing she should be concerned about.

She knew the truth.

Gian wouldn't have sent her away if he didn't absolutely have to. Of course, something was wrong. Of course, he kept their conversations short and the depth of them at a shallow level, in order to ward off Cara's anxiety.

She didn't quite know how to tell him that it really wasn't working. She was still lonely and worried. She still wanted to go home, regardless of what was waiting there—good or bad.

Still, she stayed put.

Cara rubbed a hand over her face, wavering on whether or not to call Gian's phone. It was early to be calling—seven her time, which meant it was eight in Toronto. Gian ran on his own time, though, which happened to be like a well-oiled machine. Up before six, breakfast and a workout, and then out the door before nine, if he could help it. He ran on the same schedule like it was his default. It didn't matter if Cara was with him or not, his internal alarms rarely changed.

She scrolled through her contacts, found Gian's, and hit the green phone button beside his name. The call rang and rang, four times, then five and six. On the seventh, his answering recording picked up, and she ended the call before it even beeped.

Something wasn't right.

He *should* have picked up.

Cara tried to push the worries aside, knowing it could be a million other things, too. Like a late night which had him sleeping in, though that had never been a thing before. Or an early meeting with whomever, which caused him to silence his phone. The second option was more likely, so that was what Cara chose to accept.

For now.

Even knowing that Gian would see the missed call and realize Cara had called him, it wasn't quite enough for her. Maybe the man *did* have her a little fucked up in the head and heart. A bit too crazy about him, and them, even after she had told herself not to go that far with someone like Gian Guzzi. He was everything she wasn't supposed to like—not his business, his arrogant, overly confident attitude, or his life. None of it was supposed to attract Cara like the dumb moth to the pretty flame, and yet, he had.

He was the first damn thing on her mind in the morning.

The last thing to cross it at night.

She kind of wanted him to know that.

He does like his pictures ...

Cara grinned at her inner voice, got the camera set up on the phone, and held it out far enough to get a shot of her in the sheets, with the morning light coming in through the window behind her. The stark, white light contrasted against her body, but not quite enough to hide the fact that she had been sleeping in very little, just black boy shorts. Her hair was a curly mess, framing her face wildly, with no makeup to be seen.

It actually wasn't too bad.

It was usually Gian taking the pictures, teasing her while he did so, but constantly going back through the images whenever he got the chance. She had gotten more than one text from him with an image or short video clip of her that were nothing short of *porn*. She knew when he was doing it during their encounters, as he always told her, and she never minded enough to tell him not to.

A shot of her on her knees, with his cock in her mouth. A three second video clip of his cock filling her pussy full. Each one—new or old— was like a snapshot of memories for Cara that suddenly came back in a rushing wave. She was positive that was exactly Gian's point in randomly sending the pictures or videos for her to see.

It turned her on like nothing else. It was filthy, like his mouth and everything else about him. He managed to make her body hot in a crowded room, and he could be across the fucking *city* while he was doing it.

No one knew a thing.

She did.

That was enough.

Cara sent off the image in a text before she could think better of it. And then, not wanting to sit and stare at her phone until she finally got a response, she forced herself out of bed and toward the attached bathroom.

Gian would answer.

Eventually.

• • •

Cara's phone finally buzzed with an incoming text as she neared the dining room of the Trentini mansion. She nearly checked what the text said—likely a message from Gian, as no one else bothered to text her anymore—but stopped at the hushed, yet sharp, voices coming from within the dining room. Her brother, and his fiancée.

"Have you even *asked* her?" Abriella demanded.

A loud sigh followed right after. "No."

"Why the hell—"

"Because *why*, Ella," Tommas replied harshly, not even posing it as a question. "Why is it any of my goddamn business what she does, or with whom, for that matter? Why does that matter; why should it matter? It doesn't. It never should have mattered to anybody but you and me, when it was us and our business, and it doesn't matter with her and ... whoever the fuck she chooses to run around with. She's twenty-five, a grown ass woman. Look me in the face right now and tell me to put constraints on her, *only* because it might look bad on the rest of us. Is that what you want me to do, to be, like the rest of them?"

Cara knew right then and there that they were talking about her, and likely Gian, but she didn't have the first clue as to why. She decided to stay where she was, and see what else she could learn before she made her presence known to the couple.

"I-I ..." Abriella made a frustrated sound under her breath before spitting out, "You know that's not what I mean! You're always throwing that at me like that's my default, Tommas. And you know it's not."

"It's sounding that way, Ella."

"It's *not*," Abriella stressed, "but does she know, Tommy? Does she understand what it means to be in the position she is? That's all I wondered. And stupid me, I thought you would have—at the very least— asked her about it."

"It's been a long fucking time since I've seen my sister, and the last time was when I put her on a plane after she barely made it through a wedding she was supposed to be in with Lea. She was a mess, Ella. A complete *mess*. She's okay right now. I don't know if that's because of him, or something else, but she is perfectly fine. I'm not going to upset that by poking around in her personal business."

"But what if she doesn't know, Tommas?"

"Know what?"

"About *him*," Abriella said, exasperated. "I've said some stuff since she's been here, just to see, you know, and it goes right over her head. It's like she doesn't know anything about him, in that regard."

"She can't *not* know."

"Really, Tommy? Because it's entirely possible, given what we know about her. She doesn't take an active role in your aunt and uncle's business, she stays out of sight of the family for good reason, and she's never had any sort of interest in being in that spotlight. She has no real reason to know. I think she might not, and *that's* why you should ask, even if it's to ... be sure."

"Abriella."

"It's not for me or you, it's for her. Don't you get that? She could be jumping head first into a deep pile of shit and not even know that's what it is, Tommas. That's not fair to her. You ask, or I will."

Tommas grumbled something under his breath that sounded a hell of a lot like, "You're awfully pushy this morning. Aren't you supposed to be picking out colors and fabrics for the wedding? Why are you bitching at me before ten? We should have an agreement about this sort of thing, Ella."

"Stop trying to be cute."

"I'm not."

"You are."

Figuring she had gotten all of their conversation that she would, Cara decided to make her presence known. She walked into the kitchen as another message buzzed on her phone. Both her brother and his fiancée, looked up at her arrival.

"Cara," Tommas said.

"Morning," Abriella said at the same time.

Cara's attention was down on her phone.

Gian had zero chill, but she knew this already.

Send another, his message demanded, *but next time, lose the panties, open your legs, and get your fingers wet for me.*

Cara swore her face was burning as she attempted to stuff the phone into her pocket, foolishly thinking that would save her any embarrassment. She was going to pretend like she didn't know her fucking cheeks matched the color of her hair.

"Something going on?" Abriella asked, a sly grin covering her pretty features.

Cara waved it off. "Nothing, so hey ..." Distraction was her best friend, she decided. "Were you two talking about me just now?"

Tommas passed Abriella a look that she ignored, instead turning to grab a cup from the sink and choosing to not answer Cara's question.

Cara looked to her brother. "You were, right?"

"How would you feel about taking a drive today?" Tommas asked.

What was it with men, thinking they could change the subject of any conversation if they didn't want to talk about what was brought up?

"I was thinking we could head over to the cemetery," Tommas said when Cara didn't immediately reply.

Cara stiffened. "To see Mom and Dad, or ...?"

"Lea, actually."

"Lea," Cara echoed.

"Do you not want to?"

Cara felt the old stab of pain in her chest at the thought of visiting her twin's grave, but she couldn't bear to say no. It had been too long, and in some ways, Cara had managed to put her grief aside while Gian had swept into her life like a hurricane.

Maybe she owed it to her sister.

Maybe she owed it to herself.

"Yeah, all right," Cara finally agreed.

She almost forgot about her brother changing the subject, but decided right then, it wasn't all that important, anyway.

• • •

Cara bent down to clean the shiny marble of the gravestone, stopping for a second to admire her sister's name in heavy font, chiseled into the very center of the stone below angel wings. She traced every letter with her thumb, surprised to find that the ache in her chest didn't get worse the longer she stood there.

Lea's funeral and burial had been so difficult for Cara. She barely remembered the day, but that was mostly because she had been drugged up on a mixture of antidepressants, sleeping pills, and anxiety meds. She wouldn't have gotten through it otherwise.

"It stopped for a bit—the world, I mean," Cara said to the headstone, "but it started turning again after a while. I wasn't ready for it to."

Cara went back to wiping off the stone, though she really didn't need to. Someone had been caring for the grave beyond the groundskeeper's job of mowing the grass or clearing the snow, depending on the time of year. The stone was clean of debris or dust, and fresh flowers rested along the bottom and on the top of the headstone.

She set the bouquet of tiger lilies—Lea's favorite flower—along the bottom with the rest. "You could have told me about what you were doing, Lea. I mean, I get why you didn't tell me about Frankie, but you *could* have."

"Who is Frankie?"

Cara stood from the grave, brushing off the bottom of her jeans as she faced Tommas. Her brother had been standing back on the path, far enough away that she didn't think he would overhear her conversation with her dead twin, but apparently, he had moved closer.

"You shouldn't spy," she told Tommas.

He shrugged. "Believe it or not, but spying has saved my ass more times than I care to count."

"Not this time."

"So you won't tell me who Frankie is?"

Cara pursed her lips, deciding there was no harm in giving the bare bones of the details. "Someone Lea was involved with. I didn't know about it until a while ago."

"Ah."

She turned back to the grave, pulling a string of rosary beads from her jacket pocket. They had belonged to Lea, before her death, but her sister had left the rosary behind in Toronto on that fateful trip to Chicago.

Cara wanted to return them, as it was only one thing, but it was something she could let go of. She had been able to make a quick trip to her apartment before leaving Toronto to pack a bag, and had grabbed the rosary last minute. She hung the string of beads around the stone, letting the ivory cross hang over her sister's name.

"The grave is well kept," Cara said, wanting to fill the silence.

"I come a couple of times a month to say hello, and replace the flowers."

"Do you think she hears you?"

"Do *you*?" Tommas asked right back.

Cara blinked away the tears threatening to fall. "We're the same, her and me. Even our DNA is identical, Tommas. It's like that time when we were five, and I fell off the swings at the park while she was home. I broke my wrist, and she screamed and held hers the whole way from the house to the park to find me; everyone thought she was crazy. Of course, she hears me. She's always been inside of me, listening. I was the one who wasn't talking for the longest time."

"I think there's a difference between her and you, now."

"Oh?"

"She's not alive, anymore, Cara. You are. What was cannot now *be*."

She still felt like she was living for two some days.

Sometimes, it helped.

Other times, she thought she was failing somehow.

"I still wish they had cremated her," Cara admitted. "Then I could have taken a piece of her with me."

Tommas frowned. "I think you've taken quite a lot of her with you, if you think about it."

Maybe.

Cara didn't know.

"Are you going to tell me what that whole discussion was between you and Abriella this morning?" Cara asked, keeping her back turned to her brother. "I listened to the whole thing, by the way."

Tommas snorted. "I figured you did."

"That's not an answer."

"I have another question instead, Cara."

She pivoted to face him. "Shoot."

"Are you happy?"

Cara didn't even have to think about it, not for long. "I wasn't. I was living in a black hole all the time, and I couldn't escape from it. I felt like I was drowning nonstop."

"And then you weren't," Tommas supplied.

"I guess not."

"Would that happen to be because of *someone*?"

"Do you mean Gian Guzzi?"

Tommas smiled a little. "Yeah, that's who I mean."

"I think he helped," Cara admitted, "but I think he made it possible for me to drag myself out of that black hole, too. And maybe that's the more important part."

Her brother nodded. "Then that's all that matters. It's all I need to know. The rest is details, and I've never cared for those."

Neither had Cara.

• • •

"Come sit, go through these albums with me," Abriella said from the couch, as Cara walked into the living room. "I'm sick and tired of doing wedding things, and I need a break."

From her position, Cara could see some of the albums *were* weddings.

"That kind of defeats the purpose, doesn't it?"

Abriella shrugged. "It's not mine, so not exactly."

Who was Cara to argue with the bride-to-be? She joined Abriella on the couch, curious about where Tommas was. After he had brought her back from the cemetery, he had disappeared upstairs. He hadn't come back down since.

"Maybe not this one," Abriella muttered, tossing an unopened photo album aside.

"What was that one?"

"Damian and Lily's wedding."

Oh.

The wedding that Lea was supposed to be in with Cara, but had died before she could attend. Cara did not need physical proof of how messed up she had probably looked that day, not the reminders of how it had made her feel to plaster on a smile and get shit done when she had been two seconds away from taking her own life. She opted not to open the album.

"Will you come for the wedding?" Abriella asked. "I know Tommy really wants you there."

Cara smiled. "I'll try. No promises. I have a co-op set up with a woman's shelter to do work in the summer, too, and I won't be able to take time off when it's required hours."

"Is it really that bad to be here?"

"Not as bad as I thought it would be. But it's not always easy, either."

Abriella frowned and looked away. "I get that. I guess if it was Alessa, I wouldn't want all the reminders, either."

"It's not the reminders," Cara said quietly. "It's what *isn't* here. Lea isn't here, not like she is at home. And as much as it sometimes suffocates me, I would rather her be everywhere than nowhere."

"Huh."

Cara cleared her throat, willing away the sudden emotions lodging there. "It's hard to explain."

"No, I think you did pretty well there, actually."

Cara knew all too well that Abriella Trentini was not unaccustomed to loss. In a few short months, she had lost her grandfather, both of her parents, and her brother. All that she had left now for her close family was her surviving sister. And Tommas, she had him, too.

The pain may not have been the same, but it was familiar enough. It surely stung and ached and ate away at Abriella in her quiet moments, much like it did for Cara in hers.

She didn't doubt that.

"All right, enough of this," Abriella said, blinking away the wetness gathering in her eyes. "No tears, or Tommas has a fit. Let's look at some pictures, huh?"

"Sounds good."

Although, Cara would much rather get Gian on the phone and figure out when exactly she could go back home.

She settled on the pictures, instead.

Cara found that the albums actually weren't too bad. Most were older family photos of the Trentinis, their vacations, and the kids as they'd grown up. There were other albums of weddings from other families, Christening of babies, and more. There were even some memories that Cara had forgotten, things that had brought all the Outfit families together.

It surprised her to see herself and Lea in a few of the albums, sitting off to the side in a corner, people watching as they sometimes had done together as young teens.

"Canada Vacation and Wedding," Abriella read from the front of the next album.

Cara wasn't really paying attention at that point, as she was focused on the album in her hand, and the few photos of her and Lea that were hidden inside.

She only looked away from the photos when Abriella said, "Guzzi Wedding—Gian and Elena."

"What?"

Abriella was already flipping pages, moving past decorated halls, silk-lined tables, and an ornate cake. Cara saw a familiar man in a suit standing with his father, and his younger brother. One of his mother, too, putting his boutonniere on.

No.

Cara couldn't trust what her own eyes were seeing.

She didn't believe it.

Abriella flipped the page again.

The woman was beautiful, and her white dress, modest at the top, yet covered in satin, tulle, and jewels, made her look like a proper princess.

A *Mafioso principessa*, actually.

Cara did a double take, not recognizing the woman with her perfectly done makeup and her upswept blonde hair. The ice in her brown gaze as she stared at the camera with a learned smile said she wasn't exactly happy, but her posture spoke of elegance and grace, regardless of her emotions.

Gian and Elena, Abriella had said.

Was that the woman's name?

Elena?

"When was that?" Cara asked.

Abriella turned the page, showcasing new photos, with Gian standing next to the very obvious *bride*. Both wore rings, as that too had been photographed, their hands laying one on top of the other.

"Abriella, when was that wedding?" Cara demanded, ripping the album from her.

"Whoa, relax."

Cara flipped through more photos, progressively getting more irritated as she went. "*When?*"

"Three years ago. I flew in with my grandfather. Joel came, too. The invitation was basically for everyone, but only a couple of us went. Pretty common for *famiglia* weddings."

Cara couldn't breathe.

"He was married."

It didn't even come out as a question.

Abriella cleared her throat loudly. "Is, Cara."

What?

Her inner question must have been as clear as day on her face, because Abriella shrugged and added, "Men in a position like Gian Guzzi—an heir to a Cosa Nostra family, a good Italian and Catholic, a *Mafioso*, do not get divorced. There is *no* acceptable divorce. He *is* married, Cara."

It was that moment when her brother finally decided to make his presence known again, walking into the living room as though he didn't know Cara's whole world had been tipped upside down. This was what Tommas and Abriella had been discussing, she realized. *This* was what they knew, and that she hadn't.

Cara felt dumb.

So fucking stupid.

Flashes of memories filled her mind, statements by people that she had let fly over her head, or reactions people had made when Gian took her out publically.

He had a wife.

That meant Cara …

She was his mistress.

A *goomah*.

Whore.

"What's wrong?" Tommas asked, his gaze shooting from Cara to Abriella. "What happened?"

Abriella didn't look all too concerned. "We were going through some albums and—"

Tommas was at Cara's side before she had blinked, grabbing the album from her, only to see the last photo she had been looking at. One of Gian, and this *Elena* woman, kissing on an altar. Likely their first kiss, Cara didn't know.

She didn't care.

"Why would you do that?" Tommas asked Abriella.

"He's married," Cara said faintly.

Abriella stood from the couch, stoic and stone cold. "She deserved to know. I let her figure it out."

"*Abriella.*"

She was already walking away.

Cara wished she could be angry.

She was, but not at Abriella.

Not even at her brother.

"Tommas, he's *married*," Cara said.

How had she not known?

Tommas looked down at her, wariness filling his eyes. "I don't know much about it, just that he is, and that's all."

"I'm going home."

"I don't—"

"I'm going *home*."

It wasn't for her brother to decide.

Not on this.

TWENTY

"Do we know who showed up?" Gian asked.

Dom looked to Stephan for an answer.

"All of them," Stephan said, the cigarette on his lips bouncing with every word.

While Gian despised Stephan for a great many reasons—including the man's attitude and ways—he had to admit that the Capo was honest and honorable when it came down to business. After carefully going through every man Gian could find, he was surprised to find out Stephan had no hand in Constantino's plots.

Given how fucking hard it was to find trustworthy people lately, Gian chose to allow Stephan into his very small circle. At least, for the time being. He didn't have to particularly like the guy, he only had to trust him.

Gian found his brother watching him, doing that damn thing that Dom always did whenever he was uneasy about a situation, and needed a steady, yet invisible support to walk him through. He didn't blame Dom for being that way at twenty-five. Shit, years ago, *Gian* had been the stupid kid, wading into the mafia with unrealistic expectations, needing guidance just the same.

He had looked to his grandfather. Who else fit the bill with his last name? Domenic only had Gian to look to, now.

"*Ça va?*" Gian asked Dom in French.

Dom shrugged one shoulder. "*Je vais bien*, Gian."

He didn't look fine.

Apparently, his attempt at using French to probe his brother's inner emotions without embarrassing him was not lost on Stephan.

"He's got to learn this shit and how to deal with it somehow," Stephan muttered, walking forward and leaving the brothers behind. "Treat him like a fragile *figa* that needs special handling, and he'll never be more than a walking, talking pussy, boss."

Dom glared at the Capo's back. "I don't like him."

Gian blew out a breath. Now or never, he supposed. Dom wanted to be *in*, he wanted his button, he wanted the title of a made man. He needed to understand what all of that meant, too.

Gian slapped his brother on the back and said, "You don't have to like him; you do have to respect him. Especially now."

"Yeah, *cazzo*."

Fuck was right.

"Let's get this over with," Gian said.

Like any good made man would do, Stephan waited for Gian to catch up with him at the entrance of the old pizzeria. Gian was careful to hold the heavy duty garbage bags out at his side, lest any residual fluids leak onto his leather shoes. Stephan held the door open, allowing Gian to go in first, but making Dom hold the door for himself before he, too, could enter.

Dom was lower on the totem pole, and so the actions of those around him would reflect his status until he earned a better title or position. Even if it was something as simple as not holding the door open for him.

It was all about the respect in Cosa Nostra.

A man had to show it long before he was ever given it.

"Look who finally showed his goddamn face," came a call from within the pizzeria as Gian strolled inside.

Gian ignored the older Capo's half-taunting tone, but only because for the moment, the man didn't know the position he was in, compared to his younger counterpart. The older generation of made men in the Guzzi family would always have some left-over feelings after this was all said and done, Gian was sure of it, but he hadn't been given much of a choice.

At the end of the day, it was *Guzzi* for a reason.

He was not willing—no matter his age, his lesser years compared to other men, or anything else he might lack—to allow his family's name to dim in the Cosa Nostra world. His grandfather would never have handed off the boss's seat, nor his status and respect, to anyone who didn't share his last name.

Gian wouldn't do it, either.

He passed a look around the old pizzeria, taking in the many faces of men he recognized, some he'd grown up alongside, others whose feet he had chased under for years. He understood far too well that his actions would have consequences, but he sincerely hoped these men didn't make it harder on him than it needed to be.

He would hate to have to kill people he considered family and friends.

He would do it, of course.

He simply wouldn't like it.

"Where's Edmond?"

"Yeah, where's the boss?" another Capo asked.

A few men shifted in their seats, ignoring the gazes of the Capos who had asked after the boss. Or rather, who they *thought* was still the boss.

Gian had figured that word would have traveled by now throughout the ranks of the family, considering how many men had witnessed him murder and take the boss's seat from Edmond. It certainly would have made part of this whole shit show easier.

No matter.

It seemed only a couple were out of the loop.

They would know soon enough.

Stephan and Dom stayed standing directly behind Gian, ready and willing to keep any man from leaving, if the need arose. Neither of them spoke as Gian tossed the extra large, heavy duty garbage bag to the checkered tiled floor a few feet in front of him.

All eyes went to the bag.

Gian didn't make a move to acknowledge it, or even to open it.

"Seems we have a lot of problems in this family lately," he said, still looking from man to man and never skipping a single one. "Seems we can't get along like proper made men."

They needed to know—all of them—that what had happened over the last several months, and the blood that had spilled throughout their streets, were all caused by their own hands. It didn't matter if they had been the ones to pull the triggers. Their culture of avoid, evade, and ignore was enough to make them guilty in Gian's eyes. Beyond that, the lines that had been drawn between the older generation and the younger made men, had not simply popped up all on its own. It was a divide that had come from unhappiness on one side, and entitlement on the other.

"*You* did this," Gian said, loud enough for each and every man to hear.

He was not going to repeat himself after today.

A boss didn't have to.

Not if he spoke properly the first time.

"Whether you looked away when things happened, or you personally held one of the weapons that took away members of this *famiglia*, you all did this," Gian said with a shake of his head. "And you never considered who would be left cleaning up the mess."

Gian pulled a pocketknife from his slacks, and bent down to slice a hole through the top of the garbage bag at his feet. Carefully, he grabbed the corner of the bag with the tips of his fingers, and used the toe of his shoe to kick it over.

The contents didn't even empty completely from the black bag before the men in the pizzeria reacted to what they were seeing.

Chairs scraped.

Shouts echoed.

He was sure he heard someone gag, too.

It wasn't a pleasant sight—bits and pieces of bodies spilling out of a garbage bag. A hand, a few fingers, a leg from the knee down, a bit of teeth, some congealed blood and gelatinous fluid, along with two battered heads.

As loud as the men's reactions had been, their silence came on as strongly, and just as quickly, as they took in the faces of the severed heads resting on the restaurant floor.

Edmond Portella, their former boss.

Constantino Rossi, a fellow Capo.

"One from each side," Gian said, drawing in the attention of the room again. He ran his fingers through his hair, knowing good and damn well, each man would be focused in on his actions, and therefore, would not miss his grandfather's ring in its rightful place. *On his fucking hand.*

Gian waved at the random pieces of corpses at his feet. "One from each side, you see? A traitor—my friend," he murmured, referring to Constantino. Then, he gestured to Edmond's head, its mouth opened grotesquely, the nose shattered. "And another traitor—my mentor. They both thought that they could manipulate me to get them, or their agenda, where they wanted it to go. This is our family because of that."

He smirked a little, adding, "None of you considered who would be the man to clean up the mess at the end of the day. Make sure each and every one of you takes a piece of this *mess* with you when you go, and dispose of it properly. You each had a hand in creating it, after all, so take equal part in cleaning it, too."

It took a second.

Then, two.

That beat of silence didn't worry Gian. He expected shock. He was *going* for shock. His men answered exactly as he expected them to.

"*Sì*, boss."

And …

"Yes, Don."

• • •

"Are you going to do it, give your brother what he wants?"

Gian stared out the window of the town car, trying to decide how to properly answer his father's question. There was no right or wrong way to answer. There was only the truth to give, and his father would not be pleased with it.

"Well?" Frederic asked pointedly.

"It's what he wants."

"He's twenty-five! He doesn't *know* what he wants, Gian!"

His father's sudden burst of anger wasn't shocking to Gian, he'd expected it. Maybe, in a way, he even felt like he deserved it, too.

"I knew what I wanted at twenty-five, and even younger than that. I always wanted to be a made man, Dad."

"Did you *really*?"

"Of course."

"He promised me," his father said quieter. "Your grandfather promised me, Gian."

Gian finally turned away from the passing streets to look at his father. "What?"

"He had two sons. He chose the older brother, not me, to bring into this life. I didn't mind—I didn't *want* it, anyway. And then my brother died, but I was already older, married, and had my own children."

He didn't like where this was going.

"You think you chose this?" Frederic demanded harshly, leaning forward in his seat, closer to Gian. A fire burned in his eyes as he stared down his oldest son. "Is that truly what you believe? You have to remember all those holidays and vacations that you would go on with your grandfather, while Dom was left behind. You have to remember all the extra gifts you were given, and the attention Corrado gave to only *you*."

Gian held his tongue, but barely.

"I don't blame you for holding him on a pedestal, Gian, because I wasn't allowed to let you see anything different than what he wanted you to see. And you loved him so much. *Mio Dio,* look how much you loved him! Right to his death, into his grave, my boy. But don't be foolish. Don't be a stupid man, still seeing things through a child's gaze. You're too old, and far too intelligent, for that now."

"I see things exactly as they are," Gian replied quietly.

"You were the bargaining chip," his father said, that bitterness never wavering. "You were the one I gave up, to spare the others. Your brother, your sister. He wouldn't bother with them in this life, when he didn't need to. He had you, like he had my brother all those years ago, and that was enough to carry on the name, Gian. He promised me—do *not* make your brother a made man."

Gian wanted to deny the things his father said, but in all honestly, he couldn't. His life had been privileged, both by the wealth of his family, and the status of his grandfather. It was *only* because of the affection his grandfather had given to him, that respect in his life came far easier than it did for the others. Corrado's attentions had always focused more on Gian. Sure, he had brushed it off as a younger man, but he was not dumb enough to pretend that his grandfather's actions had no intent behind them.

Actions always had intent.

It still didn't change a thing.

"It's Dom's choice," Gian told his father.

It would hurt him, Gian knew.

His father would be mad for a while.

It changed nothing.

"To refuse now, after everything," Gian murmured, "would mean to kill him."

It was the way of Cosa Nostra. Once a man had made his intentions clear with *la famiglia* to join their ranks and ways, there was no going back. There was no restart button, only a bullet and a grave, for those who could not follow through.

Frederic's frown grew deeper. "And what if it kills him anyway?"

Gian had a better question. "Did you consider that for me, Dad, all those years ago, when you were made to make a choice between Dom and I?"

His father didn't answer.

The silence was enough.

Gian had been the bargaining chip.

Frederic had made the sacrifice.

"And what about you, now?" his father asked gently.

Gian's brow furrowed. "What about me? I'm the boss. I did what I needed to do. I'm *fine*."

"You forget what that position means, son. Your image is now on display, and your weaknesses will become your biggest targets. This may have seemed easy standing on the outside looking in, but it becomes far harder to manage once you sit in the seat, and the only things keeping you worthy to be there for those men are your reputation, your image, and your actions. So far, you've not been doing well in that regard."

Gian's jaw ached from clenching so fiercely. "Say what you mean. Don't dance around it with pretty words."

"You know what I mean. Or rather, *who* I mean."

Cara.

• • •

Gian nodded to the doorman as the older gentleman opened the door to the building. "*Merci*, Benjamin."

"Have a good evening, Mr. Guzzi," the doorman replied as Gian walked through.

He had just entered the private elevator that would take him up to his penthouse when the cell phone in his pocket began to buzz with an incoming call. Gian almost considered not answering it, and letting it go to voicemail. After the day he had, a hot shower, food, his bed, and a phone call to get Cara back home in Toronto—at his side—sounded *perfetto*.

She wanted to come back, and he wanted nothing more than to bring her back.

Unfortunately, being a boss meant when phone calls came in, issues usually followed.

That phone call to Cara would have to wait.

Gian picked up the call on the fourth ring, his usual Italian and French greeting at the ready. "*Ciao, bonjour.*"

"I have Cara booked for a flight in the morning—she'll be in Toronto by noon."

Tommas Rossi didn't fuck around with pleasantries, it seemed.

"I didn't call to ask her back, yet," Gian said, "but I was ready to do that tonight."

"You don't want to do that, Gian. Call her, I mean. Not right now."

Gian's shoulders tensed as the elevator dinged, and the doors opened to allow him entrance into the penthouse. White walls and gray marble stared back at him, but he wasn't quite ready to leave the elevator.

"She texted me this morning. She can't be that pissed off at me that I haven't called her today, can she?"

Cara was not that kind of woman. She wasn't spectacularly jealous, and she didn't demand every breathing, waking moment of Gian's days. Though if she were one of those women, and she did want those things, he would give them to her.

All of them.

Love was so messed up in that way.

He'd never understood it before.

"Listen, I tried," Tommas muttered. "She wasn't willing to stay here another minute. Seriously, don't call her tonight. Give her the evening and morning to work through some of her mood, and maybe it won't be as bad tomorrow when you see her."

"I don't understand," Gian admitted.

"She knows your secret, asshole."

Gian's hand tightened around the phone. "What?"

Shit.

No.

Gian knew he should have been the one to tell Cara about his estranged wife, a marriage that had taken place under a set of circumstances driven by his grandfather and his wife's father. He had not loved her, and even now, had very little to do with Elena.

That had always been by her choice.

Gian no longer cared.

"You heard me." Tommas sighed heavily into the phone. "She deserved to know—from *you*, though, not like this."

"I was going to—"

"*When?*"

"Soon," Gian admitted.

"Not soon enough."

Tommas hung up the phone without a goodbye.

Gian didn't blame the man a bit.

• • •

"Who is she? What's the whore's name, Gian?"

Ouch.

That one kind of stung.

Especially, to hear it as an insult to Cara, when this woman—his *wife*—had no business throwing that sort of word around at anyone, given their history.

Gian wasn't able to hide the rage. "Watch your fucking mouth, Elena."

His estranged wife stiffened across the room, her arms crossing over her chest as she frowned. "You could at least tell me something, Gian."

"Why should I?" he asked quietly. "Have I asked you about your lovers? Have I ever expected you to sit back and wait for me, when you clearly didn't want to?"

Elena glanced away. "You don't know anything about—"

"I know *enough*," Gian said, hurling the words at her. "I know we haven't lived in the same space together for two years. We haven't *fucked* in three! I know why you agreed to the marriage, because you were scared and you were young. You needed to get away from your father, and you thought to use me to do it."

Gian scrubbed a hand down his face, ready to be done with the entire conversation. He hadn't wanted to be there, sharing a conversation with Elena at all, but he didn't have much of a choice. She was, whether he liked it or not, his wife. And in their world, in Cosa Nostra, that meant something *important*.

"I gave you that, I let you lie to me, because I was trying to please my grandfather, too," Gian admitted, his anger rising to the surface all over again. "But the moment you didn't have to pretend anymore, you stopped. I've never asked you for anything—never demanded you act like my wife, unless it's absolutely needed. I've never shared your bed without you wanting me there, and when you couldn't stand to have me in the same room without throwing something at the back of my fucking head, I left! I've never asked you for more than what this has always been, Elena."

A defiant glimmer lit up her eyes as she stared him down. "You've never been so blatant with a whore before, either."

He'd never hit a woman.

Never had the urge to hurt one.

Until this goddamn moment.

Gian shoved his clenched fists into his pockets, determined to stay on the other side of the room from his wife. Elena was good at these games—too good, really. She was known for her manipulations, something she had picked up from her bastard of a father, and she used them on Gian without blinking a lash about it. He had no doubt that was exactly what she was trying to do here. If she pissed him off enough to react, then it would be to her favor, and not his, when someone came to ask for his behavior toward his wife, and he would need to answer appropriately.

"You say that," Gian murmured, "like you've known for a while that I've been seeing someone on more than a casual basis, Elena."

He saw the tightening of her jaw.

It was her one tell for when she lied.

"And?" she asked.

"If you had such a problem with it, why not call me, or send someone over, write a fucking email, or whatever. Why *today*, of all days, is it that you have the problem with this? We're not together, we don't even fuck when we do have to pretend for an evening, and I am more than happy with letting you drain my bank accounts, as long as you're content on your side of the city. Why call me and demand answers from me *now?*"

Elena tipped her chin up, looking away again. "You made me look like a fool, Gian."

"Excuse me?"

"You had her all over the city, taking her out, dressing her up, and playing pretend with your people and even some of your family. You made me look like a goddamn fool. Does she know about me, when I didn't even know about her?"

"Now she does," Gian said, offering little else in that regard.

He would deal with Cara when she arrived that afternoon.

It was none of Elena's damned business.

"The least you could have done was give me the benefit of *knowing*," Elena spat at him, that fire returning to her gaze before she had even blinked. "You couldn't even do that. My mother called, which means my father knows, too."

"I had no reason to tell you. Beyond the fact we're not even together, we haven't spoken in ten months, and the last time we did talk, it was for you to tell me to get your fucking credit card fixed because it expired and the new card didn't come to your address. I *know* you were asked to the funeral for my grandfather, and you didn't even show face for that, as a wife should do. I didn't *care*. I have never cared. We're not together. We haven't been together in—"

"Then fucking give me a divorce!"

Gian stilled on the spot, letting each one of those words stab into his skin like little daggers, tearing him apart, piece by piece.

How simple her demand was.

How much he wanted to agree.

He *should*.

He needed to.

They would both be happier, they could both put the years of shit behind them to rest, and move on to better things—better *people*.

It wasn't that easy.

"I can't," Gian said quietly.

Dio, he wished that didn't have to be his answer.

Elena let out a sound that came off broken and frustrated, all at the same time. She threw her hands high, and glared at him as she said, "I don't want to hear that anymore, not now!"

"You come from the same world as I do. You know there's no other acceptable answer. Divorce doesn't exist to made men, or their wives. It never has, it never will, and we won't be the exception. I won't give up my life as a sacrifice, simply because three years ago, you tricked me into marrying you."

"I didn't *trick* you."

"Then what would you call it?" he roared back. "What would you call the things you did and how you lied to me?"

Elena's eyes watered, but that sight didn't affect Gian like it once had. "You knew what he was like to me, the things he did to me. Don't pretend like I had a choice, Gian."

He believed that, but very little else that came from his wife's mouth.

"So be it, but here we are, because of it," Gian replied. "I have an image to maintain, rules that need to be followed, the agreement to uphold between our families, and we can continue on like we have been for the past three years—"

"You mean where it's fine and great for you to fuck any whore that glances your way, but I have to sit pretty and quiet in the corner, not bringing you any shame, right?"

"Cara is the first and only woman I have ever been in a relationship with beyond sex, not that it's any of your fucking business. And you *know* that, or you should, considering this is the first time you've ever brought it to my attention that you knew I was involved with another woman. I have always been careful as far as other women were concerned, for your sake, Elena, not mine. My status demands I remain married to the woman I spoke my vows to—'til death do us part—but it says *fuck all* about remaining faithful to you. But I would have, had you given a single shit about me. And don't pretend that you've ever held fidelity in high esteem, where I was concerned. What was his name, the last one, Matteo?"

Elena barely blinked. "Cara, that's *her* name?"

Gian cleared his throat. "You want me to confirm it, but I think you already know exactly who she is. I've never said anything to you about who you've been seen out with, or the things I know you have done. I have only asked that you be mindful of your affairs because of your father, certainly not for *me*. As long as you're careful about whoever you—"

"Go to hell, Gian."

He barked out a laugh. "Surprise, sweetheart, I've already been living in hell for years. It started with you, and I have a feeling that isn't about to change anytime soon."

He hated her for that, too.

Much like she hated him, he knew.

TWENTY-ONE

"Early boarding for flight T1457."

Cara grabbed the carry-on bag at her feet, and readied for the regular boarding call for her flight. Tommas sat in the seat beside hers, yet he didn't speak. Likely because all someone had to do was look at Cara's face, and they would know she wasn't in the mood for any sort of conversation.

Tommas hadn't needed to do more than escort her to the airport, but he took it a step further, went through security, and decided to wait with Cara at her gate. She wanted to be thankful, at least her brother cared on some level, but she really wanted to be alone.

"You're always welcome to come home," Tommas said quietly.

Cara glanced up at the ceiling, and let out a slow breath. "Yeah, I know."

"But I don't think that's in your plans, is it?"

"Probably not."

"Even now, with … Gian and all?"

A flash of irritation settled in Cara's gut, but she pushed it away. It wasn't Tommas' fault that Gian had lied to Cara for months. Beyond that, she knew her brother thought that Cara had already known the truth about Gian and his … *wife.*

"I was getting back into a routine," Cara said, "before all this happened. I was getting better—finally—after losing Lea. I'm not going to push myself back several steps because of one man."

She had said the words so flippantly that anyone would believe them. Shit, even *she* wanted to believe them.

Cara didn't know if they were true.

"Cara."

She was lost in her thoughts, barely present as it was, and didn't hear her brother's call of her name.

Tommas reached out and placed his hand to her arm. "Cara."

"What, Tommas?"

"I'll never tell you what you can and can't do with your life. You know that, right?"

Cara nodded. "You never have."

"And I'm not going to start with this. But I do want to tell you one thing, if you'll hear it."

"Shoot."

Tommas smiled, but it was measured, and not entirely genuine. "Be careful, Cara, especially in this situation. You've always been careful not to step too deep into the piles of shit left by the family, and right now, I'm worried you're knee-deep and don't even realize it."

"I'm not involved in that side of his life, Tommas."

Her brother shook his head. "You may not see it that way, but I can assure you that you are."

"Well, not for much longer."

"Maybe, maybe not. A day ago—before this came up—you said you loved him. That sort of feeling doesn't go away because bad things happen. So, today, you want to skin him alive, but maybe in a week, you won't be so angry, and you might even remember what he was like *before* you knew about his wife. I won't tell you what to do, but you do need to be careful. Whether you like it or not, you've already put yourself into a position where a label is stuck on your relationship. I get that *you* didn't know it was there, but the people around him certainly did. And if you understand what it means to be ... that woman—"

Cara scowled. "The other woman. The whore. A *goomah*. Say it, Tommas."

He didn't even flinch at her truth, simply kept staring at her like it didn't change a thing about how he thought of her or saw her in his eyes. "If you understand what it means to be that woman, and you can handle it, then I'll never say a word against your choices and wishes. It is your life— live it how *you* want to, Cara. Live the way that makes you happy with the person who makes you happy. But the very second you find yourself in too deep, and you want to get out, you know where to find me. Okay?"

"*Now beginning regular boarding for flight ...*"

Cara stood, slinging her bag over her shoulder.

Tommas stood with her. "Okay, Cara? Say the word, that's all you have to do."

She smiled, or as much as she could manage. "I won't need to after today, but thank you."

"That's easy to say now, sure."

"Tommas—"

"*Okay*, Cara?"

Her brother's expression hadn't changed from the moment he'd started talking. Never once had judgement shone in his eyes. He hadn't shamed her for the things that she had overlooked, or the mess she now found herself in. No, he only cared for her, and her happiness.

Wasn't that what family was supposed to do?

She forgot what that felt like, to be looked out for, and cared about, by someone who shared her last name and blood.

"Cara?" Tommas pressed again.

"Yeah, Tommas. Okay."

He nodded, and then waved a hand toward the gate where other passengers had started lining up to hand over their boarding passes. "Have a good flight, Cara. Call me when you get home and have a minute."

"All right. Thank you, Tommy."

Tommas shrugged. "It's what big brothers do, right? Or, what we're supposed to do."

Yeah, it was.

She had forgotten that little fact.

• • •

Customs was not half as bad coming back through Toronto International Airport as they had been when Cara entered through them in Chicago. The customs officer gave her passport a glance, barely opened her carry-on and purse up fully, and sent her on with a smile.

That was one damn thing to be grateful for.

While the flight from Chicago to Toronto wasn't a long one, her emotional turbulence meant that Cara wasn't in a particularly good place. She was exhausted—mentally, and physically. The only thing she wanted to do was get home to her apartment, give her brother the call she promised him, and then lie in her bed for several hours.

She needed sleep.

Cara pushed through customs, and headed toward arrivals where her luggage would be waiting, and a line of taxis outside the exit doors. She had stepped off the escalator when she spotted the guy standing at the very front of a large group of waiting people.

Several held signs with last names scrawled on them, waiting to pick up someone from their arriving flights.

Not this man.

Chris didn't need to.

Wearing all black, his hair smoothed back, and a flat smile plastered on his face, Cara let out a sigh at the sight of Chris.

She had wanted to go home. She'd hoped for a little bit of time before she would need to have an actual face-to-face meeting with Gian. Some breathing room to get her thoughts and feelings in order, so that when she did see him, her raging emotional vomit didn't spill all the way out, making a mess of everything it could reach. Surely, she wasn't asking for a lot.

Apparently, Gian was not going to give Cara that option. Well, he would have nobody to blame but himself when he faced her anger. He could have given her a day or two—anything—to let his lies sink in.

"Miss Rossi?" Chris asked as he came to stand in front of Cara.

She looked him over. "Gian sent you, Chris?"

"*Sì*, miss."

"I suppose if I said that I didn't want to go see Gian, it won't make much of a difference, huh?"

He smirked a bit. "I'm to deliver you to his penthouse, nowhere else. I only follow orders. It would be best if you didn't make a scene. Either way, the penthouse is it."

"Wonderful." Cara crossed her arms.

"I will take you home once you're done with the boss."

The boss.

Cara didn't miss the man's choice of words, in regards to Gian. Was that what had happened while she was gone? Was that what he had sent her away for, so that he could take over the new boss's seat, and get his revenge for his grandfather at the same time?

She wasn't stupid, of course, and she knew how volatile and dangerous things had started to become before Gian sent her away. Incidents that had come far too close to Cara *and* Gian. Still, he never talked *details*. He was always careful, in that sense, and only gave her the barest bones of information. Just enough to tide her over.

For good reason, her mind taunted, *you're not his wife.*

Nothing Gian ever told Cara would be safe.

Not in court.

Goomahs didn't get that sort of closeness with their men.

Whores got nothing.

It only pissed her off even more. Cara had thought she knew everything about Gian that was important, things a man who loved her *should* tell her. Even a man like him, involved in things that put a constant target on his back.

She thought he cared enough.

He clearly hadn't cared at all.

"Your brother called ahead of time and let the boss know what time your flight would be arriving this afternoon."

Cara wanted to be angry at Tommas over that fact, but she couldn't summon up the emotion. All of her anger was being saved for the one person who deserved it the most, and she knew Tommas had only been doing what was expected of him, as he'd allowed Cara to return to Toronto before Gian gave the okay.

"Am I at least allowed to grab some food on the way?"

"The boss has a lunch waiting, if you're hungry," Chris said.

Cara scowled, and walked on past the guy. "Lunch he can choke on."

• • •

"You'll be heading up alone from here," her escort said as Cara stepped into the elevator. "The boss said it would be better if no one interrupted you two for the next little while."

Cara turned to face Chris who was holding the elevator door back from closing.

"If I wasn't so pissed off, I would thank you, but ..." She let her unspoken words hang in the air, unsaid. "You know how it goes."

The man nodded once. "Given the circumstances, I understand."

Cara frowned, her embarrassment rising. "Do you know the circumstances?"

"I've known since the day he married his wife. I was invited by his grandfather to attend, since I had kept an eye on Gian for a great many years before that day. I have been around for more things that I care to mention at this moment, and you happened to be one of them."

Ouch.

Just another name to add to her list of people who'd known, while she hadn't.

"You must have thought I was foolish, then."

Chris's expression gave nothing away. "I think you were happy, and you made him happy. So, what business is it of mine, to tell my boss that he shouldn't be happy, when I've watched him simply exist for too long?"

"That's quite a black and white way of looking at it."

"Maybe so."

"Except I have the feeling that neither of us are happy now," Cara said, "and that's his fault, too."

Chris nodded again, stepped back, and let the elevator door close.

Cara grew silent as the elevator began to move upward, and she eyed the security camera in the upper left corner of the tin box, pointed right at her. She wondered if Gian was watching, knowing that the elevator was solely used for entrance and exit from his penthouse, and none of the other suites in the building. Someone had to be watching that camera.

She shot it the middle finger for good measure.

Just in case.

Childish, maybe.

Who cared?

As the elevator came to a slow stop at the top, Cara was surprised to find her inner turmoil had almost calmed completely. She didn't know what to expect from herself—more nerves, perhaps, but definitely well-deserved anger.

None of those feelings came immediately as the door opened.

White walls, a vaulted ceiling, and the huge brass and crystal chandelier caught her eye first. She stared upward, soaking in the familiarity of the penthouse, and remembering how the first time she had seen it, it had damn near taken her breath away. She almost wished that Gian had given her the decency of choosing somewhere else to have this fucking meeting. He had to know how the penthouse would affect her, how the memories would *sting* her.

Cara shook the heavy sensation off her shoulders, and walked further into the penthouse, down the entryway, and toward the main floor of the place. She didn't have to be told to know that's where Gian would be waiting for her. Not close to the elevator, where she could make a quick exit if she needed to, but deeper into the penthouse, where he might have a chance to convince her to stay.

She had news for him.

Cara wouldn't be staying.

Ever.

Gian stood in front of the floor-to-ceiling windows, staring out over the busy city streets as Cara entered the dining room. As Chris had said there would be, a lunch spread was waiting on the large table. It looked as though it hadn't been touched. Cara didn't make a move to go near the food, or Gian as he finally looked over his shoulder to acknowledge her presence.

A wariness settled in his eyes as he looked her over, and his usual grin—that sexy, confident smirk that was always in place—had vanished. He seemed older standing there staring at her, like the weight of the world had come along and sat itself down on his shoulders for the moment. His hair, the longer strands at the top, were messier than normal. A clear sign he had been running his fingers through the dark strands, speaking of his hidden stresses.

"Cara," he murmured.

She still didn't move.

Not when he spoke, or when he turned completely to face her, and certainly not when her heart ached to *go to him*.

She didn't realize how hard this was going to be.

Not being angry, or even knowing what she had to do, but actually *doing it*. Saying this would be final—the end of them, whatever they were. *That* was the hard part.

"I'm sorry," Gian said.

"I wish that made a difference, Gian."

"I know that I should have told you, *dolcezza*, there's no reason why I didn't, except that I was being selfish."

"You're right, you should have told me, and you are selfish." Cara shifted from one foot to the other, restlessness settling into her heart. "Aren't you going to ask how I found out?"

"It doesn't matter, really. You know, and that's the important part."

She was going to tell him anyway.

"Pictures," Cara said quietly, "of your wedding. She looked beautiful, like a proper bride should."

"Can I explain a few things about Elena and the marriage? Her and I, we're not together in that sort of way. We haven't been for years, we don't even speak on a regular basis. Just let me—"

Cara shook her head, cutting him off with a quick, "No."

"Cara, please." He took one step forward, and Cara moved one step back accordingly. "You might understand—or shit, maybe not, but I need you to know why and how this happened, please."

"No, Gian. I don't care, because you didn't care enough to tell me the truth from the start. You've lied to me. Maybe not in your words, but in your omissions, and the things you kept from me. You didn't let me have a choice, you made them for me. You made me look stupid—like your foolish little whore, constantly running back to your bed whenever you snapped your fingers."

He flinched. "That's not what I meant to do, *amore*."

"You didn't have to mean to, your actions did it for you!"

"I'm sorry, Cara."

"Sorry won't fix this, Gian. It's not a fucking time machine."

"I know, I just—" His words cut off as he looked away, his strong jaw working as he chewed over his next words. "I want to explain, but it won't help, will it?"

"No."

Honesty was the best policy.

He should have followed that rule, too.

Gian rubbed a hand over his lower jaw, bringing Cara's attention to the glint of jewelry on his ring finger. Never had she seen him wear the wedding band before, and in that moment, it felt like nothing more than a slap to her face.

He caught her stare, and dropped his hand when he realized that's where she was looking.

"I have to wear it, given how things have changed, for appearances and—"

"Stop," Cara whispered. "You don't have to explain. It's a little late for that, anyway, and I'm not in any position to need an explanation. Not like your wife would need one, you know?"

Pain colored Gian's brown gaze, darkening them briefly.

"That was low," he said.

Cara shrugged. "Sometimes, the truth hurts, Gian. Seems I'm not the only one who needed to learn that lesson, lately."

With that statement, Cara turned on her heel and headed back to the elevator, determined to let those words be her final goodbye. It had said much more than she could. It wasn't a proper goodbye, but it would have to do.

"Cara, wait."

His footsteps echoed behind her, but she kept walking.

The elevator came into view fast, but not fast enough.

Gian grabbed her arm, spinning her back around to face him. "Wait, I said."

Cara glared right back at him, letting her anger swell for the first time since she had entered the penthouse. "Don't manhandle me, Gian. You don't get to order me around, not now."

"Let me speak for five minutes. Let me explain, and then you can do whatever the fuck you want to do."

"What is there to explain?"

"I—"

"Are you married?" she asked.

"It's not that simple."

"Are. You. Married."

"Yes," he admitted.

"For three years."

"And a couple of months."

Cara took a deep breath. "Did you lie to me about it?"

"In a sense, yes, by omission."

"Then nothing else matters."

"It might, if you would let me explain, Cara."

She doubted it.

"Let me go, Gian, I don't belong here. You have a woman who can stand at your side, be in your bed, and whatever else you want, but I'm not her. I am not your wife. And I won't pretend to be, when you want something different for the evening. I won't be a *goomah* for a made man, and I certainly won't be your whore."

Gian released his hold on her arm, but it took a few passing seconds. "I didn't mean for this to happen."

"You should have known it would. All lies unravel, eventually, no matter how good you are at telling them. And you're so good, aren't you? You made sure no one said a single word to me, but they all knew, didn't they?"

"It wasn't like that. They had no reason to speak up, and maybe some even thought you knew. Shit, at first, I thought you might have known."

"Why would I have *known*, Gian? I knew barely anything about you!"

"I know." Gian raised his hands high and wide, as if to offer nothing but air. "I do love you, Cara. You know that's true. You *have* to know that's true."

"Do I? I don't think I know anything about you at all."

Cara blinked, and the tears she had been holding back made lines down her cheeks. She didn't make a move to wipe the wetness away, instead, letting Gian see them, so he knew. She needed him to understand how much he hurt her.

It couldn't be fixed.

He'd done this.

"I've not been in a romantic relationship with my wife from damn near the day we married, though you might not believe it, and I certainly wasn't with her when I was with you. For what it's worth, I have only loved you, ever," Gian said.

"It's not worth very much now."

More tears fell, but she didn't make a sound.

Gian didn't try to stop Cara as she took those last few steps toward the elevator. She wished that she could say it was only relief in her heart as she did what she knew was *right*.

It still hurt like hell. Her heart shattered when she stepped inside. She broke apart as the doors closed.

That was her goodbye.

Gian deserved to see every fucking second of it.

He was the entire reason why.

Every single reason.

ENTANGLED

BOOK TWO

ONE

It was possible to be entirely alone in a room full of people.

Gian Guzzi had never had that experience before, but now it was all too common. He had wrongly assumed that taking the highest seat in his Cosa Nostra family would leave him with very little time to consider or wallow about his personal problems, but that couldn't be further from the truth.

Already, it was August. A hot, humid summer month that Gian had planned to spend with someone else, ignoring the heat as best he could. Three months had passed since his last encounter with Cara Rossi, but not a single fucking day went by where he wasn't reminded of her in some way.

Part of that was by his own hand, of course.

Being a boss, on the other hand, forced Gian to keep his personal issues quiet. He certainly couldn't afford to let the men around him think that he was distracted by his emotions, never mind a woman that he could no longer have. He needed for them to think that at all times, he was on his very best game, no matter what.

Duty first.

Legacy second.

And only then, love.

Gian finally understood what his grandfather, Corrado, had been trying to tell him for years. He had assumed that it was a sacrifice all made men needed to make for the sake of *la famiglia*, but he was wrong.

Only the boss made that sacrifice.

Cosa Nostra had to be his one constant. He had to breathe the business. He had to bleed the life. He was the one who was expected to repeat the rules and enforce them. He was the only one who was looked to when something needed to be heard. His voice spoke for everyone.

That was what a *good* boss did. Then, if he did his job well, the boss's men would never know that he was just like them, affected and ruined by silly things like love and a woman.

Duty. Legacy. Love.

Always in that order.

Always.

Oh, yes.

Gian understood those words perfectly well now.

It was better to listen to the people around him, let them talk, and then form his own opinions and give orders from what he learned. He learned that quickly enough as a boss. It also left him with too much time, when he was alone with his thoughts.

All he ever did was think.

"Happy birthday, boss!"

Gian tried to smile as a hand clapped his back with enough force to shake him from his inner hell. It brought his attention forefront to the VIP section of the club and the men, again. Men celebrating *his* thirtieth birthday.

He should be celebrating, too.

"Here, another drink," Stephan said.

A whiskey was shoved into Gian's hand.

He sipped at the strong liquor, as it gave him something to do. "*Merci.*"

Stephan said something else but Gian wasn't listening. He was not a big partier to begin with. He had only agreed to this night with his men because they had asked for it. Given how quickly tensions could flare in the family, peace-keeping was a constant part of the business. Especially for Gian.

Earlier in the day, he had spent too many hours sitting around a dinner table with the older generation of Capos in the family and their important people. They, too, had wanted to celebrate their boss's birthday in some way, but not like the younger men did. Which was understandable.

While the divide between the generational lines had closed enough for Gian to consider it comfortable, he still preferred to keep the two groups separate. He allowed everyone their voice, and their chance to express it. As much as was acceptable, anyway.

"Happy birthday to you! Happy ... "

Gian was urged forward in the group of men as a server strolled forward with a cake in her hands. It was a two-tier cake, gold in color, with black trim. The Guzzi family colors. His name and the proper birthday greeting had been scrawled across the side. It certainly looked good, but even his appetite was seriously lacking lately.

Happy birthday, boss.

Dirty thirty, Gian.

The platitudes kept coming from everyone. Gian smiled and nodded, laughing when he needed to. He wasn't shocked anymore that no one seemed to notice his cheer and good-nature was nothing more than a carefully-crafted lie.

He had perfected this shit in no time at all.

"Set it down," someone told the server with the cake.

A table was pulled over, and the cake was set down. Another man passed Gian a knife, while paper plates, napkins, and plastic forks were set out on the table by another one of the girls who worked in Gian's club.

"This one is all you," Domenic said, nodding at Gian, and then to the cake. "Go for it. Might as well add some diabetes to the alcoholism these fools already have."

Gian smacked his brother in the back of the head for that one. "You're one to talk. How many nights a week are you in a club drinking, never mind at home alone?"

Dom shrugged. "It's how I meet people."

"Right. Good excuse."

"Just cut your fucking cake, Gian."

"You know I didn't ask for a cake," Gian said to his brother, lowering his tone so only Dom would hear. "I only agreed to a few drinks."

Dom nodded. "They want to celebrate you, man. Let them."

Gian sighed.

Right.

Celebrate.

It was only *him* that wasn't feeling the party.

"Just cut the cake," Dom said. "After that, they won't even notice when you go. They'll be too drunk and working on a sugar-high."

"You get to be the lucky—or unlucky—fuck that stays behind to make sure they don't tear my club apart," Gian warned.

"I can do that."

Fine.

As long as Dom knew …

Truthfully, Gian was grateful for his brother. Dom had been one of the very few constants at Gian's side since he'd taken over the family. He had made his brother, as he promised to do, and given Dom his proper *in* to the family business. Besides, it was a hell of a lot easier to make Dom his consigliere when he was already a made man.

Dom became Gian's right-hand man practically overnight. But that was how it needed to be, and Gian didn't give fucking anyone the chance to argue or question it. Dom was better suited for the consigliere position rather than a Capo or underboss, simply because the men knew him, Gian trusted him, and he was not in the family for everyone else, only his brother.

As he had always been.

His underboss, on the other hand, had been something he allowed the men of the family to pick. It was unusual, and certainly not the norm, but they had their voice and vote in *someone*.

Stephan was who they chose.

Somedays, Gian wanted to kill the bastard.

Other days, he was worth his weight in arrogant, ignorant gold.

"Hurry up!" someone shouted from behind Gian.

Dom chuckled. "Let them eat cake, Gian."

"Didn't saying that get someone killed once?"

"She didn't give them the cake, though."

Gian didn't think that was the point.

Still, he went ahead and sliced into the cake. While the outside had been a gold and black-trimmed masterpiece, the inside was a vibrant crimson color. Red velvet, it seemed.

Like blood.

It was oddly appropriate, considering how much blood he had already spilled.

"All right, move over, let me handle this," Dom said.

Gian willingly gave the knife to his brother, and let Dom get to work. If there were two things Dom liked, they were food and good conversation. Gian was able to step aside, and barely anyone noticed as they were too busy drinking their liquor and shoving their faces full of cake.

Gian knew, in that moment, he should take the time to appreciate what he was seeing. Calm and peace. Content men. Vanishing violence. A family ready to *work*.

He should have been happy.

He should have been ... a lot of things.

Being a boss was not as easy as he had thought it would be. He had only been given a glimpse of what the position was like when his grandfather filled the spot. Now, sitting in the seat himself, Gian had his eyes wide open.

It was fucking lonely at the top.

Gian was constantly surrounded by people.

He had too much work to do.

He never stopped moving.

His time was thin.

His patience was thinner.

And yet, more than he cared to admit, he found himself entirely alone. No amount of work, Cosa Nostra, or distractions would help with his problem.

Only one person could—Cara.

She was out of his reach, now, to an extent. Physically, she wasn't his to have, no matter how badly he wanted her. Emotionally, she had every fucking one of her claws buried into his heart, and she didn't even know it.

His soul was entangled with a woman who no longer wanted him, even if he would still die for her.

Gian had no one to blame for that but himself.

• • •

Gian buttoned up his suit jacket as he stepped out of the back of the black town car. Chris held the door open until Gian stepped away from the vehicle, and then promptly closed it shut once he could. Standing in the middle of the large, circular driveway, Gian stared down the mansion that had become a private hell of sorts for him.

He did not want to enter that house.

He couldn't even call it a home, now.

Once upon a time, it had been exactly that. A *home*. His grandfather and grandmother's home, filled with memories of years long past and happier times. Now, whenever he entered the mansion, invisible weights fell on his shoulders, while a pressure built in his head, ready to burst at any moment.

That could happen to a man when he was expected to share a space with his wife, especially when said wife was Elena Guzzi. Gian was expected—in his current position—to behave a certain way regarding his wife and marriage. It looked better on his image, and his family, when he treated his wife *as* his wife. Regardless of how he felt about it, he needed to be seen with his wife. Out and about, at the mansion, and more.

Elena was no happier about Gian's presence in her life than he was, frankly.

And that only made it that much more difficult.

Gian could have moved Elena into his penthouse, and sold his grandfather's mansion for a few million, but he had chosen a different route. For one, because neither he, nor his wife, wanted to be together in a smaller space than they had to be. And for two, because the penthouse was his, much like her previous penthouse had belonged solely to her. They were not accustomed to living together, and Gian had built his life around the fact that his wife was not going to be involved.

He was not going to change his lifestyle entirely, simply to suit the desires of a few people who watched him like a hawk.

Thankfully, Elena didn't put up much of an argument when Gian suggested the mansion as a sort of middle ground. He spent a couple of days and nights there, though usually in an entirely different wing from his wife, and a few nights at his penthouse in the city where he was easily assessable to his men and business.

That certainly didn't mean either of them liked the arrangement, which only made nights like these that much fucking harder to get through.

"You good, boss?" Chris asked.

Gian kept his features schooled as he replied, "Why wouldn't I be?"

"You just seem … quiet."

"When have you ever known me to be loud?"

The enforcer chuckled. "Point taken."

"Are you in the mood for dinner?" Gian asked. "You're more than welcome to join us. Elena does seem fond of you."

Or at least, the woman was slightly more pleasant when someone else was nearby.

"I could eat."

That was that.

Elena barely blinked a lash at one of Gian's men entering the mansion behind him. Wearing one of her usual dresses, with her blonde hair perfectly done and her makeup flawless, she greeted Chris first, and only turned to Gian once the enforcer headed toward the dining area of the right wing.

"I didn't know you were coming tonight," Elena said.

No greeting.

No hello.

Nothing.

"It's Saturday, Elena. I always come here on Saturday nights."

"Not usually this late."

"Do you want a daily update for when I plan to come and go from different places, and when I might show up here?" Gian asked.

Because if that would keep her from meeting him at the door, he would happily try to provide her with those details.

"You're being a smartass," Elena said, "and I could do without the attitude."

"It's been a long day."

"Well, you certainly had a long night, didn't you?"

Gian resisted the urge to roll his eyes. "If you're talking about the dinner, and then the birthday party at the club last night, yes, it made for a long evening."

Elena crossed her arms, her jaw stiff as she stared at him hard. He always thought blue eyes would have fit his wife far better than her brown eyes did—the iciness in her gaze couldn't quite be matched by any other woman he had come in contact with. Sometimes, her brown gaze gave off a sense of warmth simply because of their color, but it was a lie.

She was colder than ice.

"And why wasn't I invited?" Elena asked. "I am your wife, Gian."

"Because it wasn't a family thing," Gian replied dryly.

"Still—"

"I wasn't asked or invited to bring you, so I didn't. Don't act like that bothers you because we both know it doesn't. The only thing that might bother you is not being able to buy something pretty to wear out for an evening. If that's what you want, decide where you want to go *next* weekend, and I will take you. Not for my birthday, though."

"Fine."

Gian sighed internally, taking that as a battle won.

"Also, my birthday is coming up," Elena added quickly.

"And what would you like for it?"

She smiled sweetly, as though she was pleased with his question.

Another false invitation into her web.

It never failed to surprise Gian how easily men could be caught up and then subsequently killed in the maze of Elena's games and manipulations. He had been one of those men, once. Years ago, it had been him who saw her distant eyes and perfectly-styled appearance and thought, *something is wrong with her, she never smiles.*

She seemed sad, alone, and too quiet. She had been young at just twenty-three, with no siblings and only her father raising her. Her mother had died long ago.

Her beauty, sweet nature, and soft voice had drawn him in easily enough. Her world had been a malevolent place, and certainly not meant for her.

He had been stupid.

A foolish man caught up in a hero complex.

It was a mistake Gian would never make again.

Not with Elena.

Gian wrongly perceived what he thought to be Elena's innocence and naivety as a direct result of her upbringing, under the hands of her violent, awful father. He had never once considered that every single thing that Elena offered to a man, whether it be emotionally, verbally, or physically, was a game. Her words were meant to placate and soften. Her touch was meant to disarm and trap.

For her, men were a means to an end.

She had simply found the *right* man in Gian to use.

It was a particular sport that she had been taught all too well, and had yet to lose.

Gian hadn't realized he had been playing Elena's game until it was too late. He had fallen for all of her lies, they were only a few weeks short of being married, he was stuck in the agreement made, and his life *shattered.* Just like that, she ruined what should have been his free choice and will.

And she had done it for no other reason than to be free.

She trapped him so that she could fly.

"Well?" Gian asked. "What do you want for *your* birthday?"

Elena shrugged. "Nothing spectacular."

"But something amazing."

"That is what your wife deserves, isn't it, Gian?"

"She certainly deserves *something,*" he said as he moved past her.

Elena reached out to pat his cheek. It took every ounce of willpower he had not to flinch away. He did not share a life with this woman beyond the one they were forced into, and they certainly didn't share affection. He didn't want her touching him, and he had no interest or desire to touch her.

Once, before they'd married, all he had wanted to do was touch her, and to save her. And then he'd figured out her games, but it was already too late.

"Don't," Gian murmured, stepping out of Elena's reach.

"So touchy, Gian."

"I wonder why, Elena."

"You're no fun tonight."

With her, he was never fun.

"If you want something, then ask for it. Don't, however, try to manipulate me into giving you something by pretending to be nice or that you give a shit. You don't. I don't. It's that simple."

Elena shot him a look. "Fine, whatever. Shiny and pretty things, people to sing me happy birthday, the usual."

Gian nodded. "It'll be done."

"*Out* somewhere, too. Not here."

"Pick a place."

Elena was the one to walk past him that time. Her smile was serene and her sarcasm oozed as she spoke over her dainty shoulder. "You're too good to me, Gian."

As he should be. As he *had* to be. Because she was his wife.

Little else had to matter, apparently. Certainly not his *feelings*. Those disgusting fucking things were meant for weaker men, and Gian had no time for weakness. The only time he did indulge his feelings were when it came to a certain woman that was out of his reach.

"Well, are you coming to eat supper, or are you going to stand there in the entryway all night?" Elena asked.

"Did you cook it?"

"God, no."

"Then yes, I'll eat," Gian said.

He didn't even trust his wife not to try and kill him with food, honestly.

This was how their life was lived, now that they had to be together in some shape or form. Carefully, circling around each other with the occasional sharp word quick to show itself and cut the other person standing too close. Maybe it was easier for them both this way.

If they stuck to what *was*, they would not dig too deep into what had *been*.

Neither of them wanted that mess brought up.

Not again, anyhow.

• • •

The priest waved his hands upward in a sweeping motion to the parishioners, and everyone stood at the same time to be blessed a final time. Gian was grateful—it was almost over.

And by *it*, he meant his time with his wife for a couple of days.

Church was meant to be one of his peaceful times, but even that was becoming tainted by the fact that he now sat in a pew with his wife, instead of with his family like he once had. Appearances were everything, after all.

Some needed to be kept happier than others, in that regard.

"Finally," Elena grumbled under her breath as the priest dismissed the congregation. She stood, brushing down the skirt of her cream-colored, knee-length dress that matched her shoes and hat. "Mass never ends. I hate it."

And yet, she was one of the best dressed in the entire congregation.

"Church is good for the soul," Gian replied tiredly.

"People like us have no souls, Gian. This is nothing more than a farce, and if there is a heaven, we will only be allowed entrance because we paid our way in."

Touché.

"Chris can drive you home," Gian told his wife as he picked up his aviator sunglasses from the pew. "I have things to do today."

Elena pursed her lips. "I'm sure."

She didn't push him or argue his demands, though. Chris would be waiting outside to return Elena to the mansion, and she had another driver on speed dial to take her wherever in the hell she wanted during the week. She had a license and could drive perfectly well, but she preferred to be chauffeured about like a queen.

Gian didn't give a shit, as long as it wasn't him doing the driving.

It wasn't long after Elena was gone down the aisle that Dom slid in beside his brother in the pew. Gian allowed a few more people to head down the aisle, opting to stay behind with Dom to get his weekly update.

It always fucking hurt. It sucked like nothing else.

Gian did it to punish himself, surely. It still helped him to *breathe.*

"Well?" Gian asked.

Dom sipped from a to-go cup of coffee like he had all the time in the world. "Nothing new, really. Cara's been pretty quiet the last week. She's still working at that women's shelter over on the Fifth."

"Carolina's House," Gian said, naming the shelter.

He knew it, because he'd donated to it often over the years, given his family's history with the place. Cara didn't know that, though.

She didn't know Gian watched her at all.

Dom nodded. "Still there. She'll be back in school next month, probably. I'm not sure about the shelter after that."

Knowing Cara, and what she wanted to do with her life, if the shelter allowed her a position while she remained in university, she would take it in a heartbeat. Gian hoped they gave her the chance. Dreams were worth following, after all.

"That's about all I have to tell on that side of things," Dom noted.

"*Nothing* else?" Gian asked.

Dom gave his brother a side-long look. "She's not been out with anybody, you know. And you could just outright ask that, instead of posing it like it's something else. I don't think she's even got time for a man, Gian."

He doubted that. Cara had time, if she wanted to make it. For whatever reason, she just hadn't made the time. *Yet.*

Jealousy burned hot and heavy in his gut at the thought. Gian ignored the reckless, violent emotion, because what in the hell else could he do?

He couldn't force his wants upon Cara.

Hadn't he already hurt her enough?

"You could go see her," Dom suggested.

Gian scoffed. "Our last encounter did not end well. I doubt me showing up would go over spectacularly, either."

"Then why not leave her alone, man?" Dom nodded down the aisle where Elena had disappeared to. Most of the people had also cleared out of the church. "You do have a wife, Gian. Focus there, maybe."

"Right, my wife."

Fuck that. Gian decided their conversation was going nowhere, and turned around to leave, only to come face to face with his father and mother. Frederic and Celeste made no attempt to hide the fact they had been standing there eavesdropping on the brothers' conversation.

"Do you have something you would like to add?" Gian asked his scowling father.

Frederic had no qualms about sharing his opinions with Gian, especially regarding his unconventional marriage, and the affair his son had had with Cara for months.

"Your brother has a point," Frederic said. "Don't go getting yourself caught up into another mess with the Rossi girl. Not now, Gian. You have better things to focus your time and energy on, and Elena is just one of those things."

"Or you could mind your fucking business."

"Gian!" his mother said, horrified and glancing toward the pulpit.

Gian wasn't in the mood to tone down his attitude for the sake of sensibilities. "I said what I said, Ma. I meant it."

"You married your wife," his father said, paying no attention to his wife or what his son had told him. "You chose to marry that girl, and now you have to live with it."

"I never got a choice, actually. I was given the illusion of a choice, which you're aware." Gian slid on his aviator sunglasses, and pushed past his father to head down the aisle. "It still makes no difference to what I told you. Mind your fucking business."

TWO

There was something about the city of Toronto in the summer that Cara Rossi loved. People seemed happier in the summer.

It was definitely *not* Chicago.

Speaking of Chicago …

"Seems my sister is so busy, she can't even be bothered to phone me on a regular basis," Tommas said the moment Cara picked up her brother's call.

"I don't even get a hello, huh?"

"Do you think you deserve one?"

"I think I'm your only living sister, so a hello would be *nice*."

"Hello, Cara. Call me more often, please. I like to know you're still alive and kicking. Without having to call to ask if you *are*. Okay?"

Cara rolled her eyes upward. "I'm sorry I haven't called in a while; I *have* been busy, regardless of what you think."

"Do tell."

"I beg your pardon?"

"What has you so busy that you can't afford a five-minute phone call?" her brother asked.

"You're such a nosy little shit. I think you get that from your wife."

Tommas snorted. "Believe me, out of the two of us, it is me who is the nosiest. Abriella gets all the dirty details from me."

"I bet."

"I worry about you, Cara. That's all."

She slowed a bit in her walk to allow an older couple to go ahead of her. "You don't need to be worried about me at all. How was the wedding?"

"That was a month ago."

"I did call to congratulate you. You were gone. I left a message on the house phone."

"I have a cell phone, too."

"Which you turned off for days," Cara argued.

Tommas grunted under his breath. "Fine, my bad. I'm shit at keeping in touch, too. I get it."

"So, the wedding?"

"It was wonderful," Tommas said. "I waited a long time for that day."

Cara smiled. "Good, Tommy."

"We headed to New York after the wedding, and then took a trip to Italy for a bit. It took us a good two weeks after we got home to settle back into a routine. That, and Abriella had to find a new doctor that she liked and we had appointments for that to catch up on."

"A doctor, for what?"

Tommas cleared his throat. "So, we might have found out some good news the morning we got married."

"Like?"

"Like Abriella is pregnant," Tommas said quietly.

Cara came to a full stop on the city sidewalk, and people blew on past her like nothing was amiss. "*What?*"

"We haven't told a lot of people, but it won't be long before the news starts to travel. I wanted to be the one to tell you."

"Congratulations, Tommas. You're going to be a great dad." Then, Cara thought to add, "I don't talk to anyone from Chicago who would tell me, so no worries there."

"Word still has a way of getting around," Tommas said. "Which happens to be part of the reason I am calling you."

"I don't understand."

"I should have called the week after the wedding, when something got brought up in New York, but with Abriella and the honeymoon—"

"I don't need details on that," Cara jumped in fast.

Tommas laughed. "Relax, that's not what I'm talking about. I just meant to say my mind was elsewhere for a bit but now that I'm back home and shit is settled, I figured it was time to call."

"Again, not understanding, Tommy."

"Is something happening up there in Ontario that I might need to be aware of?" Tommas asked.

"Not that I know of."

"You visit Aunt Daniele and Uncle Claud."

"Yes."

"And nothing seems off in the family business?"

Cara sighed. "Tommas, you know I don't stick my nose in the mafia side of the family business. I stay far the hell away from it, and for good reason."

For one, because her twin sister had been killed by the mob. For two, because the last person she did get involved with, who happened to be mixed up with that, tore her fucking heart out and might as well have laughed about it.

She was *not* making that mistake again.

"Yes, but—"

"Tommas, you're seriously asking the wrong person. I don't have any idea what's happening in the Guzzi family. I haven't ever known, even when I was with Gian. Which by the way, haven't seen him in three months, and it'll be a few more before I do, if I can help it."

"Three months?"

Cara hummed out her confirmation. "I'm not any man's *goomah*. I don't give a fuck who he thinks he is."

Tommas coughed. "I'm not sure Gian ever thought that's what you were, either."

"You don't know that and besides, he didn't have to see me as his anything. What he did made everyone else see me in that way. That is bad enough."

"Point taken," her brother agreed quickly.

Cara was never going to allow another man to make her blind and stupid to his real life. She didn't give a shit how good-looking and charming he was on the outside. Gian Guzzi had seriously damaged Cara emotionally and publicly. She loved him—still did, really—but that meant nothing when his lies came into play.

She hoped he was happy with his wife.

Tommas' voice brought Cara from her thoughts. "But it was strange not to see someone from that family at the New York meeting. Do you remember what I told you three months ago?"

Cara didn't even have to think about it. "You said if I ever found myself in over my head with anything, all I needed to do was tell you and you would fix it."

"Good. Nothing's changed with that, Cara."

"I got it, Tommy."

"And call me more, for fuck's sake."

• • •

The first thing Cara had learned about Carolina's House was that it had been named after its unintentional founder. Carolina Demaske had taken in over a hundred women during the span of her ninety-four years of life. Women who were old and young, sick and helpless. She had nursed their bruised faces, cleaned their sick bodies, and helped raise their young children without ever asking for a single thing in return.

After Carolina had passed away, *her* daughters began the foundation that would eventually lead to the women's shelter Cara stood in front of.

Carolina's House was quiet when she strolled through the front doors. It wasn't unusual for a mid-week day. The women's shelter took in victims of domestic abuse, along with older teenage girls, and young mothers who needed help in various areas of their lives. Some needed the ability to safely get away from their abusive partners. Others needed a place to sleep, and the chance to get on their feet.

Cara had been incredibly lucky to be offered a spot at the shelter as a counselor of sorts. She worked alongside a registered therapist and counselor to help the women get their lives, business, and futures sorted out. Whatever they needed regarding legal things or even just *surviving*, Cara helped.

Or, she tried.

Cara wanted to be one of those people who *helped*.

She stopped at the drop-off room—a daycare-like space in the center where two volunteers watched over younger children while the mothers did whatever they needed to do for the day. She dropped off a bag of snacks she knew the kiddos loved. One of her favorite children noticed her presence instantly.

"Cara!"

"Hey, Mikey," she said, letting the three-year-old boy hug her around the legs. "What are you building today?"

"A train station."

"A train station, huh? Can I help?"

Mikey nodded enthusiastically. "Momma said she would help when she was done with Miss Jenny, but you can help, too."

Cara didn't hesitate to get down on the floor and help Mikey begin the building of what looked to be a huge train station. It was only once the kiddos noticed the treats that she was able to sneak out.

Carolina's House survived because of volunteers. Amazing men and women who came in with no expectations, only the desire to make life a bit better for someone struggling. People brought food. Some brought items for the babies and kids, or things the women needed. Every little bit helped.

Cara had learned something incredibly important since beginning her co-op program with the shelter. Money could only go so far, and while it could buy a hell of a lot for those in need, sometimes care, love and support helped even more.

"I hear someone wanted to see me today," Cara said, leaning in the doorway of her boss's office.

Jenny smiled from behind her desk. On the other side, Tiffany flipped through documents in a folder.

"You weren't busy, were you?" Jenny asked. "I know it's your off day."

"Nope. Never too busy for this." Cara slipped into the office, closed the door behind her, and took a seat beside the seventeen-year-old Tiffany. "Mikey is working hard on his train station, by the way."

At the mention of her son, Tiffany beamed. "I'm trying to save up enough to get him the big Lego set he wants for his birthday. It's a whole train. He saw it at the store. Killed me to tell him no."

Cara held back her frown. She had so much, when others had very little.

"When is his birthday?" Cara asked.

"Two months."

"You'll get it."

Cara would make sure of it.

The teenaged mother hadn't been given an easy life, and Mikey had been one of the final things to send her running from her abusive father. She had hopped from couch to couch with her son, never staying in school, and barely being able to hold down a job. Child Services had eventually caught up to the teen, and sent her home to live with her father.

Tiffany ran away with her son *again*. The second time, she came to Carolina's House. So far, Tiffany had gotten a job, and her GED testing was a month away, which Cara had no doubt the girl would ace. Tiffany's court appearance to be legally emancipated from her father and keep him from trying to take her son away, was in just two weeks.

"So, what's happening?" Cara asked Jenny.

Jenny nodded to Tiffany. "She had something she wanted to ask, and while I could have done it over the phone, I felt it better she ask directly."

Cara turned to the teen. "You have my cell number. You know you can call me anytime, right?"

Tiffany nodded. "Yeah, of course."

"What do you need?"

"I know the House set up a volunteer to take me to and from court, but I was hoping … well, that *you* might do it, Cara. I know you're busy, and you start back at university next week, too. But—"

"Absolutely," Cara interjected quickly.

She was honored that Tiffany felt better having Cara there than anyone else.

"You won't have to miss anything?" Tiffany asked.

"It doesn't matter if I do," Cara replied. "Lots of stuff can be worked around. This, for you, is one thing that can't be. No problem at all."

Tiffany's hesitance left her eyes. "Thank you, Cara."

"Don't worry about it."

They fully suspected that Tiffany's father likely wouldn't even show up to court, but either way, *they* still had to go.

"I'm going to go find Mikey," Tiffany said.

Cara said goodbye, and once the girl was gone, turned to Jenny. "That's all? Did you want me to stick around and help with dinner or anything?"

"Extra hands for dinner would be great, but there is one more thing."

"Oh?"

Jenny shrugged. "Tiffany did mention something important. Your classes are starting up next week."

"So?"

"Your co-op term actually ended last week, Cara. You've already gotten your grade for this, sweetheart."

Cara just stared at the woman. "I'm here because I want to be, because this place is amazing and so are the women and the people who run it, not because of a grade."

Jenny nodded. "I know."

"Why mention it?"

"I wanted to ask if you would like to stay on, even after your classes start. We can work out days or evenings, weekends. It doesn't have to be a five-day-a-week thing, or whatever. The women love you, and the staff—"

"Yes." Cara didn't need to think it over. "You don't even have to ask."

• • •

The first day back to class was always a shit show for Cara. It meant rushing between halls and buildings to be early for professors that were almost always late, but had zero issue with calling out a student for coming in *after* they finally showed up. It also meant orientation for smaller classes, plus going over what could be expected for the coming semester.

Cara had another year left, and she was done. Not only did she already have her Masters of Social Work, but once the year was up, she would also add her master's degrees of science and in public health. *If* she decided to take her education further, she could choose a residency program for psychiatry and continue on that path. But for now, her three master's would allow her the ability to work in several fields, including with children and mental health.

It was every goal she had wanted to achieve, and it was almost a reality.

She wasn't used to the early morning routine after the summer, though. Cara had even managed to forget to feed herself, which sent her running to the café she liked just a couple of blocks away from the university, when she had thirty minutes to spare.

Cara groaned at the sight of a long line when she stepped into the café. Unfortunately, another swarm of people came in right behind her. She quickly filed into line in order to not wait any longer.

By the time she did get to the front of the line to place her order, Cara was damn near terrified to check her watch and see how late she already was for her second to last class. She quickly asked for a coffee, bagel, and cookie to-go. Though she was hungry for more, her stomach would have to wait until she got home.

"Your order will come up down there," the barista said, pointing at the end of the counter.

"Great, thanks."

Cara fiddled with her bag as she waited for her order. She kept glancing down at her watch to check the time, but her solitude didn't last long.

"Are you waiting for someone?"

Looking over her shoulder, a pair of striking blue eyes met her gaze. The man was handsome enough, with a disarming smile and a sports coat slung over his arm. He leaned against the counter right behind Cara.

"Are you talking to me?" Cara asked.

The man nodded. "Sure am. It's a friendly thing to do, when the only other option is standing around waiting and talking to yourself."

Cara managed a laugh. "That's true. And no, I'm not waiting for someone."

"You kept looking at your watch. I just assumed."

"I'm late," Cara explained, "and getting later by the second."

"I'm Nathan," the guy said.

Cara spun around to take the hand he offered, noting his short-trimmed nails and smooth skin. He looked to be in his early thirties, if that. "Cara."

"Well, Cara, I'm glad you're not waiting for someone. At least no one is standing up a beautiful woman."

She arched a brow. "Are you working toward something?"

Nathan shrugged. "Would it get me anywhere if I was?"

"I'm not on the market for dating, sorry."

He glanced down at her hand, still firmly held in his. "No ring."

"None on yours, either."

"To be fair, a lot of surgeons take their rings off when they're on a shift. I just got off mine, though. But no, there isn't a ring."

Cara smiled. "A doctor."

"You don't sound surprised."

"Your hands give it away."

Nathan chuckled. "I'm going to take that as a compliment."

"Miss, your order is ready."

Cara dropped Nathan's hand with a shrug and turned to grab her waiting goods. "Thank you for the conversation, but I really am late."

"No problem." He flashed her a smile. "Have a good day, Cara."

"You, too."

Cara had only taken a couple of steps toward the door, when a familiar figure passed by the café's windows outside the business. She recognized the man for two reasons—one, he shared similar features to his brother, and for two, she had seen his face on the news over and over again several months earlier.

Domenic Guzzi.

Gian's younger brother.

For a second, Cara simply stood there, watching Domenic pass by the café without as much as a look inside. She didn't even know if the guy would recognize her, but it didn't much matter. He didn't matter, really. It was just the fact that Cara almost expected to see Gian, too.

How long could they be in the same city without running into one another? And she *really* hated how a part of her wanted that run in, too.

Move on, she told herself.

Before she could think better of it, Cara turned on her heel to approach Nathan again. It didn't have to mean anything, but a date was a date, and it meant she wasn't wallowing on a man who had severely fucked her over in the emotions department.

"Did you forget something?" Nathan asked when Cara approached him. He already had his order in hand, and looked like he was ready to head out, as well.

She held out her phone, the screen unlocked and ready to input a new contact. "Plug your number in—no guarantees, though."

He glanced down at her phone before taking it from her. "No promises here, either."

Cara could work with that.

THREE

There was nothing more irritating to Gian than seeing a pair of Royal Canadian Mounted Police detectives waiting for him at the front desk of his building. At least, the managers and ladies working the front desk knew better than to allow the RCMP detectives straight up to Gian's penthouse.

Ever since Corrado died, the police attention on the Guzzi family was … rough. Damn near constant. It didn't help that following Corrado's murder, several more deaths followed in the organization, and most done in a public way.

For the most part, the Canadian crime family managed to keep their heads down and their noses clean where police were concerned. They lived under the rule that less attention was better. This, unfortunately, was blowing that all to hell.

"Gian," the taller of the two detectives—Seeley, Gian thought his surname was—greeted.

The shorter of the two, the one with wide-framed glasses and a suit that always needed pressed, hung back from his partner. He was usually that way whenever the detectives showed up for another round of *make-Gian-talk-and-get-shot-down.*

"Detective Seeley," Gian replied dryly. Then, he nodded to the quiet detective. "Shaw."

Seeley glanced upward at the tall ceilings of the building, and then quickly back to Gian. "*Je voudrais—*"

"English only, please," Gian interrupted.

Seeley's jaw clenched.

Gian made pissing these men off into a game.

"You speak French," the man said firmly.

"Today I want to speak English," Gian replied. "Serve me in my language of choice, as you're *supposed* to do. I know how the police works in this country. We're all on a nod and greet basis out there on the streets, aren't we? Use English."

"Fine, English it is."

Gian stuffed his hands in his pockets, and rocked on his heels, pleased as fuck to have once again, annoyed the cops. Maybe if he did it enough, they would leave him the hell alone for a week. He doubted it, but he figured the risk was worth it.

All Royal Canadian Mounted Police were required to speak both official languages of the country. English and French. Gian found the detectives assigned to irritating him preferred French, and because *he* spoke

French fluently, they expected him to converse in that language.

Gian was just as unpleasant in French when it came to cops as he was in his other languages. Cops all held the same distinct stench. Their job was to *seem* nice to him, to placate his distrust with them, and bring him in closer to their schemes. They put men like him away all the damn time, and Gian refused to be their next foolish sheep.

"I want to discuss some things that came up in your grandfather's case, and see if you could confirm anything for me," Seeley said.

Gian passed the man a look. "Corrado has been dead for months; you should leave him that way and let his soul rest in peace."

"Don't you want justice for your grandfather?"

How little they knew …

Justice had already been served.

"What information do you have?" Gian asked, determined to get these idiots out of his building so he could get back up to his penthouse. "And what do you want from me?"

Seeley took a folder from Shaw and opened it up. The very top item happened to be a photograph of a man with half of his face blown off, but the other side was perfectly recognizable. Gian focused on the recognizable part instead of the grisly bits with brain matter and fluids soaking into the green grass under the body.

"Nik Tradek," the detective said. "Hired gun. We did a bit of digging and found some interesting emails and numbers between him and another dead man of the Guzzi Cosa Nostra—Constantino Rossi."

"And?"

"It wasn't exactly made quiet *why* Constantino was killed, I mean, not when it came to rumors on the streets."

There was a reason for that; Gian wanted it made clear that anyone who came up against him or his family would meet the same fate. Their closeness to him mattered for *nothing*.

"Rumors are not admissible in court," Gian reminded the detective.

"Be that as it may, word only travels when there's a ring of truth."

"Again," Gian drawled, "*and?*"

"Nik showed up dead last month. As you can see, his face was blown off, or most of it."

Yes, because it'd taken two months to find the bastard. He lived his life underground and off the grid.

Gian wanted him dead.

He got his wish.

Gian made a dismissive noise. "Well, I guess that's one less killer in Canada, then, isn't it?"

Seeley sighed, closing the folder and passing it back to his partner. "Gian, I know you're not a stupid man."

"You're right, I'm not."

"Then let's talk."

"I'd rather not, I'm not stupid, after all. You said it first."

"Then let *me* talk," the detective said.

"You did waste your time coming all the way here, so be my guest, Detective Seeley."

The man gestured at the file his partner held. "You should be aware—if you aren't already—that this really is no longer about Corrado's murder, or the many deaths that followed after his. This is about the Guzzi organization as a whole, and putting an end to the reign your family has had in this city—"

"Country," Gian corrected smoothly. "We're the largest organization in this country, at the moment, and for the unforeseeable future, too. We have always been the reigning organization, and that isn't going to change. Even when the cops couldn't handle something like the biker gang wars, *we* did. And for the most part, the Guzzi organization keeps a tight leash on gangs and other violent entities that cause us issues, which in return, cause the people and *you* issues."

Seeley tipped his chin up, defiant.

Gian smirked in response.

"I mean, you could be grateful," Gian added.

"Right, that's the word police are known to use for *criminals*."

Gian waved that off. "Those are semantics. If you're here to tell me that the focus of the police has changed from putting away murderers, to bringing my family down, then you're too little too late. You see, I took care of the issues that needed taken care of, and *you* can take that however you want to. What it means, however, is that you're left with the rest of us on your side of things, including me. So, here I am. I've even made it easy on you."

"I beg your pardon?"

Gian held out his wrists, offering them to the detective. "You didn't even have to ride an elevator to arrest me. Here you go, do your job."

"I—"

"Can't," Gian interjected. "Yeah, I know. But hey, I'm really starting to look forward to these weekly meets and the games we play, so maybe in a few more, we'll actually get to the point where we can sit down and have coffee. Or maybe not."

"And how are those growing pains coming along in the organization?" the detective asked, moving an inch closer. "How difficult it must be for a boss of your age—even with your last name—to gain any traction with some of those men?"

Gian let his cool, calm expression take over as he answered, "So you're watching, then? Good, see if you can keep up. *Je suis désolé, mais je dois y aller,*

Detective. Have a good day."

"We're not done talking, Gian."

Gian had already turned back and was heading for the elevator. His response was a flick of his hand over his shoulder, even when the detective called out for him again.

Oh, they were done.

Entirely so.

• • •

"Explain to me, boss, how a man who gets driven around ninety percent of his time, has managed to get two parking tickets and one for speeding, in three months?"

Gian glared at the back of Christopher Basso's head from his spot in the rear seat. "You know they only pulled me over on the speeding ticket just to get a look inside my car."

"Says you."

"I wasn't speeding," Gian muttered.

"You are aware I know that you drive like a bat out of hell, right?"

"Shut up, Chris."

"What about the two parking tickets?" the enforcer asked.

Gian scowled. "I couldn't find a spot. I used a fire lane a couple of times—whatever."

"You'll be lucky if they don't demote enough points from your license to take it from you today."

"They're not going to take my license, for fuck's sake."

"Well, if they do, I'll still be here to drive your ass around."

"You sound like you're enjoying this," Gian accused.

In the rearview mirror, Chris flashed a grin. "I *enjoy* keeping you on your toes, sure. You're the only made man I know who doesn't spend all his time in court for offences related to the organization, but instead, his shitty driving habits. I'm serious, they're going to take your license one of these days."

"You know what, fuck—"

"Here we are," Chris said, pulling the car over to the side of the road. "You've got a half an hour to get through security and see the judge. Tamper down the attitude, and pay your fines again."

Gian flipped the enforcer off as he pushed out of the car. Leaning back in, he pointed at Chris and said, "This isn't over."

"Maybe they'll send you for Driver's Ed, boss!"

Gian slammed the car door closed as hard as he fucking could in response to that nonsense. Chris wasted no time pulling back onto the road, likely knowing he had pushed his luck with his boss enough for the day. Turning, Gian faced the courthouse and the busy steps filled with people coming and going. This wasn't his first rodeo at the place, and likely wouldn't be his last.

It took Gian twenty-five minutes, just to get through security because of the long line of waiting people. He slipped into the courtroom designated for traffic offenses and had just enough time to sit his ass down before his name was called. Like a robot, he went through the motions of the court as he had done many times before.

The only ticket Gian chose to dispute was the speeding ticket, because fuck, he had *not* been speeding that day. Since the officer in question didn't show up, the judge tossed it out. Gian was still left with two demerits off his license, and a nearly thousand-dollar fine.

"Pay within thirty days, or on floor four," the judge ordered, his gravel hitting down with a loud enough bang to make Gian's headache pound.

Great.

Chris was going to have a field day with this nonsense.

Gian wanted to get the whole day over with, and while he could pay at home on the government website, he headed through the maze of people for the bank of elevators. One elevator opened, and a flood of people came out. Gian bolted for that one, not wanting to wait for the next. A few climbed in behind him, and the doors closed. From ground floor, the elevator went up one, stopped, and dropped half of the people off. Only one other person climbed in.

At the third floor, one used mainly in the courthouse for private consultations before appearances, the only other person got off the elevator. In their haste, they bumped into the one person coming on.

Cara Rossi.

She didn't see him right away, as she was too busy glaring at the asshole over her shoulder who hadn't even bothered to apologize for running into her. But when she did see him, the door was starting to close, she was already on the elevator, and Gian was frozen in place.

Cara seemed to be in the same state.

"Gian," she said.

That was it.

That was all she said.

Just his *name.*

And good God, how he missed that sound coming out of her mouth.

The elevator moved up, closer to his floor.

Gian didn't know *why*, as he knew better than to corner Cara, but the part of him that hadn't seen her in three months, the piece of him that had been lost and torn and so fucking useless, made him move. He pulled the emergency switch, and the elevator jerked to a halt. A red light came on, illuminating the space. A bell-like sound dinged through the speakers.

He was well aware of the camera just above his head, but since he didn't plan on doing anything that would get them in shit, he ignored it for the moment.

Cara shifted in her heels, the black dress she wore showed off all kinds of leg and skin, but was still long enough to be appropriate. "This is a courthouse, Gian, not your personal place of business or something. You can't just shut off an elevator."

"I just did," he said quietly.

"And someone will start it back up if you don't push the switch again."

"So be it, but it gives me a minute."

"To do what?" she asked.

Gian wasn't sure how to answer that, so he went with the blunt truth that had been stabbing at him for months. "To just look at you, say hello, anything, Cara."

"And if I'm not interested in any of that?"

"Then say so."

Cara only stared at him, pain reflecting in her blue eyes. It killed him that he had been the one to do that to her—that his lies did this to *them*. He no longer wanted to excuse his actions, and he knew they couldn't be explained away, but he still wanted *her*.

He loved her.

So badly.

"I did tell you," Cara whispered, "three months ago when I left your penthouse. I told you then, Gian."

"And I've left you alone, haven't I?"

"Yes, but—"

"You should know that I think about you all the fucking time, Cara, even when I know it's the last thing I should be doing. I miss you, constantly. I'm alone all the time, too, even when I'm not, and it's not even your fault. I know I did this. I fucked up, I know. I'm sorry, *mon ange*. I would do it a thousand ways differently, if I could, now."

"Except you can't," Cara said, a fire returning to her eyes and a heat in her tone. "You lied and lied and lied *more*, Gian."

"I didn't tell you the whole story, but I didn't purposely keep it from you."

"It, you say. *It*. Come on, say what *it* is. Your *wife*."

Gian drew in a slow breath, murmuring, "Yeah, my wife. Estranged, spoiled, difficult, hateful, bitter, but yes, *my* wife, Cara."

"And how is she? Your wife, I mean."

"Pleased in her place," he replied frankly.

He had nothing else to offer in that regard.

Elena wasn't worth it to him, not after everything.

"I hate you," Cara said so softly he strained to hear the words. "I hate that I want to say things right now to hurt you, *only* to hurt you, Gian. I hate that I want you to know what it felt like to trust you, and then watch you fucking ruin it like you did. I hate you for doing that to me."

He could work with hate, maybe.

Hate was passionate, too.

Like love.

"You broke my heart, Gian."

"Well, I hope my heart has been a suitable replacement, Cara. Because you still have mine, and you didn't bother to give it back. It's like waking up with a giant hole in my chest every single day. I can't *not* know it's gone. I always know. And maybe I don't have any right to say that at all, but there it is."

Cara glanced away, but he saw the wetness in her eyes all the same.

"I'm sorry," Gian said again as the first tear slipped from the corner of Cara's eye. "I hate me, too."

Tears meant something—she wasn't numb and she wasn't cold. Not to him or what had happened, anyway. It meant there was a part of her that wasn't done or hadn't entirely moved on from everything. She hadn't moved on from them.

"Are you done now?" Cara asked. "Have you gotten what you wanted? Can I go?"

He wanted to say no. He had her barricaded in an elevator, and God only knew how long he would be able to keep her there. He could finally force her to listen to the shit he had to say, if he wanted to.

Gian had a feeling that would not help him with Cara, only hurt him. He couldn't force her back to his side, he couldn't demand her there, and he wouldn't ever lie to her again to have her with him, either.

If she wanted him, wanted to be *with* him, he needed her to do that on her own. She would then understand it was because she wanted that, too, and had done so, knowing exactly what it meant for both of them.

He couldn't give her what she deserved. He couldn't be her husband, or live with her in a public fashion. She would never be looked at with the same respect his wife would, and in fact, would face a barrage of shit *just* because she wasn't his wife.

And the titles she would wear because of his selfishness?

Homewrecker. Whore. Mistress. Slut. *Goomah.*

Gian could keep going, too. He'd heard them all be slung at the woman his grandfather had loved for decades, a woman Corrado barely spoke about to anyone. How could those same people justify shaming someone, when they didn't even know her or why she made her choices?

Why would Gian knowingly do that to Cara?

He loved her, so why hurt her more?

Gian stepped closer to Cara, and she didn't move away. Instead, she watched him carefully, with a stone-still body, painted red lips, and eyes that cut him to the core. He reached up, the side of his hand brushing along her cheek to push back the stray curl, before his thumb swept under her eye to wipe away the tear stain.

She was still so beautiful. Like fucking life in his hands.

"I didn't mean to do this," he told her.

Cara nodded. "Yeah, I know, but you still did, Gian."

"And what I said, before you walked out on me that day, remains the same."

"You tried to say a lot."

"I have only ever loved you," Gian murmured as he leaned forward and pressed a soft kiss to Cara's forehead. His thumb stroked her cheek, and she didn't move away, but he felt the wetness of her tears slip down to his skin away. "And I'm sorry that it hurts you, Cara. I'm sorry that I hurt you. I'm sorry that I love you."

"Me, too."

Gian reached behind Cara and pushed the emergency switch on the elevator. It took a couple of seconds for the machine to respond, for the red light to go off, and for the elevator to move again. Cara turned away from him, then, pressing the second-floor button.

At his floor, Gian expected the people and security waiting there as the door opened to let him out. He shrugged off their questions, giving no answer as to what happened to stop the elevator.

Behind him, he heard Cara whisper as he walked out, "I miss you, too."

For them, he had been sure it was far too late. He had done that, not her.

But was it?

• • •

"Drive," Gian demanded the second he shut the car door.

Chris glanced at his boss through the rearview mirror. "Shit, that bad?"

"*Drive.*"

Quickly, the car pulled off onto the road, but the enforcer was still keeping one eye on Gian. It made him feel like a bug under a microscope. He couldn't hide the fact he was emotionally unsettled—sad, haunted, and angry all at once.

He couldn't hide shit when it came to Cara.

"You know I was just joking about the whole losing your license thing, right?"

"I didn't lose my license. I paid the fucking fines. Take me home."

"Boss—"

"Shut up and drive," Gian snapped.

"You got it, boss."

Chris didn't ask or say another thing. The man made no jokes as he navigated city traffic, and headed in the direction of Gian's penthouse. Gian, on the other hand, stewed in his fucking mess of emotions the entire way, alternating between glaring out the window, and hiding his clenched hands in his pockets.

He had paid his fines, and then gotten the hell out of the courthouse as fast as he possibly could. He feared that if he ran into Cara again, he wouldn't have as much control the second time around. He thought it was very possible that he might just grab her, make her listen, and have her talk to him more than what she already had.

Gian was an *idiot*.

It was only the ringing of his phone that brought him out of his frustrated daze. He didn't even bother to check the caller ID as he swiped the screen and then put it to his ear. The usual, causal Italian and French greeting he answered with was gone because of his current mood, leaving a rude bark in its place.

"What?" he snarled into the phone.

"Well, hello to you too, asshole."

Gian's anger kicked up a notch or two at his wife's voice. "What do you want, Elena?"

"Rough day?"

"Do you care?"

"Not really," she answered sweetly.

"Why are you calling me on a Tuesday?"

He wasn't due back at the mansion until tomorrow evening, at the latest. He didn't spend every day and evening there, if he could help it. Usually, he found excuses. As long as it *appeared* that he was in a relationship with his wife, then no one would bother to look too deeply into what was actually going on.

That was good enough for Gian.

As it was, this façade took enough work.

"Dinner, with my father. It's coming up. He called, and wanted me to remind you."

Fuck.

Gian's irritation managed not to spill over into the phone when he said, "Great, anything else?"

"Nope."

Wonderful.

He hung up without a goodbye, and didn't feel guilty for it. After all, Elena would do the same for him.

FOUR

"Quaint little place, isn't it?"

Cara's head popped up, and her nerves instantly bloomed at the sight of Frankie Ricci. He seemed relaxed, with his hands shoved in his pockets and a small smile on his face.

The coffee shop buzzed with noise around them.

"Frankie, hey," Cara greeted.

"Studying?"

She closed her spread-open books. "Trying. Sit."

He did, taking the only other chair at the table. She couldn't help but wonder, when he looked at her, was he seeing Lea and not *her*?

"You all right?" Frankie asked.

Cara shrugged. "So, so."

"I didn't expect to get a call from you, and especially not one to meet up."

"I, uh … was in a shitty place for a bit."

Cara packed her books away. It had taken her months just to gain up the courage to contact Frankie, never mind considering what they would actually talk about. She had *lots* to ask and say. Whether he would answer … that was the question.

"Thanks for agreeing to meet me," Cara said.

Frankie leaned back in the chair, his posture softening. "No problem. I noticed you've been quiet lately."

"Quiet?"

"Not so … out and about." Frankie smiled, adding, "With the boss."

"Gian."

He lifted a hand as if to say, *who else*.

Cara cleared her throat. "I haven't been out with Gian in three months."

"Ah."

"You don't sound surprised."

"Because I'm not," he replied. "I'm even less surprised because I know his wife has taken a more active role in his business side of life. More than she ever did when they first got married. Kind of forces you into the back seat, doesn't it?"

Cara bristled. "I'm not *with* him at all."

"I didn't assume that, either."

Cara checked her impulsive defensiveness. "I'm sorry, don't mind me. It's a knee-jerk reaction. I feel like everyone I met knew what was happening, everybody except for me. No one thought to tell me that he was married, or that I was an affair."

Frankie's expression didn't change. "Define 'affair' for me, Cara."

"Why?"

"Because your definition of it won't fit with a lot of people's opinions of the word."

"Really?"

Frankie nodded once. "That's what I said."

"He's married."

"Yes."

"He was involved with me in a relationship."

"Again, yes," Frankie said.

"Then that is an affair," Cara pointed out.

Frankie still didn't look entirely bothered by Cara's reasoning. "I mean, technically, sure. But only because men who join our ... thing, aren't allowed to be divorced, for the most part. Some do, sure, but they know they're never going fucking anywhere. Gian, being an underboss at the time, couldn't afford something like a divorce, given the circumstances of his marriage."

"Circumstances like?" Cara pressed.

"That's something he'd have to answer. I just know arrangements aren't usually made to be broken."

"He was still having an affair with me. He made me his mistress and he didn't even have the decency to tell me."

"Because he didn't have paper stamped from a proper divorce," Frankie replied softly. "After how many years of being separated from his wife, is he allowed to have a relationship with someone else? Even though they were clearly separated, why do words like affair have to be tossed into it? Why does the fact he's married—but again, separated—have to be the first thing to be brought up in conversation? Seems unfair to him."

"That's easy for you to say, to defend his actions, sure. But people still consider her to be his wife. They are still married." Cara glanced away. "Does it seem unfair because you, too, were miserable in your relationship with your wife, and occasionally found a happy pause with my sister?"

Frankie blew out a slow breath. "A happy *pause*?"

"You're still with your wife, aren't you?"

"Yes. We have one child, a girl. Our first boy is on the way, due in a month. We're very much together. Happily, I might add."

"Happily. Even after what you did?"

"My wife and I were a lot like Lea and I were, before the pregnancy thing got in the way. Casual, no strings, and we didn't get too deep with one another on an emotional level. And then the pregnancy came, so our family forced us to do the *right* thing." Frankie's tone twisted bitterly, and his lips curved into a sneer. "We didn't want to be married. She didn't want me around, and I didn't want to be there, either. You think she *didn't* know? She knew, but she didn't care. She didn't consider us together, even if everybody else did because we weren't divorced."

"Oh," Cara murmured.

"Our unhappiness meant nothing to everyone else, as long as we continued doing the right thing for who we are," Frankie continued with a heavy sigh.

"And so, Lea ..."

"Was there," he said, "and it was stupid and easy, but it hurt us both a lot, too."

"And what about your wife?"

"Our daughter was born, and I was over there a lot more. I stayed with her, to help with the baby and whatever else. You could say the baby brought us closer, as silly as that might sound. It'd been a while since I had seen Lea at all when she died," Frankie admitted, frowning. "There was no proper breakup or goodbye, whatever. It was hard, and it set me back for a while with my wife because I felt like I couldn't explain what was happening inside my head. Circumstances being what they were, and all."

"But did you?"

"Eventually." Frankie chuckled. "She's pretty amazing, my wife."

"Did you love my sister?" Cara dared to ask.

"Not in the right way," Frankie said without even thinking about it. "Not in a way she should have been, not like I do with my wife now. It took a while to figure that out, too."

"In an unhealthy way?"

"Exactly."

Cara tapped her fingernails to the table, settled in her heart, yet restless in her soul. "Thanks for meeting up with me to talk about this. I know it's private, and you really didn't need to tell me anything, if you didn't want to."

"I don't think this was only for you to talk and learn about Lea."

"Well—"

"I mean, you can say that, but I don't think it is. I think that you've gotten yourself tangled up in your own situation with a man, and like your sister, you keep running—"

"I haven't gone back once, actually."

"But you consider it. You *want* to."

Cara wouldn't look Frankie in the eye. "I'm not like Lea, and I'm not like your wife, Frankie. I have a line that I don't want to cross, and I didn't appreciate being forced over it without even knowing what was happening."

"Fair enough. Question for you, then."

"Sure."

"Had Gian said upfront that he had a wife—estranged for years, basically separated from, whatever—would you have continued seeing him?"

"I don't know," Cara answered.

But her voice wavered.

She had taken a second to answer.

Frankie continued staring at her, and in that moment, she didn't think he looked at her and saw Lea at all. He just saw a confused, sad woman.

"I think you do know, Cara. Again, circumstances, and all. They make all the difference."

Cara made a dismissive sound. "Well, it certainly does now, anyway. Like you said, his wife is present, apparently."

"Public opinion counts for too much in this life, unfortunately, and we made men are entirely to blame for that, too."

She didn't reply to that.

She didn't know how to.

• • •

Cara fidgeted in an attempt to soothe her nerves as the maître D' of the posh restaurant scrolled through reservations on a tablet. It didn't help, and considering it had been months since she had dressed up and gone out on a formal date, she felt all kinds of awkward.

"Name?" the man asked.

"Rossi. Cara."

"Ah, here we are. Follow me."

Cara managed to get distracted by the high-vaulted ceilings of the restaurant, and the crystal chandeliers hanging over every single table. She was led closer to the open concept kitchen of the restaurant, and further away from the bar.

"Miss," the maître D' said, bringing Cara from her daze. "Your table."

Cara thanked the man, and sat down at the empty table. Checking her phone, she noted she wasn't early, but she wasn't late, either.

Nathan—the doctor she met at the café—arrived less than five minutes after she had sat down, wearing a proper suit and a smile. "Cara."

He took her hand, bent down, and kissed two of her knuckles, allowing her to stay seated. Then, he too took the only other chair available at the table.

"Why do you seem surprised to see that I showed up?" Cara asked.

Nathan laughed, taking the menus from the server before shooing the man away. "No promises, remember? That's what you told me when we met. I get a random text, just as I'm coming out of a routine surgery, that asks about dinner, and nothing else. That doesn't seem a little on-the-fence to you?"

Cara had to give him that. "All right, fair enough."

"You look beautiful."

"Thank you. And this place is ..." Cara waved a hand high. "Amazing."

"It helps to know people sometimes," Nathan joked. "The owner is a friend from way back. I always get reservations last minute, when others can't.

"Nice to know."

"Drinks before food?"

"No on the drinks. I think I'll let you order the food for both of us. Surprise me."

Nathan flashed her with a smile. There was nothing necessarily wrong with the man. He was charming, good-looking, and decent, by all standards. He looked fit, well-dressed, and had a good path in his life. He was everything that she should want in a man, because he was safe and nice and appropriate.

Cara felt nothing looking at him.

Nathan did nothing for her.

Sad, really.

She just wanted to feel normal again.

It didn't help that it felt like someone was watching her. Cara tried to brush the odd sensation off and ignore it. Despite regretting her spur of the moment decision to text Nathan for a date, Cara decided to stick it out.

It was only after the food had arrived, and Cara picked at the dish set in front of her, that Nathan cleared his throat loudly.

Cara glanced up at him. "Yes?"

"You didn't hear a word I just said, did you?"

Had he been talking?

Ouch.

"Sorry," Cara said. "I'm not very good company, am I?"

Nathan smiled, but she could see the truth in his stare. "Let's be honest here, Cara. We're not going to repeat this, are we?"

"Probably not. It's not you ... it's me, really. I've got no business going on dates at the moment, I think. I thought trying might help. It didn't."

"Yet, you asked me out tonight."

"A shitty attempt at something different," Cara said in explanation.

Nathan didn't look like he understood, but who could?

Cara was a mess.

And not in a good way.

Nathan took her rejection in style, thankfully. Although, he was quieter through the rest of the meal. He offered to walk Cara out of the restaurant once they were done, but she only agreed to let him walk her to the bar. She didn't want a drink, just a second to sit alone and think.

At the bar, Nathan leaned in, his hand resting on her lower back, and kissed her on the cheek. "Thank you for coming out with me tonight."

Cara laughed lightly. "You've got to be one of the strangest men I have ever met. Rejection doesn't bother you a bit, does it?"

"We win some, we lose some."

"Thanks for … not being an asshole."

Nathan's grin widened, and Cara let him kiss her cheek once more. "Enjoy the rest of your evening, Cara. You *do* have my number, in case you ever want to use it."

But she wouldn't use it.

Cara watched Nathan stroll out of the restaurant with his hands in his pockets, and no worse for wear than he had been when he first arrived. The bartender took her order for ice water in a glass, and Cara surveyed the rest of the restaurant while she waited.

It was only when her gaze landed on a familiar pair of dark eyes that she finally understood why it felt like someone had been watching her.

Gian.

He sat at a corner table, tucked away in a quieter part of the restaurant with dim lighting, and what looked to be a glass of whiskey in front of him. Across from him sat an older gentleman, dressed just as well as he was, although the man was several pounds heavier around his middle. His guest seemed entirely oblivious to the fact that Gian was no longer engaged in their conversation, but rather, focused on Cara at the bar like she was the only person in the room.

His stare did not feel like it usually did.

It was hard.

So cold.

Angry, even.

Those dark eyes of his pinned her in place, lips smoothed into a thin, grim line, and his sharp jaw tensed as he looked her over. She didn't miss the slide of his gaze darting to the left, in the direction Nathan had gone. His hand clenched around his glass tight enough for Cara to see his knuckles go white.

Great.

Cara would recognize that look anywhere, even if Gian had no business sporting it. He was fucking jealous.

All over, unnecessarily, completely *jealous*. And fuck, it looked good on him. Like every other goddamn expression he wore, from his indifference to his rage, to his sweetness in the mornings, and the way he looked when he fucked her. It all looked damn good.

She had just spent a little more than an hour with a man who was everything that Gian was not, in certain ways. She hadn't managed to feel anything for him, not even an ounce of the confusing mess she felt with just a *glance* at Gian Guzzi.

How was that fair?

She should be over this ridiculous mess by now.

Even *Gian* had told her that she would be fine—that she was the kind of woman who could fall again and again, yet manage to brush herself off and move on with her life. Yet, there she was, *not moving the fuck on.*

Frustrated, Cara turned away from Gian, refusing to meet his stare again or acknowledge his presence. She had gone months without running into him in the city, and now, in a matter of just a couple of weeks, she had run into him twice.

Someone from up above was laughing at her. Clearly, she had no guardian angels looking out for her.

She snatched up the glass of ice water when the bartender finally brought her the drink, and took a sip. Maybe, if she just pretended like she hadn't noticed Gian twenty feet away, he would opt to go the same route she did.

Cara hoped for too much.

Just as she finished her water and slid the glass back across the bar, she felt his presence slip in behind her. It was fucking crazy and stupid and intense how that worked. The very fact that he didn't even need to speak, or make a noise, and she just *knew*.

Knew that he was there.

Knew that he was looking at her.

Knew him.

"Are you going to corner me somewhere and make me talk again?" Cara asked without turning around.

"No," Gian said, his voice a rough murmur.

"Good, because I'm about to leave."

"Is your date waiting outside?"

"That's none of your business," Cara replied.

"Maybe not, but I asked, Cara."

She turned slowly to face Gian, taking note that he still seemed a hell of lot more tense than he normally did. Even with his hands shoved in his pockets, she could still see his unease in his narrowed gaze and tight jaw.

"You have no business asking anything," Cara reminded him.

Gian's jaw ticked. "So you don't want to answer, then?"

"There's nothing to tell, and you *don't get to ask.*"

"I—"

"Don't you have a guest at your table?" she interrupted, her annoyance rising fast.

"It was over ten minutes ago, but it took him this long to realize I wasn't interested in the conversation he was offering. Enough about me, let's get back to you."

Cara bristled. "Excuse me?"

"Who was that man?"

"None of your bus—"

"Cara." The quiet way he said her name, so heavy and thick, made her back straighten as a shiver crawled up her spine. *Damn him.* Gian took one step closer to Cara, ensuring she couldn't move, as she was backed into the goddamn bar. "At least tell me who he is, that's all."

"A date, someone I met. Happy?"

Gian's eyes flashed with his jealousy, and she hated him for that, too. "No, I'm not *happy*."

"Well, don't ask if you don't really want to know."

"How long?" he asked.

"I'm not answering that one."

"I've seen him here before, with the owner. I could always … ask around."

Cara stiffened a bit. "You have no right to do that, Gian. Whether or not I see someone, or go out with someone, or *fuck* someone, isn't for you to know or have an opinion on. I'm not yours, now. You don't get a say in anything I do. Learn that, and fast."

By the time she had finished her tirade, her voice had turned into a harsh whisper.

Gian barely blinked a lash at her rage.

"It fucked me up," he said, shrugging one shoulder, "seeing you out with somebody else. Smiling like you do, and it just … fucked me up, Cara. I thought, who the fuck is he, and what in the hell is she doing, and *why?* And it's fucking disgusting how fast I thought about finding out who he was just to kill him. And you—Jesus, Cara—you don't even realize how pissed off it makes me that you *smiled* for him, *mon ange*."

Cara sucked in a low breath, willing it to give her some sense of calm. It didn't help.

Screw him for the fact he made her hot and bothered, and all he had to do was *threaten* a man he didn't even know. God, she hated this and the confusing way it left her feeling.

"You don't get to say those kinds of things to me. We're not together. I can date whoever I want. I already told you that. And stop calling me your pretty French pet names, Gian."

"Why? It still fits. My angel."

"I'm not *yours*," Cara snapped. "Not anymore."

Gian smirked, his arrogance becoming all the more apparent. "Oh, Cara, you're always going to be mine. *Sempre, amore*."

"I beg to differ."

"Do you want to play this game?"

"Gian—"

"You *are* mine, Cara, even if you're not with me. And do you want to know how I know that, sweet girl?"

Cara refused to look him in the eye. He stepped close enough that his body pressed against hers, but she couldn't move away. She kept her head turned to the side, even when his hand slid up to cup her cheek and his fingers threaded into her hair.

"I know you're still mine, because there's no way on earth you could tell me that man, or any other man, knows anything about you worth knowing."

"Stop, Gian."

Why was her voice so goddamn weak?

And why did she want to turn into his palm, not away like she was? *This isn't fair.*

"Has he, or anyone else, even touched you since me? Can you even *stand* to let someone have you the way you let me have you?"

Cara's gaze cut to his fast. "*Gian.*"

"Tell me."

"No."

"No, you won't tell or no, no one has touched you?"

Both of them.

Cara refused to say that out loud. Gian only smiled like he already knew the fucking truth, like he could see it written all over her face.

"Right. I would be willing to bet he knows *fuck all* when it comes to you," Gian said with a dark, husky laugh. "Like the way you won't get your ass out of bed in the morning, or all the little secrets you like to hold onto because you're locked up way too tight in your heart, and it takes a fucking sledge hammer to get through."

Gian inched closer, his unique scent soaking into Cara's lungs like a familiar drug. Liquor and leather and *man*. "Let's be honest, Cara, he doesn't know the shit that matters, really. He probably doesn't know what you like, either. I bet he doesn't know how you liked to be choked when you come, or the way you beg like a good little slut to have your ass filled when your—"

Cara's hand came up swift and *hard*. She didn't even think about it. Her palm cracked against Gian's cheek with enough force to silence the nearby tables of people.

"Excuse me, miss, do you need anything?"

The sound of the bartender's voice had Gian's burning gaze flying over Cara's shoulder, probably burrowing a fucking hole into the poor man who dared to intrude.

"It's fine," Cara said. "We're perfectly fine."

"If you're sure …?"

"She's sure," Gian uttered through clenched teeth.

Emotions warred within Cara, heating her cheeks and making her body vibrate. Her palm stung, but she didn't care. She glared at Gian, daring him to say another word, even when her hand dropped back down to her side. He didn't look away, but rather, his smirk grew sinful, like he had gotten exactly the reaction he wanted.

"I can say more, if you want," he said.

"Shut your mouth. How dare you, Gian?"

"Tell me I'm wrong. Tell me any man, except *me*, knows those things, and owns those things where you're concerned. *Tell me*."

She couldn't.

"You can't say it, can you?" he asked.

"Fuck you."

"Tell me to get the hell away from you, then."

Cara didn't.

She hated herself for that, too.

What she despised even more, was when he kissed her—hard, demanding, and rough, just the way she liked the most—she didn't push him away. No, she fisted his jacket and bought him closer, she sighed at the familiarity of his hand curving around her throat and his tongue dancing with hers. She soaked in his scent, reveled in his taste, and hated herself for every second of it.

She wanted more, so she just pulled him closer.

Every bit of anger and disgust came out in Cara's kiss, and even more bled away the longer she didn't force Gian to stop. Not when his thumb pressed into her racing pulse, or his teeth bit into her lower lip.

She couldn't breathe, but fucking hell, she was awake and alive again for the first time in months.

Why did it have to be like this?

Why him and her?

Why?

He provoked her, she knew. His words had been *meant* to provoke her into this. She was weak enough to let him.

Cara's lips tingled from the brutality of Gian's kiss long after he had pulled away. *God*, she loved it.

Gian watched her like a predator, refusing to move his gaze even an inch, and not letting her drop her stare. She saw his jealousy still lit up like fireworks in his eyes, but she found so much more staring back at her, too.

A man she had missed for months. A man she still loved, though she knew it was bad. A man she wasn't even sure she knew.

So, why was he so familiar?

"You did that on purpose," Cara said, her accusation coming out quieter than she meant for it to. "You provoked me on purpose, Gian."

"I did nothing that you didn't want me to, *mon ange*."

She hated that pet name, too, because she didn't hate it at all when he said it.

Cara had damn near forgotten they were still in the restaurant, standing at the bar. It became impossible to ignore when the sound of clattering utensils from a nearby table broke her from her daze, and she realized how very public of a scene they had just made.

She finally dropped Gian's stare.

"Come with me," Gian murmured.

Cara shook her head. "No, and you know why."

"Don't do that, Cara. Don't refuse me when you know damn well that it's the very last thing you want to do. Come with me, be with me for a night, and fuck the rest. What's the issue?"

"You know exactly—"

Gian stepped away from her, cocking an eyebrow high as he did so. "We both could be doing far better things than standing here, arguing about nonsense and details that will never matter to me when it comes to us. And before you even spit it out of your pretty mouth, I don't think they matter all that much to you right now, either. I am leaving, my car will be waiting at the curb. I'll give you ten minutes, and then I'm gone. Come with me or don't, but I won't stand here and argue with you for another second."

Cara thought he was joking, or bluffing. She should have known better. Gian didn't joke or bluff.

He gave her a soft kiss on her cheek, and then he turned on his heel and headed for the front of the restaurant. There was so much she had wanted to shout at his back in that moment. Fuck him for the *details*, as he called them. Fuck him for making her choose like this. Fuck him for making her love him, breaking her heart, and then doing this to her too.

Why wasn't she stronger?

Why wasn't she a better woman?

When it came to Gian, apparently Cara was nothing more than a stupid, foolish girl who had no control over herself, nor did she want to have limits where he was concerned.

She watched the clock behind the bar.

At eight minutes, her heart won out.

Gian said nothing when Cara slid into his car.

FIVE

"I thought you didn't do angry sex," Cara said from her perch on the edge of Gian's bed. "Wasn't it you who said that was unhealthy?"

"I'm not angry."

She might be.

He sure as hell wasn't.

How could Gian be angry when, at the moment, he had Cara stripped down to nothing but her skin, in his penthouse, on his bed? How could he possibly be *angry*?

"You're not even a little bit mad?"

"About what?" he asked, shedding the final bits of his clothing.

"I did hit you."

He shrugged. "I *did* provoke you."

"I knew you did that on purpose."

"And look where you are now, my sweet girl."

Cara's eyes flashed with her desire and irritation. "Yes, how stupid of me, I fell right back in your bed."

"Where you belong, Cara."

Her red lips curved at the edges in a half-hearted smile. "You're impossible."

"So you've said a few times before."

Gian shoved his boxer-briefs down, not missing Cara's gaze dropping to his prominent erection. He'd been as hard as fucking steel from the moment he'd touched her at the restaurant.

It was a serious problem. He intended to rectify it as soon as possible.

Gian crossed the small bit of space between him and where Cara sat on his bed. She stared up at him, still and waiting. He wanted nothing more than to feed into the dark, debasing shit running through his mind. All the urges he couldn't fulfill elsewhere, and the needs that weren't helped with his memories of Cara.

He held back.

Barely.

"Could you snap your fingers for me?" she asked sweetly.

Too sweetly.

"Why?"

"At least then I can say I came running for something when you called."

Fuck.

Gian let out a hard breath. "Cara, stay or go."

She didn't move, neither did her blue gaze—the window into the most beautiful soul he had ever had the pleasure of knowing.

"But don't sit here and make it seem like I'm not giving you a choice," he continued when she stayed silent. "I want you here. I have wanted you here since the day I let you walk out, but don't make this into some hate-fuck session. It's never going to be that and if you need that to justify how you're going to feel tomorrow, then leave. Right now."

Her stare slid away from his. "You can't let me have anything, can you?"

"Not when I can see right through your shit, *bella*."

"You're making this hard on me."

"From where I'm standing, it seems pretty fucking easy."

"Of course it would, to *you*."

Gian opened his mouth to respond, but his air caught in his throat when Cara's hands reached for him, her fingers circled tight around his cock. She slid her palm under his sac to cradle his balls. Firm, long strokes of her hand—tight as fuck at the base, and a little looser at the tip—had his head falling back, and a thick groan escaping his chest. His cock jerked in her hand, when her thumb rolled one of his balls between her soft palm and her fingers. Gently, and not too rough, but shit if that didn't make him flex his hips forward into her strokes for more.

He didn't give a shit if it was her hands, her mouth, or her cunt. As long as his dick was on it, in it, or soaked by it. As long as she was touching, fucking, or doing *something* to him, all was well in his world.

Whatever it was, she was his heaven.

It was his *drug*.

How long had it been since she touched him?

Too damn long.

"You were right," Cara said, "at the restaurant, I mean."

"Do tell."

"There's been no one since you. There *can't* be. They're not you, Gian."

"I'm not sorry for that," he murmured.

"I didn't think you would be."

He was *far* too pleased about it, actually.

"Don't be *nice*," Cara said softly, making him look down at her. "Don't be soft, and sweet, and *good*. Don't do that tonight because you want to fuck with my head after everything that happened. *We* don't do that, Gian."

"Cara—"

"*Don't.*"

"Cara," Gian murmured in a half-groan, his fingers weaving into her hair and tugging firmly enough to make her stop. He found a familiar lust and love swirling in the blues of her eyes, but he saw a wariness there, too.

It cut him deep. "When have I ever done that to you?"

She didn't hesitate. "Never."

"And I won't."

A single nod answered him back.

"Now … *Jésus Christ*, get that mouth of yours on my fucking cock. I better see those goddamn lipstick stains of yours where I like, Cara. Be a good girl, like I know you can be, and suck my fucking dick."

She did what he demanded, and it was glorious. A warm, wet familiar bliss that cleared his mind and made him silent in one single second. All she had to do was wrap her pretty red lips around his cock, suck him hard and deep enough into her throat that her muscles contracted along his length, and he was done for.

God, did she know how to suck cock.

It made Gian *crazy*.

Her tongue flicked against the throbbing vein on the underside of his dick, while her sharp teeth scraped along his length on the withdrawal. Gian didn't need to urge or help Cara on when it came to sucking him off. She knew exactly what to do. That didn't stop him from tugging harder on her hair to feel her happy little moans vibrate his shaft. It didn't stop him from flexing his hips forward when she took him deeper, just to see her sly grin form around his dick as her eyes watered.

"You're so good with that mouth, *mon ange. Succhiami il cazzo*."

Suck my cock.

Suck my cock.

He said it three times—once for each language he spoke.

It was only when his spine started to stiffen and his balls got too fucking tight that he finally pulled Cara away. As much as he wanted to watch her suck him dry, he *needed* to be buried as deep as he possibly could be into her cunt when he finally came.

Too damn long, he reminded himself.

Cara was already reaching for him before he could push her back to the bed, her thighs opening for his body to fit against hers as his mouth slammed down on her parted, wet lips. She sighed when he pulled her hair, making her head tilt back so he could kiss her throat, and bite her shoulder hard enough to leave a mark. He could feel her heart race like thunder when she slipped a hand between their bodies and fitted his cock to her cunt. The wetness of her arousal soaked the head of his dick, and he thrust in.

Home, and *heaven*, and *bliss*.

Those were the things he found when he finally buried his cock balls-deep inside Cara Rossi for the first time in months.

Love, and *selfish*, and *more* were the words that slipped through his mind when she shuddered under him, and her nails raked stinging lines along his back.

"Fucking take me," he ground out against the hollow of her throat. "Take all of me, Cara, and show me how much you want it. Show me how good you are for it, sweet girl."

Cara only mumbled a broken cry of his name. Her back arched hard from the bed while her legs opened even wider. She pushed her head back farther into the sheets, and her teeth clenched around another whine as he fucked her harder.

He couldn't get deep enough.

He couldn't fuck hard enough.

Not enough to feel like he was ever going to satisfy how much he needed, loved, and wanted this fucking woman.

"I want ... *I want* ..." Cara's words melted together in a gasping breath that he couldn't understand. But with every thrust of his body against hers, with every slide of his cock inside the wet clenching heat of her cunt, he knew what it was. She wanted to come, and he needed that too. More than his own pleasure, he needed *hers*. "*Please*."

He knew what she wanted for that, too.

Not nice, not easy, and not soft or slow.

She wanted his hand on her throat, taking away her air, and a brutal fucking that would ache when she was finally done coming. He gave her exactly that, reveling in the way her cunt clamped down on his cock when his fingers curved tightly to her throat and how the blues of her eyes sparkled with bliss when his rhythm turned harsher.

Shit, her orgasm came on fast.

Even with his hand on her throat, her scream was *beautiful*.

Gian thought he might be able to hold off his own need to come long enough to fuck her through it, and then get her on her knees to finish him off.

He was *wrong*.

He came hard, emptying every bit of cum into her cunt as the last shudder racked its way through Cara's body. His fingers loosened their hold on her throat—he'd never trusted his control to choke her while he came and he wasn't about to start testing the waters right then.

"Fuck, fuck, *fuck*," Gian mumbled.

He was too fucking sensitive and too damn weak all of the sudden. Pulling out of her warm pussy was the hardest thing he ever had to do, but he needed to so he could breathe.

Cara's light, breathless laughter echoed into the room. His cock—covered in their fluids—rested semi-hard against her thigh. He felt her fingertips slide along his length, and looked down to find her using their mingled cum to lubricate her clit as her fingers started stroking fast circles.

"Shit," Gian breathed. "That's fucking hot, Cara."

Her smile was sinful. "Watch me come again."

Jesus Christ.

His cock was already perking up.

"Watch me, Gian," Cara whispered.

All. Fucking. Night. Long.

• • •

"*Tabernac.*" Gian's curse came out as a low rumble, his irritation rising as he was forced to roll away from soft, naked skin in his bed. He couldn't let go of Cara completely, so he picked up the ringing cell phone on the nightstand and stroked a hand up her spine with his other. All of his frustration leaked into his tired voice when he answered the call with, "Do you know what goddamn time it is, and what in the *fuck* do you want?"

"Yeah, it's after nine and *Sunday*, Gian. Since when do you sleep in and where in the hell are *you*?"

Dom's voice made Gian sit up in the bed, but he still didn't stop touching Cara as he moved. She grounded him—her presence calmed him. He had been a mess for months and for a moment, he was okay.

"It's Sunday, Gian," Dom repeated. "Mass started already. Elena put out a call to a couple of people when you didn't show up this morning at the mansion, though you were supposed to be there last night. What the fuck?"

Saturday at the mansion.

Sunday at church with his wife.

Merda.

Gian had entirely skipped those plans after seeing Cara the night before. He hadn't intentionally done so, but something better came along, and those plans no longer mattered. He was surprised that Elena cared enough to call anyone and ask around about him, but that was probably because she was hoping his body showed up somewhere.

"Weren't you having dinner with her father last night?" Dom asked.

"Yeah, I had dinner with Gabriel."

"*And?*"

"And nothing. I forgot, I guess."

"You for—"

"Gian, is everything all right?"

Cara's question came out too loud in the quiet bedroom to be hidden. He shot her a reassuring smile, and stroked her back again, saying nothing. She tucked back into the blankets, happy as could be, but Gian knew his brother had heard her.

"Oh, well, shit," Dom said quickly.

"So, something came up," Gian muttered.

"Some*one*, you mean."

"Semantics."

"If you say so. Cara Rossi?" Dom asked.

Gian sighed, scrubbing a hand down his face. "I'm not in the mood, nor do I have the patience, to listen to anyone's bitching this morning, man."

"Yeah, sure. When did that happen again? How long?"

"*Or* your questions," Gian added. "I answer to God, my priest, and the Pope, but certainly not to you. Don't expect me to."

And Cara ...

Gian answered to her, too.

"What do I tell Ma and Dad ... or your wife, for that matter?"

"Apologize, say I wasn't feeling well. I'll be at the mansion before noon to deal with the other bit, since I need to grab some stuff anyway."

"Sure, sure," his brother said, sounding anything *but* sure.

"*Au revoir*, Dom."

Gian didn't bother to give his brother the chance to say goodbye back, before he hung up the phone. Setting it back to the nightstand, he immediately went back to Cara, his arms ensnaring her warm body and bringing her closer to him under the white sheets.

He didn't want to talk or think.

He just wanted to *be* for a while.

Cara's rhythmic breathing was too light, telling Gian that she hadn't fallen back asleep. He waited out her inevitable questions, but what she eventually said was not what he expected.

"I don't want to be that woman, Gian."

"Cara—"

"I don't want to be the other woman."

He swept her wild curls off her shoulder, giving him soft skin to kiss. He felt Cara's shiver work its way through her body, and so he kissed her again, just to feel it once more.

"I know," he murmured, his lips still pressed to her body.

"But here I am."

"Those are details, and I know they're the kind of details that matter to some, but they are *only* details, *bella mia*. You're not the other woman for me. You've always just been mine. There is no *other* here. There's one man and one woman. One man who loves *one* woman—I love you, Cara. That's it."

"One man with a wife," Cara said softly.

"She's certainly not mine, not in that sense," Gian said dryly. "On paper, maybe, but the rest ... no."

"I'm not sure if that makes it better, but I want it to. I wish it did, and I'm pretty sure that makes me a horrible person."

He pulled her closer still, letting her legs tuck in around his under the sheets, while his arm tightened around her midsection to keep her in place.

"Do you want to know anything about her or the—"

"No," Cara interjected swiftly, shutting him down.

Gian kissed her shoulder again. "All right."

"Do you have to go?"

"In a while, yes. I have to go to the mansion and grab some things for the week. I missed church, too, so my mother needs a visit now, to be sure I'm not dead."

"So, the mansion. Is that where … Elena, right?"

"Mmm."

"Is that where she lives?"

Gian let out a slow breath. "Yeah."

At his quiet confirmation of her suspicions, Cara stiffened in his arms.

"Would you stay, though?" Gian asked.

"For what?"

"I'll be back later today or tonight sometime. I'd like to come back to see you. We should talk, or something. Just talk, Cara. Without yelling or slapping, or fighting and fucking. Just *talk*."

"I don't want to be that woman, Gian," she repeated.

She hadn't refused his request, though.

Gian took that as a win. "But?"

"But I love you, too. I love you, and I want to hate you."

Yeah, that was the hard part.

It was every single reason why she was in his bed, instead of in her own. Because had he loved her even a little bit less, or perhaps in a better way, he would have left her alone to her business and life the night before.

Except he couldn't.

Because *love*.

Or, that's what he was going to keep telling himself. Otherwise, he would be forced to admit how selfish of a fucker he truly was.

"Stay," he said, kissing along the curve of Cara's shoulder. "Stay for me."

"Maybe."

It wasn't a no.

• • •

Gian grabbed one of the five new garment bags hanging in the walk-in closet. He used the second largest bedroom in the mansion, while his wife used the master bedroom, just across from his. He only kept clothes when it came to personal effects at the mansion, so that he could come and go as he liked, and it actually appeared as though he lived there.

Occasionally, he did business at the mansion, too. He had dinners for the men, and other nonsense that invited people into his "personal" space, though it was complete bullshit. Home was his penthouse, not this mansion.

He stripped down from the jeans and leather jacket he had tossed on before leaving the penthouse. He'd called his mother and promised dinner to make up for missing Mass, but she wouldn't appreciate him showing up in jeans.

A suit it was.

He had just pulled the shirt up over his head, when a clearing throat froze him in his tracks. Turning slightly to face the opened doorway of the walk-in closet, he found Elena standing there, staring at him.

"Do you need something?" he asked.

"It's good to see you're still alive."

"Is it?"

She just shrugged.

"Where were you when I came in?"

Elena flicked a loose, blonde curl over her shoulder. "Changing out of church clothes. I saw your car, so I came looking for you. Also, I could ask the same, Gian. Where were you last night and this morning?"

"Busy. Something came up."

Gian turned back to the suit he had set out, picking up the pants as he said, "Ma is expecting us for dinner. You don't have to go, but I would appreciate if you did."

"Whatever. How did dinner go with my father last night?"

"Same as it always does. Gabriel is … Gabriel."

Elena made an agreeable sound under her breath. "Did he want anything specific?"

"You have more contact with him lately than I do, so you tell me."

"He asked *you* to dinner, not me."

Gian rolled his eyes. "Like I said, it's the same shit it always is. Business, family, and you. Nothing new, nothing to worry about. He isn't about to climb through a window and steal you back in the night."

Elena didn't respond immediately and Gian shot a look over his shoulder to find she was staring at the floor, silent. She was as cold as ice, but there were buttons that a man could push, and she reverted into a shell of herself.

Gian had pushed that button.

"I could have phrased that better," he said.

Elena shrugged one shoulder. "I choose not to underestimate my father. He used me from the time I was fifteen to do his bidding and play his games, right up until the day I met you. It's only because he believes I'm no longer useful to him that he keeps a distance now, you know."

Gian grunted, displeased. "Yes, and then you used me. So how different are you two, really?"

"I used you to get away."

"It doesn't justify the mode, Elena."

She only smiled. "It got me what I wanted. I never needed to fuck another man to benefit my father, I only needed to fuck you. And after that, I didn't even need to do that, Gian. So yes, I got what I wanted."

"Yes, stuck in a marriage with me. Where we despise one another, where you lied to me about everything and tricked me with a fake pregnancy, and then losing—"

"I apologized for all of that!"

Gian spun fast on his heel, not hiding his anger. "That's the problem. You think because you spit out a few sad words, that it fixes what you did. It doesn't fix it, Elena. You've trapped me into this fucking hell with you. I'm so goddamn happy that you don't mind because of all the wonderful things you have, because fuck me, right? Fuck me and everything I might have wanted from life, Elena."

"I was taught that feelings didn't matter in this life, Gian. Only the end goal. Perhaps you should learn the same. My bad, that I happened to meet my goals before you did."

Feelings only mattered when they were hers.

That was what she meant to say.

Gian was not stupid.

"Get the fuck out, Elena."

"In a minute."

Gian snarled a warning at his wife over his shoulder, done with her nonsense and games for the day. Elena barely reacted. In fact, she continued standing in the doorway with her arms crossed and her eyes nailed to his back.

"What do you want that you haven't already bothered me with?" he asked, reaching his limit of patience.

"Who were you really with last night?"

Gian's shoulders stiffened. "I beg your pardon?"

"Who were you fucking?" Elena carefully enunciated each word. "That's why you didn't come here last night or to church this morning, right? You've got scratches all down your back. Jesus, she must have liked whatever it was you were doing to her. Doesn't that hurt? That's one thing you're quite good at—making a woman come again and again, I remember that well. Did she scream your name like a good little whore? Was it loud enough to drown out me and everyone else filling your thoughts?"

Gian reacted only to the fact Elena used the word whore. He spun fast on his heel. Elena took a giant step back, far enough out of the doorway that Gian was able to grab the door and slam it closed without hitting her.

Her voice stopped him before he closed it completely.

"Oh, someone's touchy. Is it her again, Gian, the one from before?"

Gian let the door slam in her face, determined not to give Elena a thing unless she pried it out of his dead hands. When a man gave her an inch, she took a mile and ran with it until he was a bleeding, useless, broken mess trailing behind her. It was just what she did, it was what she had been taught and Gian refused to *ever* play those games with his wife again.

The last time he had, he'd lost. Lost his freedom. Lost his rights. Lost what he thought was his child. He just fucking lost.

So no, fuck her, and her games.

"Cara, right?" Elena asked from behind the wood. "That's her name, isn't it? Are you screwing that whore again?"

"Go to hell, Elena, before I fucking send you there."

She laughed at him.

He wasn't surprised.

Story of their life …

• • •

"Elena didn't want to come?" Celeste asked as Gian kissed his mother's cheek.

He readied to speak the lie he had prepared, but whether or not his mother would fall for it was another story.

"She's not feeling well," he said.

Celeste frowned. "She was fine at church this morning. Wasn't she, Frederic?"

Gian's father nodded. "Seemed so, *Tesoro*."

"Well?" Celeste looked to Gian. "See, even he—"

"She's not feeling well," Gian repeated, "and I can't make her come to dinner when she isn't up for it, Ma."

"Fine."

His mother didn't sound particularly happy about it, though. He wasn't about to complain that Elena stayed home.

"What's for dinner?" Gian asked.

Celeste waved a hand, beckoning her son and husband to follow. Gian walked alongside his father, a few paces behind his mother, as Celeste described the meal that was waiting for him. As good as it sounded and for as hungry as he was, he only wanted to eat, spend a few minutes talking, and then get the hell out of there.

Cara would be waiting at his place for him.

Maybe …

He'd sent her a text earlier and gotten a reply. She had been at the penthouse then, but whether or not she still would be was another story.

Cara had a bad habit of overthinking.

Not that Gian blamed her.

"Sounds delicious, Ma," Gian said.

Celeste preened over her shoulder. "Of course it does."

The family had just sat down for their meal when the phone call came in. His parents' maid handed the phone over to Gian with wide eyes before she bolted out of the room. Celeste and Frederic watched him like two hawks as he put the phone to his ear.

Gian tried to hear what Elena was saying through her panic, but he could only make out a few words.

They were enough. They were too much.

Cops.

Warrants.

The mansion.

Get here, now.

Gian only made it outside of his parents' place. The cops were already waiting for him there, too.

Apparently, the mansion was one of many places served with warrants, and he was just one of many men to find themselves in hot water with police. His father-in-law's house that was just an hour outside of Ottawa was another. Gian found himself in the back of a police cruiser and his hands cuffed, before he could even tell his father what to do.

"The charges?" Gian demanded from the officer.

The man shrugged, but before he shut the door, he said, "Ask Seeley when you get to the station. He said you two had missed your meeting this week."

Gian realized then that he was fucked.

He just didn't know *why.*

SIX

Cara had forgotten how comforting and familiar Gian's penthouse was for her. All the tall ceilings, the warm whiteness of the rooms, and the wide windows that could make someone feel like royalty looking down on the city—it was beautiful.

The walls of the penthouse had heard her secrets and given her a safe space, all those months ago. They had shut out the world and let her learn who Gian Guzzi was underneath his charming, mysterious mask. Or rather, who she had thought he was.

He's still the same man, her mind whispered, *but with added baggage.*

Yes, if only it was that fucking simple.

Cara learned, as she snooped through Gian's office and wandered into his walk-in closet, that the penthouse still held pieces of her time from before. One of her chokers hung from a small brass hook in the jewelry case, resting alongside a half of a dozen Rolex watches. Bangles she had slipped off her wrist still sat in a glass bowl. A jacket she remembered tossing over the bedpost one night in her haste to get in the bed with that sinful man had been hung up in the closet alongside Gian's things.

Gian had no reason to keep her things; to leave the items where she had placed them, or to move them to safe spots where she could find them again.

And yet he had.

Gian kept the tiny pieces of her with him. Cara didn't know if that was because, one day, he planned to return them. Maybe he wasn't willing to scrub her from his penthouse or his life.

There was something else that became *painfully* obvious as she snooped. His wife held no place in his personal spaces. The woman was nowhere. No clothes, makeup, pictures, or mementos. It was as though— only here—she did not exist.

Or perhaps he didn't want her to.

Cara also didn't want to think on it for too long. Thinking for her almost always led to overthinking, and that was a problem. She already knew Gian loved her, and she didn't think for a second that he would say something he didn't mean, but it was all the rest of the details that came along with it where she hesitated.

Cara didn't *want* to hesitate.

Not for Gian ...

She decided, when it was just after dinnertime and she was *still* at Gian's place, that it was the only reason why she was there. Comfort and

259

familiarity. Nothing more, nothing less.

Cara was also pretty damn good at lying to herself.

And overthinking.

She should have been gone hours ago. Instead, she stayed, putting the shower in the master bath to use, and then ordering in food for lunch *and* supper. She had answered the one text from Gian earlier in the day, but he had yet to send another.

Cara didn't know if that was a purposeful move on Gian's part, or not. It would certainly be smart of him, to let her have the few hours that kept them apart without his voice in her head so she could work through her shit. She was always working through something.

It was only after supper time had long passed, that Cara began to think something might be wrong. She shot Gian another text and got nothing in response.

Cara was just slipping on her shoes to leave the penthouse, after sending *another* text to Gian that explained he could call her when he had time, when the elevator into the penthouse opened. Chris—Gian's man that had kept an eye on Cara months ago—rushed into the place with a black messenger bag clenched in his hand.

He only hesitated when he saw Cara coming down the hall.

"Sorry, I thought you might be Gian," Cara said.

Chris cleared his throat and glanced back at the elevator. "Boss brought you over?"

"Last night."

The man didn't even look surprised. "All right. You should head out."

The lilt in Chris's tone made Cara stay right where she was. "What's wrong?"

"Nothing that you need to worry about, miss."

"It's Cara."

"I still know your name and I still prefer what I use."

Cara frowned. "Because I'm not his wife, or—"

"Because respect matters," Chris interrupted as he slid past Cara in the hallway. "Now, I'm serious. Get out of this building, preferably within the next ten minutes or so."

"Why?"

"You didn't leave anything behind, did you?"

"Why aren't you answering my questions?" Cara demanded.

Chris pulled open a drawer in the decorative hallway table, and yanked out a gun, dropping it into the bag. Cara gaped like an idiot, wondering how she had never noticed that weapon there before and how many others might be hidden in the penthouse.

Then, she had an even more pressing thought.

Why was Chris here?

He *never* used to come inside Gian's penthouse without permission. No one had ever done that, from what Cara remembered. If he was doing this now, was it because of the weapons? Did he know where they were, or most of them, and did he need to get rid of them for some reason?

"Chris—"

"Okay," Chris said, turning to face Cara with a blank expression. "*Cara*, you need to go unless you feel like getting dragged down to a police station to explain why you are in the boss's place, and what you were doing here with him, amongst many other things they'll ask. If you left something that will say *you*, specifically, were here, then get it and go. I don't have the time to baby you out of this place, I have shit to do."

Cara still didn't move. "Where is Gian?"

"Right now, he's either in lock up or being questioned. Based on whatever they picked up at the mansion, their warrant for this place was on the way. Do you want to be standing there when they get here or what?"

Shit.

"I should go," Cara said.

Chris nodded. "Yeah, do that, and fast."

Cara had just walked out of the front doors of the building when the first cruiser and unmarked car pulled up on the side of the road. The officers and one plain-clothed detective with his badge hanging around his neck, walked past her as though they had no interest in the redhead leaving the building.

She hailed a cab, and didn't take a real breath again until she was back at her place, and hidden in her bed.

What just happened?

The question kept banging around in her head. Cara didn't even know how to answer.

• • •

"I'm starting to think that you don't know how to return a phone call."

Cara almost fell off the stepladder she was using to put away groceries in the pantry at Carolina's House. "Jesus, *Zia*, make some noise."

Her aunt, Daniele, only cocked an eyebrow in response.

Carefully, Cara climbed back down the ladder, ignoring the way the floor swayed a bit under her feet when she wasn't so high up anymore. Her new issue with heights and vertigo was becoming annoying, but she ignored it.

Ignoring it was easier than dealing with what it meant.

"I've called you three times this week," her aunt said.

Cara shrugged. "I've been busy."

And avoiding.

She had been avoiding everyone and anything related to the Guzzi family, the police, and the current investigation into their business for three entire weeks. That also meant ignoring her own family, mostly her aunt and uncle, who had been just one of many to be dragged into the city for questioning by police.

Cara knew better than to get involved.

Gian wouldn't want her to, she was sure of that.

Of course, Cara *had* been keeping up with what she could. It seemed Gian had found himself in jail under a half of a dozen weapons charges, and according to the news, the weapons had been found at the Guzzi mansion. The weapons didn't entirely relate to the investigation's main objective—whatever that was, as the info hadn't been offered—but the unregistered, illegal weapons were still grounds for charges.

Canada did not like guns on the streets, especially not illegal guns.

Given Gian's name and affiliations, a previous arrest for assault with a weapon, and his ability to up and leave the country, simply because of the amount of zeros in his bank account, he was remanded to the jail until his trial. A trial which was likely going to be sped up when Gian accepted a shorter sentencing term for a deal that was offered regarding the charges.

Or so Cara heard …

She was trying not to get involved. She was trying to keep her head low and stay the hell out of it all, so then she didn't get dragged into a mess, too. That was the message passed along to her during a late-night visit from Chris. The man had shown up at her door with those instructions from Gian, and very little else.

Cara didn't have much of a choice but to agree.

As it was, her life was already a fucking mess for more reasons than just Gian's arrest. She didn't plan to add to it with stupidity.

"Did you need something specific?" Cara asked her aunt. "Because I really need to get done here, so I can go home and work on my essay due next week."

"No, I just worried about you, Cara. You haven't called, or been around. I wanted to check up on you. I know you're here a lot throughout the week when you're not at school, so I thought I would drop by today since I was in the neighborhood."

Her aunt seemed sincere enough.

Cara decided to placate the woman.

"I am fine, *Zia*. But I am busy, really. I promise, I will make it up to you, and come over for dinner this weekend. I have nothing else better to do, okay?"

Daniele pursed her lips, but eventually smiled and nodded. "Fine, that sounds good. And you are *well*, aren't you?"

"Yes, why?"

"You're looking a little green today, that's all."

Cara swallowed the nauseous feeling building in her stomach and crawling up the back of her throat. It was not the easiest thing to hide—especially when the random vomiting spells hit at the most awkward of times—but she managed.

"I'm fine," Cara assured. "I'll even call you when I get home tonight after work, all right?"

"If you're sure ..."

"Perfectly sure, *Zia.*"

Cara's lies and false smiles seemed to do the trick. Her aunt left with a demand that she had better call that night, *and* show up for dinner on the weekend. She barely heard her aunt's footsteps fade away before she made it to the garbage can in the corner to throw up.

Her hands shook as she tried to steady herself for the second wave of sickness that almost always followed the first round.

The biggest question of her life had been answered that morning when she pissed on a plastic stick, and a small window blinked with a single word over and over again. At seven days late, and a multitude of other symptoms, Cara knew the answer. She still took the test, half praying it would come out one way, and yet feeling a mess of relief, joy, and absolute chilling fear when she finally knew for sure.

Pregnant.

The pregnancy test was still in her purse. It was probably still blinking that goddamn word. Cara was too scared to check. She wasn't ready for it to be real.

Not yet.

• • •

"Miss Rossi."

Cara stiffened at the sound of Chris's greeting behind her. She turned the lock in her apartment door to close it up, and turned to face the man. He smiled at her. "You could have knocked on the door."

"I just arrived."

"Mmm."

Chris nodded at her messenger bag. "Going somewhere?"

"School, actually. I already missed one class this morning, I'm trying not to miss a second."

"Would it be so bad if you did miss another?"

Cara's hand tightened on her bag. "Well, kind of."

"You look tired," he noted.

"Do I?"

"A bit."

Cara hinted at nothing being wrong. Eight weeks after Gian's arrest, and five weeks after finding out she was pregnant, Cara still hadn't told *anyone*. Not a single soul knew her secret, and for now, she wanted to keep it that way.

She had been going through a rough patch with her early pregnancy. Exhaustion and morning sickness were taking its toll. She slept a hell of a lot more than she normally did, which said something, considering she wasn't a morning person at all, and she still couldn't smell meat cooking without throwing up.

It was not particularly fun.

At only eight weeks pregnant, Cara was wondering how she was supposed to make it another thirty-two weeks. The doctor had assured her that the tiredness would wane in the second trimester, as would the sickness, but she wasn't sure that she believed the woman.

"Care to go on a drive today?" Chris asked. "There's someone who would like to see you."

"Isn't today Gian's sentencing?"

"It is."

"Is it him who wants to see me?"

"He does."

Cara frowned. "How, exactly? He's always transferred directly from the jail to the courthouse, in cuffs and a cruiser with a guard."

Chris shrugged. "Some strings may have been pulled today, that's all I can say."

"He hasn't even called me."

"His calls are monitored and he calls no one. Messages are passed back and forth during visits, and that's how shit gets done."

"Oh."

"Jail isn't a vacation, believe me."

Cara rolled her eyes. "I never said that. A call would be nice, though."

"You probably won't get one. Maybe a visit, once the media fades away a bit, but not a call. He wants nothing on record other than a name and date. So, a drive?"

Cara handed over her bag when Chris offered to take it. "Fine, a drive."

• • •

Cara was certain that the midtown alleyway Chris parked in was not anywhere close to the courthouse where Gian would have been sentenced earlier.

"What are we doing?" Cara asked.

Chris slid on a pair of sunglasses, turned the radio on low, and rested his arms behind his head. "Right now, we're waiting."

Given the man's vagueness, Cara had the distinct feeling that she wouldn't get any of her questions answered, so she didn't ask more. She wasn't sure how much time passed—ten minutes or maybe twenty. Then, Chris perked up, his gaze shooting to the rearview mirror. Cara glanced over her shoulder. A police cruiser parked behind them in the alley.

Chris said nothing, simply exited the car after grabbing a large envelope from the passenger seat. Cara watched from the back window as Chris passed the envelope to the first police officer who left the cruiser. A second officer, younger than the first, headed to the back of the car to unlock and open the door.

Cara's thoughts of the odd scene, and the obvious bribery happening, drifted away when Gian stepped out of the police cruiser. His hands were cuffed in front of him, but the younger officer quickly undid the cuffs when Gian offered his wrists out. The suit Gian wore belied the fact he had already spent eight weeks in a small jail cell, as it looked perfectly pressed and fit him handsomely.

A few words were said, the officers turned to talk between themselves, and Gian headed for Chris's car. Cara didn't realize she had been holding her breath until he slipped into the backseat with her.

At first, he said nothing. His hands—God, she missed his hands—drifted over her cheeks with the softest touch, and then he was pulling her close. For a moment, a blissful few seconds, all of Cara's stress and fear and worries drifted away. His dark eyes lingered over her features, his thumbs stroked her skin, and Cara remembered how to smile again.

"I missed your face," Gian murmured.

Cara let out a low laugh. "That's all you have to say?"

"No, not all. I'm sorry. I love you. There's a few more, but those stand out the most."

Before she could think better of it, Cara closed the distance between them. The kiss started out innocent and sweet enough, but took no time at all to burn deep with something far more sinful and desperate. She loved the way his fingers tangled into her hair as his tongue warred against hers. She nearly forgot about the people outside of the car, but she still didn't care.

Not when her heart was suddenly thrumming a familiar tune.

Gian, Gian, Gian.

That's what the song sounded like. That, and *love, love, love.*

Cara knew it was bad and wrong. She had no business being involved with this man after everything, never mind hoping for a future with him that could never *be* anything. Yet she did.

She hoped and wished, and she thought the risk of crashing and burning might be okay, if she could just love him while it happened. Maybe.

"I heard you pulled some strings," Cara said when Gian kissed a soft path over her cheekbone. "Aren't they worried you might run off?"

Gian chuckled, and kissed her mouth again. "Not in the slightest."

"How much did you bribe them?"

"A lot."

Cara let Gian pull her closer, and soaked in the wonderful sensations of his fingers sifting through her curls. It was the intimate, comforting action that he usually only did in private with her, but it was her very favorite thing.

"I don't have too long," Gian said. "A few minutes, that's all."

Cara nodded. "Okay."

"I'll get Chris to bring you in for a visit sometime over the next few months, if possible. I need the news programs and the fucking media to just … lay off for a bit. I don't want you mixed up in any of this nonsense, Cara, not if I can help it."

Cara's heart stopped for a split second. "A few months?"

Gian let out a hard breath. "Seven months, five with time already served. It'll be done and over with before we know it, no worries."

That was easy for him to say. That was easy for him to *think*.

"You've gone stiff on me," Gian said. "Why?"

Cara tried to let the words form, she tried to explain her reaction away, but nothing came out. She was still hearing *five months* in the back of her mind.

"Cara," Gian said gently.

She looked up at him, and the words were right there on the tip of her tongue. *Say it*, and *tell him*, she thought. He needed to know about the pregnancy, especially now.

A light knock on the window interrupted her from saying anything at all. Chris stood just outside the door, and then gestured back toward the police cruiser. Gian sighed, but nodded once in response.

"I'm sorry, *mon ange*."

Cara let him disengage from her, though it cut her up. "Wait."

Gian already had the door open, and one foot out of the car. "What, Cara?"

She grabbed her bag, and dug through it, searching for a small paper she had shoved in there. Her doctor had made an appointment for her to have an early ultrasound when she had complained about cramping. As it turned out, nothing was wrong, and it was perfectly normal for her muscles to cramp a bit as her uterus grew a baby. She got a little picture of a peanut-shaped blob to keep.

Cara found the sonogram picture, and shoved it into Gian's hand. The due date of the baby, how far along Cara was, and other information was listed at the top.

Gian's gaze drifted between the grainy, black and white image in his hand, to Cara, and then back to the picture again. "Is this … uh, what I think it is?"

"Yeah," she whispered, "that's exactly what you think it is."

He didn't question her on a thing, only leaned back into the car, and kissed her hard on the mouth.

"I'm a little scared," Cara told him.

Gian cupped her cheek with a firm hold, but a soft touch. "Yeah, I get that now, *bella.*"

"Five months is like almost the whole time."

"But not all, okay? Not all, sweet girl."

"Boss, the cops need to get on the move, so…"

Gian held his hand out, shutting Chris up instantly. Never once did his gaze move from Cara as he did so. "If there's anything you want or need, Chris will get it for you, or Dom. Someone. Do you understand?"

Cara nodded. "I'm sorry, it was busy with school starting and everything. I missed a couple of my pills and—"

He kissed her again, quieting her. The shiver that worked its way through her spine was wonderfully familiar.

"I don't care, Cara."

"Boss—"

"*Fuck off,*" Gian barked over his shoulder.

Chris stepped back with hands up. "My apologies."

Gian's gaze was back on Cara in a heartbeat. "Five months is nothing. We already did three months, right?"

"We didn't even fix the problems or talk about all of that, either. We fucked and here we are! Not the same thing, Gian. It's like a big bomb ticking down that's going to blow the hell up one day."

"Close enough, Cara. And who cares if it blows up, as long as it's spectacular? We're pretty fucking spectacular, love. *Je t'aime, ti amo,* I love *you.* Always."

That, she did believe.

He loved her crazy, but she didn't entirely know why.

He loved her stupid, and she liked it too much.

It was all kinds of bad. They were all kinds of wrong.

Maybe that's just how they were supposed to be.

"You do need to give me a choice in this—in *us.*"

Gian laughed in that sexy way of his. "I did give you a choice. You chose to get in my car. You came with me. You're mine, and you know it."

Jesus. Why was he so damn right?

"Always, Cara," he repeated, kissing her quickly again.

"Always," Cara echoed.

SEVEN

"This was not what I expected."

Gian waited for Cara to sit at the round table, making sure to keep his hands visible for the watching guards. It was really their only request, besides no overt public displays of affection.

Not that he cared at the moment …

Gian's attention was snagged by something *far* more beautiful. Cara, that was, and the way her hand curved protectively around the slight swell of her stomach. He wanted nothing more than to stand and greet her the way *he* liked, but the guards wouldn't be pleased.

He enjoyed having visitors. It kept him sane.

Two more months, he told himself.

That was all he had left, and he would be out of this fucking hell.

"And what did you expect, *mia cara bella*?" Gian asked as she sat down.

"A Plexiglas window and phones, maybe," Cara said, taking in the visitor's area.

"It's a jail, not a prison. I'm in on a non-violent offense. The only prison they would be willing to send me to, is halfway across the country, and by the time they got me the spot, I'd only have a month to spend there. It's pointless."

"It's easier here?"

Gian nodded. "Quieter, less issues. Not so many inmate politics. More visitations. The guards aren't … completely fucking useless."

Cara gave him a look. "It's not supposed to be a vacation, Gian."

He shrugged. "Hey, if they make it easy, then they make it easy."

"I'm also kind of shocked at the attire." She waved at him.

Gian glanced down at the drab, gray uniform he wore on a daily basis. "I miss a good suit, to be honest."

"At least there's no cuffs."

"Not until I'm escorted back to my cell, anyway."

"I wasn't told what to expect here," Cara admitted.

"But you still came."

Her blue eyes flashed to him instantly, a love and wariness reflecting there. "Of course, I came, Gian."

"I'm sorry it took this long for us to have a visit."

"I had a lot going on, anyway."

Gian chuckled. "Or you're making excuses so that I don't feel like shit."

Cara winked. "You'll never know."

Oh, he did.

He loved her for it, too.

"Your brother didn't say much, though," Cara said under her breath, shooting a look over her shoulder. "Not about *anything*, Gian."

Dom stayed just far enough away from the table to allow the two privacy. Gian sent his brother a grateful nod, which was quietly returned. Dom had too many opinions to name where Gian and Cara's odd relationship was concerned.

"Dom is ... Dom," Gian said lamely.

"I don't think he likes me very much."

Gian tried to hide his frown. "It's not you personally, Cara."

"What is it?" His gaze dropped down to her rounded stomach, and Cara's hands cupped the swell quickly. "Oh, well then."

"He doesn't know what to think of it all," Gian explained.

Cara nodded once. "So it's more you, that's what you want to say. Not me, *you*."

"In a way, sure. Except he can't say shit to me because I'm the boss, brother or not. He's in a shitty situation where his opinion is not welcome, but he still wants to give it. Not that any of that matters. Enough about this, Cara, tell me about my baby."

The sweetest, prettiest smile bloomed on her features, lighting up her whole face. *That* was one of the things Gian missed seeing the very most. Even worse, he missed being the one to make Cara smile. He felt that he had given her far more reasons to frown.

"Halfway there now," Cara said. "Twenty weeks this week. He's very active, makes for interesting prenatal appointments when he keeps moving away from the wand as they're trying to hear his heartbeat. I would let you feel, but he's quiet right now. For once."

Gian was sure *his* heartbeat had stopped for a split second. "*He?*"

Cara pulled a small roll of sonogram photos from her purse, and slid it across the table to Gian. "A boy. So far, a very healthy, active boy, Gian."

He looked over the sonograms, taking in the shadowy profile of a baby in the middle of the picture. The tiny slope of a nose, and the roundness of his cheeks and lips were the most prominent features. Another photo showcased five small toes of a perfectly formed foot. The final image was a strange mixture of shapes that Gian didn't understand at all.

"What's this?" he asked.

Cara used the tip of her finger to outline the central image. "What do you think?"

His laughter rung out in the quiet visiting area, gaining the attention of several other inmates and their family. "Shit, really?"

"Yep."

"Definitely a boy, then."

"You couldn't miss it if you tried, once it's pointed out," Cara said, shaking her head.

"Thank you for bringing this, Cara."

"I have copies for me, too."

"I know, but—"

"He's your son, Gian, so why wouldn't I bring this to show you? We might have unfinished business, but he's brand new and he has no baggage. You know?"

"Yeah," Gian agreed. "Come here."

He hooked his finger at her, willing to take the scolding or whatever other issue that might pop up for what he was about to do. Cara, always trusting when it came to him, even when she didn't have the first clue of his motives, leaned closer at the table, until he could cup her face and bring her in the rest of the way.

Gian kissed Cara quickly on her painted red lips, feeling her smile grow when he kissed her twice more in quick succession. "God, I love you. You know that, huh?"

Cara nodded. "I know, Gian. I just don't understand why sometimes."

"Because you're *you*, Cara. And you're mine."

He figured that should be simple enough.

It was enough for him.

Having Cara close was not necessarily a good thing for Gian. Now that he had her there, he wanted to drag her into his lap, tangle his fingers into her hair, and hide away from the world that never left him alone. She was his peace, even if she couldn't possibly know it.

Gian settled for resting his palm over the slight, hard swell of her stomach. "Two more months, Cara, and then we'll have all the time in the world to deal with the unfinished business."

"Don't look forward to doing that too much, Gian."

"I love you. The rest doesn't matter."

"It matters," she argued, "to me."

"The details matter to you. The details aren't us in the grand scheme."

"We're part of the details, whether you want to admit it or not."

"Cara—"

"Yeah, I know," she mumbled when he kissed her cheek. "You're impossible."

"I am," he willfully, and happily, admitted. "More so when it comes to you."

That didn't mean that Gian was stupid, of course. He knew there was a lot that had been left unsaid between them. There were details of his life and his marriage that bothered Cara on a moral and ethical level. She didn't want to be the other woman in his life, but his only woman. He knew these were all things that would somehow need to be dealt with, but he believed—stupidly, maybe—that because he loved her, and he knew that she loved him, it would work itself out.

It *had* to.

Gian only noticed the guard approaching when the man was just a few steps away from the table. "My apologies."

The guard gave a short nod. "Hands in view, Guzzi."

Gian put his hands on the table, and moved an inch or two away from Cara. She frowned at the guard, as the man walked back to his previous post.

Before either of them could talk again, Dom had stepped up to the table, and cleared his throat. "We've only got a few more minutes left, Gian."

"Oh," Cara said, looking to Gian. "Well, I'll step out into the waiting area, and let your brother sit and chat for a minute."

"You don't have to do—"

"Sure I do, he's your brother."

Cara gave Gian another quick kiss before she left the table. Dom offered her a strained, awkward smile as she passed him by. Gian waited until Cara was gone completely before he turned his attention on his brother.

"You're here every week," Gian grumbled. "I get ten minutes with her and you interrupt me. *Why?*"

"I always have people with me," Dom said like it was obvious. "*I* never get the chance to chat with you privately. Now seems like a good time."

Gian grinded his teeth, irritated with Dom's justification. "What do you want to chat about?"

"How do you know you can trust her?"

"Who?"

"That woman. Cara."

"Because I just do, Dom. That's how."

"So, she says she's pregnant, that it's your child, and you just believe her, no questions asked?"

"I'm trying really hard right now not to get pissed off at you, but you're making it difficult."

"Why, because I'm asking you hard questions?" Dom asked.

"No, because you question *her*, asshole." Gian looked back in the way Cara had gone, wishing she had stayed right where she was instead. "You question the motives and morals of a woman who you don't know from a hole in the ground. You question her actions and her behavior with me because *of* me, Dom, because of the choices I made. You're so easily willing to think ill of her because I love her, not because she's done anything to deserve it. That's why you're pissing me off. It has fuck all to do with me, and everything to do with her."

"You said yourself that it'd been three months since you two were together. Then what, one night does the trick?"

Gian sighed, and rubbed a hand over his face.

He needed a fucking shave.

"I'm just saying," Dom muttered, "because the last woman who told you she was pregnant with your kid—"

"The last woman was Elena, and Cara Rossi is the furthest thing from her. The two are not comparable. Cara has no motives to lie to me, Dom, not like Elena did."

"One would think you might be a little more careful."

Gian shook his head. "It's my child and she's mine, too. You don't have to like it, you don't have to approve of it, because you don't matter where she and I are concerned. It would be great, if you and a lot of other people learned that fucking lesson, and fast."

"What about everybody else?" his brother asked.

"What about them?"

"Ma and Dad. Your wife. When do they get to learn you've got a child on the way with your mistress?"

Gian bristled at that title being so easily thrown at Cara like she deserved it. Maybe it was then that Gian could truly understand why the details bothered Cara so much. It was never him that would be questioned for their choices or the results of their behavior together, it would always be her that needed to answer for it.

That was unfair.

"All right," Gian said, standing from the table, "I'm done here."

He gestured at one of the guards.

Dom stood, too. "Gian, you owe me—"

"I owe you and everyone else, fucking *nothing*. That's why I'm the goddamn boss, and no one else is. I answer to those I choose to and you are not one of them."

"And your image, your respect, your wife, or our family? What about that? How do you think Ma is going to feel when she finds out you knocked up some woman when she's spent the last couple of months trying to befriend your wife?"

Dom didn't get it.

He wasn't listening like he needed to.

"I gave you the button too soon," he told his brother. "I spent *decades* under Corrado, learning how to be this man who didn't question what he was told to do, or how to do it. I learned how to not speak out of turn, even when it killed me to stay quiet, and who knew his place amongst other made men. *Decades* of my life were spent this way, Dom, from the time I was a child, until he gave me my button, so that I could sit where I am today, and have my given respect. Clearly, you could have benefitted from that same upbringing, but because you didn't, I have to deal with your disrespect and bullshit. I should have listened to my instincts instead of my feelings where you were concerned this past summer. You're not ready for a button—to be a made man—when your disrespect clouds a discussion with your boss."

"You're my brother first."

"Then, when you were unmade and just a man, you were my brother first and could afford to have a damn opinion about my life," Gian snapped back harsh and fast, uncaring of who heard him say the words. "*Then*, I was your brother first, Dom. Now, I am your boss. Learn the fucking difference. Learn it fast, before you force my hand and my gun. If I were any other boss, you would not be alive right now. Do *not* forget that the next time you feel as though your opinion should be shared."

Gian didn't wait to hear Dom's response or for the guard to make his way over. He headed toward the guard, meeting him in the middle with his wrists already out and ready for the cuffs, so he could be transported back to his cell.

He would rather spend the rest of the day in his cell than deal with his ignorant brother.

Another day, he told himself.

There would always be another day.

• • •

Gian would have been pleased to say that the remaining two months of his sentence had flown by before he even knew what was happening, but that hadn't been the case. He had never been more aware of how long sixty days could be until that was what his freedom had been reduced to.

It probably didn't help that for the majority of the time he spent in his cell, he was thinking about Cara, and when he would be able to see her next. It gave him something to do, and something to look forward to. Visits had been planned, but shit just didn't pan out properly.

Not even a conversation was had. The silence in his head when he was alone could be deafening.

As he dressed in the three-piece suit that he had handed over to the jail in exchange for their uniform, and fixed the Rolex watch around his wrist, Gian only had one thought in mind.

Cara.

He had come to a few conclusions when he was kept from her—more so than when he had *chosen* to stay away before. She was the blood in his body, the breath in his lungs, and the sun in his life.

273

She just was.

Everything, for Gian, was Cara Rossi.

Gian had always known those things, of course, but it was a much more intense understanding to come to when a man was alone with nothing but his thoughts and feelings. He had never done particularly well with feelings, after all.

More so, Gian now wanted to make sure Cara understood that she was all of those things to him and more. He wasn't sure if he had properly explained all of that to her, and didn't she deserve to know?

Maybe if she did know, then Cara might finally understand why details never mattered to Gian where they were concerned. The only details that had ever mattered to him were her.

Gian also needed to make sure he kept his ass out of jail, because he had too much time to think, and he didn't want a repeat. He was tired of jail-house nonsense, their fucking schedules, and going to bed when he was told to.

This was fucking ridiculous.

He wanted home, Cara, and a good meal.

It didn't have to be in that order.

So, as he slipped into his clothes, fixed his jewelry to his wrist and slid his rings on his fingers, Gian was more than ready to get his freedom back.

"Sign here," the nasally-voiced woman behind the Plexiglas window said.

Gian scribbled his name across the dotted line.

Just a few steps away now.

Freedom was so close, he could taste it.

Gian collected the folder with his release papers and headed for the doors that separated him from the outside world. It could have been worse, he knew, as those five months could have just as easily been spent in a prison.

It didn't matter.

He was ready to be out.

He wanted his life back.

"You're looking terribly happy about something, boss."

Gian smiled at the voice that greeted him as he walked out of the jail doors. Chris waited there for him, as that was who he had requested pick him up. He didn't want an affair for his release. As it was, his mother wanted a dinner, and he had men to meet and greet after being locked away for five months. Because of those things, he already had to put off seeing Cara for at least a day or two, which was bad enough.

"It's a nice day for the end of April," Gian noted, glancing up at the bright sky. "Tell me you brought the SUV with the sunroof."

"I did," Chris said.

"Good man."

"I also brought your wife."

There went Gian's good mood.

"What?" Gian asked, feeling the beginnings of a migraine. "Why would you do that?"

Chris jerked his thumb over his shoulder at the SUV. The windows were tinted too dark for him to see inside, but he had no doubt that Elena was sitting in the back seat.

"She had to come," Chris said, "and apparently her father knows you're getting out today, and wanted a meeting before you did anything else. According to Elena, he requested *she* be there, too. Sorry, boss."

"I don't answer to Gabriel Canali or his fucking wants, and he knows it."

"Yeah, I know, but you also don't go out of your way to irritate the monster that man happens to be, so I made the middle-ground choice that I figured you would want me to."

Gian scowled. "I'm going to be late for dinner with my mother, now."

Celeste would *not* be pleased about that.

"I already took care of it, boss."

"Oh?"

"She's going to come for breakfast tomorrow, at that restaurant you like downtown. Just you and her, maybe your father, too. Also, I figured if you were in a public place, she would be less likely to make a scene about you getting out of jail or the fact you were *in* jail to begin with."

Gratitude flooded Gian where Chris was concerned. The enforcer was decent. He did his job, even if Gian wasn't always pleased about the way he did it, and he took care of his boss. That was the most important thing.

"All right, then," Gian muttered, shooting a look at the SUV. "A dinner with my father-in-law it is."

And a car ride with his wife.

Fun.

"Here," Gian said, digging his cell phone out of the paper bag. The device was dead, and needed a charge. "You brought something to charge this, right?"

"Sure did."

Chris never failed.

• • •

"I should have brought you a new suit to change into," Elena said.

Gian passed her a look, noting the red dress, matching heels, and wide-brimmed sunhat she wore. For the most part, the hat had been a good shield between them, keeping them from needing to look at one another, never mind *talk*.

"Why would you do that?"

"You know how Daddy is," she said quietly.

Gian went back to staring out the window. "He's the one who wanted this dinner, Elena, knowing I was fresh off release. He can deal with a wrinkle in my shirt."

"Still …"

"And you don't need to be bringing me anything," Gian added.

Elena sighed. "Sure."

Gian glanced back at his wife again, taking note of the nervous edge in her posture and her hands fidgeting in her lap. Chris caught his boss's reflection in the rearview, but quickly turned his gaze back on the road.

"You haven't seen Gabriel since I went in, then?" Gian asked.

Elena shrugged. "I didn't have to. He was in for a while, too."

"He was released a month before me."

"I made excuses."

"Two blocks away, boss," Chris said from the driver's seat.

"*Merci*," Gian replied, though he continued watching Elena. "Smile pretty and nod at whatever he says, because that's what he likes to see from you. Keep your replies quiet and well-mannered, as that forces him to be polite, too. Don't give him shit to pry into, where our lives or this marriage is concerned; neither of us wants or needs that. Thirty minutes, at the most, and I'll excuse you. How's that?"

Elena frowned. "You don't have—"

"What good is your husband, if he doesn't at least look out for you, Elena?"

Her posture softened a bit. "I don't always treat you well, or I haven't, I guess. Don't be surprised when I don't expect the same in response, Gian."

"I have always looked after you where your father was concerned, Elena. Even before I knew that's what you were using me to do for yourself. Let's not pretend like this is anything different. It's the rest—the lies you told, the way you fucked me over, and the shit we don't have together that I can't be bothered with now. I'm not going to work toward any kind of real marriage with you, and you don't want me to, either. I need to stay married to you for appearance, respect, and an oath I took, and you need to stay married to me to keep your father away. Nothing more, nothing less. This, your father, I will always protect you, and you know it. *You* shouldn't expect any different, not when I have never given you a reason to think otherwise."

She didn't reply.

He didn't need her to.

"Well, fuck," Chris grunted as he pulled the SUV over to the side, and killed the engine.

Gian would have asked what the problem was, but he didn't need to. A news van had parked outside the restaurant, with cameras turned in their direction. "Why in the hell are they here?"

"Your guess is as good as mine, boss."

Jesus Christ.

"Your release *was* publicized," Elena pointed out.

"So then a news van shows up at the jail," Gian replied, "not the restaurant where I'm meeting your father."

"Gabriel, then?" Chris asked.

"Why would he do that? He's not in any better of a position than I am at the moment, and could afford to stay out of the fucking spotlight for a bit."

Gian hadn't been the only organized crime boss arrested in those raids. Gabriel's sentence had been lighter by a month, sure, but the man still went in. Besides that, Gian wasn't exactly low profile in the city of Toronto.

Long before his family's name had been synonymous with crime, the Guzzis had become rich by striking gold in one of Canada's only gold mines. They were old money and with that had come a socialite lifestyle that spanned generations, his included. He didn't enjoy that side of life as much as his parents had, or even as much as his sister currently did, but his face was well known, much like his last name.

"Pay them no mind," Chris said, "and I'll scare them off when you're inside, boss."

Gian nodded, thankful. "Great."

Unfortunately, the second Gian stepped out of the car, he could feel the fucking camera burning into him. He was *very* aware that his face would likely be on the news that night, and that didn't exactly make him jump for joy.

The born and bred gentleman he was sent him to Elena's side of the SUV. He opened her door, and offered a hand to help her out. She didn't pass the cameras a single look, but she did lean in and give Gian a quick kiss on his cheek.

Then, just as fast, she murmured in his ear, "For Daddy to see."

For them, it was always a show.

It always had been.

It had to be.

He hadn't expected the kiss, and it took a great effort for him not to pull away from Elena, but he managed.

Elena kept her hand firmly tucked into his elbow as they entered the restaurant. Unsurprisingly, Gian found the place quite empty of patrons, and only a couple of wait staff waiting for them at the front.

"Your father owns this place, doesn't he?" Gian asked.

"Yes."

Wonderful.

"How nice of him to close it down for the day, just for us. That's a great way not to draw any fucking attention."

It was a great way to make a scene, by closing down a busy restaurant for a day, only to have two crime bosses of rival families show up for a sit-down together.

Fuck.

Gian hated Gabriel Canali for many reasons, including the woman hanging on his arm currently. The bastard could not be trusted.

Elena's false smile grew as the woman wearing a standard black dress led them through the restaurant, closer to the front windows. His wife leaned into his side, her hand tightening on his arm with a fierceness that damn near hurt. Yet, her smile never faltered, not even when she first caught sight of her father.

Gabriel was a bull of a man, with his torso as wide as he was tall. Dark-eyed, black-haired, and with a soul as dirty as shit, the man was intimidating at first glance.

A Camorra boss of a clan that liked its violence to the extremes, and its money as dirty as it could get, Gabriel held no loyalties to anyone but himself. He didn't follow the same kinds of rules in life that Gian, or other made men did, as Camorra clans were, simply put, out for the betterment of their own positions.

Gabriel had killed nearly every single one of his rivals off. All except for the Guzzi family.

Gian had too much pride to let a cocksucker like Gabriel force his hand more than he had already done. As it was, he'd married the man's daughter, was stuck with her until the day one of them died, and that was more than enough punishment for Gian, regarding getting mixed up with the Canali Camorra clan. *Far more than enough …*

"Gian," Gabriel greeted, pushing his large girth up from the head of a table. "Beautiful day, isn't it?"

Gian nodded, taking the man's hand for a shake. "It is."

Then, Gabriel turned his gaze on his daughter. "Elena, *mia reginella.*"

My little queen.

Gian felt his wife's fingernails dig into his skin through his suit jacket.

"Daddy," Elena greeted politely. "How are you?"

"Well, although not as good as your husband, seeing as how he's free today. You only get one free day to have fun after a sentence, and then it's back to work. I'm happy to see he's spending it with you." Gabriel chuckled darkly. "I can't say I ever did that for my wife when she was alive."

Elena said nothing, but she didn't move from Gian's side, either. She had her sore spots, and her father was one of them. In a way, Gian thought it might do him well if he cared less, that he had a colder heart, so he could send Elena right back to her father's cruel hands to do with as he wished.

Fortunately for Elena, Gian was not that cold, callous, or cruel.

Even if he wished he was.

No woman deserved to be beaten, used as a toy, or traded for the pleasure of men and blackmail like Elena had been for the majority of her life under Gabriel's demands. It wasn't exactly a secret in their family. It was not freely talked about, either.

"Sit, sit," Gabriel demanded, waving at the table. "The food is coming soon."

Near to the second they were all seated at a table, food was brought out from the kitchen by a chef and a waiter, served to each of them. Gian was at least grateful to get a few bites of a decent meal shoved into his face before the Camorra boss began talking again.

"Are you ever going to give that husband of yours a *bambino* or two?" Gabriel asked his daughter. "I might like a grandchild, too, Elena."

Elena kept her head down as she replied, "Someday."

Gian forced the lump of food down his throat. "Not everyone wants children."

"All good Italian men do," Gabriel said. "Although, considering it's been four years since the two of you married, is it more that you don't want any or that you *can't* have any?"

Elena stiffened in her seat.

Gian kept his focus on his father-in-law. "Children are not on the conversation menu tonight."

"Just curious. She did lose your first child, didn't she? Shortly after the wedding. Perhaps those abortions Elena had didn't serve her well, after all. How many was it again, *cara*, five?"

"Daddy, don't start—"

"Elena, are you finished?" Gian asked, interrupting his wife from taking her father's bait. "Eating, I mean."

She nodded. "I am."

"Chris is waiting outside for you."

Elena didn't need to be told again. She got up from the table, said a quick goodbye to her father, rubbed a hand on Gian's shoulder as she passed, and then she was gone.

"I was only asking," Gabriel said with a smirk. "No need to send her out. She can handle her own, Gian, I assure you."

Gian held back from punching the man in the throat. "Yes, and then I'm the one who has to deal with her emotional backlash from *handling* you and your nonsense for the next week. No, thank you, Gabriel. If you're going to throw my wife's abortions in her face, maybe stop to consider who forced her into those, as well. What was she, sixteen the first time? The police chief, wasn't it?"

Gabriel didn't even blink at the accusation. "It kept me from getting tossed behind bars on a five-year sentence."

"Shame. Those five years could have done her a world of good."

"She's not as innocent as you think, Gian. You're under some impression that she didn't understand what she was doing for all those years—she knew. She knew *perfectly* well."

This was an emotional, manipulative game that Gabriel liked to play with his daughter, far too often. He couldn't use her to do his bidding now, so he liked to mess with her in other ways. Sometimes, Gian thought his wife and father deserved one another for their despicable behavior toward each other and other people. Other times, like now, he didn't want to sit back and watch Gabriel hurt Elena simply because he could.

"What did you really want today?" Gian asked. "What did you want by asking me here?"

"To warn you," Gabriel said before he took a hearty sip of whiskey from a glass. "I couldn't do that when you were in jail, and your men are already well versed on staying away from me and mine."

"For good reason. Warn me about what, exactly?"

"I was arrested and put in for four months because of *you*. Or rather, my affiliation to you was enough to have them watching me, and then serving me with warrants that garnered the charges I received. I don't care about the details, Gian, I care about my freedom."

"Don't we all?" Gian asked dryly. "Get to the point, so we can go our separate ways and pretend like this didn't happen until the next time."

"*The point*, you arrogant fuck, is that you've clearly got a rat problem somewhere. Someone, likely one of your fucking men, is feeding information to the police. And that's not surprising, considering all the shit you stirred up after your grandfather was killed. Corrado was a good man, fit for his position. You, on the other hand, are a spoiled, cocky, ignorant—"

"If we're going to trade insults, my demand is that you let me go first," Gian murmured. "It's only fair, considering. Otherwise, I'll take a pound from you for every name you throw at me without it being deserved."

Gabriel ground his teeth loud enough to be disturbing. "You find out which one of your useless cunts are talking to the police, or I will do it for you."

"Who's to say it's not coming from your end?"

"It's *not*."

"Well—"

"Figure it out," Gabriel interrupted, "or I will tear through your streets and do it myself."

"Are we done?" Gian asked, standing from the table.

"Very much so. Tell my daughter to behave, Gian, though I am sure you're keeping a proper eye on her. Women like Elena need that sort of control. She needs to be on a *very* short leash, because her bite is far worse than her bark, believe me."

Gian didn't bother to respond to that, instead turning on his heel and heading for the front of the restaurant. He was gone from the business, and into the waiting SUV, before the cameras even realized he had stepped back out.

This time, Gian sat in the front seat beside Chris.

Elena sat in the back, glaring out the window.

Chris handed over Gian's charging cell phone, still plugged into the cigarette lighter. "Here, it's been going nuts. Probably trying to catch up with all the shit that it's missed out on these past few months."

"Thanks. Drive."

The enforcer did as he was told.

"What did he say when I was gone?" Elena asked from the back seat.

"Ignore that fucking bastard," Gian replied.

He was more interested in checking his phone. A brand-new message scrolled across the screen, one sent within the last few minutes.

From Cara. *Twenty-eight weeks today*, it read. He could see, through looking at her messages for the past several months that she had sent him a text like this for every week that he had been locked up. Gian smiled.

Elena leaning over his shoulder quickly made his brief happiness dissipate. He turned his phone's screen off, but he wasn't sure if Elena had seen the messages, or not. Of course, if she had, that didn't mean she would understand what they meant.

"I'd like to go to the mansion," his wife said.

"Be my guest. I'm going to the penthouse."

She sat back in the seat, unbothered and cold once more. "Good."

Elena dropped her pretense and her mask, as she had gotten what she wanted where her father was concerned, and didn't think she would have to worry about him again for a while.

Gian expected nothing different.

EIGHT

"Good God, be careful, Claud!" Daniele leaned over the railing, shaking her head. "You're going to throw out your back again, you stubborn mule."

"I could have gotten the landlord's son to help bring the box up," Cara said, two steps above her aunt.

"Will you *donnas* shut up? Knock it off," Claud barked down below in the stairwell. "It is one goddamn set of stairs and a crib. I can handle this."

Daniele sighed. "I see an emergency room visit in our near future."

"Oh, just go get the apartment door open!"

"Fine, throw your back out! I don't care."

Daniele cared, Cara knew.

Even as her aunt stalked down the hallway, huffing, she still looked back over her shoulder with concern to see if her husband was coming. Cara leaned over the railing to see her uncle scratching at his jaw while he stared at the crib.

"I'll get the landlord's son to come help," she told her uncle.

"*I* had a son to help, but where is he now, Cara?"

She only stared at her uncle, unsure of how to answer that. She had no idea where Constantino was. There had been no funeral, no memorial, or anything to suggest he was dead, yet her uncle spoke like Constantino was buried somewhere, or dead in a ditch.

"So, do you want me to get you help, or not?" she asked.

"Not, girl. *Not.*"

"*Zia* was right, you are a stubborn mule."

"She only uses that word because she's too polite to call me an ass!" Claud shouted as Cara followed the path her aunt had taken.

"I'm not too polite, you fucking ass."

She *was* grateful that her aunt and uncle had been sweet enough to pick out a nursery set for her, as once she was no longer able to hide the fact she was pregnant, they were the first people she had told. She had told her brother second.

A whole lot of questions followed, from both ends. To be fair, Tommas asked a whole lot less questions than her aunt and uncle. Questions about the father, or the fact she was just a few months off graduating. That led them into the fact the baby would come soon after, or shortly before, graduation. Then, even more questions about the baby's father.

Cara supposed the questions were normal, given her circumstance. She chose not to answer specific ones, while she gave vague answers for others.

She rubbed a hand over her twenty-eight-week pregnancy swell to soothe the jabbing elbows of her unborn son driving into her organs. Inside her apartment, Cara found her aunt moving a few pieces of small furniture out of the hallway to make it easier to get the crib inside what had been Lea's bedroom.

Cara finally got around to cleaning it all out.

She had a reason to now, after all.

"The rest of the nursery set will be delivered," Daniele said, "so at least for the rest of the furniture, you won't need someone to carry it in."

Cara agreed. "Thanks for all of this, *Zia*."

"No need to thank me, Cara. You work hard and I know you'll be a good mother, so you deserve all the help and whatever else you can get, believe me." Daniele went back to her work, randomly asking, "Of course, you could get lots of help by way of the baby's father."

Cara side-eyed her aunt, trying not to be too rude when she replied, "*Zia*, I am sure he will help, but right now, I am handling this on my own. And I am okay with that, as I have told you many times. The father is my business. Please respect that."

"I worry about you, Cara, that's all."

"I'm perfectly fine, *Zia*."

"Yes, yes, I know. You keep saying that." Daniele waved a hand at her. "Go check on your uncle, and make sure he hasn't had a heart attack in the stairwell."

Cara set her purse and phone on the couch, before going to do as her aunt wanted. Just as she reached the end of the hallway, Claud was finally pulling the large crib box through the stairwell door.

"See, I managed just fine on my own," Claud muttered.

"Huffing, puffing, and red-faced the whole way," Cara agreed.

Her uncle shot her a dirty look, but didn't respond.

"I think just setting it in the bedroom will be good enough for today," she added with a smile. "No need to put you through the torture of setting the crib up today, too."

"Who *will* do it for you, Cara?" Claud asked, pulling the box down the hallway toward her apartment. "Gian? His brother, perhaps?"

Cara froze, her back turned to her uncle. "What did you just say?"

"Nothing. I was thinking out loud. It was nothing."

She slowly turned around. "It was not nothing—you specifically said a name, not that I have given you a reason to use that name, so why did you, *Zio*?"

Claud wiped a hand over his face, effectively removing the sweat from his brow at the same time. "Word travels in this business, between us made men, I mean. I happen to know you get occasional visits from the boss's men, and I also know you were seen out and about with him last year before your trip to Chicago."

"*So?*"

"I also know you had a visit with him in the jail a couple of months ago, Cara."

She grinded her teeth in an effort to stay quiet.

It didn't work.

"*Zio*, this is not your business," she said firmly.

"You're right, it isn't. And your brother told me that, too, when I called him to chat about your current predicament."

"You called Tommas?"

"Lower your voice," her uncle snapped.

Cara's back straightened at the sound of a man scolding her.

Fuck. That. Shit.

"I am not in a *predicament*. I am pregnant, and by whom, is my fucking business to handle how I please."

"I know Gian Guzzi is the father, Cara. Or I have a strong enough suspicion to use his name, for good reason. And considering your reaction, I am not wrong. Tell me I am wrong."

"And so what if he is?"

"He's a married man!"

"Do you think I don't know that?" she cried, throwing her hands wide. "I *do* know that, Claud!"

"Have you considered how difficult this road will be for you and the child?" her uncle asked quietly. "To be the mistress of a made man and the bastard boy, born to a *goomah* mother? Have you considered that at all?"

Cara felt the familiar prickling behind her eyes that signaled her tears were trying to fall. She held them back, and settled for hiding the trembling of her hands at her sides.

"I know I made choices that might not be what everyone else would make," Cara replied, level-toned and stone-faced, "and I know this won't be easy, but don't toss those words at me *just* because they're the ones everyone else wants to use. You only see the surface, and how that looks, but you don't care about the rest. You don't care to know the details, about me and him, about us, or *why*. So that also means you don't get to tell me *fuck all*. Not what to do, how to handle this situation, or anything else about me, my baby, his father, or what I should do with my feelings. Take your opinion, and shove it up your—"

"Cara," her aunt called softly from behind her.

She turned to find her aunt standing a few feet down in the hallway. No doubt, Daniele had heard every single word.

Walking past her aunt, Cara said, "Well, there you go. Now you know *who*. Does it make it better, *Zia?*"

284

Daniele didn't say a thing.
She didn't have to.
Cara knew the answer.
No, it was not better.

• • •

Cara dug into a takeout container full of noodles, as the news program on the television repeated the highlights of the day. She checked her phone, seeing a new message from Gian, one in reply to her latest update on the baby's gestation.

I like Marcus for a name, Gian had wrote. *It's my middle name, and my grandfather's father's name. A family name.*

Cara thought to reply, but she decided she would do that after she finished eating. She had just taken a good mouthful of noodles when a shot of Gian came across the screen.

New Guzzi Crime Boss Released, the headline read across the bottom of the screen. That wasn't exactly news to Cara, as she had known Gian's date of release for a good month, and had counted down the days. She also knew, through Chris's last update, Gian might need to lay low for a few days before she would see him, it really just depended on circumstances.

That, Cara had also understood.

What she didn't understand—or like, for that matter—was seeing a shot of Gian fresh off release, walking into what looked like a restaurant with his wife on his arm.

Then, the shot changed.

Gian stepping out of a car, moving to the other side, and then helping his wife out. She kissed his cheek, her wide-brimmed red hat that matched the color of her heels and dress, hid half of her face, but not enough.

Cara had not been able to forget what Elena looked like since the moment she had seen those wedding pictures. It was burned into her fucking retinas.

"Gian Guzzi, heir apparent and new boss to the Guzzi Crime Dynasty is free today," the anchor said. "We were unable to question the purported Don on his release, or the investigations the police say continue to be active, as he moved directly from the jail to a restaurant, where he seemed to meet with his father-in-law, while his wife was close by. Guzzi's father-in-law, Gabriel Canali, is another well-known gangster from an Ottawa organization, a leader of a Camorra clan, who was also recently released from jail."

The anchor continued talking, but Cara shut the television off, and tried to focus on eating her food. She no longer had an appetite.

Cara didn't want to be that woman—jealous because she saw Gian with his wife, and not her. She didn't want to become irrationally angry anytime a news program mentioned something about Elena.

She had *no right* to feel those things.

And yet she did.

Cara quelled her irritation and useless jealousy by rolling her hands over her unborn boy's movements. Each little kick and jab, calmed her a bit more. There wasn't much else she could do.

It was the loud knock on her apartment door that broke Cara from her daze. She wasn't expecting visitors.

Cara quickly got up off the couch and made her way to the door, when the knocking became slightly more persistent. "Just a second, I'm coming."

She pulled open the door to find an unknown, older woman standing behind it. For a long moment, she only stared at the woman, taking in her ashy blonde hair, green eyes, and the way she smiled ever-so-slightly at the sight of Cara. The woman's gaze dropped to Cara's slightly rounded midsection, and then just as fast, flew back up to her face.

"My, you are quite a beautiful thing, aren't you?" the woman asked. "He always did have an eye for the ones that could stand out in a crowd. I believe it's because he never learned how to blend in, either. He always had to be front and center, a prince waiting to be a king."

Cara held the door, unsure if she wanted to close it or not. "Do I know you?"

She looked familiar.

"Under different circumstances, I am sure we would have known each other very well," the woman said softly. "It's Cara, right? Cara Rossi?"

"I am dangerously close to shutting this door," Cara warned.

The woman laughed, her crow's feet becoming more apparent around her eyes. It was that laugh, and the way her features changed enough, that Cara thought she might know exactly who this woman was. It also could have been the French accent coloring up the woman's words that did it for Cara, too.

But that woman wouldn't come here, would she?

She wouldn't seek Cara out, right?

After all, Cara was the whore, the mistress, the piece of ass on the side. She wasn't worthy of the family name, she couldn't sit beside her man in church, and her very presence was a dirty word for some.

Surely *that* woman, would not come to Cara.

Surely not.

"Celeste Guzzi, Gian's mother," the woman said, smiling softly again. "It's nice to finally meet the woman I'd heard all those rumors about nearly a year ago. Gian wouldn't budge an inch, when I asked. Your aunt is an old friend, from way, way back."

"Oh," Cara said dumbly.

"She thought I might like to meet you." Celeste's gaze dropped to Cara's stomach again. "For obvious reasons, sweetheart. And she was right."

"Not that you've given me a reason to think this, but to what, tell me to crawl in a hole somewhere?"

Celeste frowned. "Not at all, dear."

"Sorry, knee-jerk reaction."

"I can understand why."

Cara stepped back, widening the apartment door a bit more. "Would you like to come in, and maybe have a tea or something?"

Celeste nodded once. "*Oui*, I think I would."

"Does Gian know you're here?"

"Oh, no." Celeste laughed as she walked into the apartment. "I get to wait until tomorrow for breakfast to see him. We're going to have *so much* to talk about now."

Cara shot Celeste a look from across the way. "I'm not sure if you mean that to be a good or bad thing."

"Well, it's both. I understand the predicament my son found himself in, and not just with you. Between his grandfather, all the rules and expectations they shoveled onto him over the years, and then his wife ..."

"I'm not sure I want to know anything about her," Cara said, trying not to sound trite.

Celeste shrugged, as if to say, *do what you will.* "Perhaps you should learn about Elena, or at least, learn why she is where she is with my son. I wish more people had looked beyond the surface when they married years ago, or for that matter, paid attention to it all. No one thought to, and it's no wonder he's found himself—" She looked over to Cara, then said, "It's no wonder he's found himself in this situation. A man or woman can only be so unhappy in every aspect of their life, before they eventually start looking for something—or someone—to fill that void."

Cara turned the electric kettle on. "I never thought about it in that way."

"You don't know *her*. Elena, I mean," Celeste said, her assumption spot on. "But that is not my place to say, either."

"Is it your place to be here?"

The older woman didn't even hesitate. "No."

"Yet here you are."

"Here I am, Cara." Celeste smiled wider. "Now, tell me about my first grandbaby."

• • •

Cara stared at the tubs of ice cream in the store's freezer, trying to decide which flavor—or rather, favor*s*—she wanted to buy. Shrugging, she pulled several mini tubs out and dropped them into her cart. If she couldn't decide on just one flavor, then she would try them all. *Winning*, Cara thought. Pregnancy was no fucking joke.

Neither were the late-night cravings.

"Is that one any good, do you know?"

The question came from Cara's left. She had been so involved in her task of getting the last, but most important, thing on her grocery list, she hadn't been paying attention to her surroundings.

Cara found the woman who the voice belonged to, and damn near tripped over her own two feet. *Elena Guzzi.*

Elena stood only an inch taller than Cara, but that was probably because of the sky-high heels the woman had on her feet. She certainly didn't look dressed to be grocery shopping in a black knee-high, pencil skirt dress with a beige trench coat overtop. Her makeup was flawless—impeccable, with nothing over or under done. Even her blonde hair laid straight down her back, and not one stray hair was out of place.

She was beautiful. Perfect, even. Yet, cold in her eyes.

Cara recognized her instantly, but Elena looked at her as though she didn't have the first clue in the world who she was.

"I-I'm sorry?" Cara managed to ask, finally coming out of her shock.

Elena leaned over Cara's cart, balancing her basket with nothing but wine inside, on her hip. "That one right there—the peanut butter one. Is it any good?"

"That one is, but I don't know about the rest."

"Oh, good. I like peanut butter." Elena moved around Cara's cart, seemingly unaware that she was being watched like a bug under a microscope. "Although I don't think I have the same excuse as you do to be snacking on these, do I?"

"Pardon?"

Elena pointed at Cara's stomach peeking out beneath her opened jacket. "How far along, if you don't mind me asking?"

Oh, God. Cara did not want to be having this conversation with her lover's wife, especially considering the woman didn't seem to know who in the hell she was. Didn't that make it even more wrong on some level?

She was going to hell.

"Twenty-nine weeks in a couple of days," Cara said quietly.

"Almost there, then. Boy or girl?"

"Boy."

Elena smiled, but Cara couldn't help but notice how it didn't *feel* true. It certainly looked warm enough, but the iciness in Elena's gaze was hard to hide. Cara wondered if that was just a part of who Elena was inside her soul—perpetually cold, always distant.

Cara didn't have any right to speculate on those things, anyway.

"Have you thought of any names?" Elena asked as she put a couple of tubs of the ice cream in her basket.

"Um, his father likes Marcus. A family thing, I guess. I haven't said yes or no to it."

Cara's awkward tone did not go unnoticed.

Elena shot her with an apologetic look. "Oh, my gosh. I'm so sorry. You probably think I'm a creep or something, randomly questioning a stranger in a grocery store about her pregnancy. Don't mind me, really. Babies just make me curious, and so does pregnancy."

Cara knew better than to ask, and she should have just taken the chance to get out of the conversation while she had it, but she didn't. "Why is that?"

"I lost a baby, nearly four years ago, shortly after I married my husband. We haven't been able to … well, you know."

Guilt and shame compounded hard in Cara's chest, squeezing the fucking life out of her heart.

"I'm sorry," Cara said lamely.

What else could she say? *I'm sorry your husband knocked me up?*

Elena smiled widely at her, as though her admission meant nothing, and neither did Cara's apologies. "Well, enjoy your ice cream, and have a great day."

"You, too."

Cara watched Elena disappear down the aisle. It was the strangest, most random interaction of her life.

Worse, was the fact Cara didn't even know if it *was* random.

• • •

Cara balanced the four bags of groceries in her one hand and arm as she tried to get the main doors to her apartment building open. She felt his presence slide in beside her before he even spoke. He slipped the bags from her grasp easily, and his sweet kiss landed on her cheek without a word.

An arm slid around her waist, and Cara's body reacted as though heaven had just come to wrap around her soul. She leaned into Gian's embrace as he kissed her cheek once more.

"What did I tell you, *mon ange?*" Familiar, comforting dark eyes looked her over, before moving onto the contents of her grocery bags. "Come on, tell me."

"About what?"

"When you need something, Cara."

"Gian, I am not getting someone to grab my groceries. I can handle it—"

"Then take someone with you to help you carry all this shit, love."

Cara shrugged. "You showed up. All is well."

Gian sighed, and gave her a quick kiss on her forehead. Cara smiled, and managed to get the main doors open at the same time. Quickly, the two slid into the building, and Gian led the way. His arm stayed firmly tucked around Cara's waist, his palm hidden under her jacket, resting flat to her swelled stomach.

"I didn't expect you so soon," she said as they climbed the one stairwell to her floor.

"I should have come sooner," he replied. "Things got in the way."

"Like what?"

"Life," Gian said roughly, "and nothing that matters, to be honest."

Once the two were safely hidden away in Cara's apartment, she stood back and let Gian put all the groceries away. He never missed a beat, sliding things into cupboards as though he had lived there for as many years as she had. He really did pay attention, and he didn't forget things.

At least, not where she was concerned.

"I want to apologize for something," Gian said, his voice muffled by the freezer as he shoved in the mini ice cream tubs.

"What's that?"

"My mother showing up here the other night."

Cara's tension released in a laugh. "She's a wonderful, interesting woman."

"Wonderfully interesting is one way to put it." Gian closed the freezer door, and looked back at Cara. "Still, you shouldn't have been put in that position. I should have told her first, and then—"

"You're right, you should have."

Gian nodded. "She let me know that. *Repeatedly*."

"I like her."

"She likes you," he replied with a smirk. "I knew she would, it was just everything else that I didn't know about, I suppose."

Everything else, like his wife.

Cara thought to tell Gian then and there that she had run into Elena, but only decided against it because what would be the point? His wife clearly hadn't recognized her, and she hadn't done anything wrong or rude. If anything, wasn't Cara the one in the wrong, just by being pregnant with Elena's husband's child?

The meeting was random. Nothing more, nothing less.

Cara did have other questions, though.

Things she wanted to know.

"Gian?"

"Yes, *amore*?"

"Why did you marry her? Why her, Gian?"

NINE

"Why her, Gian?"

Gian tensed at the question, but only because he knew there would be no one, easy answer. It was several events, mixed-messages, and dumb feelings that had led him into the mistake of marriage with Elena. A sense of duty.

When he stayed silent, mulling over his reply, Cara took a seat at the table. "So, you're not going to tell me?"

Gian meet her gaze, unashamed. "Of course, I'll tell you. It's just not an easy question."

"You've asked me before, if I wanted to talk about her or the marriage. What is so different this time? Because I asked?"

"Because I wasn't expecting it. Because back then, I was prepared to explain and knew how to say things. When you spring it on me, I don't have time to consider ways to wall myself off from shit I don't like to feel."

Honesty was the best policy.

Gian had learned his lesson about lying.

Cara played with the tablecloth as Gian got one of the mini tubs of ice cream from the freezer, and then spoons from the drawer. He pulled a chair out from the table, and set it opposite to Cara, so the two were facing one another.

"Wine would probably be better for this conversation," Gian said with a smirk, "but since you can't drink, neither will I, and the ice cream will have to do."

"It's that bad for you that you need wine?"

"Whiskey, preferably. Even beer wouldn't be enough." Gian shook the ice cream container. "And today, it's ice cream only."

"So, why her?"

Gian handed Cara a spoon, and used his own to pull through the top of the ice cream. He stared at the rolled-up treat on the tip of the spoon, considering whether or not he wanted a bite before he spoke. His mouth worked first.

"I met Elena Canali shortly after her twenty-second birthday, at a restaurant, actually. We married when she was twenty-three. Just a random pass by, she was at one table alone, and I was at another with a date, of sorts. I recognized her, but only because we had previous run-ins with her father. Gabriel is a boss of another organization—one not entirely like ours, less controlled, but still Italian-based. Not that it matters."

"Then get to what does," Cara urged.

Gian sucked the ice cream off his spoon, then waved it at Cara. "I'm picking out important details. Think, stuff I overlooked, or should have paid more attention to. Things like a boss's daughter being alone, without any sort of watcher or protection."

Cara frowned. "All right."

"She was exceptionally beautiful, and it's one of the first things someone notices about her, even from afar. I was not an exception to that rule. She kept looking over at me, ignoring the fact I was with a woman at my table, and I caught her staring a few times. It made me curious."

Cara took a bite of the ice cream, too. "She is beautiful, but cold, too. Even in your wedding pictures, I could see it. It's strange."

"It's not strange if you know her," Gian murmured. "Back to my story, though. I let my date go early; my mother had set it up, and back then, I didn't mind playing into Celeste's meddling from time to time, but nothing was coming from that."

Gian shrugged. "Anyway, she left, and I asked for the bill. The waiter hadn't even brought it over before Elena approached me. By the time he did get there, we were already five minutes into a conversation about who was going to run for mayor that year in the city, as the Ford family seemed like loose cannons, which teams had the best shot at the Stanley Cup, and some movie she wanted to see that was coming out."

"Oh?"

"I offered to take her to see it," Gian said dryly. "Call that a first date, I guess."

Cara took a huge scoop of the ice cream. "And then what happened?"

"I mean, you could say we started dating, but it wasn't like that really, and it was clouded by all sorts of other shit going on."

"Like what?"

"Elena's father was in the midst of a street war with a gang, so I had to be careful about my involvement with her seeming … to their side of things and making it appear like the Guzzi family would get involved. Petty street wars aren't worth much except a growing body count, and the Guzzi family doesn't get mixed up in those sorts of things unless it'll benefit us in some way."

"Details again?" Cara asked.

Gian laughed. "Sort of. I thought *I* was the one being careful, taking her out occasionally, or having her stay over at my place, but never hers. She didn't meet my family or friends, and I didn't meet hers. It turned out, *she* was the one being careful. Elena didn't want her father to know about me, or that she was messing around with me—that's the best way to describe what it was, anyway."

"But you liked her?"

"Well enough," Gian answered, choosing his words carefully. "I liked what she gave me, the pieces of her on the surface, because she never went beyond that. I liked how she was attentive to *me*, only. Especially when we were together, other people didn't exist to her. She doted on the stupid male side of a man's brain that feeds off being *the* man, you know what I mean?"

Cara shrugged, but said nothing.

"Elena works best when she controls a situation, no matter what that situation might entail. And she does that with men, specifically, because she knows she is beautiful, and she knows that using her sexuality and her sweetness is disarming to men who aren't looking for her manipulations. They are unprepared for the attack, for the gut-punch or the knife in their back when they turn away. She makes you trust her, because why would she want to hurt you, this person she so clearly adores? And then she strikes."

"Huh," Cara said quietly, frowning.

"I know, I jumped ahead a bit in explaining that. It'll make sense in a second."

"Go for it."

Gian took a deep breath, and another bite of ice cream, letting the chocolate and peanut-butter flavors wash over his palate before he spoke again. "We had been doing our thing for a few months or so, when she came up pregnant."

Cara stiffened.

Gian didn't miss it.

"Or so she said," he added, knowing it wouldn't make a difference. The words were out there, and they hurt to know. "I had no reason not to believe her, or to think, if she was pregnant, the child might not be mine. Things moved very fast from that point—her father was suddenly involved, and all the things people heard or whispered about that man were right in front of my eyes and very true. He's dangerous and he's volatile. He's manipulative and evil. But aren't we all, in some way?"

Gian shook his head, adding, "Elena wanted to get away from him, and that much was clear. I understood why, too, because he used her and he abused her. He was angry that she had been seeing someone behind his back; he's so abnormally close to her, and controlling of her. At least back then. And when she refused to abort the pregnancy, he nearly beat her to death, and then had her sent to me."

He dropped the spoon to the table with a clatter. "I saw a different Elena then, Cara. One that was scared and small, a victim of a man she just wanted to get away from. And to this day, no matter what that woman has done to me or what she might do in the future, I still see the Elena from that day. Bruised, and swollen, with a bloody, busted mouth, and dried blood matting her hair. I see her, and I never have to think *why*? I think, *why not*? Why not hurt, use, and manipulate to be free, to be happy? Why not use all the things your father taught you to do, in order to protect and advance him, to protect and advance yourself? It doesn't give her a pass, sure, but it certainly makes more sense, in a way."

Cara cleared her throat. "She was lucky she didn't lose the baby, then."

Gian chuckled darkly. "There was no baby to lose, Cara, but I'll get there. Corrado pressured me to do the right thing, with Elena, but also where our family was concerned. He didn't want to face a war with Gabriel on the streets, and he knew how dangerous the man could be. So, a marriage it was."

"And that obviously happened."

"Quite fast, within a couple of months of announcing the engagement." Gian took Cara's spoon from her, scooped some ice cream, and fed her the bite, waiting for her to finish before he continued. "Leading up to the wedding, we had to deal with the usual family things. Which put Elena front row and center for her father. His way of hurting her emotionally when he couldn't hurt her physically, was to shame and embarrass her in front of me, or others. *Does he know*, her father would say, *how you sucked the cock of the mayor's son to pay off my debt?* Things like that."

Cara let out a shaky exhale, and looked away. "That's terrible."

"It reinforced my belief that I was doing the right thing, though I didn't love her, and I knew what a marriage with someone meant in my world. It is for life, there is no out, except for death. But I thought, I was doing the right thing."

"And then?"

"And then a week after we married, I caught Elena drinking wine. From the moment we walked out of the church on our wedding day, something changed with her. She no longer focused on me like she had once done—all that attention, the doting and the adoration, was gone. She didn't need to pretend, you see. Not once she had gotten what she needed from me. I was pissed about the wine, because of the baby."

"But there was no baby, you said?"

Gian nodded once. "She tried to say she had miscarried. We weren't even having sex; we hadn't fucked since the night we married, so how could I say for sure that she was or wasn't losing the baby?"

"Was she?"

"No, there *was no baby*. I had her records at her doctor yanked, though it wasn't my right to, and found there was no pregnancy, at least not within the months she had been with me. Six months *before* we had met, there had been an abortion on file. One of several over the years. She was actually on the depo shot, and had been since the last abortion, so a pregnancy was highly unlikely to begin with."

"Oh, Gian."

"Don't do the pity thing," Gian said, shooting Cara a lopsided grin.

"Not for me. I overlooked a lot of things because I didn't want to question a woman that was clearly in need of help. I was too busy feeding a hero complex and trying to do what everyone else wanted me to. By the time I realized how incredibly fucked I was, and how much Elena had manipulated me, it was too late."

"You were married."

Gian's smile faded. "For life."

"But—"

"There is no but, not for this. Not in the position I was, and while I wanted to send her back to her father with a fuck you and a smile, I couldn't do it. And she fought with me daily, she raged at me. I gave her the things she wanted, a beautiful penthouse, new cars, furs, nearly a million in diamonds. I gave her everything she wanted, just to keep her happy for a short while, but that was the problem."

"It only lasted for a short while," Cara said.

"I couldn't keep her happy, because she had gotten what she wanted from me, and as of that point, I was only a nuisance. So, I moved out, about a year after we married, though we hadn't been even sleeping together or using the same bedroom from almost the day we married. We did it quietly, we were careful about our public side, making sure it still looked like we were a happy couple. We didn't want to provoke her father, after all. Then, as time went by, we stopped pretending unless it was something big or important, like a wedding, a funeral, somewhere our faces might be shot on the news, or whatever."

Cara reached out and stroked Gian's cheek, surprising him at the tender touch. "I'm sorry."

"Don't be, *bella*. It's circumstance and details. That's all it's ever been, Cara. I don't have a paper to say I'm divorced, because I can't. Men like me can't be divorced without ruining everything we worked for. And a divorce might push an already violent man over the edge—something else my family can't afford right now."

"What about … other relationships?"

Gian shrugged. "I haven't had other relationships. For a while, even after we separated, I was faithful. Then one night, I met someone, and I was out of her place before morning even came. I didn't have time to be in a relationship, or the effort it would take to keep up the charade. When you came along, I wasn't so jaded toward women, because I hadn't needed to be in a long time. I had no reason to distrust you, not when you showed your cards that first night, telling me what you did and didn't want. And my God, there was something about you that made me sit down and pay attention. It just blew up from there."

"And you were fucked again."

Gian smiled sinfully. "I didn't mind, Cara. Not with you. You made me love you, and I wanted to be with you, so I was going to try and do that. I just didn't know how. I *was* trying to tell you before you found out in Chicago. I knew I should tell you, but it isn't the kind of conversation that is usually brought up when you first meet someone. As time passed, it became more of me not knowing whether you were going to be with me, or go your own way, so I held off again. I asked what you wanted with me, in the future, and you only said me. You said *me*, love. I just didn't know how to tell you the situation without ruining us. I didn't want to ruin us. And then you were gone."

"I should have listened to this when you offered to tell me before," Cara said sadly, her hand still cupping his cheek, and her thumb stroking sweet lines on his jaw. "I'm sorry that I didn't."

"Circumstance and details have put me back in the position where I have to play house with a woman I despise, who I don't trust. I wish I could be rid of Elena, but I can't send her back to her father. Not that it would do me any good, because she would still be my—"

"Wife," Cara interrupted gently.

"Exactly. I'm sorry that I can't give you the things you deserve. I'm sorry that I love you, Cara, but I can't shout it to anyone who will listen, or make a huge show of getting a ring on your finger and walking you down the aisle. I'm sorry that I was selfish and put you in a position where your worth is tied to my choices. I can't make a home with you, not one that will ever feel proper or permanent, because I fucked up once, and here we are."

"*Gian.*"

"I'm sorry," he repeated. "I wish I could say something different, but it's the only thing I have right now. I'm sorry."

"Me, too," Cara whispered.

• • •

"Gian?"

Gian reached for Cara through his groggy haze of sleep, hearing her call of his name, and wanting to bring her closer. He found her side of the bed empty, and promptly opened his eyes wide. Cara stood in the bedroom doorway, rubbing at her eyes with the back of her hand. A quick check of the clock said it was way too early in the morning for her to be up. Cara didn't get out of bed before eight, not if she didn't have to.

"What are you doing out of bed?" he asked her.

Cara pointed at her rounded stomach, pouting in the darkness. "He makes me pee a lot."

Gian's tired laughter rung out in the bedroom, and he fell back into the bed. "Go to sleep, Cara."

"In a minute."

"What is it, *mon ange?*"

"Did you set up the crib?"

Gian cleared the sleep out of his voice, saying, "Yeah, it needed set up, didn't it? You fell asleep early, I had nothing to do."

"Could have woke me up. There's all sorts of things we could be doing that are fun in bed, you know."

"You need to sleep more than you need me waking you up to get a good fuck."

Although, he was down for that, too. Just not when he could see she was tired as hell.

Cara slipped into the bed, and tucked herself close to Gian's side. Rolling over, he brought her head to his naked chest, and let his hand rest on her lower stomach. A possessive, protective swell washed through his bloodstream at the feeling of his son shifting under his father's palm, one of the first movements Gian had felt of his child.

"Cara?"

"Hmm?"

"I would rather set up a nursery in the penthouse, if you would be willing to stay there, I mean," he said.

Cara let out a soft sigh. "I don't know about that one."

"I don't have to be there, if you don't want me to—"

"Aren't things complicated and difficult enough with all of this? Do we need to add in that sort of thing, too?"

"I'll do whatever you want, love. You know that."

"I do."

"But my son is, and will always be, non-negotiable between us. For him, and for you if you would let me, I will move the world. I won't compromise about my child. Not when it comes to caring for him, or providing him with whatever he needs, not to mention his mother."

"I should hope not."

"Then consider the penthouse now, and what it would mean to be somewhere that's safer, better watched, closer to certain places you frequent. It would also be easier for me to come, on that side of things."

"And go," she added quietly. "It would make it easier for you to come and *go*, Gian."

"I can't help that, Cara."

"I know," she murmured.

"Consider it, for him."

"And for you."

Gian smirked, pressing a kiss to her soft hair. "And for me, yes."

"Gian?"

"What, *amore?*"

"Shut up and fuck me now."

"Cara, you should sleep while you can. You need to slee—"

She was the one to shut him up, instead, by leaning up to catch his moving lips with a hard kiss, and in the next breath, she had climbed on top of him under the sheets. In no time at all, she had discarded his boxer-briefs, and the short nightie she had on did little to hide the fact she was naked underneath.

Cara shivered under his wandering hands, and she let him pull that damn nightie off her body entirely, baring all of her to him. The heavy swells of her breasts fit perfectly into his palms, and she sighed happily when he tweaked her nipples under his forefinger and thumb. Her back arched under his touch, moving her closer to him when he shifted in the bed to sit up. He traced the gentle curve of her stomach with his fingertips, watching pretty goosebumps bloom over her skin.

Her hands were between their bodies before Gian could even demand it, circling his length and fitting his cock at her cunt. He held Cara's face in his palms as she lowered down on his length, hard and fast. Heat shot through his cock, and straight up his spine, when she was seated on him fully. There was no waiting for her, no slowing or careful movements.

She rode him crazy, so wild. Her nails dug into the hard muscles of his arms as he dragged her closer for a kiss, keeping her there while their tongues warred until he was forced to pull away for a burning breath.

"Oh, my God. Oh, my God," Cara mumbled again and again.

A record on repeat.

All her pretty cries.

The way she looked riding him.

How her body shook and shivered.

It was all such a familiar tune.

Gian loved it.

She was so wet, her cunt squeezing the fucking life out of his body through his dick. He angled his lower half into her lowering body, making it so that her greedy little clit was rubbing against him every time she came down on him fast and hard again.

Gian wanted to give Cara what he knew she liked the most—his fingers tight around her throat, his body pounding into hers until she was a mess of tears and sweat into the bedsheets. But he held back, and only because he thought that might not be okay, given her state. Instead, he settled on letting his hand rest against the thrumming beat of her pulse on her neck, and his teeth leaving marks on her lips and tits. He let her set the pace, and how rough she wanted to fuck him, not the other way around.

His words spilling out were damn near constant, though, and unstoppable. Whispered harsh and fast in her ear, because he was worried he was going to lose all train of thought before he could get them out in their entirety.

"You're so beautiful, *mon ange*. My good girl, fucking me like you are. Take what you want, Cara, take my cock."

Cara's first orgasm came on like a tsunami of sensation that even Gian could feel, from the way her body tensed and then shook, to the loud, broken cry she released. Her eyes flew wide, the blue of her irises a darkened wave of color, while her pupils had blown wide in her bliss.

So fucking beautiful.

And apparently, it wasn't nearly enough. The second she had calmed, her demands came sure and quick in his ear.

More, and *now*, and *only you, only you, only you.*

How could he refuse?

How could he refuse *her*?

• • •

"Seems we have some work to do," Stephan said.

Gian nodded in agreement with the Capo. "Lots of digging and prying into whoever might be feeding the police information."

"There's a lot of men in this organization," Dom pointed out.

"I'm aware."

"It won't be too difficult," Chris added.

All eyes moved to the quiet enforcer in the corner, who had mostly been playing on his phone and sipping from a glass of water. While the rest of them drank whiskey or a beer, Chris drank water.

"And why do you think that is?" Gian asked his man.

Chris looked up at his boss, shrugging. "Once word begins to travel that the boss is looking for a rat, you'll find that the men who don't want any fucking part of that shit will be the first to point you in the direction you need to be looking. They all pay attention, they simply choose not to speak up unless they need to. Make it so that they need to, boss. That's all."

Dom's gaze swung back to Gian. "How do we even know for sure that the rat *is* in our family?"

"Gabriel is pretty convinced on that fact," Gian replied.

"And he is a voice of reason here?"

"No, but since we all know how he treats someone he likes, imagine how he treats those he doesn't like. If he says he doesn't think there's a rat in his family, it's because he's already made his rounds. It's our turn to do rounds on our end, now."

Gian let the men have their opinions, but he was firm on what he wanted. Soon after, the three men cleared out of his office at the mansion, leaving him alone once again. He had only called the meeting, because he had spent the week keeping a low profile, and trying to spend as much time with Cara as he could. When he knew he had no choice but to head home, he decided to call the meeting.

"You look stressed, Gian."

His attention flew to the new presence in his office. Elena leaned in the doorway, a silk robe cinched tightly at her waist and her arms crossed under her chest. Immediately, he was on edge at Elena's sudden entrance and it had a whole lot to do with the bare legs and black heels she wore. Why did she need a robe and heels like those on at the same time?

It was a dichotomy.

Unless she was looking for something.

He wasn't about to provide it.

"Do you need something?" Gian asked.

"I saw the guys leave. I thought I should check on you."

Right.

"I'm fine, about to head to bed." With that, he stood from his desk, closing his laptop down and putting away his papers. All the while, Elena never moved from her spot in the doorway, forcing Gian to come incredibly close to his wife as he passed her by. Her hand coming up to press against his chest over his dress shirt stopped him for a moment. "What, Elena?"

"I don't interest you at all, do I?"

His gaze lingered over the delicate column of her throat, to the peeks of her breasts at the top of the robe, and then down over her trim waist and the expanse of her legs. "You did once, but it was a game you used to hurt me with. Nothing about that interests me at all, Elena."

"Why her, then?"

Gian stiffened. "I beg your pardon?"

"What about Cara Rossi is so special? She's pretty, sure. Red hair, tall, slim. But she isn't … spectacular, is she? Or did I miss something?"

He realized in that moment how delicate of a line he was walking with his wife. It was not one he wanted to walk at all, but it seemed Elena was not going to give him a choice in the matter.

"Cara—"

"Did you think I wouldn't know about her visit when you were in jail? Or how curious it is that you are bringing her to visit … not to mention, when she's pregnant? Or that you hole yourself up in her place for days, hiding away from the world?"

"Elena, that's enough," Gian warned. "This isn't your business, and you have no reason to care, either way."

"Someone told me she was pregnant," Elena continued, not heeding his warning in the slightest. "I had to see, so I did. I approached her in the grocery store. I don't think she even knew who I was, or if she did, it probably wasn't until after. A boy, she told me. Marcus for a name, maybe. You're going to give your bastard—even if he is a firstborn boy—your family's name? And not even for a middle name, but a *first* name, his given name. I don't understand, I guess, what about her that does it for you. Like I said, nothing about her is spectacular or amazing. She's just a woman."

"Because she isn't you," Gian said, "she is the complete opposite of you, Elena. And that is *everything*. Stay away from Cara, understood?"

His rage simmered through his bloodstream, but he managed to hide it for the moment. How long that would last, he couldn't say.

How dare she approach Cara?

How dare she seek her out?

Had Cara even realized?

"I will make your father look like a saint, if you hurt that woman or my child," Gian murmured in Elena's ear. "We both know the only reason you're still a problem for me is *because* of your father. You have things in this life that she doesn't, where I'm concerned. You have my last name, my homes, my money, and my grandmother's rings on your finger. And you don't deserve a single fucking one of them. You know it, too. So, try not to let your need to play games with the lives of others cloud the smart part of your brain that knows you're safe and comfortable in your good little life here, Elena. I don't love you and you will never have my children, because those are things *she* has. And if you try to take them away from her because you are jealous or bitter, I will scatter you from one end of this city to the other."

Gian smiled, but Elena stayed stone-cold.

"Just so we're clear," he added.

Elena stayed where she was in the doorway. Gian went to bed. Cara, however, got an enforcer to watch her the very next morning.

TEN

"Eight weeks left—let the countdown begin," Jenny teased.

Cara huffed as she bent down to pick up the rest of the art supplies on the small kiddie table. "Don't remind me."

"You're thirty-two weeks pregnant, Cara. How can you not know it every second of your day?"

"That's my point. I don't need more reminders."

Jenny laughed. "Uh-huh. Are you nervous, is that it?"

"Excited, but mostly …" Cara waved at her very large stomach that made it hard to sleep, eat, and almost every other function of life, including breathing some days. "I'm just over all of this."

"Don't worry. It will all be worth it in the end. Once you have the little one in your arms, all of the hells of pregnancy and birth will be forgotten."

Oh, Jesus.

Birth.

That was another thing Cara was not looking forward to. Not by a *long* shot. That, she was scared of. Terrified, even. A *baby*—a small human—was going to come out of her *body*. Women might have been doing it for millennia, but sweet Jesus, Cara had *not*.

"Wow, you just went white," Jenny noted.

Cara tried to be nonchalant as she put all the supplies away into their proper places. "I guess birth makes me a little worried."

"When a baby gets in, Cara, it has to eventually come out."

"Yes, that is the only guarantee about pregnancy. I'm well aware of that."

"Women's bodies are made for this, too."

"Again, I know."

"Then perhaps you should stop squeezing that glue bottle before you bust the top of it off," Jenny pointed out.

Cara instantly dropped the bottle of glue into the container. "Okay, so maybe the idea of birth freaks me out a bit."

"A lot, you mean."

"Make it easy on me, Jenny."

The older woman laughed, saying, "You know I won't do that. My whole job is to make people talk about their deepest, darkest issues. Since no one else is around right now, I might as well work on you."

"I'm not in need of a therapist, but thank you." Cara shot the woman a smile. "Really, though, I know it'll be fine. I'm just freaked out because I'm twenty-seven, *very* pregnant, and it's almost at the end."

"Which means?"

"My whole life is about to change?"

Jenny nodded. "But you know that, too. You know little man is going to change things for you, from your daily life, to school, to work, and that's just the surface. Emotionally, physically, and mentally, change will come there, too. The fact that you know these things means the transition will come easier for you, from a woman, to a *mom*. Too many live in the clouds when they're pregnant, and then baby comes, and boom, back down to reality. It's a hard pill to swallow."

"You make motherhood sound … like war."

"For some, it can be," Jenny murmured.

"I'm lucky that I have people to help," Cara said, shrugging. "Like the ladies here, or my aunt and uncle. The father and some of his family, too."

Cara said that last sentence quieter, and offered little to no information about Gian, his family, or who she meant.

"You say that like you're leaving someone out," Jenny noted.

Cara frowned, and turned to face the woman. "It would be nice to have my sister, too. You know?"

"To wish for things you cannot have, is human."

"Maybe so, but I don't like to dwell."

"And I think it's more than acceptable for you to wish your *twin* sister was here for this, even if it hurts a lot to think about. You shared your whole lives with one another. Boys, graduation, smiles and tears, laughter … *life*."

Cara cleared the emotion lodging in her throat. "Yeah and this is one of the very few things we won't get to share, so that's a little hard. But it doesn't matter, right? What's done is done, so let's get up, brush ourselves off, and move on."

"It *does* matter, Cara. My advice is that you don't hold those feelings in, or push them aside in pursuit of happier days, especially not now," Jenny said, coming close enough that she could soothingly rub a hand over Cara's back. "Because even if you think not dealing with those thoughts and feelings is better, you're actually doing yourself, and the baby, a great disservice."

"How so?"

"Babies have a way of reminding us of everything we are without once they come into the world, although unintentionally. The wash of hormones, all the changes, and everything else comes together like the Big Bang to make one hell of a combination on new mothers. Deal with how you feel now, so that when he is here, those things don't surprise you."

Cara nodded. "Okay."

"And I am always here to talk," Jenny added.

"Sometimes, I think you just like making people cry."

"Hey." Jenny covered a spot on her chest with her hand. "My heart. Did we not just have a deep conversation, of which you will take something away to use to help yourself?"

"So?"

"Remember what I said, Cara. Seriously."

"I will," Cara promised, "and thanks for making me talk. Too many people are fine and happy with me brushing them off when I say I'm fine, or something similar. You don't."

"Not my job to," Jenny said, ticking a finger over her shoulder as she headed for the door. "Oh, well, hello there. Can we help you?"

Cara turned to look at who Jenny had greeted, only to see a waiting Gian standing in the doorway. "Gian."

He pointed at Cara, a sexy smile growing on his handsome features. "I'm actually looking for her, as she has an appointment today, and I would like to join her."

"You don't have to do to that, Gian. They just want to make sure he's turned properly now."

"My son, so yes, I do."

Well, now someone else could put a face to her baby's father when Cara refused to.

Jenny shot a wink back at Cara. "Well, there she is. Why do you look so familiar to me?"

"My family is well-known in Toronto. We're often on the news, or something similar."

It took the older woman a moment to put together *who* she was looking at. A horrible sensation of dread dropped heavily in Cara's stomach as she waited for it to click.

"Does the name Guzzi help at all?" Gian asked Jenny.

"Oh … my." Jenny lost her happy disposition, but quickly plastered on a false smile. "Are you sure you're in the right place, then, Mr. Guzzi?"

"Jenny," Cara warned.

Gian rattled off something that sounded like a business name, but Cara couldn't be sure. Jenny tensed, and then stared at Gian. "Really?"

"Yes. I thought I might take a look around while I was here, if you wouldn't mind."

"Does she know?" Jenny asked.

Gian's gaze darted to Cara, and then quickly back to the woman standing in front of him. "There was no reason for her to. It was a common thing long before her appearance and work here."

"And the use of the business name?"

"No affiliation to a family name that may make some uncomfortable to be attached to, except in details that no one has time or need to dig into," Gian replied with a smirk. "It does the same job as anonymous donations, of course, but simpler come tax time."

"I'll have to take your word for that." Jenny looked back at Cara once again. "Thanks for helping to clean this place up. I will see you on Monday, right?"

"Monday," Cara agreed.

Once Jenny was gone, Cara looked to Gian.

"What was all that about?"

"Pardon?" he asked.

"That vague, weird conversation."

Gian shrugged his shoulders, his lips curving teasingly at the edges. "I have no idea what you're talking about, *mon ange*."

"Gian."

He glanced away, shoving his hands in his pockets. "So, the woman who started this whole place—"

"Carolina Demaske."

"She was a good friend to my grandmother, on my mother's side, especially throughout her life, long after she no longer needed the safe haven that Carolina provided. There was a time when my grandmother had no one else but for Carolina, and it was a message she passed down on us all."

Cara took in those words and what they meant. "You donate money to the shelter?"

"Monthly," Gian admitted, "and it is just one of many that I donate to, personally. I know my mother and father, and even my sister and brother, donate to other places or things they want to support. Carolina's House has always been one I focused on, personally."

"That's ... wonderful, Gian."

"I have too much, I don't need it all, Cara. I can afford to give some away. Unfortunately, there are those who are not comfortable with taking money from a man with my last name and affiliations, so I have become smarter about donating, using businesses as a shell of sorts, where my name is too deep into the paperwork for people to care."

"And I take it, this started long before I ever stumbled upon this place?"

He laughed, dark and husky.

It nearly killed her every time she heard that damn sound come out of his mouth. It was so fucking unfair that all the pregnancy hormones running through her body made it even more difficult to control herself around Gian. All it took was one of his chuckles, a look, or a smirk, and she was a stupid pile of hormones and desire.

And oh, God.

Being *touched?*

Apparently, Cara's body had nerves where they never existed before.

Gian *loved* that.

Cara was just … overwhelmed.

All. The. Time.

"Long before you," Gian said. "I may have upped the amounts I donate over the last few months, but I tend to do that whenever I have a particularly good year, money-wise."

"Oh."

"So, the appointment?"

Cara picked up her jacket and purse off the back of a chair. "You don't have to come for that, I told you. It's just a checkup to make sure he's where he's supposed to be."

Once she was close enough for him to reach out and grab her, Gian did just that. Cara found herself tugged into his side, his arm wrapped around her lower back, and then he pressed a soft kiss to her temple. Cara's smile grew as her eyes fluttered closed.

"I want to go," he murmured against her skin. "And then I would like to take you out to eat, get you home, relaxed and comfortable, and see what happens."

"That does sound nice."

Gian's fingers danced over the column of her throat before he pushed her wayward curls aside. Just the feeling of his fingers against her skin was enough to make heat and lust bloom.

This was heaven *and* hell.

Cara had been trying to let Gian in more, and not be so guarded. Especially not where his wife was concerned, or even just them in general. She finally understood what he meant about circumstances and details muddling up a situation that most people only saw from the outside, and never what was below the surface.

He made her so happy.

He loved her so much.

Why did she have to give up those beautiful things, and Gian, because others said they were wrong? She wouldn't. Certainly not now.

"I love you, Cara," Gian said.

Like he could read her fucking mind.

"I know you do. You can say it in three languages, remember?"

He never forgot to tell her he loved her, in the loud moments, the quiet ones, and all the times in between. He never once forgot.

"And I can mean it in every one of them, Cara."

No, they weren't bad or wrong.

• • •

"I can't believe it's June already," Stephanie said.

Cara glanced over her laptop, the dissertation she had been working on for the better part of two hours finally drifting from her mind. She welcomed the distraction. "I can't believe I have one week left to finish this damn paper."

"You'll kill it, no worries there."

"Thanks," Cara said, smiling.

"But are you going to make graduation, or …?" Stephanie trailed off with a nod at Cara's stomach. "How far along now?"

"Thirty-three weeks, and I probably won't make graduation."

"That sucks."

Cara shrugged. "Late July ceremony is not going to coincide for me, unfortunately. I mean, I probably *could* make it, if I wanted to. But I'm going to be *really, really* pregnant, if I haven't already had the baby by then. I figure since I already took time off from the shelter for around that time, I should probably use it to chill as much as I can."

"I get that. And hey, the university does do the mini-ceremonies in the beginning of the new semester for those who took the summer to earn their final grades, or whatever."

"Yeah, Professor Madele told me about it. She made it clear that if I didn't participate in the coming one, I had better be there."

Cara leaned back in her chair, resting her hand to the top of her swelled stomach. She thought the baby boy was already like this father, constantly wanting to move, never satisfied with staying still, and far too restless for his own good. Even in the womb. She could only imagine what he would be like *after* birth.

Still just like his father, probably.

"Miss Rossi?"

Two men dressed similarly in plain black suits approached the table, one already holding out a badge to identify himself. Not that Cara would have needed to see the badges to know the men were cops, or detectives. Growing up the way she had, cops were easy to detect. They all walked the same, dressed the same, spoke the same, and smelled the same.

Like a *cop*.

"Detective Seeley, and this is my partner—"

"Yeah, that's nice, hello to both of you," Cara interrupted. "What can I do for you?"

"Actually, Miss—"

"Cara, please."

"Cara," Detective Seeley said, drawling her name out for longer than was necessary. "Actually, Cara, we were hoping you might be able to do something for us. Or rather, help us with some information regarding Gian Guzzi."

Cara passed her friend a look, although to Stephanie's benefit, the girl was trying to look *anywhere* but at the detectives. "Hey, Steph, could you give us a few minutes?"

Stephanie nodded quickly, and gathered her things. "Sure can. I was about to head out anyway. Call me when you wanna meet up to sprint again, Cara."

"Okay."

The detectives kept quiet until Stephanie was gone. Thankfully, the library was mostly empty, as it was only mid-day, and the girls had picked a quieter part of the library to work. One between the bookshelves, where only two tables were set up in the large rows.

"All right, ask," Cara said, glancing up at the detective once she knew they were alone.

"Can you confirm you have personal ties to Gian Guzzi?" the detective asked.

"Define personal for me."

The man's gaze dropped to Cara's stomach. "We have reason to believe he may be the father of your child."

"What reason is that?"

"Well, we can't exactly give that information away, Miss."

"Again, it's *Cara*. I'm not married, I'm twenty-seven years old, and I'm pregnant. We have far passed the *respectable lady* stage in my life, thanks."

"Is Gian Guzzi the father of your child?" Seeley asked.

Cara sighed heavily. "And if he is? I don't see what that would have anything to do with detectives approaching me mid-day, in the library of my university, when I'm attempting to finish my dissertation so that I can get my diploma before my son is born."

"Our apologies for intruding on your time," the shorter of the two men said quickly. "But we have reason to believe your personal affiliation to Gian may help us with our current investigations."

"And what investigations are those?"

Cara did not plan to make this easy on the police, but she also had to be careful with how much she pushed. Given her dual citizenship, trouble with officials could put her back across the border without so much as a paper to sign.

"Surely you're aware that Mr. Guzzi is affiliated to some … criminal business in Toronto? We're aware you visited him while he was serving time in jail, just a few months ago. We would like to discuss your relationship with him, and what else you may know."

Cara took her time to save her document, shut down her laptop, and put her things away. She knew that no matter what, she didn't have a choice but to play along with the detectives, and keep her nose out of trouble. That didn't mean she planned to give them anything.

"Would you mind a trip to the station, just so that we can get our questions and your answers on an official record?" Seeley asked.

Cara waved a hand, as if to say, *whatever*. "Could I make a phone call before we go?"

"If you think you need to."

"I think I do."

The detectives probably assumed Cara planned to call a lawyer. She called Gian. He and a lawyer met her at the station.

Cara answered *nothing* after that.

• • •

"I can't see anything," Cara grumbled.

Gian's hands rubbed her shoulders, his dark chuckles echoing in her ear. He kissed the spot behind her ear and then said, "That's the point, *mon ange*. It's a surprise."

She reached up to try and readjust the blindfold over her eyes, but Gian quickly rerouted her arms back to her sides.

"Nope, hands stay down."

"But—"

"Little ledge here, and then some steps, love, so be careful."

Cara rolled her eyes behind the blindfold, but managed to get up whatever stairs were there with Gian's help. "Can you at least give me a hint?"

"Where's the fun in that?"

"Where's the fun in being told you're going to have a nice night with ice cream and a back rub, only to be made to dress up and be taken out. In *kitten heels*, Gian. I couldn't even wear my comfy shoes!"

"You will be happy that I made you wear the kitten heels. Someone might take pictures, and those shoes you wear do not look nice with a dress."

"Says you."

"And you, when you're not thirty-four weeks pregnant, Cara."

She huffed under her breath, hating that he was probably right. Then, she had another thought. "Why would anyone take pictures?"

"You'll see," her lover replied vaguely. "Gilles will drive you back to the penthouse once this is all done and over with, as it's not the kind of event men are usually invited to and I have something to pick up across the city."

"What happened to Chris?" Cara asked about her previous enforcer, who still refused to call her by her name.

"Chris has other things to look after at the moment. Sometimes, it's better to put people where they get the best business done. Chris happens to be very good at getting information from people, and I need that right now."

"Because of the cops?"

"Amongst other things," Gian muttered. "We're not talking about that tonight. This is all for you. And I thought you liked Gilles?"

"I do, he just …"

"What?"

"Talks a lot," Cara said.

Gian laughed, his hands tightening on her as he directed her around a corner, or so she assumed. "He is a talker."

"Chris barely talks at all, except to repeat orders or something."

"Okay, enough of this, smile, *bella*."

Cara didn't know what he was talking about, but the blindfold was suddenly pulled from her face, allowing her vision to clear. It took Cara a couple of seconds of blinking, and a few shouts of "Surprise!" from the people standing around one of Gian's restaurants for her to realize what was happening.

Pretty, pale-blue and green decorations littered the restaurant. Each table held different items—a spot for gifts, one for a massive cake decorated in similar colors, and the like. A banner hanging from one chandelier to another read *Baby Shower!*

Cara took in the people around her. Women she worked with at the shelter and the women *from* the shelter. Her few friends from university, and the professor she enjoyed spending time with and who had helped her through her difficult moments. And surprisingly, nearing the front of the guests, Cara found Gian's mother and another woman, who, guessing by her features and how she kept close to Celeste, was probably his sister.

Crystal, Cara thought her name was. Gian didn't talk about her a lot.

"You've been busy," Gian said. "And working far too hard, *mon ange*. Ma asked about a shower for you, because she wanted to—at least—send something over. And then a couple of weeks ago, Jenny contacted me about helping with something like this to surprise you. You're not too angry, right?"

Cara just *blinked*.

"Why would I be angry, Gian?"

How could she be angry?

"You don't like surprises," he said.

She had assumed, given the circumstances of the pregnancy and Gian's marriage, and how busy her last few weeks before birth would be, that something like a shower was out of the question. She didn't even think she knew enough people to have a proper shower, not that it was acceptable for her to plan her own, anyway.

She didn't have to worry about anything, apparently.

Gian took care of things.

Always.

"It's wonderful. Thank you."

Gian kissed the back of her head, never hesitating with all of the eyes watching them. "Enjoy your party, Cara. I love you, pretty girl."

• • •

"I can certainly understand why Gian adores you so much," Crystal said quietly, giving Cara a small smile.

"It's a shame things are so … complicated," Celeste added.

Cara cleared the awkwardness from her tone before speaking. "Thank you for coming, and for helping them set up, and everything else. Really, it was too much."

"Nothing is too much. Not for my grandbaby." Celeste waved her hand as if to dismiss that statement. "What a silly thought."

"Cara, are you ready?"

She looked over her shoulder to find Gilles—the enforcer Gian had said was non-negotiable for the unforeseeable future—waiting at the front doors of the restaurant.

"Just a second," she told the man.

"I'll grab the last bit of stuff and put it in the truck."

"Thank you." Cara turned back to Celeste and Crystal, the last two guests she had yet to say goodbye to. Everyone else had already gone and the staff had mostly cleaned the place. Cara had managed to sneak a few keepsakes to put in her baby's memory box of the day. "Time to get home and sleep, I do have to put in hours tomorrow at the shelter. It was very nice to meet you, Crystal. Thank you for coming, again. Really."

The woman shrugged. "Maybe we'll do something again soon, Cara. It just all depends."

Cara didn't ask what their future meetings would depend on, because she already knew. Privacy. Public opinion. Gian's wife. She didn't need the verbal reminders. Her mind never let her forget, now.

"Okay, let her go," Celeste ordered. "And I want one more of those pretty blue drinks before we go, too."

One more hug later and Cara headed out of the restaurant behind Gilles, whose arms were filled with his fifth round of baby shower gift bags, filled with too many items to count.

"Do babies really need all of this?" Gilles asked.

Cara helped to open the back of the truck, since her enforcer's arms were otherwise occupied. "I don't think they need *all* of it, but it certainly is cute."

And Cara swore everybody oohed and awed over every little outfit, pair of shoes, and tiny rattle she pulled from the gift bags.

"But look at it. Look at *all* of it."

She did.

The truck bed was filled.

It was a lot.

"I'm grateful," Cara said, laughing.

"But it's too much for a baby, right? Since when do newborns care how many outfits they have, or if they have a swing thing that bounces? Does the baby really need twenty pairs of socks, or bibs that look like bandanas?"

"He'll use it all, eventually."

Gilles shook his head. "It's crazy. Women go nuts over this stuff, and I just don't understand why."

"I take it you don't have kids, then."

The man looked *horrified*.

"Jesus, no," he muttered, glancing up to the sky at the same time he made the sign of the cross over his chest.

"I'm not sure God will help to keep the babies away, Gilles. They're not demons or evil spirits."

He stared at her with wide eyes. "That depends on who you ask."

Well, she would give him that.

"To the penthouse?" Cara asked.

Gilles nodded, urging her around to his side of the truck. "The penthouse; boss's orders."

The backseat was also filled, as was the front passenger side, so apparently, she would be sitting directly behind him in the back.

Cara turned to thank Gilles as he opened the back door to help her climb in the lifted truck, but she didn't get the words out. The last things she saw were dimmed car lights, before the vehicle turned sharply off the road, and headed directly for them. She felt the strong hands of the enforcer shove her into the truck at the very last second, but it was all black after that.

She could still hear the sound of metal crushing against metal when she woke up in the hospital screaming.

Gian.

She screamed for him.

And for her baby.

ELEVEN

"Gian … *Gian!*"

Cara's hoarse, panicked cry had Gian sitting straight in the uncomfortable hospital chair. His eyes flew wide, not that he had been sleeping. He couldn't sleep, really. In his daze of watching monitors and waiting, he had settled into a headspace that kept his anxiety and rage at bay, but forced him into a still state of semi-consciousness.

"Gian!"

"Shh," Gian murmured, "it's all right, *mon ange*. Everything's fine. You're fine. The baby is fine. I'm fine."

He was leaning closer to Cara's hospital bed, instantly, already squeezing her hand that he hadn't let go of since he came into the room. His other hand swept through her mess of curls, sweeping the hair from her face so that her searching blue eyes could find his, and she would relax.

Again.

This was the third time since he had arrived that she'd woken up confused, in a state, and unable to calm down. The first two times, his presence had done very little for her. Nurses had rushed in, then, needing Cara calm again for the baby's sake, had administered something into her IV that put her back to sleep.

She was lucky.

So fucking lucky.

At first, Gian had thought a concussion was likely, given the gash on Cara's hairline, and the bump behind her right ear. The doctor had agreed, and every thirty minutes, Cara had been woken up, checked over as best as was possible, and then allowed to rest again. Not that she had understood much of what was going on.

Cara's frightened gaze finally met Gian's and for the first time, she relaxed without the help of added medication. She slumped into the bed, but not before her arm—tacked and taped with an IV and tubes—snaked around his neck, and dragged him closer.

"The baby is perfectly fine," Gian told her again before she could ask. He could already see her questions forming. "He's great, his heartbeat is strong and they brought in the portable ultrasound machine to look everything over."

Cara's hold on him loosened, but barely. "Okay."

"Do you want a drink, or something?"

"Water."

"Sure, *bella*. You have to let me go first."

She did but it took a while. He quickly got the glass of water ready, with a bendy straw, and then helped her to drink until she was satisfied. Her voice wasn't as dry when she spoke again.

"My head hurts and my side, too."

Gian nodded. "You hit your head pretty hard inside the truck, and—"

"He pushed me."

"Hmm?"

"Gilles," Cara said, her brow furrowing and her gaze dimming with memories. "He pushed me into the truck, out of the way, when the lights came out of nowhere."

Ah.

Well, yet another reason for Gian to thank the enforcer and make sure he was given a proper send off to the heavens. For now, though, Gilles' body was still chilling on a slab in the morgue.

"You probably hurt your bottom rib at the same time," Gian explained. "Not broken, but it took a hard hit, like your head."

Cara's fingers danced along her hairline, and she winced at the feeling of the stitched slice that was a good two inches long. "Ow."

"Don't touch," he said, moving her hand away and tucking it into his own. "It's going to be sore for a while, but it'll heal nicely, given the way they stitched it."

Her wince deepened into a scowl, and her body tensed.

"*Ow.*"

Gian looked over at the monitor, recognizing how Cara's body tensed with that specific pain. He watched the little paper coming out of the machine spike but quickly drop. It had been nearly forty-five minutes since the last time it did that, and this time, the duration had been significantly shorter.

According to the nurses, that was a good sign to see.

"What in the hell was that?" Cara asked when the spike dropped and tapered off completely.

"A contraction," Gian said gently. "You were having them pretty steadily for a while, and they gave you some meds to slow it down, if possible. It worked, anyway. Soon, the contractions will taper off to nothing at all, and it'll be fine. That's what these are monitoring."

He moved the sheets covering Cara aside, so then she was able to see the bands and circular monitors wrapped around her middle.

"A *what?*"

"A contraction," he repeated, "though they're pretty short and not spiking high when they do hit now."

"I shouldn't be having those yet, Gian. It's too soon."

He shushed her again, kissing her softly on the mouth to quiet her fears. "The accident set them off, but he's *fine*. They're stopping. They checked and there was no dilation. He's got a bit more time to be safe in you, no worries there."

How Gian managed to stay calm, and speak carefully as to not panic Cara more than she already was, he didn't know. Inside, he felt like a raging fucking hurricane. A very small part of him knew that right then, Cara needed his calm, controlled demeanor.

He could do that.

For a little while.

Cara blinked, her panic subsiding slowly. "Where is Gilles?"

Gian sighed, his gaze darting away. "He didn't survive the impact."

"What about the other car—the driver? Are they okay?"

His rage flooded back into his veins, hot and heavy, demanding attention and wanting soothed in some violent way.

Gian would get to it.

Eventually.

"Hit and run," he said as calmly as he could manage.

In other words: *entirely fucking intentional.*

Gian wouldn't tell Cara that, though. At least, not while she was recovering in a hospital bed. These were the kinds of conversations that shouldn't be had in a hospital, simply because the walls had ears that were always listening.

And the cops would be back soon enough ...

Gian, on the other hand, would be looking for the fucker behind the wheel that killed his enforcer, and damn near took the love of his life and his unborn child away from him. *Soon.* He already had a suspicion of who might be involved, though he had no particular reason to suspect her, except he wouldn't put it past his wife.

That, and he didn't trust Elena as far as he could throw her. He certainly didn't have a reason *why* Elena would have set something like this up, but sometimes, she didn't need a reason. She just needed to be able to do something and she would. Especially if it meant hurting someone who had hurt her.

"All those things," Cara said quietly.

"What things?"

"The baby things. The gifts from the shower. They were beautiful and tiny. They're all ruined now."

"You don't have to worry about those things, Cara. They can be replaced. They're just *things*, they're not you or the baby. Some of it is probably okay, whatever was in the back under the truck bed cover. But it doesn't matter right now, don't focus on it or worry."

"I know, I just ..."

"Your mind's way of processing," he supplied.

Cara nodded faintly. "I'm tired, Gian."

He could see that in her, too. In her dropping lids, slack lips, and weakened grip on his hand. Another nurse would be in to check on her soon, but he figured she could get a bit more sleep before that happened.

"Rest, *amore*."

"You won't leave, right?"

"Not tonight," he promised.

"Did you see the baby on the ultrasound when they checked him?"

Gian smiled, cupping Cara's face in his hands, and stroking her cheeks with his thumbs. "I did. He looked like he might have waved, but I think he was just swiping at the thing pushing on him. He didn't like that very much."

"He does that every time. And he's okay, you're sure?"

"He's beautiful and perfect, Cara."

Just like her.

So beautiful.

So, so perfect.

And fuck *anybody* who tried to ruin that or take them from him.

• • •

Gian stepped out of his Mercedes, and surveyed the cars parked around the Guzzi mansion's circular driveway. Too many cars for a Saturday. And none he particularly recognized right off the bat.

A flash of irritation settled in his gut, as he had come to the mansion for a fucking reason, and he wanted to deal with it right then. Not at some later point, when his wife was alone.

Despite it being the weekend, and knowing he *should* stay put as he had been doing for several months without fail, Gian didn't bother to even grab his keys out of the ignition. He was all too aware that he still needed to keep up appearances with his wife, but he also wasn't interested in playing to the mafia's politics at the moment. Once he was done with his business here, he was heading right back to Cara, to get her settled in at home and comfortable again.

Or as comfortable as she could be, given the circumstances.

Inside the mansion, Gian found his wife, and *several* of her very loud friends in the common sitting area. Drunk, apparently. On a Saturday afternoon.

Elena rarely had parties and it wasn't often she brought over guests. Gian might have even taken a second look when his wife said she had friends, because she never spoke fondly of anyone except herself and her dead mother.

Her friends, however, were not what Gian would consider suitable pals for Elena. All women who had made their names and money from marrying men with deep pockets. Men who happened to be beyond a certain age. A few of the ladies had too much plastic and silicone pumped into their bodies.

Sure, the women were Toronto Elite. They regularly graced the society pages. They were also constant, unrelenting, non-stop drama. Those stupid fucking Housewives reality shows had *nothing* on these women.

Gian certainly didn't approve of whom Elena called her friends, but the very sad fact was, she fit right in. Perfectly. Then again, Elena could fit in everywhere. She only needed to want to, and make an effort.

And hell, if her time and efforts were distracted by these awful *femmes*, then he didn't give a shit. As long as it wasn't on him.

Gian stood in the entryway of the sitting room, shaking his head as the maid attempted to clean up what appeared to be a wine spill. Her effort was fruitless, because one of the women leaned toward Elena, and clearly drunk, simply spilled more right over the same spot.

"Mariana," Gian said loudly, calling their maid out by name. He also gained the attention of the rest of the drunken women acting foolish, including his wife. "Mariana, if the ladies can't manage to keep the wine in their glasses, please stop refilling them. Why don't you take a break for a little while? You look like you need it."

Mariana stood quickly, her aging face flustered. "Yes, sir."

"Just about time to break up the party, ladies," Gian said, turning back to the room. "Sorry about that."

But not really.

"Gian," Elena whined, "you can't just come in here and ruin my lunch with the girls."

Gian arched a single brow at his wife, silencing her from saying anything further. Mariana scooted by him in the entryway, her head tucked down. "Actually, Mariana, take the rest of the day off. You won't see funds deducted on your pay. It seems Elena has forgotten that your job is *not* to cater to her every whim and fancy, but rather, to keep her house clean because she refuses to do it herself."

Mariana hesitated, looking back at him with wary eyes. "If you're sure?"

"Positive. Say hello to your husband for me. I haven't seen him in a while."

"I will. Thank you, sir."

Gian faced the sloppy drunks in his sitting room once more. "Elena, have your friends leave, or join me in the kitchen. *Now.*"

"Gian!"

Elena's mortified shriek grinded on every single nerve that Gian had left. He managed to ignore it, but it was goddamn hard. Not bothering to wait on his wife's decision, Gian headed for the kitchen, listening to the voices he was leaving behind.

"My, he's certainly in a mood, isn't he?" one of the women asked.

"Oh, he's always in a damn mood," Elena muttered. "Don't mind him. He'll probably head upstairs for the rest of the day. We won't even know he's here."

"We never see him out with you, Elena."

"It's better that you don't, trust me."

Gian rolled his eyes upward, feeling the tension headache beginning to build in his temples. Fuck no, he would not be staying. Even if that meant coming back to find the entire mansion trashed from Elena's nonsense.

"What in the hell do you want?" Elena hissed at his back.

Gian had heard her enter the kitchen behind him, but he focused on his task of getting a glass of water. That way, he could resist the urge to put his hands around her throat and choke the fucking life out of her.

"No calls came in from you last night," Gian noted. "You weren't concerned when I didn't make it home?"

He looked back at her, noting her glazed eyes and messier than normal appearance. Drinking before supper could do that to a person.

Elena shrugged. "You come and go, Gian. This isn't the first weekend, recently, where you've stayed away until we have to be seen at church. What does it matter? You told me to fuck off, so I have. Isn't that what you want, for me to leave you alone?"

Yes, but he *needed* to believe she was actually doing that, too.

"And where were you, anyway?" Elena asked.

Gian stiffened a bit, but chose to answer partly honestly. "With Cara."

He decided not to mention the accident, or the hospital. His best defense against Elena's games—or any that she might be playing—were to let her set a trap, and then subsequently fall into it with her usual lies and manipulations.

Elena sighed. "You don't have to just … throw that in my face, you know."

"I didn't mean for it to sound that way."

"Well, it does. And that's kind of awful of you. I'm aware you have a mistress, and that she's pregnant with your child, you don't need to add onto it by giving me a play-by-play of your activities with her. It's embarrassing enough."

"You asked where I was, and I told you."

"Yes, for *no* reason."

"Actually, there was one. Cara was involved in a hit and run last night. It seemed, from onlookers, that it was very intentional. A man of mine was killed, too."

"So?" Elena asked.

She didn't ask about the baby, or Cara, or anything else. She didn't make one of her haughty proclamations about his whore, as she so affectionately called Cara whenever she got the chance and wanted to hurt Gian. Nothing. Simply a *so*, as though it had no affect or bearing on her life, because it didn't. And Elena cared for nothing that didn't involve her in some way.

That was the only reason why Gian chose to believe—at least, for now—that his wife was probably not behind organizing the hit and run. However, he put Elena on a very short leash where giving her any sort of trust was concerned.

"I'm going to head out again," Gian said, "I may or may not make it to church on Sunday, it depends."

"If you don't come here before church, then can I not go, too?"

"I don't give a shit. Make an appropriate excuse, when asked."

Elena nodded. "I can do that."

"And I'll try to keep my … activities, a bit more quiet," Gian said. "I certainly don't mean to toss them, or this, in your face, as you said."

"Well, you do. Often. More than you realize."

"I'll be more aware of that, or try."

It was the least he could do.

"Oh, and Elena?"

"What, Gian?"

"You have no reason to be jealous or to compete with any of those women out there, so I'm not sure why you continue to play these games with them like you do."

Elena shot him a look over her shoulder. "Don't I?"

"What do they possibly have, that you don't?"

"*Freedom*, Gian."

"Well, we both know why that is, don't we?" he asked.

Elena only smiled fleetingly and coolly in response.

He would much rather see another woman smiling at him.

• • •

"Here, love," Gian said, offering Cara his hand to help her from the car. She took it, her fingers warming his as she carefully maneuvered her way out of the backseat. "There you are."

Cara eyed the walkway from the side of the road to her apartment building's entrance, and frowned. "That's a long walk."

For a heavily pregnant woman with a bruised rib and lingering headaches from trauma? Yes, it certainly was a long walk. He could fix it for her, and he didn't mind doing just that.

Gian chuckled, and before Cara could refuse him, he swept her up in a cradle-like hold. Her arms flew around his neck, her eyes wide. She was still as light as a feather to him, but he was careful not to jostle her too much in case it caused her unnecessary pain.

"There, that's easy enough."

"Gian, put me down."

Chris strolled behind them, carrying what few bags had been in the back of the car. The enforcer said nothing, only grinned as Gian ignored Cara's demands.

"You're fine where you are, *mon ange*," Gian said. "Enjoy the view."

"I'm too heavy—"

"No, you're not."

"The scale says I am twenty-five pounds heavier."

"The man that loves you says you're *perfetto, bella, mia tesoro*."

She pursed her lips, half-heartedly glaring at him. "Why do you always do that?"

"Hmm, do what?"

"Say the right things all the time."

Gian smirked down at her. "It's a gift."

"It's certainly something."

Chris stepped up to unlock the building door and hold it open, but stayed behind them as Gian carried Cara to the apartment.

"Just set the bags inside the door," Gian told Chris as Cara unlocked the apartment.

"Got it, boss."

It didn't take them long to get inside, for Cara to turn the lights on, and for Chris to head back out. Gian urged Cara toward the couch, despite her protests to want to clean, or cook. He wasn't having that shit—she was resting.

"You do realize that no amount of talking is going to change what I want you to do, right?" Gian asked.

Cara sighed heavily, resting into the couch. "I need to sweep, and pick things up."

"I will handle it. You will relax."

"This isn't your—"

"I will handle it, Cara."

She scowled. "You're so stubborn."

"You're one to talk." Gian smirked at the sight of her frustrations. "Now, what do you want me to get you to wear from your dresser? Something comfy?"

"I'm fine."

"Cara."

"Oh, my God, Gian. Don't hover."

He was down on his knees in a flash, resting his hands on her thighs. That wasn't nearly good enough for him, though, so he pushed the over-sized shirt she wore up high enough to get his palms against the swell of her stomach. Quickly, he leaned in and pressed a kiss to her skin, just above her naval.

"I'm not trying to hover," he whispered against her skin, "but I can't help it. Let me do things, Cara, even if you're capable and I'm driving you crazy. Let me help, because I love you, and I need you to be okay. I need to make sure you're okay."

Her fingers drifted through his hair with soothing strokes. "I am fine."

"Now, Cara."

"And the baby is fine."

"Again, *now*." Gian kissed her stomach again, though the baby was quite still. He figured that the boy didn't have much room to move around in anymore. "You don't allow me to do a lot for you as it is. And I understand why, though I want to do more."

"You do enough," she replied.

Gian shook his head. "No, I really don't. I shouldn't be living separate from you, or worried I might miss the call when he finally decides to make his way into the world. You shouldn't have two nurseries in two different places. I shouldn't have to keep a fucking wedding ring tucked away in my car or wear it on my hand, depending on what I'm doing or where I am that day. None of that is what I *should be doing*. None of it, Cara. And it kills me—it's killing me. So if that's how I feel, then I can only imagine what it's like for you."

"Gian—"

"Please just let me help, *amore*. Let me do something."

Cara ran her fingers through his hair again. "Something comfy, then. And a glass of water would be nice."

"All right."

"And you," she added quieter. "You and a blanket would be perfect."

"Get one of those ugly Rom-Com things you like on, too."

Cara smiled beautifully. "You always call them ugly, but you laugh when you watch them. I think secretly, you like them."

He shrugged. "Don't say that too loudly."

"Mmhmm. Blanket, water, comfy clothes, and you. Hurry, Gian."

Standing, he kissed her mouth, soft and sweet. He had to keep it short and pull away fast, because the longer he kissed Cara, the more he wanted to stay right there and keep doing exactly that. Between them, kissing *always* led into something more—fucking was not resting, Gian was forced to tell himself.

Even if he could think of a dozen ways to have Cara *be* resting *while* he fucked her. This was more difficult than he thought it would be.

Gian gathered all the things Cara wanted, including the large, fluffy comforter from her bed. He let her change out of her clothes and into the clean, comfy things he had brought her as he went for the water. By the time he got back to the couch with a glass in hand, Cara had draped herself in the blanket with only her head peeking out from a small hooded bit.

"You look like a human burrito," Gian said.

"Don't judge. Also, the movie is starting, so be quiet."

Chuckling, Gian settled into the couch. Cara crawled, in her blanket burrito, closer, and then snuggled into his chest. He was far more interested in her than the movie, but that was okay, too.

"Why Marcus, again?" Cara asked randomly. "That's the name you like for the baby, isn't it?"

"It is. A family name."

"But all the men I know about in your family don't have that name."

"All the first-born men have it somewhere," he replied. "Usually middle names, like me, and my grandfather. My great-grandfather, and my uncle who died, their first names were Marcus, too."

"Is that why you got the family name, then? Because he died, and you were a first-born boy."

"He died when I was a toddler, actually."

"Why did you get the name being born to a second son?" she asked.

"My uncle didn't have children, and he wasn't married. The name had to pass on to someone, and my parents agreed to give it to me, on the stipulation they chose my given name. Gian Marcus it was."

Cara glanced up at him, her brow puckered in that way of hers. It told him she was overthinking something, which wasn't unusual for her.

"What?" he murmured.

"It seems like it's an important thing to your family—the name, I mean."

"It is. It's very important to us. It's as important as our last name. This is a legacy, Cara. All the men carry it on in one way or another, and it begins with a name."

"But ..."

"Just ask, love. Whatever it is, ask."

"He's not going to be ... legitimate, Gian."

He stiffened, hating how she said that word a little quieter than the rest. The last thing she should be, or that he wanted her to be, was ashamed. Not of innocent life or love.

"He's still mine," Gian said firmly, "and he's still a first-born Guzzi boy, which means it's my legacy to pass on, like it was given to me once. It's my choice to make for my son, not someone else's. It may seem silly to others, something insignificant, but I *know* what this name means. I know what comes of it and what's expected of the man who is given it. He's my boy. He's *my boy*, with a woman I chose and love, not one that was forced upon me. Whether he's legitimate or not is fucking nonsense; it means nothing to me. He was made because he was meant to be and because I love you. I want to give him *my* names because he deserves them."

Cara glanced away. "All of them, even the surname?"

"Why wouldn't I?"

"Your wife, for one."

"It's not a card I want to pull, Cara, but she is well aware that to keep her place and her respect in it, she can say nothing about what I do, so long as she is treated well and is held up as the wife I married. Nothing more, nothing less."

"But isn't a baby with your mistress the utmost *dis*respect, Gian?"

"For some. Not for others. It depends on the man, and at the moment, I am the most powerful man at the table. I am the only one with the voice that matters. I speak, they listen. Her included. This—the baby, his name, all of it—is no different."

"I don't know what to think about that," Cara admitted.

"You don't have to think anything."

"Marcus Gian, then? I like the sound."

"Marcus Gian *Guzzi*," he said, kissing the top of her head.

"Marcus Gian Guzzi."

• • •

The enforcer standing in front of the old barber's shop nodded to Gian in greeting as his boss approached. Sure enough, through the window, Gian could see inside the business, and the man waiting that he had been called in for.

Gabriel.

It was a meeting that, for all purposes, had been meant for Gian and his Capos. Somehow, Gabriel must have gotten word and decided to crash it.

"Has he been here long?" Gian asked.

"Since we called, boss," the enforcer replied.

Gian scowled.

That was long enough.

"*Merci.* Keep an eye on the road."

The enforcer agreed. Gian stepped inside the barber shop, noting the tension had already settled thickly in the air. His men, those he had called for the meet, had shoved themselves to one side of the business, while Gabriel and his men had stayed on the other side.

Resting back in the barber's chair, Gabriel looked to be in his glory. His forehead and thick neck were covered with hot, wet towels, while his cheeks and jaw had been slathered with a foaming cream. The careful hands of the barber—one who had cut his hair and shaved Gian from the time he was fifteen—made clean lines with a blade over Gabriel's face.

"Gian," Gabriel greeted without so much as looking at him. "You don't mind me joining your meeting today, do you?"

"You know I do," Gian replied, "and more so, that you're in my seat."

"Well, here I am."

Yes, there he fucking was.

Quietly, Dom and Stephan entered the barber shop. Better late than never, Gian supposed. Truthfully, he had been closer to the spot when the call came in, so he wasn't about to throw a fit at his consigliere and underboss.

"What do you want?" Gian demanded.

"Right now, a shave."

"No, *being* here."

The barber's hands stilled and he shot Gian a look. Gian could tell the man wanted him to relax, and not cause any problems for his business. As it was, the barber shop was well-known for the *Mafioso* that came and went daily, most notably, Gian at least once a week.

Carmen had always been able to shave Gian far better than any razor ever had.

Gabriel looked over to Gian, though only his eyes moved. It was disconcerting to have this man stare at him, Gian thought. He knew the things Gabriel was capable of and he purposely tried *not* to poke the man's beast. That was just good business.

"I want an update on our little situation," Gabriel said, "and to talk."

"The *situation* is being handled."

"Good, then you've found the rat amongst your men. And disposed of it, I assume."

Gian felt the coldness and distrust that automatically came from saying that word waft from his men. A few murmured between one another, but most stayed quiet. "No, I haven't found him."

Gabriel *tsked* under his breath. "Wasting time, you foolish boy."

"That's your one insult, Gabriel. Any after that, and I'll begin taking a payment for it. A pound of your choice."

"Touchy," his father-in-law muttered.

"No more than you." Gian stayed standing, although he waved to Dom and Stephan to find seats closer to him. Then, he turned back to Gabriel. "We're still working on that issue. It's not as simple as it seems, and whoever it is, they're not obvious."

"Or you're distracted."

"I beg your pardon?"

"Your whore, Gian." Gabriel smirked as Gian went cold all over. "Cara Rossi, that's her name, isn't it? *Quite* pregnant. While I certainly wasn't faithful to *my* wife, I would have never taken you for the type, too."

Gian's molars ached from clenching so fiercely.

He would not talk about Cara with this man.

He would not give Gabriel that ammo.

Gabriel said nothing more, letting the barber finish his shave and wipe his face down with the hot towels before he stood. Then, he faced Gian, as hard-assed and as big of a bastard as ever.

"You *are* distracted," Gabriel said, "and it shows. Otherwise, you would have found your rat by now. I gave you time to do it, but since you're too busy making a fucking spectacle of that whore of yours all over the city, time has now run out. I'm not going to jail again, Gian. For every week that passes without you delivering the rat to me, I'll take one of yours. And just so we're clear …"

Gabriel looked over Gian's shoulder, and waved a fat finger at the line of men who had come to speak with Gian only. "Just so it's clear to *them*, every minute you spend with your whore is a minute you could have been working to spare one of their lives. Make the choices *wisely*, Gian."

Apparently, Gabriel intended to start his plan immediately. He had only just left the barber shop along with his men and gotten inside a waiting vehicle, when a black van pulled up. The enforcer outside the barber shop was grabbed and gone before anyone had blinked. Gabriel watched from the backseat of his car with a smile.

Gian was going to kill that bastard someday. *Somehow.*

TWELVE

At first, Cara didn't notice the police cruisers and unmarked vehicles parked along the front of her apartment building. She was too busy reading the letter from her university, inviting her to take part in the autumn graduation ceremony for late graduates of her class. While she wasn't a late graduate, she had passed on attending the main event.

When Cara did finally notice the police attendance, she was halfway up the walk. The early July air was hot and humid, as the majority of the entire summer had already been. She cradled her thirty-seven-week pregnancy swell overtop the flimsy summer dress that helped to keep her cool.

"Cara Rossi?"

She turned to see an officer in full uniform approaching. Her nerves picked up another notch.

"Yes, that's me," Cara said.

"I'll escort you to your apartment."

"Why? Did something happen?"

The officer smiled thinly. "Normal procedure, that's all."

"Normal procedure for *what?*"

"Follow me, miss."

"What is going on?" Cara demanded.

The officer answered nothing, simply urged her toward the front doors of the building. Cara wondered if maybe her place had been broken into, though that seemed unlikely. She lived in a good part of the city, and the cost of her rent proved that little fact. Her building—in all the years she lived there—never once had a crime taken place inside or on the outside property.

It was possible that the cops were there because of her accident weeks ago. Her rib was healed and no longer sore, as was the gash on her hairline. Thankfully, that had healed with a scar that wasn't noticeable, due to skilled stitching by a doctor.

"Is this about the accident?" Cara asked. "I answered all the questions I could at the hospital the next day, and then another round the next week when detectives came with pictures of vehicles for me to look at. I don't know what more to tell you."

The officer still didn't answer.

Now, Cara was just getting peeved.

She didn't have to wonder for long, as the door to her floor was pushed open. From her spot way down the hall, she could plainly see evidence boxes and bags resting along the wall outside of her apartment door. Inside a few of the clear, plastic bags with red tape sealing the tops, rested items that belonged to Gian.

A shirt of his.

A book.

An empty bullet clip for his favorite Berretta.

Wait, where in the hell had he put that damn thing?

"You're raiding my place?" Cara shrieked, heading down the hall fast. "What fucking reason do you have to justify a search warrant on my apartment?"

She dropped her bag and the papers from her university, uncaring about the items. Inside her apartment, it looked like a hurricane had ripped through it. An officer identified her and Cara confirmed it, before another paper was shoved into her hands. She barely glanced at it, seeing what it was and only getting more irritated.

A search warrant.

Signed by a judge.

"Nice to see you again, Miss Rossi," said a familiar detective. The man walked toward Cara with a small stuffed animal in his hands. A tiny elephant that had managed to survive the accident weeks before and Cara had put on the baby's dresser as a decoration. "Cute little thing, this is."

Her baby's nursery?

Cara's rage spiraled out of control, and she pushed past the detective, heading for Marcus's room. Sure enough, even it had not gone untouched by the search. Each and every one of the baby's dresser drawers had been pulled open. Carefully folded, tiny clothes spilled across the room in piles, while cute knickknacks and decoration items had been upended in a messy search.

The closet, a space Cara had kept a few boxes of Lea's remaining things, was open. The boxes of her twin's belongings had also been ransacked and searched through.

"We have reason to believe you or your apartment, is a regular stop for Gian Guzzi," the detective said behind Cara, "and so, here we are to check for any information related to recent investigations into his business."

Disbelief swept through Cara.

"And what did you hope to find in an unborn baby's nursery?" she asked.

"Oh, we didn't expect to find much in this apartment at all."

"Then *why?*"

She had been the victim just weeks ago. She had been the one nearly killed by a hit and run driver. And now it was *her* that needed to be treated like a criminal?

Why?

"Gian will understand exactly why," the detective said smugly.

Cara's hands balled into tight fists, her fingernails cutting into her palms. "Where is my purse and cell phone? I want to call Gian and my lawyer, now."

"As soon as we're done taking a look through the bag, Cara."

Fuck him.

• • •

"Cara, just consider—"

"Gian, it's fine. I've almost got the apartment back to normal. The baby's room is all organized and ready again. There's really no need."

"Well, *no* need is kind of wrong. There is a need, *mon ange.* Thirty-seven weeks pregnant with my son is a very good reason to move into the penthouse now, while you have a bit of time left to settle in."

Cara sighed, and shifted the bag of heavy text books on her shoulder. "Okay, I know I was pissed off about the search on my place, but it's still not a good reason for me to upend everything right now to move into the penthouse. We're a little late into this pregnancy to be doing such a big move, Gian."

"Except *I* would like for you to, Cara."

"Listen, we'll talk more when I get out of the university's library."

"Don't hang up on me because you don't want to discuss this."

"I'm not. I'm at the entrance doors right now. I want to get these books out of my place. I will call you back."

"*When* you're out, right? I want to talk about this, even if you don't."

"I have to head over to the shelter, too," Cara reminded him.

Gian grumbled under his breath. "Isn't your time off supposed to start soon for the shelter?"

"Next week, yes."

"Don't work too hard, Cara."

She smiled. "Why not? You happen to be very good at massages. It gives me an excuse to ask for one."

"You don't need an excuse, pretty girl."

"I'll remember that."

"Do so."

Thankfully, Gian dropped the prickly topic of Cara moving into the penthouse. With a quick "I love you" and another demand for her to call him back when she could, the call ended. Cara headed into the university's library, ready to get rid of her textbooks she had needed for the year.

The university had a program that allowed students to drop off textbooks to be used for students the subsequent year who were low income, and couldn't afford to buy the expensive books on their own. A lot of private libraries would pay a small amount for the textbooks, but the university's program was non-profit. It was all by donation and they didn't charge the students to get the used books. Cara didn't care about the money, she cared about being able to help someone.

It didn't take long for Cara to get her textbooks dropped off and head back out the way she had come. She fully intended to call Gian back as soon as she could, but he would have to wait. As it was, traffic in the city had been terrible all day, and Cara was running short on time to get to the shelter for her shift.

She would usually take the bus, but flagged a passing cab instead. Just as she slid into the back seat and tossed her mostly-empty tote bag to the floor, something caught her eye across the street.

Or rather, someone.

Two people, actually.

Elena Guzzi was just coming out of a specialty boutique, her arms loaded with several bags. A large-brimmed hat keeping half of her face hidden, but Cara would recognize the woman anywhere. At the end of the street, Domenic—Gian's younger brother—waited for Elena, already holding the passenger side door open for the woman to get inside the car.

That was all Cara saw before her cab pulled away from the side of the road, leaving the scene behind.

Still, an angry ache had settled in Cara's chest at the sight of Gian's wife. After their first run in, Cara had been left feeling so ashamed for her involvement with Gian and the pregnancy. But after, once she had learned more of the story, and the things Gian told Cara, she didn't think that run in with Elena had been accidental at all.

And neither had her pity party lies about losing a baby, or not being able to have more children.

Was Cara imperfect?

Were her actions immoral?

Was she a sinner in this?

Absolutely.

Yes, on every single account.

But something told Cara that Elena Guzzi was not all too innocent, either.

None of them were.

• • •

Cara held the hands of the young, high-risk domestic abuse victim across from her while Jenny continued to explain what was going to happen from there on out. Melinda, at only twenty-two, had just been dealt another difficult blow in what was an already horrible time in her life.

Two weeks after the beating her husband had served down on her, and the woman was at least beginning to look better. The black and blue bruising on her face had faded to a yellow that was easy to cover. Her broken nose was no longer swollen, and she was able to open her right eye again. The busted vessels in her left eye were also healing, and no longer drew attention, as they had when nearly the entire white of the eyeball had been a bloody, ghastly red.

Melinda tried to smile when Cara offered her hands a squeeze, but it faltered at the last second. Outside appearances were deceiving, and there had never been a better example of that than a woman who had learned to hide the signs of her spouse's abuse.

This woman had been hiding hers since she was eighteen.

"So, he got bail," Melinda whispered.

So soft spoken.

Still afraid.

Never weak, though.

Cara repeated that sentiment to Melinda when the woman was willing to listen. She was not weak. She was brave, courageous, wonderful, and deserved beautiful things. All the beautiful things she wanted would and could be hers.

"He did get bail," Jenny said, "and since this is his first charge on his record, we expected that. The restraining order is still in place and the police officer on the case was kind enough to alert us that he is free on bail, until the next court date."

Melinda wet her lips, her gaze darting between the floor and the wall. "He knows where I am."

"The restraining order is still in place, but should he come to the shelter, we have policies in place that will keep you and everyone else perfectly safe."

"Except he doesn't care about those kinds of things. He never has. He said he would kill me; he almost did. He's—"

"Melinda," Cara said softly, "take a breath. Take a moment to breathe."

The young woman did, but Cara could plainly see it didn't help all that much.

"This is the first time I've ever left him," Melinda mumbled. "This wasn't even the worst beating, it was just the first time someone helped. I don't … He won't … I'm scared."

Jenny nodded. "I know. We consider your situation to be high-risk, which means at the moment, the shelter is currently on a level red watch."

"What does that even mean?"

"It means that because there is a risk of an altercation between you and your husband while we get things settled with the court, your divorce lawyer, and everything else, everyone here will be more alert for a problem. Until we have a reason to move you—say, he shows up here, or approaches you when you're out with one of our escorts—then the shelter is where you will remain. So, while you are here, because of the risk level, the staff and volunteers, and even the other women currently housed here, will be on a high alert for safety."

"So, wait and see if he tries to beat me to death again?" Melinda asked.

Cara winced. "*We* understand the situation and why you're afraid of him showing up. But given this is his first actual arrest and the past years of abuse haven't been documented officially, the courts were already unlikely to deny him bail. Trust that we will do absolutely everything to keep you, and everyone else, safe while we go through this process. And if at any single time, he gives us even a small reason to suspect he's planning something, you will be moved with a police guard. Okay?"

Melinda agreed, but she didn't look entirely convinced.

Cara understood that, too.

It was hard to trust others to keep you safe, when all you knew was keeping yourself alive.

"Are you good to go back to your room?" Cara asked.

"Or, supper is getting ready to be served in the kitchen, if you're hungry," Jenny added.

Melinda shrugged. "Food would be good."

"Wonderful." Jenny waited until Melinda had gone from the office and the door was closed once more, before she turned to Cara to speak. "I didn't want to frighten her more, but the officer who alerted us to the granted bail thought we should know."

Cara stood, rubbing a hand over her stomach to soothe the jabs of the baby boy hitting her rib. "Know what?"

"The officer figured he would keep an eye on Allen Farger for the day, as he had time, and he said there was something about the guy that bothered him."

"So?"

"He lost him about an hour after he started tailing him," Jenny said.

"Like in traffic or something?"

"No, like Allen seemed to know someone was following him and deliberately lost the officer."

Well, shit.

"Why would he do that?" Cara asked.

Although, she was pretty sure she knew the answer.

"Because he didn't want to be seen or bothered doing whatever in the hell he was going to do." Jenny loosened her ponytail, and tipped her head side to side, stretching her neck. "*That* was why I put the shelter on level red watch, not because of the bail."

"Don't you think Melinda should know?"

Jenny frowned. "Tonight is the first night that young woman has even felt comfortable with eating dinner in the main dining room, around others. She is medicated just to be able to sleep. She is terrified enough, so no, I don't want to pile more on to her, and watch her regress. We've got a long way to go with this one, Cara."

"Yeah, I see your point."

"What time were you planning on leaving today? You should rest, you're nearly thirty-eight weeks pregnant, Cara."

Cara dismissed the suggestion. "I'm fine and I think after I make a call, I'll stick around."

"You really should relax. Once your baby gets here, you'll have no time to rest at all."

"Don't worry about me, Jenny."

"I worry about all my girls, regardless of who they are, Cara."

Yeah, she knew that, too.

"I'll be fine," Cara assured her boss once more.

Fifteen minutes later, Cara had holed herself in her small office, and finally gotten Gian on the phone. She probably should have called him back earlier after their conversation while she dropped off her books, but the hectic pace of the shelter that day hadn't given her the chance.

"*Mon ange,*" Gian said the moment he picked up Cara's call from her office phone. "How's my girl?"

"Honestly?"

"Of course."

"Tired. A little stressed. Craving that shredded ice with the cherry flavoring you brought me last week. Nothing I can't handle."

Gian's chuckles were dark and wonderful on the other end of the line. "I can have some for you when you get home. Just let me know when you're leaving."

Cara blew out a slow breath. "Yeah, that's the thing. I probably won't be out of here until later than I thought. I know you were going to come over, but why don't we just figure something out for tomorrow instead?"

"Cara, you're supposed to be taking it—"

"Easy, I know. But shit came up."

"Are you actually going to take your time off for maternity leave starting next week, or what?"

"Yes, Gian. I am going to take my leave."

"You make it hard to believe, that's all. You work harder than I do, *amore.* And that says something because I never stop."

"I promise I'm going to take my leave. But tonight, I'm going to stay later. We have a new woman on the floor—domestic abuse, and it's a risky situation right now. I feel like she just needs someone to talk to a bit more, and maybe she'll feel less anxious about the shelter and what we're trying to do to help her."

Gian grunted something under his breath that Cara didn't understand before adding louder, "Your soul is too good for this world, love. You better take your leave, and enjoy every minute of it. You deserve that, Cara. So fine, we'll do something tomorrow, but something tonight, too."

"I'm going to be too tired for anything tonight, Gian."

"I'll surprise you."

"With what?"

"I'm actually not too far away with my brother, having dinner. How about—"

Gian's sentence cut off, and a nothingness sounded in Cara's ear. She looked down at the office phone, only to see the call had been cut off, but there was no dial tone. She hit the receiver button, but each time, the same nothingness came through the speaker.

"What the fuck?" Cara asked out loud to herself.

Then, the lights went out.

Instantly, backup emergency lights lit up over Cara's head in one corner of her office. There was absolutely no reason for the phones to cut out, nor for the power to shut off. Cara might have overlooked the power thing, as sometimes that happened in the city when a car accident took out a transformer, but she hesitated on thinking that was the issue.

Why?

Because even without power, the phone lines would work. The phone lines would have needed to be cut, deliberately, for them not to work.

Instinct made Cara grab her cell phone from her purse as she headed out of her office. The shelter was a complex-style building, comprised of different areas from housing wings, to the kitchen, the offices wing, and the downstairs section, where things like the daycare, reception, a small library, and more was set up for the women to use.

Cara went for the stairs first, deciding on heading down that way to see what in the hell was going on. She had just stepped foot on the lower floor when the first gun shots rang out. Screams followed.

"Holy shit," someone murmured from the front.

Cara stayed behind the safety of the wall that separated her from being seen by the people at the front entrance of the shelter.

"Allen," she heard Jenny say, "please put the—"

"Shut the fuck up. Where's my wife?"

Cara heard the patter of fast footsteps heading her way, and the second gunshot split through the air. The body of one of the volunteers landed so close to Cara's spot that she heard the woman take her last breath.

Oh, my God.

"Let's not do that again," Allen—Melinda's husband—said, his tone cold and bored. "Lock the place down. I'm not leaving until I get my fucking wife."

Cara took a breath, and then another. Her slight touch of PTSD from Lea's murder made things like gunfire into a huge monster she didn't want to battle. She certainly couldn't afford to battle it right then.

She didn't realize it but she had squeezed her hands so tightly, her fingernails cut into her palms. It was only the slight movement of her baby that brought Cara but of her daze, back into the present, and reminded her what she had in her hand.

A cell phone.

One that worked.

And there was still a whole floor of people that needed to stay where they were and go into lockdown mode. It was likely that because of the cut phone and power lines, the staff in the upper floors were not aware of what was happening downstairs. A proper alert couldn't be sent over the speakers to lockdown and hide-in due to a dangerous situation.

Thankfully, given the time of day, the bottom floor was mostly empty. A lot of the staff and women would be in the kitchen on the second floor, readying for meal time. A lot of the woman might even still be in the housing wing, readying to head to the kitchen.

Cara hit the stairs running, though she tried to keep her steps as quiet as possible. Already, she had her phone turned on and was dialing nine-one-one.

"Nine-one-one emergency services, what's your emergency?"

Cara rattled off the address to the shelter. "Active shooter, at least one dead."

"You're sure it's *active*, ma'am?" the woman asked.

Another gunshot rang out from down below as Cara headed for the housing wing first. "*Very fucking sure, thanks.*"

"Okay, please remain calm and on the phone."

Cara pulled the lock-in bar from above the housing wing's entrance doors and set it up as firmly as she could against the bottom, hearing some of the women come out of their rooms. The dispatcher continued to ask Cara questions, and she rattled off as much information as she could while she placed the metal bar in under the doors, opened it wide so that it used the cement walls as support. Now, the door couldn't be opened from the other side.

"Ma'am, do you know—"

Cara ignored the dispatcher, and turned to the women coming out of their rooms, and the few staff there, too. "There's an active shooter on the main floor. Door one to the housing wing is closed, secure, and locked-in. I'm going to exit out door two and head toward the kitchen. Someone needs to put the lock in bar behind me. *Do not open those doors.* Do not open them until you hear police declaring a non-active situation. Get in your rooms, close the doors, lock them up, and get under your beds, in your closets, or your bathrooms if you have one in your unit. Turn the lights off. Be extra quiet. Police have been notified, so let's not get on a dozen cell phones and block up the emergency lines. Okay?"

She could plainly see the questions the waiting people wanted to ask, and their fear. She was grateful that they simply nodded, and she continued on, heading for the exit door.

"I take it the shelter has codes in place for this sort of thing," the dispatcher said. "That's good, very reassuring."

"Just because we have them, doesn't mean we want to use them."

"Good point. The police are on their way."

Cara's phone vibrated, an incoming call on the other line, but she focused on making sure the housing wing did as she asked, and locked in the exit door that led to the stairs. Instead of going down the stairs to the bottom floor, she went down the U-shaped hallway that would lead her into the offices and kitchen area.

Once again, her phone vibrated with a call on the other line.

Cara checked it, seeing Gian's number.

"You're still on the line, ma'am, aren't you?" the dispatcher asked.

"Yes, but—"

Another burst of gunfire rang out behind the doors that lead to the offices wing where Cara had first come from. The noise and shock alone sent her spinning back into the wall again.

Shit.

Shit, shit, shit.

She couldn't lock in the offices wing when she knew there were people inside that might be able to get out. Not to mention, the lock-in bars were *inside* the doors, not outside. Because the people within needed to be safe, and keep the bad guys *out*.

Cara hadn't meant to, but in her panic, she had clutched her phone the wrong way, and ended the call with the dispatcher. She could hear the shouts of Melinda's raging husband just a few feet beyond the office wing's doors when her phone started ringing.

Loudly.

Loud enough for someone to hear behind the doors.

Utter fear sent Cara running for the only safe zone left. *The kitchen.* Attached to the dining hall, she could get inside, have the doors locked down, wait for the cops, and hope for the fucking best.

She slammed into the back section of the kitchen like a bat out of hell, shouting and waving at the staff to help her get the lock-in bar in place. Her words mostly came out in a jumbled, panicky mess of jerky sentences and orders in the dark space with only the dim emergency lights up above.

Someone seemed to hear her, though.

Or they understood.

They just got the lock-in bar spread at the bottom of the door when the first kick hit it. Then, another round of gunfire sent Cara and the man who had helped her get the bar in place, flying backwards. She stumbled over her own feet, suddenly thankful the doors were metal and could take a bullet or two.

"The other door," Cara mumbled to the confused, frightened staff working in the kitchen, "get the lock-in bar in the other door!"

A nagging pain started to ache in Cara's side, but she pressed the heel of her palm against it to soothe it as best she could. Her phone rang once more, and Gian's number lit up the screen.

Even though every single part of her *screamed* to pick up the call and hear his voice, because it would calm her like nothing else, Cara didn't do it. She didn't want to scare him, or worry him. The situation was ... well, bad.

Really fucking bad.

Cara decided to call the emergency line back, just to let them know an update on the situation, and why the call had been ended in the first place.

"Nine-one-one, what's your—"

"Active shooter at Carolina's House on the Fifth," Cara interrupted, keeping an eye on the locked-in door. "I was just on the phone with a dispatcher, and accidentally ended it. We have the housing and dining wings locked in, but the main entrance, bottom floor, and offices are not secure."

"Units are on route to the scene, and one has already arrived, ma'am."

"Thank you."

She still didn't relax.

Not for a minute.

And especially not when the dispatcher said, "We have a confusing report coming in from the first unit, could you clarify the situation? One shooter or two?"

Cara's brow furrowed. "Just one, why?"

"There are running vehicles outside of the shelter's main entrance and a witness told police that two men entered the shelter five minutes ago. With weapons visible."

"This began at least fifteen minutes ago," Cara whispered.

"Yes, I can see when your first call came in, ma'am."

Cara wasn't sure *why* she felt the need to ask, but the question spilled out anyway. "What are the models of the vehicles outside the shelter that the witness saw the men come in?"

"Um ... a Lexus and a Mercedes."

Gian.

THIRTEEN

Gian couldn't get rid of the image of the brain matter splattered across the welcome sign behind the shelter's receptionist desk. He'd *thought* something was wrong when his phone call with Cara ended abruptly. He knew something was wrong for sure when—after driving like a bat out of hell—he found the front of the shelter dark, without the usual warm lights brightening the entrance.

Inside, two dead women sent him running for the offices wing. Dom stayed in the entrance to help the frightened, shocked women that had been spared.

"Cara!"

Gian checked office after office, but found nothing. A few of the staff had locked their doors, too, but he didn't think Cara would be in an office with someone else. She had called from her office phone, and that was why he went looking there first. He'd put together what she had said about the risk level for an altercation due to a new woman at the shelter, and figured … the altercation happened.

Halfway down the hallway, he heard a snarling voice coming from behind the exit doors. He wasn't sure where that led to, but he knew the shelter was sectioned off to make it feel more home-like, and less like a complex.

"Get those fucking doors open," a man barked. "Right now, or I'll blow your fucking head apart."

"Please, listen. The doors *can't* be opened. Please don't—"

"Open the fucking doors!"

"I can't open them!"

The woman's resounding cry that followed her statement had Gian picking up his pace. Already, he had his favorite Berretta at the ready. He shouldn't be walking around with a gun, anyway, not with the cops being so hot on his ass, and the time he had just served for illegal weapons possession.

Gian figured having a gun now was a damn good thing.

"Bitch, I'm gonna kill you."

Gian's foot hit the latch on the wing exit door at the same time he aimed his gun and turned toward the voices. The guy with the semi-auto rifle pointed at the cowering woman on the floor didn't see Gian either.

Not until it was too late.

The trigger pulled back smooth and easy under Gian's finger. The bullet plugged into the forehead of the guy, sent his eyes flying wide, and then he stumbled back several steps. His head cracked morbidly against the wall on his way to the floor.

Gian considered putting another bullet in the fucker, just for good measure, but the horrified shriek of the woman stopped him. He passed her a look and recognized her instantly. Cara's boss.

Jenny, he thought her name was.

"You okay?" Gian asked.

Jenny just stared at him, blinking.

"Did someone call the cops?"

She still didn't talk.

"Where's Cara?" Gian demanded.

Jenny swallowed hard, her gaze darting to the corpse bleeding out between his eyes on the floor, and Gian standing just a few feet away. "Probably inside the kitchen and dining area, if she's not locked in her office."

"She's not locked in her office."

"You killed him."

"He was going to kill you," Gian offered with a shrug. "Which was the better option? I think we both like this one more. I can have the carpets replaced before the weekend is up. It'll be like he never even happened, no worries."

The man might have hurt Cara.

Or Gian's child.

Rage filtered in through Gian's numbed senses, but he pushed it down. It was done with, and handled. A problem came up, and he fixed it. It was just what Gian did.

"RCMP, show your hands!"

Gian tossed his Berretta aside the second he heard the police shout their warnings from behind the doors where he had just come. He shot Jenny a smile as he put his hands behind his head, and moved down to his knees on the floor.

This way, he was not a threat.

This way, it would be faster.

He *really* needed to see Cara.

• • •

"Gian!"

Gian turned at the familiar sound of Cara's shout. Just in time, too. She barreled into him, her arms snaking tight enough to choke him, and then she pulled him closer still. Her kiss landed fast and hard against his mouth, taking his breath away.

Finally, he could *feel*.

He wanted to hug Cara, to bring her in closer, but all he managed to do was press his cuffed hands along the swell of her stomach. It was enough and the baby's kick had his heart beating a little faster.

"Hey, it's all right, *mon ange*," Gian soothed in Cara's ear. "All's well, now."

"What is this?" Cara demanded, pulling away to grab the cuffs. "They arrested you?"

The cop keeping watch on Gian near the back of the police cruiser gave a little shrug when Cara glared at him.

"Details," Gian said, "nothing more. I had a gun on me and no papers for it, not to mention a license for a concealed weapon. It's just details."

"Gian, those *details* put you in jail for five fucking months last time!"

"Yeah, not so loud, Cara. And it was a little more than one gun last time, but it doesn't make this look very fucking good on me at the moment."

She frowned. "But you were the one who … who …"

"Came in and saved the day?"

"I mean, yeah!"

Gian sighed. "Just relax. You don't need to be worrying so much that you worry my son right out. All right? Also, there's a couple of EMTs here, so have you been checked over yet?"

"I'm fine," Cara said, huffing.

She might have thought so.

Gian needed to be sure.

"Officer, could you have this woman checked—"

"Gian, stop it!"

He ignored Cara, and nodded toward her when the officer grinned. "I mean, if you wouldn't mind. I'm not going anywhere, really."

"I'll escort her over, Mr. Guzzi."

"You ass," Cara muttered under her breath to Gian.

"Just get checked, love. And the baby—his heartbeat and whatnot. I'll still be here, where the hell am I going to go?"

Cara's narrowed gaze didn't relent, but the officer was quick to urge her toward a waiting ambulance, fifty feet down the street. Gian took the second he had alone to breathe, and get whatever story he needed to tell straight in his brain. Not that it was going to help him on the legal side of things.

All too soon, the officer was back, without Cara.

"Well, Mr. Guzzi, it's time to head down to the station."

Gian looked in the direction Cara had gone. "Could I at least wait for an update on her?"

"She seems fine, and the EMT got an earful when he was a little rough-handed checking the baby."

"Oh, is that so?"

He couldn't even try to hide his rage, or the way his tone edged dangerously.

The cop eyed Gian, amused. "You killed one man tonight. Isn't that enough?"

"Not when it comes to her."

"Let's go, Guzzi."

• • •

Gian rested his head against the cinderblock wall of the jail cell, thankful he was alone for the moment. He'd been shoved into the cell with a half of a dozen other detainees, but throughout the evening and into the morning, the others had been moved elsewhere, or released once they'd slept their drunken stupors away.

He reached for his pocket to pull out his phone, and cursed under his breath, realizing he didn't have it on him. Everything—from his phone to his keys, and the bit of change alongside his wallet—had been taken from him.

This was not where Gian wanted to be.

Not again.

"You're looking mighty comfortable."

Gian didn't bother to even turn his head at the new—yet familiar—voice. The RCMP detective that had become a second shadow of sorts for him loomed just beyond the bars.

Seeley looked at a file in his other hand. "Quite the mess you've found yourself in again, Gian."

"*Oui.*"

"Why on earth would you think it was a good idea to go in guns blazing, when you damn well know you're not to have any weapons, legal or otherwise?"

Gian shrugged. "I wasn't thinking."

That much was the truth. He had gotten that call from Cara, decided to head over, and shit had gone south from there.

"The cops said you refused to give a statement," the detective noted.

"I want my lawyer there when I do."

"It's the weekend. You know these jails don't bring in lawyers and have all that nonsense done on the weekends."

"Then my statement can wait."

"Make it easy on them, give them the statement," Seeley said. "What's it going to hurt? We already know what happened, just repeat it for them."

"When my lawyer shows up," Gian replied.

Seeley grunted under his breath. "You've got these damn Mounties split down the middle, Guzzi. Half of them think they should release you for what you did, and the other half thinks you're nothing more than a—"

"Criminal, I know. That half is right."

"At least you're aware."

"Is Domenic being held in another cell because we're brothers?" Gian asked, getting tired of the same old conversation that would go nowhere. He'd also been wondering about his younger brother, and how Dom had faired through the weekend. "I mean, I get why you wouldn't want us together. It would be a shame if we concocted some kind of story to get me out of here, right?"

Seeley's face turned to stone. "Domenic wasn't arrested."

"Oh?"

Gian didn't hide his surprise.

"No need to, as his weapon was registered and legal. He also didn't shoot anybody, and he was helping in the main entrance with victims. He was brought in for a secondary, more thorough statement this morning, though."

Something in the lilt of the detective's tone caught Gian's attention.

"Was he now?" Gian sat a little straighter on the bench. "Do tell."

"Where did you get your gun from?"

Gian said nothing.

"How long have you had it?" Seeley questioned.

Gian stayed quiet.

There had to be a reason for these questions, after all.

Frustrated, the detective pushed away from the bars with a scowl. "You've got everybody fooled, Guzzi, but not me."

"I beg your pardon?"

"You owe your brother—big time."

Gian hid his inner confusion well. "We do look out for one another when we can."

"Seems *this* is no different. Domenic took the rap on your gun. Said the illegal weapon was his, in his vehicle, and that you had grabbed it when you two arrived. There's no way to prove otherwise, especially considering he too had a gun on him, though his was legal and registered. Your charges have been dropped, except for the discharging a weapon, but—"

Gian released a dark laugh. "It'll be thrown out in court, given the circumstances."

Seeley's face reddened. "Likely."

"When am I getting out?"

That was all Gian cared about.

He had a pregnant Cara to get back to.

Life was waiting.

He didn't have time for this shit.

Seeley perked a bit at the question, happier than before. "We're a bit short staffed this weekend, and nobody seems to be around to properly discharge you. Shame. Monday, likely."

Gian resisted the urge to flip the man his middle finger. Instead, he rested back on the bench, much more comfortable than before. "*Merci*, Seeley. See you next time, we both know there's going to be one. Oh, and do see if someone will bring me something decent to eat. I have restaurants that will deliver."

• • •

"Good to see you're smiling," Stephan said as Gian approached his waiting underboss.

Gian stuffed his hands in his slacks pockets, enjoying the sunshine. "Why wouldn't I be? It's Monday, it's a beautiful day, and I am not in a jail cell."

"Lucky, boss."

"Very. Where's my brother?"

Stephan shrugged. "Dom said he had some shit to catch up on. I didn't mind coming down to pick you up and take you home."

Gian kept his features blank, but disappointment filled him. He hadn't been able to have a conversation with his brother while in the jail, and knowing that Dom was taking a charge on possession of an illegal weapon for him, he owed him thanks. He'd hoped to do that first thing, and then get on with his day.

"Your vehicle is still in impound," Stephan said.

"I'll worry about it tomorrow."

"Maybe not even then."

Gian cocked a brow. "And why not?"

"You have bigger problems to worry about at the moment, boss."

He wasn't so sure of that.

"Bigger than Cara being two weeks away from delivering my first-born son? Bigger than convincing her she needs to move into the penthouse, so I can take care of her? Bigger than barely escaping more jail time? Tell me what's bigger than those things at this very moment, Stephan."

The underboss shot a look down the street, as though he was expecting someone to be watching them. No one was, or so it seemed. Gian wouldn't put it past their shadows, though.

"You made another show, boss."

Gian tipped his head to the side. "*Excusez-moi?*"

"We're all walking a fine line out here on the streets, trying to keep our noses clean, stay quiet and out of sight of the cops, not to mention away from that fucking prick Gabriel. And then there you go, making a show of yourself and all of us again. All because of your mistress, boss. I'm not saying this to be disrespectful," Stephan added quickly, likely seeing the rage growing on Gian's features. "I'm saying it because someone's got to be the one to warn you and nobody else is stepping up right now. As it is, we've been battling the cops *and* Gabriel's men, not to mention tip-toeing around one another, thinking there's somebody among us that's feeding info to the police."

"I hear you."

"Do you?" Stephan asked. "Are you listening now, Gian?"

Gian bristled. "Try that again."

"*Boss*, are you listening now?"

"I didn't intend to make a scene," Gian said quietly. "Not with this or with Cara. I reacted. Like any man would have done."

"Any man that wasn't in your position, maybe," Stephan agreed.

Gian hated how Stephan made damn good points.

"It'll smooth itself over, surely. Over time."

"Except it won't, not really. Let's not even consider the cops for the moment, just Gabriel. Already, he's threatened us, he's taken from us, and he's pointed the finger at you each and every time as a reason why. Maybe before, the men in the family would overlook it. But the next time, when another Guzzi man shows up dead because of that fucker, they're not going to be so compliant and forgiving. They're going to remember your face on the television, and your pregnant mistress as the reason why."

Gian no longer felt as carefree as he had just a few minutes ago. "I'll figure it out."

Something.

He would figure *something* out.

"But today," Gian said, "I have a woman to apologize to, so that's where I need to go."

Stephan nodded. "The penthouse it is, boss."

"She didn't ask to be taken to her place? Cara doesn't live at the penthouse, and never lets me forget it."

Yet.

"Well, that's where she's been. Chris says she hasn't left, either. He's been keeping an eye on her, apparently."

Well, then … maybe something *was* finally working to Gian's favor for once. He would take what he could get.

• • •

"Oh, my God. You smell like a jail cell."

Cara's words were grumbled against Gian's lips, but he still heard them perfectly fine. His chuckles did nothing to quell the way Cara's nose scrunched up as she pulled away from him in the penthouse hallway. He wanted to bring her closer again—fuck the jail cell smell—but she had a point. He needed a shower, a toothbrush, and a clean suit.

"Sorry, *mon ange*. I'll get on it."

Cara smiled in that sweet way of hers, but a wariness still remained in her gaze. "So, about the charges …"

"Everything is fine," he assured. "Things have been taken care of."

"How?"

"Carefully."

That was the best he could offer, given the circumstances.

"Enough about me. How are you feeling? Would you be more comfortable at your place?"

Cara shook her head. "I don't want to leave."

"We don't have to. Not today, anyway."

"*At all*," Cara said, looking up at him to make her point clear. "Maybe I took some time to think about things while I didn't have you all up in my head voicing an opinion, too. I like the nursery you set up across from the master bedroom."

"I told you I wanted one here, just in case."

"It's … fully stocked and ready. Everything is set up in there. The walls are even painted a pastel blue."

Gian's brow furrowed. "Of course, it is. You're thirty-eight weeks pregnant, *bella*. I'm not sure when you think it would be appropriate for it to be done, but *before* the baby arrives is a good time for me."

"But I kept saying no about living here, Gian."

"So?"

"You have everything he needs."

"Why should you travel a bunch of stuff back and forth if you don't need to?" Gian asked.

"Why don't you demand things of me? I'm having your child, we're in … whatever we are, this relationship together. Why don't you want more? Why don't you demand more?"

"Because I don't think you want me to, and I'm not sure it would make a difference if I did demand you do what I wanted," Gian answered honestly.

Cara just stared at him, barely reacting at all. "And that's all?"

"I love you, Cara. I will love you whether you live with me or not. I will love you if you're *with* me, or not. I will love you even when you don't love me. So, we don't get to be entirely normal, and circumstances kind of fucked us up along the way. Who cares? You make me happy; you give me every reason to be happy. Why would I mess that up by demanding that you change what you're fine with giving me?"

She didn't answer right away.

Instead, Cara said, "I'd like to stay here."

"*Live* here," Gian clarified.

"I want to be with you, Gian."

"I think we can make that happen."

He'd been waiting for this day; hoping for it, really. Living there was one thing. Gian wanted to give Cara something far more permanent where the penthouse was concerned. Something that no one could take from her. He only needed her signature on already finished documents, but that could wait for another day.

The prettiest, widest smile bloomed over Cara's lips, and Gian couldn't help himself but take another kiss. Cara relented to his wants, letting him take and take until she was breathless and laughing.

"But you do stink," she said.

"Showering now, *Tesoro*."

Her tinkling laughter followed him down the hallway, but he didn't mind her teasing. He didn't waste time showering, because he had something far better waiting for him outside the bathroom. He quickly showered up in the attached master bedroom's bath, didn't bother to shave like he should have, and walked out with nothing but a towel in his hand to run through his hair.

He found Cara staring at herself in the large mirror opposite of the bed.

She let out a heavy sigh. "I can't reach it."

"Reach what, love?"

"The stupid zipper on this dress. I got it up earlier, and now I can't get it down."

Gian held back his laughter. "Why bother with a dress at all? You have those comfy clothes you like."

"I wanted to wear something other than pants with stretchy panels, Gian."

"And now you want the dress off?"

"I miss my comfy pants," she admitted with a pout over her shoulder.

"I'll help," Gian told her.

Gian tied the damn towel around his waist, not missing for a second how Cara's gaze dropped down to his hard erection before it was covered. He couldn't help it, really. She was near, and as beautiful as ever—more so, carrying his child, if anything—which meant his cock was ready to play and do its thing.

"How can you even want to fuck?" Cara asked.

"*You*," he corrected as he came to stand behind her. "I want to fuck you because you're within touching distance and you're *mia bella cara*. If I didn't want to, then there would be a problem."

"Gian, right now I have the sex appeal of a slug. You can't be serious."

"Do you want to bet?"

"Bet on what?" Cara laughed, letting him pull the zipper on the dress down her back. "That I'm as huge as a house, and not exactly a hot fucking commodity in the sex department?"

"Cara, you are …"

Her gaze found his in the mirror. "What? *Very* pregnant. Very uncomfortable. Very—"

"Much mine," Gian interrupted firmly, hoping to quiet whatever nonsense was in her head. He began sliding the dress down her body, taking his time to enjoy baring her skin and curves while he did so. "Maybe there's a bit more of you to enjoy right now, and I think it makes you sexier. Maybe you heat up a little faster when I touch you, and your shivers come from somewhere deeper. I like this," he said, letting his palm skim over the roundness of her stomach before drifting lower to slip under her lace panties. "I like that this is where I've gotten you, and the way you look because of it, pretty and sweet with my child. Why wouldn't I like every bit of this, Cara? What man wouldn't be crazy about *this*?"

Cara's breath hitched as the dress fell to the floor, and Gian's fingers glided along the hood of her clit. Jesus, she was hot to the touch and it was *glorious*.

"A-and after?" Cara asked softly. "After, when I'm not like this or like before, either?"

Gian grinned, leaning in to get a taste of the tender skin behind Cara's ear. Her responding shiver only made his cock ache even more—got him harder. "So maybe you'll be *plus douce … doux, mon ange*. Softer, in spots. Sweeter, in others. Maybe you'll have some new lines or curves for me to explore and love, but don't you think you've earned those things? Don't you think this body of yours and what it's doing, deserves to be adored and loved, no matter if there's a little more, or it's a little different?"

"I—"

"Because I think it does," he interrupted, nipping the spot behind her ear to quiet her. "I think something that's this beautiful should know, and I intend to make sure that you do, Cara."

"So, no slug sex appeal?"

"Not even a little bit. That's nonsense. You're as beautiful and as sexy as you've always been to me, and I don't see that changing. Not with time or life. Not with more children or age. It just won't, *bella mia*. You're perfect. For me, you're perfect. And I waited so long for you, Cara, so damn long."

Cara's trembling picked up, and her breaths came out in stuttered streams as Gian's fingers continued their slow and steady pressure on her clit with each stroke. "I'm going to come."

"Yeah, that's the point." His free hand slid under her throat, turning her face just enough that she had to stare at herself in the mirror while the orgasm raced through her body. "And look at how fucking beautiful you are. Like this, with me. Why wouldn't I want to see this, Cara? *Why not?*"

And good God, she *was* beautiful when she came.

Flushed skin and a trembling lower lip. Hooded eyes and red curls framing her pretty face. Shaking from top to bottom with the most pleased sigh falling from her godforsaken mouth. He loved every inch of this woman. Every single curve and line that she owned fit perfectly into his own. He loved her.

"*Gian.*"

"Hmm?" His fingers slowed on her clit as she hummed her way through an orgasm that seemed to go on and on for ages. He explored lower, finding her wet and hot at her slit, just like he expected and wanted her to be. "Talk to me, Cara."

"You said it all pretty well without me needing to."

"I do try," he murmured. "And I know you miss when I choke you, when it hurts so good, or when I use you harder; I know you want me to fuck you crazy, and I *will*. But never like this, not when you're like this, sweetheart."

Not when she was fragile.

Not when she was growing something oh, so precious.

Not when he could worship her for being *everything*.

He just couldn't do it. He wanted to love her differently, then. Not that it was a better way, but he liked it just the same.

Cara's gaze darted to catch his in the mirror, and love stared back. "This is good, too."

Gian tipped Cara's head back far enough that he could catch her mouth in another burning, long kiss. Her tongue tangled with his, while his fingers weaved into her hair to hold her in place for as long as he wanted. He couldn't quite get enough—not of her softness, sweetness, her taste and smell, or all the rest that made up her wonderfulness.

It was never enough.

"Show me how good, then," he urged. "Show me how good you are, how good you look with me, Cara. Show me you *see*, too."

Cara was bent over before Gian could get another word out of his mouth. Her pretty ass was high in the air, while she used the sides of the mirror for support to keep her steady. Gian used those few moments he had to admire the woman begging for his hands to touch her, for his cock to fuck her, and how absolutely perfect she looked bent over, ready, and so damn willing. He dropped his towel and filled her full of his cock while her gaze stayed locked on him in the mirror.

He felt every fucking inch of her take him in, squeeze tight around him, and promise something wicked and heavenly was on the way. Still, he kept his gaze locked on hers. With each hard thrust that she met, and every long pull that came a little faster than the last, he watched her.

She had to see what he did, even if he spent the rest of his life making it happen.

Gian would do it.

Happily.

• • •

Gian rubbed his forehead to ease the tension settling there, and went back to looking over the emails in his inbox. What he needed to do was get some sleep, but as he was already behind on work, he couldn't afford to take the extra rest.

It never ended.

Life was always getting in the way.

"Gian?"

The cell phone on his desk rang at the same time Elena's voice filtered in from the doorway of the office. Gian answered the phone, and held up a finger to ask for a moment from Elena.

"*Ciao, bonjour,*" Gian greeted, not even checking the caller ID.

"It's time."

It took Gian far too many seconds and a few more blinks of his eyes to realize who was speaking on the other end of the call, and what exactly they were trying to tell him.

Cara.

And her words could only mean *one* wonderful thing.

"You're sure?" he asked.

Cara blew out a hard breath that crackled the speakers. "Oh, yes. Definitely sure, Gian. These contractions are nothing like those fake ones I was having. It fucking *hurts.*"

Gian winced, and kept the panic he was suddenly feeling out of his tone. For one, because he knew Cara didn't need the extra worry, and for two, because Elena was just a few feet away, listening to one side of the conversation.

"Have you been timing it?" he asked.

"They're ten minutes apart now for two hours, so lots more of this to go yet. Also, that kind of sucks, because if they hurt now, just think, Gian."

"Think what?"

"Think how much it's going to hurt when it's like thirty seconds apart."

"You're going to be fine," he assured.

Cara was strong as hell.

Silent strength. Steadfast love. She just *was.*

"Water?" he asked carefully, mindful of Elena's presence.

"Not yet," Cara replied, "but the doctors said it's not like the movies, anyway. Lots of women's water doesn't break until they're in active labor, so."

"I'll head over."

"Don't rush, we've got time."

Gian chuckled, and shook his head. "You're kidding, right? Of course, I'm going to rush."

"Don't get yourself killed on the highway or something, Gian. I swear to God." Cara's next breath came out stuttered and her voice strained. "All right, I'm going to hang up because another one is starting, and I don't want to talk through it."

"I'll listen to you rage, if that's—"

"*Goodbye*, Gian."

He laughed when she hung up the phone on him. He had zero doubt that Cara would be just fine through labor and birth. If anything, she was too stubborn to get overwhelmed by something as silly as pain. It would likely be *him* on the floor in a panic, passed out or something equally humiliating. Birth was not for the faint of heart, or so Gian was told.

"You're leaving?" Elena asked.

Gian closed down his laptop, packed it up, and grabbed the suit jacket off the back of the office chair. "I am."

"Congratulations are in order, hmm?"

He shot his wife a look. "I beg your pardon?"

"The only reason you would rush out at night after a phone call like that one is because your *goomah* is having the baby. Congratulations are in order, so congrats."

Apparently, Gian had not been as vague as he thought on the phone call. That, or Elena was just very perceptive.

She cleared her throat, and crossed her arms over her chest. She was ready for bed, by the looks of the silk robe she wore, her clean-face, and the messy bun of hair on top of her head. It was rare that Gian saw Elena in a state that was any less than perfect.

"I did try to be discreet on the call," Gian said.

"I could tell, but I'm also not stupid."

"I likely won't be around for a couple of days. Don't expect me, not that you'll mind, I'm sure."

Elena glanced away, her jaw tight and eyes hard. But there was a barely hidden sadness in her features, too. Gian hadn't expected that at all.

"Again, congrats," she murmured. "I hope he's everything you want, and everything we don't have, Gian. It's easier for you that way, isn't it? When everything you share with her, is nothing like what waits for you here?"

"You don't really need an answer for that, Elena. You already know."

How different they could have been, he thought. How entirely different their life could have been together.

If only she had cared enough. Gian no longer cared at all.

• • •

Marcus Gian Guzzi made his way into the world nearly twenty-four hours to the minute that Cara had called Gian. He came into the world quietly, pink, slick and bloodstained. He didn't cry at first, but not because something was wrong.

No, he didn't cry because he was born with his eyes wide open, already looking for the people that belonged to only him. The smallest thing to have ever scared the very life out of Gian. The most beautiful thing to have ever graced his life, next to his mother.

An amazing, tiny, brown-haired, dark-eyed creature that was nothing like Gian had expected, but *so much more*. Ten perfect fingers, and ten perfect toes. Soft, warm skin, and facial features, right down to the dimple in his cheek, that matched his father.

Features that matched the Guzzi genes. Cara had been so quiet through the process, measured breaths and quivering words. She wanted Gian close, but she barely spoke to him at all. He went off her cues, to give her what she wanted, and didn't ask to be told what to do. It wasn't him doing this wonderful thing, after all. It was all on her.

It was only when, in a birthing pool of her choice, she had pushed Marcus out into the world that she did so with her first and only cry.

And it wasn't so much a cry as a roar. It was kind of perfect, too.

Hours after, once Cara had finally drifted off to sleep, and Gian was awake in the private room, holding his blinking newborn son, he took that silent moment to be amazed.

So amazed and in wonder. His child was *everything*.

Gian lifted the swaddled boy a little higher, bringing him closer so that Marcus's hazy gaze could catch his father's. Sure enough, the baby stilled under his swaddling blankets the moment he locked onto Gian's face, and everything was right and good and beautiful in that moment.

"Sweet boy. First of my legacy and house, and the seventh of your name. With blood made of gold, luck, and dirt, child. You don't know what awaits you; you have no idea how amazing you're going to be, but you don't need to know, not yet. You have a whole life for me to teach you all of that, so it can wait. *Guzzi Principe*, this world is yours. This whole great, big world is all yours, Marcus."

Like all Guzzi boys, Marcus was born a prince.

And like all Guzzi men, he'd eventually be a king.

FOURTEEN

"A little more, please."

Cara tipped her head down, the action causing more of her curls to fall over her shoulder. "Like that?"

"A bit too much, actually," the photographer replied. "Now we're more like a curtain of hair, instead of a few stray curls."

"Here, let me help." Gian stepped into Cara's view, and in front of the white backdrop. He smiled down at her, his fingers sliding along the column of her throat to push back the hair that had fallen over her shoulder. Cara had all she could do not to shiver, and guessing by the way Gian's grin deepened, he saw it, too. "There, perfect."

"Step back and let me see, Gian."

At the photographer's demand, Gian gave Cara a wink, and did as he was told.

"Yes, that's much better," the woman said. Then, her camera started up again, capturing images of Cara in a stone-still pose, with a sleeping, one-week old, naked Marcus in her arms. "You do seem to have a good eye for this sort of thing, Gian. Do you dabble in photography at all?"

Cara shot Gian a look that she hoped kept him quiet from discussing his little hobby with *her* and cameras. In his spot in the corner, now sitting back in the corner chair and watching the session, he seemed content and pleased. In his suit and shined leather shoes, his dark gaze staying pinned on her, he had never quite looked more handsome. He barely reacted at all to Cara's unspoken warning.

"I certainly have an eye for someone," he murmured.

"I hope you put it to use."

"Oh, I do. I most certainly do."

"Gian," Cara said quietly.

His husky laughter filled the penthouse's living room. The photographer had chosen it amongst the many others, because of all the floor-to-ceiling windows and natural light. Cara wouldn't have minded going in to the woman's studio, but Gian said it wasn't necessary. She wanted photos, Gian had the woman come to her. It worked.

"I think we're just about—"

Gian's cell phone started ringing. "Done."

The photographer smiled. "Yep. Just let me pack up. Cara, you can keep the muslin wrap for Marcus, as I don't reuse items like those for other newborns. I have to say, he was one of the easier babies to photograph this week."

"That's because he spent an hour and a half on my boob before you got here," Cara half-joked. "Milk-drunk."

It wasn't a lie.

It *was* kind of funny.

The truth was, Marcus happened to be a wonderful baby. Sure, he clusterfed at night before bed, and he liked to have his spaces quiet and dimly lit, but Cara figured that was just his way of transitioning into the world at a slower pace. Marcus rarely cried, he barely fussed. And then there was Gian … She swore the baby just *knew* his father was in the room, even when he couldn't see Gian.

Marcus was attached to Cara, yes.

Gian was entirely different.

"Here, let me take him, *mon ange*," Gian said, coming to stand at Cara's side again while the photographer packed up her things. "Go get in that new dress I brought back for you from Ottawa yesterday. He'll be okay with me."

Already, Marcus's hazy brown eyes fluttered open at the sound of his father's voice. He tried peering around, but was only satisfied in his knowledge that his father was near when Gian scooped him from Cara's embrace. Then, the baby blinked up at his father and promptly fell back asleep.

"Gian, that's not an at-home kind of dress."

He smiled, and kissed her cheek. "Maybe not, but it *is* fit for a queen in her castle. Go put it on. I'll get him into a diaper and clothes, too."

Cara thought about Gian's ringing phone that had interrupted the end of the session, even though he hadn't picked up the call, and wondered … "Is someone coming over?"

"A couple of people, actually."

"Who?"

"Family." His stare dropped down to Marcus. "Mostly for him, though."

Oh.

"I'll go change," Cara said.

The nervousness in her tone must have been clear to Gian because he reached out and stroked her cheek with two fingers. "All you have to do is smile, beautiful girl. The world is so much better when you're smiling."

He always says the right things …

Cara still couldn't shake the nerves as she slipped out of the flowy white dress that she had used for the photo session, and into the form-fitted coral Dolce & Gabbana number hanging in the closet. She figured the dress had been a silent apology of sorts from Gian, as something had come up in the week, and he'd rushed off to Ottawa to take care of it.

For the most part, he had spent the first couple of days after Marcus's birth with her, then one night at the penthouse, before heading back to the mansion. He had promised to come right back the very next night, but the Ottawa thing came up, and ruined those plans.

Quickly, Cara checked herself in the mirror as she slipped on a pair of black pumps and a diamond choker. Another expensive gift that she had woken up to the morning after Marcus's birth. Gian had only shrugged and smiled slyly when Cara asked where it came from.

Thankfully, her fit and slim form was bouncing back rather fast. She thanked breastfeeding, good genetics, and the fact she had been in decent shape before and throughout the pregnancy for that little gift from God. Of course, things *were* different.

Her body was still different. Slightly wider in the hips. Her breasts were bigger. And her stomach had softened slightly, even as it flattened back down.

She had worried about the changes, both selfishly and vainly. She wished now that she hadn't spent time on that nonsense at all.

Cara came out of the bedroom and into the main section of the penthouse to find the photographer had left, but the new guests had arrived. Her presence wasn't noticed as she hung back in the entryway, and watched the newcomers *ooh* and *awe* over her son in his father's arms.

Gian's mother and father, and his siblings, each took their turns giving little Marcus their time and attention.

"Oh, look at his little fingers," Crystal said softly.

"Guzzi eyes," Domenic noted.

"Not *just* the eyes," Celeste said of her grandson. "Look at the boy— he's Gian's spitting image, my God."

"He is, isn't he?" Gian asked, his pride shining through.

"*Oui*, he looks just like you did when you were brand new. *Doux bébé*," Celeste cooed, running her fingers through the wisps of Marcus's dark hair.

"And her," said the quiet, tall man standing just a few feet back from the others. "He looks like her, too. You can't miss *that*."

Cara shifted as the man's gaze fell on her in the entryway. It seemed she had not gone as unnoticed as she previously thought. She knew who he was—Gian's father, Frederic. She didn't know a lot about the man, as Gian didn't offer, but she had heard things in passing.

He did not approve.

Not of her.

Not of her child.

Not of Gian's choices.

Just the way Frederic's cold gaze passed over her, and darted back to the baby boy in Celeste's arms, Cara knew all of those things were true.

"He does take after Cara quite a bit, too," Gian said, losing the happier tone from earlier. He turned to Cara, extending an arm and opening his hand wide for her to step forward and take. She did, still unsure and unsettled in her heart. "Remember what I said about today, Dad."

"I came, didn't I?" Frederic asked.

"*Sì*, but remember, too. This is not *your* home. Your rules do not apply here. Mine do. Hers do."

Dom cleared his throat, and quickly diverted the attention back to the baby. While it helped a bit, Cara still couldn't shake the coldness she had found waiting for her in Frederic's gaze, or how he all but dismissed her presence, even when he was standing directly beside her.

It was difficult.

A shameful feeling burned in her throat.

She couldn't expect anything different.

Cara only relaxed when Gian's lips pressed to her temple, unbothered by the people watching them. His lips moved with his words, whispering over her skin with assurance and love.

"You are never the lesser, not in your own home, *mia cara bella*. Demand respect in your space because it is yours, and do not let someone take it from you. You are the queen, and *this* is your castle. This is your home, and those who are lucky enough to be allowed inside should understand what that means. Smile. *Always* smile here."

He was right.

He always was.

• • •

It seemed like Cara had blinked—just *once*—and Marcus was turning one month old. Everyone had told her again and again that she needed to enjoy the time she had with her baby while he was a newborn, because before she knew it, he wouldn't be so tiny and new. Sure, Marcus was still a newborn, but just the fact that the first month had passed them by so quickly, in a haze of long nights, dirty diapers and so much more, was surreal.

And sweet.

The ding of the elevator brought Cara from her thoughts. She lifted her stare from her sleeping son in her arms, just in time to see Tommas enter through the penthouse's elevator with a wide smile and already opened arms.

"Cara."

"Tommy," Cara replied in kind, unable to stop her growing smile.

"Come here."

Before she knew what happened, her brother had wrapped her up in a tight hug that damn near squeezed the life out of her. She wasn't about to complain, though. It had been too long since she last seen her brother, though they did try to talk at least once a week.

"My God, look at this *bambino*," Tommas said, stepping back to give Marcus a good one-over. "He's going to be a heartbreaker."

Cara swatted her brother on his arm, laughing. "Don't start with that yet. He's just a baby."

"Prepare for it, Cara. Prepare."

She rolled her eyes, and turned to walk them in further. "Do you want a coffee? How was your flight?"

"Coffee would be great. And it was shit, but it always is when I'm not flying privately."

"How's Abriella?" Cara asked.

"Wonderful and beautiful," Tommas said of his wife. "Next time, she'll come, too. It's just not the right time with the little one."

Tommas, too, was a new parent. His son, Tommaso, was only a couple of months older than Marcus. Cara had seen picture after picture of her one and only nephew, as Tommas was like every proud father with a camera in his hands, but she had yet to meet the baby.

"I get it, no worries," Cara assured. "You didn't have to rush up here, either, by the way. I would have understood, Tommas."

Her brother shrugged, setting his bag to the side as they entered the kitchen. "Who else is going to come here and see this baby of yours, huh? I'm the only family you've got left—*I* need to be here for him. And you, too."

"Sit down. I'll get your coffee."

Tommas shrugged off his suit jacket and took a seat at the large kitchen table. Cara didn't miss how her brother peered around the penthouse, or the bit of it that he could see. She hadn't been the least bit surprised when he mentioned wanting to come down for a weekend to visit, but she *had* been a little shocked that he actually made time to do so.

Her brother had a busy life in Chicago, especially now that he was married with a child of his own, not to mention the fact that he was the boss of the Outfit. She suspected that her brother's time was already pulled thin in every single direction, and yet he made time for her.

Time for Marcus.

Cara appreciated that more than Tommas could possibly know.

"So, this is a nice place," Tommas said quietly.

Cara side-eyed her brother as she set a cup of coffee down in front of him. "Say what you're thinking, don't dance around it."

"When did you move out of the apartment?"

"A couple of weeks before the baby was born."

"Wasn't that when the issue happened at the shelter?" Tommas asked.

Cara made a face. "Yeah, around that time."

Tommas scowled, but hid it quickly enough by taking a drink of his coffee.

"That wasn't Gian's fault," Cara said, shifting Marcus to sleep over her shoulder as she took a seat beside her brother. "That was completely unrelated to Gian, Tommy."

"So you said before. A domestic abuse victim's husband, right?"

"Right." Cara rubbed a hand over her son's lower back. "And Gian just happened to … get himself in the middle of it, which was mostly what ended up on the news."

"And you, too. *You* ended up on the news, Cara."

"Not by our choice."

Tommas sighed, and looked around the penthouse again. "I guess he moved you in after that, huh?"

"Actually, I kind of did that by myself. He didn't really say a thing either way, because it was what he had been asking for the whole pregnancy. It was a few days later that he finally did something about me moving in."

"And what was that?"

Cara's gaze darted away from her brother as she admitted, "Signed the deed for the place over to me. This place isn't his, now. It's mine. No one can take it from me, no one can force me out of it. It's all mine."

Tommas let out an appreciative sound, surprising Cara further. "Well, then."

"I do like the penthouse."

"It's very high up."

"I feel safer here, Tommy. It feels right to be here."

"Are you happier here, too?"

Cara looked back to her brother to find he was searching her face for any sign of a lie or maybe even discontent. "I'm happy with him."

"Even knowing what you do—even after everything?"

"I don't excuse Gian. I only choose to love him. The rest is details. Those don't matter."

"They never should." Tommas nodded, and then reached for Marcus. "Now, give me my nephew. It's time for him to wake up and meet me properly. Where is Gian, by the way?"

Cara handed the sleeping baby over. "He thought I might like to spend some time alone with you first before inserting his presence, too."

"That's fine and great," Tommas replied just as fast, "but it doesn't answer my question."

"At the mansion."

Tommas' gaze cut to Cara just as Marcus woke up. "Is that where she lives?"

"Her name is Elena. His wife. You can say her name to me, Tommy."

"Again, not my question."

"It is."

"I see," her brother said softly.

"It's not always easy or pretty. I never thought it would be, though."

"But love, right?"

Cara smiled. "Yeah, love, Tommy."

• • •

"I haven't decided if I like you yet or not," Cara heard her brother say from down the hall.

She carefully closed the door to Marcus's nursery, not wanting to wake the baby up after his before-bed feed. It was like the baby thought he suddenly needed another round of milk before he could go back to sleep. Cara's well was dry for the moment.

"I don't think it's required for you to like me, honestly," Gian replied with a chuckle.

Cara kept her steps light and quiet as she walked down the hall, heading toward the office where Gian had disappeared to with Tommas when she went to feed Marcus after supper. Just a foot from the opened doorway, she held back from going further where she could be seen, and listened to the conversation happening beyond the doors.

She knew better than to eavesdrop.

She couldn't help it.

All evening, from the time Gian had arrived back at the penthouse, the two men had engaged in very safe conversation with one another. They almost seemed to be circling around one another, too, as though they were being careful about their words and actions, lest one offend the other.

Cara was not sure if that was because of their respective positions in their organized crime families, or for her.

"I like that you love her," Tommas said, "and that counts for a lot."

"I love her entirely."

"And your son, too. That much is obvious."

"He's my greatest pride and joy, and she gave him to me."

"But I don't like the rest," Tommas admitted. "I don't like that she is pushed aside in the eyes of others, or given labels and names that she doesn't deserve. I don't like that it must hurt her to spend half of her week with you, and wonder the other half. I don't like that there are nights she is alone, caring for your child, because you have distractions elsewhere."

"Responsibilities—duties," Gian corrected fast and sharp. "Distractions implies something that is not and has not ever been *there*. Use the right word, Tommas. It's the least you can do if you're going to insult me to my face."

"I'm not trying to insult you, Gian. I only want to understand."

"You're like me, aren't you? You sit in my spot, too. You know these rules, this life, and those people. Divorce would mean ruining my family's legacy, at the very least. At the most, my life would be given up as a sacrifice. So here I am, doing what I need to do."

"Certainly not what you want to do."

"No," Gian murmured.

"I heard you were having some issues on the streets, and with the police."

"The police are expected, given what happened last year and before that. The streets, on the other hand ... well, that's just my bastard father-in-law trying to force my hand with my family and men. He's been quiet the last month or so, surprisingly. And after everything he did, the issues he started, men he killed, and the threats ... it's concerning. He's gone under the radar, too, making it harder to watch him. Even his men are out of sight for the moment. He wanted to make a point to me, or rather, make a point out of me. He didn't succeed, but that does not mean he's finished."

"Why is that surprising? Maybe he finally came to the realization that you're not going to give him what he wants."

"You would have to know the man," Gian said with a sigh. "Everyone always gives him what he wants, even if it takes a while. He simply has to find the right button to push with a man to get him to hand it over."

"And so, the quietness and the disappearing act is a bad thing."

"It is always bad when a man cannot see Gabriel coming, Tommas."

Silence hung heavily between the two before Tommas spoke again.

"And all of this for what? Why is he causing these issues?"

"He believes I have a rat in my family, and he thinks forcing my hand to cull through my men indiscriminately will fix the issue," Gian answered.

"Do you have a rat?"

"A big, fat one."

Tommas grunted disgustedly. "But you're not as concerned about the rat as you are—"

"Gabriel. Exactly."

"And why is that, now?"

"He's pushed every other button he thinks I have, Tommas," Gian said, "and it earned him nothing. I only have one thing left for him to come after, to make his point loud and clear."

"You're talking about Cara."

"Every part of me wishes I wasn't."

"But you've told me you keep her presence quiet, and that you're quiet about coming and going from here. You said you were *careful*, Gian."

"I can never be careful enough, I can only be mindful now."

"What does that even mean?"

"It means I have been watching and waiting for him to try and push that button with me, because he knows very well that it's there. I do all I can to keep her safe, because I put her in this position, even if she doesn't know it."

"Why not just kill him?" Tommas demanded.

"It's never that easy. Another person on my shit-list shows up murdered. I don't need the fucking attention it's likely to bring, unless he doesn't give me a choice. I've managed Gabriel this long, when others wouldn't have bothered at all, I can manage a little while longer. Surely. We've been entangled in this mess for years. I know his games."

"So just *kill* him."

"Tell me, why didn't you just kill the person standing in your way, Tommas?"

Tommas cleared his throat. "It wasn't that easy."

"My point, *merci*."

"And if he *does* go after Cara?"

"I'm doing everything I can to make sure that doesn't happen."

"But if he *does*," Tommas pressed, not even posing it as a question.

"Then I'll slaughter him. It'll turn all eyes on me—it'll cause a war between organizations. It's everything I can't afford to have happen right now, given the state of my freedom and *famiglia*."

"But?"

"I'll do it. I'll burn the whole fucking world down for her. Imagine what I would do to just one man."

• • •

Jenny's face lit up with pure joy as Cara turned the infant car seat so that a wide-awake, one month and a half old Marcus was visible. "Look at him!"

"I do," Cara said, laughing. "Every day, all the time."

"Oh, my God. He is too *precious*."

And just like that, someone else fell in love with Cara's son. She couldn't really blame people. There was something about Marcus's sweet face and gold-flecked brown eyes that just did it for everybody. When he smiled, they all *melted*.

"He looks like his father," Jenny noted. "Those eyes are just unreal."

"So everyone keeps saying."

Jenny carefully maneuvered Marcus from his car seat. The baby peered up at the new, strange person in his world, but still grinned behind his soother. "I'm so glad you brought him in to the shelter to say hello. Everyone misses you so much. We were starting to consider you were never going to come back."

Cara waved that off. "I'll be back. Four months is all I agreed to take off, and I can bring him in with me when I do start back. No worries there."

"Well, let's go say hello to everybody, sweet boy."

For the next hour, Cara strolled from office to office, and section to section, watching as yet more people fell head over heels for her boy. She had wanted to come to the shelter sooner, as her coworkers were just as much her family as her own brother, but things always seemed to get in the way. She had pushed it aside for far too long.

Cara was grateful she had made the time today.

"So, how's it been with the new baby?" another one of her co-workers asked.

"Busy. Tiring. Wonderful."

The woman smiled as she headed back into her office. "Babies will definitely do that."

Cara stepped aside as the mail cart was pushed through the office wing. The man who delivered the mail stopped long enough to give the baby and Cara a quick hello, and then went about delivering the last bit of his manila envelopes to each office.

"We will be so happy to have you back," Jenny said, "though I understand why you want to take as much time as you can with this beautiful little creature."

Cara took her son when Jenny offered the still wide-awake baby back. "I do want to get back here, though. I feel like I'll probably have way too much to catch up on, by the time I get back into the office."

"Don't worry, you haven't missed a lot, Cara. We've just spent the last month working through what happened with the shooting, settling back in, and getting everyone settled. Nothing too strenuous."

"Still …"

"Enjoy the time with your baby," Jenny said.

Cara sighed. "I am, trust me."

"And you are *always* welcome to come in just for conversation. No one is going to turn you away with little Marcus here."

She laughed. "Yes, not because you want me here, it's all about him, now."

"Well, look at him!"

"Oh, my."

The quiet exclamation from behind Cara gained both her and Jenny's attention. The previous co-worker that had been admiring Marcus stood in her office doorway with a manila envelope in her hands. Her gaze darted from whatever she was staring at, to Cara, and then back again. A pink reddened her cheeks.

"Something wrong, Nancy?" Jenny asked.

"Um. Uh. Well—"

"Spit it out."

An odd, heavy sensation settled in Cara's stomach. She wasn't sure why, but just the way Nancy looked at her again, and then back down to the item in her hands, it was unsettling.

To say the least ...

"Whoa!"

Another shout from someone else echoed inside a different office.

"Did you get one of these?" Nancy asked, lifting the envelope for Jenny to see. She kept the items hidden behind it, though.

"I'm not sure."

Nancy's gaze darted to Cara once more. "You should probably check, Jenny."

"Just ... Jesus," Jenny said, stepping forward and ripping the items from Nancy's hands. "Give it to me. What is wrong with you?"

Jenny didn't bother to hide the items that had been inside the envelopes the way Nancy had. Cara almost wished her boss would have done just that. She could plainly see photos of her *very* naked self in the most dirty, compromising positions. With each photo that Jenny flipped through, the images became progressively dirtier and worse for Cara.

"Oh, my God," Cara whispered, horrified.

She recognized those images.

They were ones Gian had taken of her.

Some from before her pregnancy, a few early in her pregnancy, and even a couple of candid shots late in the pregnancy, although those weren't filthy in nature, simply private.

Smudged lipstick. Cum up her back. A handprint on her ass. Her mouth full of cock. Her legs spread wide open. Her pussy wet and open. All of the images had her face clearly visible.

Cara's heart rammed hard in her ribcage, taking over all other sensations. Her blood rushed in her ears as she struggled to ignore the sudden flood of absolute *shame*.

"There were a lot of those same envelopes on the mail cart," Nancy said quietly. "Probably one for every office, Jenny."

Jenny stayed quiet for longer than Cara liked, but eventually nodded. "Okay."

"I'm so sorry," was all Cara managed to get out.

Anymore, and she was sure vomit would follow her words.

Jenny looked to Cara, a wariness and pity in her gaze. "This is a very deliberate act on you, Cara."

Was it?

Cara didn't know anything.

"Why?"

"The first time you come to the shelter since taking time off, and *these*

361

get sent here." Jenny cleared her throat, uncomfortably. "Presumably to everyone in the offices."

"Oh, my God."

She was going to throw up.

"Who knew you were coming here today?" Jenny asked.

Gian. That was it, as far as Cara knew. And Chris, her enforcer, as she wasn't allowed to go anywhere without him. She didn't think either of those two people would have done this to her.

"I should go," Cara mumbled, grabbing for the infant car seat resting on the floor. "I'm so sorry."

"Cara, wait a—"

She didn't wait.

The shame wouldn't let her.

It ate her alive.

FIFTEEN

Gian found Chris sitting at the kitchen table as he stormed through the penthouse. The enforcer had set little Marcus up in a bouncy chair, and was apparently reading the newspaper to the baby. Beside him, a row of overturned photographs and a discarded manila envelope sat on the tabletop, seemingly forgotten.

He hesitated at the sight of the overturned images, but only because he knew what he would see on the other side. He, too, had gotten a package delivered while dining with a business associate.

Apparently, so had his mother.

His father.

His brother *and* sister.

Several of his men.

People he worked with.

People who worked *for* him.

His aunt in Quebec.

His cousins.

Gian suspected there were more, but the people affiliated with his life were probably too shocked, embarrassed, or unsure to contact him and ask about the dirty pictures of Cara. He had found that with a few, they didn't need an explanation. Like the ones delivered to his parents—there had been no explanation. Some delivered to his men, or people he worked with, had included a simple note explaining who the woman in the images was, and how it related to Gian.

Others, like the ones delivered to *him*, or to Elena, had been written on directly. Or so Elena told him. Gian believed her, if only because his package had also held the naked images of Cara with red ink marked across the photos labeling her *whore* and *slut*. To name a few.

"Were those sent to you today?" Gian asked Chris.

The enforcer kept his attention on the baby. "Found the package under the wiper of my car after I ran in to get a coffee while Cara was inside the shelter."

Gian cleared the rising rage clogging up his throat. "I see."

"The doorman downstairs was nice enough to let me know that the front desk also received the same package of photos."

Gian's molars ached as he gritted his teeth in an effort to calm himself down. "Destroy them."

"I thought you would prefer to, if given the option. I didn't bother to look beyond the first one when I pulled them out. It was enough for me to

363

know I shouldn't be looking at them. And then Cara came running out of the shelter like a bat out of hell … so, yeah."

"Does she know that you saw the pictures, too?"

Chris shook his head. "Didn't say a word, boss."

"Keep it that way."

"I planned to. This is bad, isn't it?"

Little Marcus seemed perfectly content to bounce in his chair, thanks to Chris helping by tugging on the bottom. The baby certainly didn't know his mother's whole world had just been turned upside down, and she would never feel safe or unviolated again. Not even in her own skin. How could she, when every time someone looked at her, she would have to wonder if they had done this to her, or if they had *seen*?

"It's bad," Gian said, "but not in the way some might think. Someone intended to embarrass me, to shame me, and what they did was far worse."

"They hurt Cara."

"Yes."

Chris sighed, and stopped bouncing the baby's seat as he turned to his boss. "Who would have access to those photos?"

"They're accessed only on my phone and you know how careful I am with that."

"But who would, boss?"

Gian had to seriously consider his answer, because he wasn't sure. Yes, his phone had a pin lock on it, but if someone picked up the device when his back was turned before the screen blacked out, they could easily see inside and explore his very personal and private life. Beyond that, phones were not infallible. Anyone with a decent computer program could plug one in and strip it of files, locked or not, with the owner none the wiser.

"Whoever it was would have needed to have my phone for a bit, I think. Some of those images are back from after the bomb was set on my car, when Cara and I were a new thing. It would have taken time to grab files that far back in the gallery."

"Then you're just knocking names off the list," Chris said with a shrug. "So, who was it?"

"Am I knocking names off?" Gian asked right back. "Because that leaves a few people who I spent enough time with to maybe set my phone down and look away, but that doesn't mean I did or would."

"Another question, then."

Gian figured he was the one who needed to be asking questions, but he didn't see the harm in letting Chris ask, too. "What?"

"Who would do it—do something that awful to someone like this?"

Gian scoffed, dark and hateful. "My wife. Her father. This stinks of them. It reeks of their kind of nonsense."

"You don't sound sure."

"I have never left my phone within reach of Elena, and she also received a package today with these photos, or so she said when she called to scream at me. I haven't seen Gabriel since before Marcus was born, and again, he had no access to my phone. It certainly stinks of them."

"Except *how*," Chris muttered.

"*Oui.*"

"Cara disappeared into the bedroom. I didn't want to interrupt her, and the *principe* is fine with me, boss."

Gian nodded. "Thank you."

Unsure of what kind of state he would find Cara in, Gian headed for the master bedroom. He opened the door to see a hurricane of devastation staring back at him. Clothes strewn about the floor in piles, wrinkled or torn. Jewelry scattered, perfumes toppled over, and makeup palates crushed in a strange rainbow of colors on hardwood. White sheets had been ripped from the mattress, and glass from the shattered mirror glittered on the floor and the shoes that had clearly been used to smash it.

Rage found him standing there.

Shame screamed through the silence.

Cara, so calm and put together, so strong even in her weaknesses, had clearly broke under a whole new kind of weight. It was not lost on him how she attacked the things that accentuated her life, beauty, or image. Her clothes, perfumes, and makeup. Her jewelry, and the mirror that showcased her reflection when she stared into it.

It killed him.

Because she was so beautiful. Because she was so wonderful. Because in her heart, she was everything sweet, good, and deserving of love, adoration, and respect.

Someone had taken that from her without care or concern. They had taken private moments of her life, things that only *he* was allowed to see or have from her, and showed them to the world.

And how dare they?

Cara's worth should never be tied to the acts of a bedroom, and yet, he feared they now would be for far too many. She probably knew it, too.

"Cara?" Gian called into the bedroom, taking a single step inside. "*Mon ange?*"

A quiet, choked sob echoed from behind the opened door of the attached master bath. Gian instantly headed in that direction, making sure to shut the bedroom door behind him.

He found Cara tucked into the corner of the bathroom, soaking wet from a still-running shower, and naked, though she clutched at a towel. She wouldn't look at him, not when he called her name again, or even when he got down on his knees and reached for her. She *flinched* away from him when he touched her, but he still pulled her into his embrace.

"I'm sorry," he said over and over.

"Why would someone do that to me, Gian? *Why?*"

"I don't know."

But he thought he did. He thought he might know. He still didn't want to tell her. How could he explain that someone had violated her privacy and life, simply to hurt him? Wasn't it bad enough that Cara had to know those photos were his to begin with? That he had not been careful enough with something like those images she trusted him with?

Cara shook from the force of her cries. No matter how hard he tried, Gian couldn't wipe the tears away fast enough before more ran down her cheeks.

"I'm so sorry," he told her again.

He couldn't make this better.

This couldn't be fixed.

Gian hated himself for that.

• • •

"Cara, look at me," Gian demanded.

She did, but the sadness that had been constant in her eyes for a week, stared back at him. He was so angry and disappointed in himself, because she asked him the same thing every day: *why* and *who*. He was no closer to being able to answer that for her, and each time he couldn't give her what she asked, he failed more.

"It'll be fine, a quiet weekend away," he told her.

Cara nodded, her attention drifting back to the sleeping baby in the car seat next to her. "Maybe it'll help to get away."

That's what he kept telling her.

He hoped it was true.

"Chris will keep an eye on you," Gian promised, "but if you need anything, if you want me, just call. Okay?"

"Sure, Gian."

He didn't for a second think she would call. She blamed him, in a way, and Gian didn't fault her for it. It had been his phone, his pictures. It was her job lost, her newly beginning career already stained and tainted, and her reputation destroyed with one selfish, vile act. It was her image and self-worth ruined, not his. And fuck him, because he couldn't even tell her who or why.

"Is it different?" Cara asked. "The Ottawa penthouse, I mean. Is it different from the last time I was there?"

Gian smiled. "A bit. I had some upgrades done. It needed them. I think you'll like it. Take some time to enjoy it, anyway. I haven't been able to yet. Not entirely."

"You could come."

"You don't really want me to, though, do you?"

Cara glanced away. "I just need to get out of this city and breathe, Gian."

"I know, *mon ange.*" He wouldn't fault her for that, either. Leaning into the back of the SUV, Gian kissed Cara on her forehead, and relaxed a bit when her soft fingertips stroked his cheek. It felt like a silent promise that things would be better ... eventually. Quickly, he laid his hand on top of his son's head, and Marcus's eyes fluttered open at his father's touch. "For *anything*, Cara, you call me."

"I will. I love you, Gian."

That, he didn't doubt.

Not at all.

"*Ti amo*, Cara."

Closing the SUV door, Gian smacked the roof with his palm, and caught Chris's eye in the front seat. He didn't have to verbalize his order for the man to do his job, Chris always did it without needing to be told.

Gian stayed standing on the sidewalk long after the SUV had disappeared out of sight. It was only as he headed toward the underground garage to get his own vehicle that his cell phone started ringing. Dom, he thought, or maybe Stephan. There was always too much shit for him to do, and he never got time to rest anymore.

He picked up the call without even checking the ID.

"*Ciao, bonjour.*"

"It's been a while, Gian."

Every inch of Gian turned to ice at the sound of his father-in-law's voice.

"Gabriel," Gian greeted as he closed in on his car. "I'd like to say it's nice to hear from you, but we both know that would be a fucking lie."

"Yes, well, I hear you've been looking for me."

Gian slid into his car, and started it up. "You heard correctly. I like to keep an eye on men who threaten me and my men, after all. You can't blame me for that."

"Of course, not. Have you found your rat yet?"

"That's not your concern."

"So, no," his father-in-law said rather cheerily. "As I suspected. Still too busy putting your attention and time where it neither deserves to be, or needs to be. Such a shame, Gian. I thought giving you some space and time to think might have changed your mind—especially now that the whore has had the baby. Babies change things, I thought. They make a man ... see things a bit differently. It's not as fun with a whore when you're not just fucking her, but changing nappies and listening to a child cry for hours on end. I *thought* the baby would send you back to where you should be."

Gian's brow furrowed. "Where I should be? What in the fuck does that mean?"

"With my daughter. Where else?"

Oh, fuck that.

Gian had no idea where Gabriel was getting this nonsense, but he wasn't even going to indulge it. "My personal life is not up for discussion today."

"It is always up for discussion when it's a man like you, in your position."

"Was this ever even about a rat in my family, Gabriel?" Gian wondered out loud.

The older man chuckled. "It was. These are things you need to learn, and fast, Gian. Tell me, did *Cara* like the gift I sent out last week?"

All over again, ice and fire spread through Gian's veins, threatening to send him into a rage before he even knew what happened.

"How did you get those photos?" Gian asked.

"I have ways."

"You just signed your death warrant, Gabriel."

He figured the man deserved a warning, at least.

"Wrong," his father-in-law murmured. "You've signed hers, and the child's. As I warned you. I would have overlooked a lot of your personal business, until you began hurting what belonged to me."

"*What?*"

"I let you have Elena. You should have taken better care with her; I won't have her crying to me over something as stupid as you. Perhaps your man will make it out alive, though. The one driving them, I mean. I hope you said goodbye."

The phone call hung up. Gian couldn't get his fucking car into drive fast enough. He hit the road already breaking the goddamn speed limit, but knowing he was probably too late.

• • •

Hospitals were both horrible and amazing places. Horrible, because just the smell alone brought memories of more deaths and nights spent in worry than Gian cared to remember. Amazing, because the smell also brought along memories of lives saved and time given.

The only thing keeping him sane as he sat in a hospital room, waiting? His son.

Marcus slept off the bottle of formula he'd downed as soon as the nurse had brought it in for Gian to feed the boy earlier. Although to be fair, Marcus had not wanted the formula at all or the oddly-shaped nipple that was nothing like his mother's breast, shoved into his mouth. In a hospital crib, swaddled in a warmed blanket, the baby had no idea how close to death he had come.

No idea at all.

Gian, despite tired legs and an aching back, kept watch over the boy. He tensed at every flicker of Marcus's lids, and each jerk of the baby's limbs beneath his tight swaddle. Marcus was perfectly fine—not a scratch or bump on his beautiful, innocent head. His car seat had made sure of that when the SUV had been run off the road, and then subsequently rolled down an embankment.

Still, Gian couldn't get the image of his son's car seat with a single bullet hole through the back rest, only a couple of inches higher than where his son's head would have been laying. He couldn't forget the pieces of broken window glass scattered across the baby's body, or the bloodstained blanket, colored red with Cara's blood.

Cara. Pain shot through Gian like a lightning bolt.

His gaze darted to the closed door of the hospital room, and he had all he could do not to go out and demand someone give him more answers. He would get none if he did, anyway. Not until Cara's surgery was either over, or unable to be completed.

Three shots. One through her hand. One to her thigh.

The final one—the most deadly and likely to cause complications—to her chest. They had been aiming for her heart, though a shot to the head would have been quicker and cleaner. Gian figured it wasn't about quick or clean, it was about making a point.

A point he heard loud and fucking clear.

"Boss?"

The sound of Stephan's voice brought Gian from his internal war. The underboss stood in the now opened doorway, his gaze stuck on the phone in his hand.

"Dom wanted me to let you know that he got ahold of Tommas Rossi, and that your mother is on her way up now," Stephan said. "Tommas can't get out of Chicago right now, but he demanded updates every hour, on the hour. I guess your mother is in quite a state and is asking to see the baby."

Gian nodded, but the numbness was beginning to seep in, taking away his desire to talk, or even think. This was better, though, as he wouldn't feel so guilty when he left his child and Cara to recover in the hospital without him while he finished a job that was long overdue.

The guilt would come later, surely.

He would deal with it then.

• • •

"Mr. Guzzi," greeted the maid as Gian walked past the kitchen's entrance inside the mansion. "I was not told to expect you tonight, sir."

Gian cursed under his breath, but turned back to Mariana with a forced smile. "I wasn't expecting to be here tonight, either. Are you the only staff left?"

She nodded.

"Good," Gian said, "you're free to leave early. Now, preferably."

"But I haven't finished my—"

"It's fine. Please head out."

Gian waited for Mariana to gather her things, and then saw her out the front door. Satisfied he was now alone in the Guzzi mansion—albeit, his wife was *somewhere*—he went back to his task. Finding Elena.

It didn't take him long.

Elena rested in a Jacuzzi tub with bubbles that smelled of vanilla and overflowed to the floor. A half-downed bottle of wine sat on the edge of the tub, no glass in sight. Apparently, she was drinking it straight from the bottle. The steam in the master bathroom was thick enough to make Gian squint down at his wife from up above. He ignored her nakedness, as it did little for his desires, and it wasn't as though he hadn't seen it before.

"Elena," Gian barked.

She jerked awake in the tub, her flailing sending water and bubbles peppering the walls, floor, and Gian. He didn't bother to move, simply continued standing above her, glaring down.

Elena met his glare with one of her own when she realized he *was* there. "Gian! What in the fuck are you doing?"

"I could ask you the same thing."

"I beg your pardon?" Elena scrambled to sit up properly in the tub, using an arm to cover her chest as she reached for a nearby towel. She couldn't quite reach it, though, and Gian didn't offer to help. "What do you want?"

"Again, I'll hand that question right back to you, wife."

Her brow furrowed. "What does it look like? I wanted to take a bath."

"And drink a bottle of wine in the process, apparently."

"It's a half of a bottle."

"Details. Get the fuck out of the tub."

She narrowed her gaze. "I—"

Gian was not in the mood to play games with this woman tonight. He yanked Elena out of the bubbly, hot water by her wrist, not caring at all that she slipped and stumbled before righting herself with an angry huff. If looks could kill, he would have been dead right there on the spot.

"We're not going to play your games tonight, Elena," he warned. "I have a feeling you've been playing enough games with me as it is. I'm going to speak, you're going to listen. I'm going to ask questions, you're going to talk. If you lie to me, I will know it. If you spin bullshit with me, I will know it. Do you understand?"

"Could I at least get dressed?"

Gian grabbed the large towel hanging off the hook and shoved it at his wife. "Cover yourself up, it's the best I can do at the moment."

"You're an ass—"

"Yes, I'm aware," he interrupted before she could insult him. "You know, your father told me again and again that I needed to watch you. He tried to get through my thick skull that women like you can't be trusted. And after all the shit you already did to me, I should have listened to the man. Except I didn't, because I listened to too much of what you were saying. You're just as much of a snake as your father is."

Elena blinked, her brown gaze icing over. "What is this even about? Shouldn't you be fucking that whore of yours across the city? I—"

Gian moved forward, crowding Elena to the bathroom wall as his hand came up to clench around her throat. He squeezed hard, feeling her swallow under his grasp as she attempted to take in some kind of air. "*I* talk, *you* listen."

"O-okay, Gian."

"I don't know why, but it seems you've been feeding your father some kind of crazy bullshit where you and I are concerned. You have him believing you actually *care* about me on some level. You have him thinking I'm *hurting* you. That you're alone here, without me, and poor little Elena is just so fucking *heartbroken.*"

Sarcasm oozed from Gian.

He couldn't even control it.

It was all lies.

"And what I didn't understand, Elena," Gian continued, "is why you would want to do that at all. We keep your father away and out of our life for a goddamn reason. He was always too fascinated with you, too close to you. Controlling. Vindictive. Dangerous. That's what *you* said. I saw these things myself, and I knew it was true. You wanted away from him, and you used me to do it, so I protected you for all these years, even after you lied and hurt me. I still *protected you.* Didn't I protect you from him?"

She nodded, though the iciness in her gaze hadn't left. She didn't look at him with fear, either, despite the fact he only needed to squeeze her throat a little tighter and she would have no air left to breathe at all. Gian figured that was because this was not the first time his wife had found herself in a position like this one.

"Then *why?*" Gian roared. "Why would you invite that man back in? Why lie to him, manipulate him with personal things about you and me that aren't even close to the truth? Why use a woman I love and my child—an innocent baby—as a sacrifice for your games? Why do any of that?"

Elena let out a slow, steady stream of air, as much as she could, and then smiled.

Goddamn.

It was cold.

Dead.

It burned.

Like her.

"Because look at you," she whispered, her voice hoarse and strained. "Look at you, Gian. Look at how angry you are, how ready to kill you are. Years ago, when you found me battered and beaten because of him, you were angry, but not like *this*. So calm and steady, but with rage so real it radiates. I thought it would have been enough back then to push you into killing him—seeing me like that, and what he did to me—but it wasn't. And because of that, I had to follow through, didn't I? To get away, I had no other choice but to follow through with the next part of the plan."

A heavy realization settled on Gian's shoulders like a dead weight as he took in his wife's words.

"To marry me, you mean."

Elena shrugged dainty shoulders. "I can't help that it's taken this long for you to finally find something you give a shit enough about to kill for it, but don't you ever fault me for using it, Gian. You know exactly who I am—I can't help that my father forgot for a time, too."

Yes, he knew.

She was a snake.

Just like her father.

Elena winked. "Hiss, hiss, Gian."

All that rage that had been beating at Gian's surface finally spilled over. The control he thought he had was gone, just like that. There wasn't a single part of Gian that was able to be rational in those few seconds. He took the greatest pleasure in seeing Elena's eyes water as he choked her against the bathroom wall—how her words struggled, and her body tensed with the urge to fight. It was one of the most beautiful sights he had ever seen, where she was concerned.

"You deserve to rot in hell, Elena. He almost killed them! Because of *you*."

"We'll be free," she croaked out under his hands. "Don't you get it?"

"You're—"

"*We'll be free, Gian.*"

He wasn't quite sure what it was that sent him jerking back from Elena. Partly, her words. Partly, her blue-lipped smile and happy eyes.

"You're fucking crazy," he said, pointing a finger at her. "You're insane."

"Why, because I figured a way out of this for both of us? All you have to do is get rid of the problem, Gian. He gave you a reason to do it, didn't he? A reason to justify all the problems that might come of it. You're angry, remember, he nearly killed Cara and the baby—your precious *things*. So, *kill him*."

"You think that'll fix this?" Gian asked, waving between them. "You think that's *enough*?"

"Shouldn't it be?"

"This is for life, Elena! And not because of your father's rules, but because of the ones *I* am forced to live by. You stupid, silly woman." He laughed darkly, taking another step back from his wife and shaking his head. "You're so blinded by your need to manipulate and control and gain by hurting others that you don't even realize how *fucked* you are. Killing him isn't going to get you the divorce. It will never get you the divorce!"

She stiffened, clutching the towel against her body with suddenly shaking hands. "But … but—"

"And the biggest problem is that I can't even kill you for what you've done this time," Gian snarled at her. "We've made such a fucking spectacle of this sham of a marriage—how unhappy you are, how distracted I am *elsewhere*. Killing you would do nothing but turn everyone against me when I need them the most. But Jesus, it might just be worth it, Elena."

Finally, a spark of fear lit up her gaze. "You can't kill me. I'm your wife, Gian."

Exactly.

And it had nothing to do with her, but everything to do with him. He was a made man—he chose this life, he lived by it, he spoke the rules, and he enforced them even when he hated them. No one could ever possibly understand the struggle it was to be *him*, and he wouldn't ever be able to explain it unless someone walked in his shoes.

No one ever would.

"The only reason I would ever give you a divorce, despite how it would ruin me," Gian said, "is so that when everyone finally stops looking at me, and you think you've finally gotten what you wanted, I could take it all away from you. I could kill you and no one would ever look to me, Elena. *That* is why I would divorce you, why I would sacrifice my name and legacy, because that is what you deserve. How badly do you want to be free? You've already taken everything from me. When is it finally going to be your turn?"

Elena only continued to stare at him, seemingly horrified and in disbelief, all at the same time. This was their life—he couldn't help the fact that she ignored things that were right in front of her face simply because she figured she could manipulate her way out of them.

That might have worked in her father's Camorra world.

It did not work in Cosa Nostra.

"You're going to get dressed," Gian said quietly, "put your makeup on, cover those marks on your neck with a scarf, and do your hair. Then, you're going to call your father, and tell him whatever you need to so that he comes over here tonight. You're going to sound pleasant and sweet and whatever else he needs to hear so that he doesn't think for a second that anything is wrong. And once he is here, you're going to do the same thing, and you'll look away when you need to, you'll say nothing to anyone about what happens here. Is that understood?"

Elena's hands trembled more. "Yes."

"*Yes*, what?"

"Yes, I understand, Gian."

He tipped his hand toward the bathroom door. "Hurry the hell up. I won't be far behind, so don't think I won't hear if you try to fuck me over, Elena."

Gian did exactly as he said he would, following behind his wife while she readied and then called her father. He said nothing as she convinced Gabriel to come to her, and Elena kept her act up the whole time.

He might have been proud, had he felt something at all.

He didn't.

Not an hour later, Gian had two snakes in his mansion instead of just the one.

"Daddy," Elena said, a false cheeriness coloring up her tone. "I've missed you."

"*Reginella*," Gabriel replied, the wet sound of a kiss meeting a cheek echoing down the hall to Gian's hidden spot. There was more affection in that one word than Gian had ever heard his father-in-law use before, especially toward Elena. It made him wonder—consider—just how much was an act those two put on for the world. How much of their vileness toward one another was simply what they wanted people to believe, not what was actually the truth. "You look tired, Elena."

"Long day," she replied. "Come in, sit down."

"I take it, your husband is not around."

"When is he ever around, Daddy?"

"Mmm," Gabriel hummed, "shame, really."

"He's just happier elsewhere at the moment."

"Not for long, *dolcezza*. I assure you."

"Oh?" Elena asked.

Gabriel's laughter rang down the hall, following along with two sets of footsteps. "That's not for you to worry your pretty little head over. I always take care of my *bambina*, don't I? Of course, I do. Now, where is that spiced rum I like so much?"

"In the main room. Are you supposed to be drinking with the medicine for your heart?"

"Never mind, *donna*. Don't lecture me on my health."

"I just—"

"Don't."

"Fine," Elena said with a quiet sigh.

Gian stepped out of the shadows of the closet enclave in the entryway after Elena and her father passed him by. He followed behind them a few steps, listening to their conversation as he screwed in the silencer to his gun.

What a mess this would be.

What a war it would start.

He wished he cared.

Gian stayed in the entryway of the main room while Elena directed her father toward the wet bar. It was only when Gabriel lifted a glass of spiced rum to his lips and turned slightly that he saw Gian waiting there, gun cocked and ready.

His finger was already on the trigger.

Gabriel took his drink, and swallowed it down without so much as a flinch before he said, "I trusted you, Elena."

The man didn't even look at his daughter when he spoke to her.

"You should have known better than to trust a snake you raised," Gian told his father-in-law. "She learned from the very best, didn't she, Gabriel?"

"*Elena.*"

Elena didn't respond, but she did do as Gian had previously told her. She moved toward him, readying to leave the room so that she wouldn't see what happened, or what came next.

"You could at least apologize to me, Elena!" Gabriel shouted at his daughter's back. "After everything I did for you!"

"Why should I apologize, Daddy? You never apologized for making me this way."

Gian waited until he heard the footsteps of his wife retreat to the second level of the wing, and then he pulled the trigger. He fired off three more shots, one with each step he took before he was standing over the dead body of Gabriel.

Just to make sure.

"*Cazzo*, Gian!"

Gian turned fast on his heel at the sound of his brother's voice. Dom stood in the entryway, his gaze darting between his brother and the body on the floor. "What in the hell are you doing here?"

He hadn't called for Dom. He hadn't even seen his brother before he left the hospital.

"I ... I thought—" Dom's words cut off as his gaze cut to the side, looking at something down the hall before going right back to Gian. "Stephan said you had to handle something at the mansion, because of what happened to Cara and the baby. He didn't explain more."

"And what, you decided to follow behind me?"

"I thought you might need help."

Gian softened his stance a bit. Things had not been good with his brother for a long while. Longer than he was willing to admit. From the day in the jail all those months ago when Gian had needed to put Dom in his place, there had been a heathy distance between the two. It wasn't necessarily a bad thing. His brother became a better made man for it, a decent consigliere to his boss. Yet, the bond of what had been—between them as brothers—was seriously strained.

"If you want to help," Gian said, tipping his head toward the body on the floor, "then an extra pair of hands tonight would be great."

"Gabriel attacked Cara?"

"He did it. The bitch upstairs helped him along into it, but not much can be done for her."

That was all Gian was going to say about it.

Dom could fill in the blanks.

"I'll help," Dom said quickly. "Just tell me where to start."

"Find the bleach."

"There was something else, too."

"What's that?" Gian asked, tucking away his gun.

"Chris didn't make it through surgery. They put him on life support when his brain function failed."

Well, *fuck*.

SIXTEEN

It was the pain Cara felt that woke her. It wasn't deep, or even sharp. Instead, it was a pulse skimming her nerves, being chased away by something cold in her veins.

The beep of a monitor had Cara turning her head to find the unusual sound. An IV pole with a morphine drip, and another for what looked like antibiotics, it seemed. She lifted her hand to find the tubes attached there.

Her other hand?

Wrapped in medical gauze and *ow*.

But almost as soon as she remembered the events that had gotten her in a hospital bed—being run off the road, the shooting that followed—the morphine chased the memory away again with its cold sweetness.

Still, Cara breathed deeply.

That hurt, too.

Worse than the hand.

It was only Gian coming in through the automatic doors of her room that distracted Cara. His attention was focused on Marcus, and a bottle of milk. He didn't notice Cara was awake as he tried to feed the baby.

"Come on, Marcus," Gian murmured, teasing the baby's lips with the nipple. "You have to eat, *principe*. I know it doesn't taste good, but it's good for you. It's not like Ma, I know. You *have* to eat, little man. What am I supposed to tell Ma, that you won't eat for Daddy? No, don't spit it—"

Gian sighed, his shoulders dropping as he used a burping cloth slung over his shoulder to wipe around Marcus's face. Then, the wailing started. Marcus's high cries resounded with his frustration and hunger.

"Okay," Gian soothed, "no crying. Ma's sleeping. Another walk around the hospital, more formula to spit on the floor while we go. Maybe you'll drink enough on the way to fill your stomach."

Gian turned around to leave the room, and Cara's panic flared. She forced herself to sit up in the bed, despite the pain in doing so.

"No, don't go, Gian."

How Gian heard her, she wasn't sure. Her voice was all but gone—too soft to make any impact. Somehow, he had.

Gian was already heading for Cara's bedside with one of his smooth, charming smiles firmly in place. Something was wrong. She could see it. His smile was forced.

Cara chose not to ask for the moment, instead, wanting her son. She held her arms out, ready to take the baby. "Let me see him."

Once Marcus was tucked into Cara's embrace, his gold-flecked brown eyes locked onto hers, she was finally *okay*. She could breathe, because all was right in her world. Her baby was okay.

Cara held Marcus a little bit tighter.

"I'm sorry," Gian said, keeping a hand on the baby's back to steady him. Cara hadn't realized it, but thin lines of tears streaked down her cheeks. With careful touches, Gian swiped the wetness away. "I tried, but he won't eat. I don't know if it's me or the shit they keep trying to shove down his throat."

"Probably both," Cara whispered through her tears.

"He doesn't want to sleep, either." Gian laughed hoarsely. "I just think he knew someone important was out of reach for a while."

"I thought he was a daddy's boy."

"Not when his mother isn't within crying distance, apparently. Kept his whole wing up last night."

Cara tucked the side of her face into Gian's palm, feeling his thumb rub soothingly across her cheekbone in rhythmic strokes. He kept her drowsiness at bay, and calmed her.

"I'm sorry for this, *mon ange*," Gian added quieter. "It never should have happened."

"I know."

And she *did* know.

She knew without him needing to tell her. Why would he want or wish for someone to hurt her and their child? He loved them; he protected them as best he could.

Cara knew all of those things because she saw him do it every single day. Sure, this was her greatest fear. It was all the reasons she didn't want to be in this life, attached to a man whose tomorrows were not guaranteed.

She also couldn't *be* without Gian. It wouldn't be living. It had just taken Cara a long damn time to settle those things with her head and heart.

Marcus turned into Cara's chest as he rooted for what he wanted to fill his stomach.

"Here," Gian said, handing the small bottle of formula over. "They said the narcotics will transfer through, so formula and bottles it is."

Cara frowned. "He's still new. I don't want to bottle-feed him. I'm better for him, Gian."

Her body ached to feed her child.

"Not my call," Gian said, leaning down to press a quick kiss to her forehead. "Besides, what's important is that he *eats*."

Cara nodded, but only because she knew Gian was right.

Marcus had to eat.

It was that simple.

Surprisingly, Marcus took the bottle with Cara feeding it to him. He drank it slower, and with a scrunch to his nose, but he certainly didn't give his mother the same kind of trouble he had given his father.

Gian took the baby to burp him—Cara didn't have the strength—and then placed a sleepy Marcus into his mother's arms. Cara took the time to look at her lover. A tired, strained smile stared back at her, but there was love, too.

Always love.

Gian dragged a chair closer to Cara's bedside, and took a seat. His arm curled around her lower half, while his other swept through her curls to keep them out of her face. His forehead pressed to hers, and his lips dotted sweet kisses along the seam of her mouth.

"This will never happen again," he promised.

"You can't know that."

"I can. At least, not by the person who did it, and not for the reasons it was done. It will *never* happen again, *mia cara bella*. Ever."

Just the way his tone dipped, and his dark gaze lit with fire, Cara chose not to ask more questions. They were things she didn't need to know, because she knew Gian.

She knew his love. She knew his providing, careful, strong hands. She knew his entire life and soul were the two things he was currently holding. It would always be enough for her.

• • •

"Let me help," Gian said, offering Cara his hand to help her from the limo.

She took it, muttering, "I'm fine, Gian."

"Maybe so, but you don't need—"

"Gian, you need to relax. It's been two weeks. The infection is gone. The doctor said I've healed well, internally and externally. I can get out of a car."

He stared at her. "So?"

"Gian!"

"Let me help you, *mon ange*."

Cara wasn't going to be given much of a choice, it seemed. She let Gian help her out of the limo. She *was* better, two weeks after being released from the hospital. It was only Gian that hovered over her like a goddamn hawk, now, constantly on edge and ready to kill someone for even breathing in her direction.

She wished she was joking.

Cara smoothed down her black dress as Gian leaned in the car to grab her clutch and wide-brimmed hat. Funerals were not Cara's favorite thing, not in the least, but this was one she refused to miss.

Even when Gian said she didn't need to go, or there were some people who may be uncomfortable with his mistress's presence. Even when he warned there would be media outside the church, although the private graveyard would be protected from unwanted attention.

Cara didn't care.

She *had* to go.

For Chris?

Of course, she did.

Cara fixed her hat, tipping the wide brim down enough to hide half of her face. She let Gian lead them into the church, her mind on her son at the penthouse with his grandmother. Her presence at the funeral would be enough; no need to go adding their child's intrusion, too.

Inside the church, Cara was acutely aware of the eyes that watched her. She didn't talk unless greeted, and only to offer her condolences to Chris's parents and younger brother, standing at his closed casket.

She had already met his mother and father once. It had taken a lot of begging on her part, but Gian took her down to Chris's ICU room where he was kept alive on machines until his parents chose to pull the plug on their adult son. She wanted to thank him—for everything.

It was in that hospital room where Cara finally learned why Chris had always used miss when he spoke to her, and not her name. His father used it for each nurse, to the female doctors, to Gian's mother, who kept watch on Marcus while they went inside, and to Cara.

Because respect is important.

Cara wanted to pay her respects and say goodbye because it was the very least she could do, after everything. Fuck anyone who thought she didn't belong there like they did, simply because she was who she was.

"Are you okay?" Gian asked as they took a seat in a middle pew.

Cara let him tuck her in closer to his side. "I am, Gian."

"But sad."

Yes, sad.

The funeral wasn't a big affair. Chris's father spoke, as did his younger brother. A friend got up to read something, as well. The priest finished it all off. Then, the mourners headed to the private graveyard to bury Chris in the cool October ground, while colorful leaves fell all around.

Gian and Cara were some of the last to leave the graveyard. Cara noticed a few men—some she recognized, like her uncle—stayed close to Gian after the graveyard cleared out.

The limo pulled up, and Gian opened the back door for Cara to climb inside.

"I have a dinner," he told her, "one I can't miss today."

Cara's brow furrowed. "You didn't say anything about that earlier."

"Came up last minute. I can't refuse, not if it'll mean peaceful streets for a while."

"Peaceful streets?"

"Chris wasn't the only man buried today," Gian said vaguely. "So, if this dinner will smooth over any possible problems with the new man in charge, I shouldn't miss it."

Cara quickly realized Gian was giving her a lot of information to take in, without actually saying a lot. She appreciated it.

"Okay, then I'll see you back—"

"*She* isn't going to show at the meet with the new Camorra boss, is she?" a voice called out from behind them. Gian tensed, scowling. Cara tried to look over his shoulder at the man making a scene over nothing. She recognized him as one of Gian's men, but she didn't know his name or how important he might be. "Wasn't bringing your *goomah* here enough, boss? We don't need to be rubbing her in their faces, too, considering."

Gian leaned in, gave Cara a quick kiss on her lips, and then closed the limo door. Or, he tried. Cara kept it open, unsure of what was about to happen.

"Don't drive off," she told the driver, not taking her eyes off Gian as he stalked toward his man.

The guy didn't even see Gian reaching inside his jacket. Or if he did, he didn't have time to react. Gian pulled his gun from within his jacket, and then *beat* the man with it. He beat him until blood spilled, and the man was unconscious on the ground. He didn't say one word while he did it. No one stepped in, either.

Then, as fast as that rage and violence had showed itself, Gian straightened to his full height, and it was gone. As though it had never been to begin with.

Cara, on the other hand, wasn't quite sure what to do.

"Would anyone—anyone at all—like to revisit this conversation?" Gian's bloodstained hands skillfully tucked the gun away. Not one man spoke up. "Good, then let's move on."

Yes, move.

That sounded like a great idea.

She closed the car door.

"Please take me home," Cara told the driver.

• • •

"When is enough going to be enough for you?"

Cara bristled at her brother's tone, and avoided looking at the laptop screen. Skype was a wonderful thing, for the most part, but not today. "Tommas, you don't—"

"I don't *what*, Cara? Know, understand, relate? Which one is it?"

"All of them!"

"I *know* you've lost your job. A job you worked incredibly hard for, and loved with every fiber of your being."

Cara tried not to show how much that comment stung. "I did lose a job I loved but I don't blame that on Gian. He wasn't the person who purposely distributed naked pictures of me, causing my boss to have to consider the ethical and moral ramifications of those images and my personal connections outside of the shelter. Gian didn't *want* that to happen, Tommas. Why would he hurt me like that or send people those photos? They were *his* private photos."

She had—at first—felt as though Gian could have done more to protect the images. She hadn't felt that he had done anything to help get those images out into the world to hurt her.

"Fine, move on from the photos," her brother said with a shake of his head, "because shit, Cara, they're just *one* thing in pile of things."

"Tommas, I didn't call you tonight to fight. I just thought you would like to see how I'm doing a couple of weeks after the accident."

"Accident?" He scoffed. "Say what it was. An *attack*. Something else that was—"

"If you say someone shooting me was Gian's fault, I am hanging up this fucking call."

"Did you do something to provoke someone into shooting you, or am I missing a whole bunch of shit?"

"He didn't pull the trigger, Tommas."

"He doesn't have to, where responsibility is concerned!"

Cara's fingers twitched to close the laptop screen. She didn't want to end the conversation this way with her brother. She knew Tommas was only expressing his concerns in the one way he currently could, and clearly, he was not doing it well.

Then, her brother said quietly, "I only want you to be happy, Cara. Safe, happy, and *loved*. By a man who deserves to love you, and who can keep you safe while making you happy. I'm worried that you're so accustomed to coming second in his life now, that you don't even see that you do."

"Tommas, I love you."

Tommas nodded. "Yeah, I know."

"But you have no idea what you're talking about. On this, you're wrong. You're so wrong, it's sad. And sure, I know you don't have much to go on, but let me make one thing perfectly clear here. Gian puts Marcus and I first much more than anyone realizes, and those who do realize it, don't like it a whole lot. Because he shouldn't do what he does with us—he shouldn't be with us so much, or provide for us as much as he does. He shouldn't love us in public, or give us presence in his family. We're the secrets, Tommas, the dirty words in his life. His bastard son born to a *goomah* woman. He has every single reason to push us aside for his own respect and image, but he doesn't. And he *doesn't care*. We come first, even if it is to his detriment."

Tommas frowned, but said nothing.

"Frankly, I don't think even Gian realizes how often he puts us first to his own detriment. I don't think he cares either way, because this is what is right for him. He's a wonderful man, and I love him. So let's be clear here, okay."

"Okay."

"He's mine. I'm fine. I'm not leaving. Not him, this city, or this life. My son is healthy and happy, *with* his mother and father. I no longer give a shit who thinks what about me, Gian, our situation, or the rest. What I care about, is that I'm happy and my son is, too. That goes for you, too, so learn it fast. I love you but I don't have to like you if you're going to make it hard on me."

For a long while, her brother said nothing.

Cara expected that. She had always been the quiet one. Steadfastly strong, sure, but silent all the same. She didn't speak up unless necessary, and this had just been one of those things she left alone. Not anymore.

"I'm just worried about you," Tommas finally said.

"Don't be, Tommy. I am fine. I am going to keep being fine. It's what I do."

That was that.

Shortly after, Cara hung up the Skype call with her brother. Marcus was fed, fast asleep, and safe in his bed, she reminded herself. She had time to relax, and that was what she had intended to do. Instead, she had gotten into a verbal sparring match with her brother.

"He has a point, you know."

Cara jerked straight in the office chair, glancing at the doorway to find Gian standing there. Solemn in his expression, with his suit jacket from earlier gone, his tie hanging loose over his chest, and his shirt sleeves rolled up, he looked … tired. Like his whole day had gone to hell in a handbasket, and he was just over it.

For the most part, Cara ignored the blood splatters dotting Gian's dress shirt.

"Who has a point?" she asked.

"Your brother."

Her brow furrowed. "You listened to my conversation?"

"Part of it," he admitted. "I came up on the last of it, I didn't mean to and I didn't want to interrupt. You spy on my conversations—don't pretend like you don't."

Fair point.

"And what was Tommas' point that you agree with, exactly?"

"Quite a bit of it, actually. I could do more, be more. I could do better things, be better. A better man. You deserve the kind of man he described, and so does Marcus, and yet, you're both very firmly stuck with me. Bit of a shame, *oui*? I'm sure there's someone out there who could have, and likely would have, made you a much happier woman. How fucking selfish of me to have kept you like I did, to have stolen you like I did, when you could have been someone else's everything, and you only get to be my something to the rest of the world. A fucking *shame*. I'm sorry for that, *mon ange*."

Ouch.

That hurt.

"What did you just say?"

"Nothing," Gian said, waving it off and turning to head out of the office. "Nothing that wasn't true. I'm tired, Cara. I'll see you in bed."

Like fuck he would.

"Gian, don't walk away right now."

He kept going.

"Gian!"

Nothing.

Cara got up out of the chair, and headed after Gian, fuming and confused. She came up behind him as he shrugged off his dress shirt and tie in the hallway and tossed it into the laundry room without a care— bloodstains meant it would all need to be thrown out.

"Gian," Cara said firmly, grabbing his arm and pulling as hard as she could to turn him around to face her. "Repeat what you just said to me."

He stared at her with hard eyes and cold features.

His best defense.

Cara saw right through it.

"Your brother is right about the things he says. Maybe not in all the details, but in theory, he's *right*."

"And didn't you hear what I said to him?"

"I heard you defending me when it's the very last thing you should be doing. I have done very little to be worthy of your loyalty, Cara. It would not be such a stretch to think you would like to have more from me, or this—whatever we are."

"We're us, Gian. And I like *us* perfectly fine."

"You like us. You like being my mistress and being seen as the dirty little secret in my life. You like being treated less than someone else, simply because you don't have my last name. You like having your child be pushed aside because—"

"You've never done any of that, and certainly not to Marcus."

"But others do. And if they haven't yet, they will in the future. Because that's inevitable, love. Don't you understand? He won't always be little, but I will always be married to someone else. As he gets older, as he becomes more present and not just a cute baby in the corner, he will become more of the awkward conversation people need to have, rather than what he is now. You don't deserve that, and neither does he, no matter what you've told yourself to believe otherwise."

"I haven't told myself anything."

"Clearly you have, or we wouldn't be having this conversation."

"*You* clearly know nothing about what goes on inside my head, Gian."

"Cara, I don't want to fight tonight. You asked what I felt was right regarding what your brother said, and I told you. There's no need for you to agree or disagree, or talk for hours on end about it. It's just an opinion."

"It's also the wrong one."

"Cara—"

"It's the wrong one!"

Gian scrubbed his hand down his face, sighing. "Just … let's have this conversation tomorrow. Okay?"

"No. Not okay."

"Well, I'm done for tonight."

With that, Gian turned on his heel and headed down the hallway again. Cara didn't even think before going after him once more. This time, she didn't bother to grab him in an attempt to stop him, but rather, scooted around his side and came up in front of him. She slammed a single palm into his chest with enough force to make her hand sting *and* make him come to a full stop with narrowed eyes.

"We're *not* done," Cara said calmly, "not until I say we are, Gian."

"Come on, *mon ange.*"

"I'm so fucking sorry that *you* have had to tell yourself some kind of shit to justify why you think I'm still here. I'm sorry you must have thought I was going to run at some point, because maybe that's just what you think I do. I'm sorry you don't think I'm a strong enough woman, or good enough, to do this with you, but I am. I have always been, Gian. And do you want to know the one thing I have never needed to know I was that woman?"

"Try me."

"For you to tell me. I don't need you to tell me anything. Not that you love me, or our son. Not that you'll be there, even when being here only digs your holes deeper elsewhere. I don't need you to tell me how you struggle, or that you worry about me, or that your biggest fear is that in thirty years, we're going to be just like your grandfather and his mistress. Locked away in a high-rise penthouse, hiding from the rest of the world on weekends, because we're so wrong and bad and isn't that just a fucking *shame*. Isn't it a fucking shame that you've got a mistress, so nobody talks about it, because I'll be your secret that's not really a secret?"

"I will *never* be that woman," Cara continued, "because you'll never be that man, Gian. I am not the one between us who needs to figure that out. What do you want to do? What do you need me to make you do so that you feel justified in what you think you've done to me? Do you want me to put you on your knees, Gian? Crawl across the floor to me, with your head low and your eyes down because you don't even deserve to look at me. Is that it? Do you want me to make you beg every time you come near me, or apologize again when I let you in close enough to touch me? Do you need to be *forgiven*, is that it?"

Gian's lips flattened into a grim line, but he stayed quiet.

Cara didn't really need him to talk.

"If that is what you're waiting for, Gian, you're going to wait a long damn time," Cara said, never once looking away from his gaze. There, she'd always found his heart and soul. He couldn't hide it staring back at her. "The things I needed to forgive you for, I already did. It's not my responsibility to forgive you for things you manifest all on your own, nor is it my job to tell you I already forgave you for the things you *did* do. I didn't do that for you, I did it for me. Because I love you. I have always loved you. I always will."

She poked him hard in the middle of his naked chest.

"And *that* is the end of the discussion, Gian, because I said so, not you."

"Well," Gian said gruffly, his hand coming up to enclose Cara's finger still poking his chest, "it's certainly the end of *this* discussion. I'm starting to think we need to have an entirely different one altogether, considering your mood."

"And what is that? Because there's nothing else for us to say about it."

He lowered her hand in his own. "There's lots to say, Cara. But you're right, and I'm sorry."

"I'm right?"

"About everything. All of it. Every single word you said is true. It's simply not a discussion I wanted to have because I felt a certain way about it all. Seems you didn't feel the way I thought you would, anyway. Much like with everything else about you and me, but that's fine, too. You're *right*, Cara. You don't owe me a thing, except what you want to give me."

She nodded. "Okay. And this *other* discussion?"

"Well … that's entirely about us, too, *amore*."

"What is it?"

He stepped closer, taking her cheeks in his warm palms and making her look up at him. "Sometimes I do forget how incredible you are, Cara. Not because you're not showing it—you always show it. I just get used to not needing to do everything for you, because you've got it handled. Or not telling you the same things over and over, because you don't need to hear me say them. I forget sometimes how strong, resilient, and amazing you are.

And that is a shame."

"Oh?"

"But I don't forget for one fucking second that you're mine, *mon ange*. I will never, ever forget that."

"You shouldn't," she said, barely above a breath. "I've always been yours, Gian."

"Maybe, but it is one of those things we sometimes need to be reminded about. Kind of like now."

Cara was going to ask what Gian meant, but found she didn't have to as his hands pulled her forward, and his mouth crashed down on hers. Her lips melded with his in a familiar battle—one she hadn't realized she had been missing. His tongue teased the seam of her mouth before she allowed him in to war with her own. There was nothing sweet or innocent about the kiss. Each stroke of his lips flamed a fire that had been dormant in Cara for a long while.

It wasn't Gian's fault on that end. The last time they had been intimate was shortly before Marcus's birth, and after that, it just hadn't been possible. She had passed her six-week waiting period to heal, and her doctor had given the okay to resume those activities, but Cara just ... hadn't thought about it.

Gian didn't give her a reason to. She was tired sometimes, and had other things to focus on. He never pushed, never asked or demanded anything unless *she* brought it up.

And good God, she was suddenly reminded why it was better when Gian demanded anything from her at all. It was better because he only had to speak, or touch her, and her whole body lit up like a fucking firework.

"Yep," Cara mumbled as her back hit the hallway wall. "Definitely missed this."

Gian's hot mouth traveled down over her throat, his hands skimming up under the silk nightie she wore to find her panties and pull them down roughly. "*Get these off right now, Cara.*"

"Jesus, you're impatient."

"You will find out exactly why in less than thirty seconds, I guarantee it."

Oh, she already knew.

Cara could feel just how impatient he was, considering the hard length of his erection was digging into her thigh as he pinned her harder to the wall. "The bedroom is like two doors down, Gian."

"So?"

Up went her silk nightie.

She didn't see where it fell.

"*Gian.*"

His response to her warning was the rattle of his belt buckle before his pants fell down to the floor, and his boxer-briefs followed. He stepped out of the items without even missing a beat or taking his hands off her body.

"The baby is sleeping almost right across the—"

His hot breath pulsed against the skin of her throat, wicked and promising. "You can, can't you?"

"Yes."

"You want this, don't you?" he grunted into her neck, his fingers sliding between her thighs to tease her sex. "You're so wet already."

Cara let out a breathless laugh. "*Yes.*"

"Then shut up and let me fuck you, Cara."

That was that.

Gian's hands found the backs of her thighs, and his fingers dug in deliciously deep, holding her tight. He lifted her legs first, forcing Cara to find a very careful balance between his hard body and the wall at her back. His sinful mouth found hers for that first hard, deep thrust. It took her fucking breath away.

She'd forgotten how her body stretched for him. She'd forgotten the heat that tangled through her blood as she adjusted to his size and how full she always felt with him inside of her pussy. She certainly hadn't expected it to be damn near the same as it had been before, but it *was*, and Jesus, Cara was spun.

He was not easy with her, each flex of his hips coming harder than the last until the pace between them was simply *brutal*. She was sure his fingerprints were going to be permanently embedded into the back of her thighs, but she couldn't find it in herself to care.

"You can do better than that, *Tesoro*," he taunted when she didn't beg loud enough. And then he turned right around and uttered, "Fucking take it, Cara," through clenched teeth, while his hand found its favorite spot. Her throat.

Well, her favorite spot, too.

Cara thought, if it were possible, her body simply didn't have limits where Gian was concerned. She needed his rough hands, his dirty mouth, and the way he choked her to a sweet, blissful finish. She needed it every single time, however she could get it.

Like a damn drug.

Her fingernails raked lines over the backs of his shoulders when that beautiful release finally came flooding through her, hot and heavy. She felt him shudder—from the pain or his own orgasm, she wasn't sure.

But she heard his breath catch against her throat, and his fingers loosened on her throat as they trembled, and she knew then, anyway. His final two thrusts came harder, before his whole body tensed and she felt his release pulse inside her body.

Sweaty, breathless, and content, Cara hummed a pleased, happy sound as tremors worked their way up her spine and the orgasm faded. Gian took a slight bit longer to catch his breath, but that could have just been because he took his time dotting Cara's neck, cheek, and mouth with soft, sweet kisses all over again.

"Careful," he murmured as he pulled from her body and let her down to the floor. "Easy, Cara."

She laughed quietly. "Easy would have been the bed."

"That's no fun."

"It is, too."

Gian kissed her again, firmer that time. "I will give you whatever you want in bed in the morning, I promise."

Cara rubbed her thighs together, acutely aware of the sticky fluids there. "You made a mess."

"*We* did."

"Same difference."

"I should have grabbed a condom," he admitted.

Cara ran her fingers through his hair. "It's all right. I started the pill again, anyway. Though, it won't be effective for another two weeks."

Gian rolled his eyes upward, then glanced down the hall at the baby's closed bedroom door. "Right, the pill. The thing that didn't stop Marcus from making his way into being at all."

She patted his cheek with a wink. "There's other ways, Gian. Besides, Marcus is wonderful, and I don't regret him for a minute."

"I said nothing about regret and I didn't say I wanted to prevent anything, Cara. I *am* a Catholic, remember? Even if I'm not a very fucking good one in almost every other aspect."

Cara's gaze shot up to Gian's, only to find his amusement lighting up his handsome features. "Is that so?"

"We never talked kids, love."

"We just had one."

"Exactly." Gian scooped Cara up into a bridal embrace, walking them toward the bedroom as she snuggled in closer to his warmth and familiar scent. "I want a whole army of kids."

"Wow."

"Boys, preferably."

"You don't really get to pick, Gian."

"A baseball team, or a half of one."

"You're killing me," Cara said, shaking her head.

"Someday, Cara."

She smiled.

Maybe.

SEVENTEEN

It was decided.

The best sight in the morning was Cara on her knees, face buried into a pillow to muffle her sounds, while Gian got a mouthful of her cunt from behind, and stuffed her ass full of his fingers. He loved the way her body trembled with the need for release, and how sweat had slicked up her spine from being teased over and over.

Crazy red hair.

Flushed skin.

Sweet pussy.

Wild eyes met his over her shoulder, when he added a third finger to Cara's ass, and replaced his mouth on her cunt with just the pad of his fingertip massaging her clit. It was the way her hips swayed and her muscles contracted that drove him crazy. She was so fucking tight around him, and he couldn't fucking wait to get his cock feeling that, too. She always begged so well when something was filling her ass.

Yes, the very best.

"You want to come so badly, don't you?" Gian taunted Cara, kissing her lower back between each word.

Her reply came out breathless and high—so very pretty and strained. "You know I do, Gian. *Please.*"

"My greedy girl. So fucking needy. Come, then."

His mouth was back between her thighs in a heartbeat, sucking hard on her clit while his fingers pounded deeper into her ass to stretch her open. She loved that, he knew, though it had been a while. He was going to make sure it wasn't as long between this time and the next time.

Cara's cries turned the sweetest kind of desperate, and then muffled into the pillow as her body tensed all over. Gian chose not to complain about being unable to hear her coming, but only because he got to taste it, instead.

And sweet Jesus, she tasted heavenly when she came.

Like his own personal tart candy.

Gian had just gotten his cock lubed up, had a fistful of Cara's hair wrapped tight around his hand, when familiar soft cries broke through his lustful haze. A baby's cries, he realized. It took Gian far too long to realize it was *his* baby that was crying through the monitor on the nightstand.

Cara laughed when he stiffened above her and let go of her hair. Turning over, she leaned up and kissed him hard on his slack lips—grinning in a know-it-all sort of way. "Sorry, Gian. Raincheck on that for tonight.

Either learn to fuck faster, or stop demanding I be so loud."

"But ... but ..." He looked down at his fully erect, lubed cock that was aching. "But ..."

He *really* needed to fucking come now.

Cara's palm patted him square in the middle of his forehead, as though she were stamping something there with her hand. "Parents call that being cock-blocked. Welcome to the club."

"Cara!" Gian shouted over his shoulder as she headed for the bedroom door. She only shrugged in response, slipping on a nightie and then a robe to fully cover up. "That's not fair at all, *mon ange!*"

"Shower, and take care of it yourself, I guess."

Holy sweet baby Jesus!

"I don't *need* to take care of it myself! Cara, I haven't taken care of myself in a decade, for fuck's sake."

Cara's head popped back in the doorway. "Seems you do, actually. No better time to get reacquainted."

She was *loving* this.

Gian knew he was bested—by a baby *and* his lover, it seemed. He could have waited, of course. Marcus liked to sleep in the mornings after his feedings, and Gian could always drag Cara back to bed and punish her for her smartass remarks, *plus* relieve himself in the process. It sounded like a good idea, except his fucking balls hurt like hell all of the sudden.

And that wasn't good at all.

Gian was a ten-minute kind of morning man. Ten minutes was all he needed to jump in the shower, get dressed, and head out for the day. It was a routine he had perfected over the years. That day, it failed him entirely. It took him thirty minutes just to get through a goddamn shower, and while he got the job done, he hated every fucking second of it.

Cara was right.

He was going to have to learn to keep her quiet, or settle with a faster fucking.

He liked neither of those options.

All dressed and ready for his day—albeit in a slightly shittier mood than he suspected he would have been, had he gotten to be balls deep in Cara before seven AM—Gian headed for the kitchen. His walk slowed as voices filtered down the back hall, and it took him all of three seconds to go from shit mood to *rage*.

"Thank you for letting us up to talk, Miss Rossi."

"Yes, Gian was never so kind, unless we had a warrant," Detective Seeley added with a chuckle.

"I didn't actually let *you* up," Cara replied coolly. "I was told I had guests and allowed entrance without asking for details. Not the same thing. My mistake. Don't think it'll happen again."

"Sure, well—"

"What do you want at seven-thirty in the morning?"

Gian held back from entering the kitchen, instead lingering out of sight in the hallway. There, he could still hear the conversation, but the detectives wouldn't know he was within hearing distance. Shit, he didn't know if they were aware of his presence in the penthouse at all.

"How long have you been living here, again?" Detective Seeley asked.

"I've *owned* the penthouse for a couple of months or so. Why?"

"Curious. Where is Gian this morning?"

Cara said nothing.

The detective chuckled. "You're not sure or he's with his wife?"

Gian stiffened, anger flooding him all over again. Using his wife to annoy, offend, or bother Cara in any way just seemed like a prick move on the man's part.

"Where Gian is can't be any more or less important than whatever the fuck you want," Cara replied sweetly.

"Little ears are listening, Miss Rossi."

"I'm sure my son will hear worse."

"With a mob boss for a father, I would tend to agree."

Another dig.

Cara only laughed. "Right. Moving on. What do you want, or again, you can leave. Mornings are busy with a baby, as I'm sure you know."

"We've gone over some of your interviews and statements with police after the latest attack, and wanted to go through other details with you that you may not have been aware of. Or rather, some suspicions we have that may be of interest to you, where Gian is concerned."

"I'm sure they won't concern me at all," Cara said flippantly, "but you can try."

"Never say never," Seeley replied all too cheerfully. "Shorty before your attack, you found yourself in a bit of an awkward situation, didn't you?"

"I'm not sure what you mean."

"Photos of you were distributed. See, the shelter reported the photos, as the owner assumed you too would be opening an investigation into such a matter."

Gian swore he could feel Cara's tension when she said, "I don't know exactly what kind of legal action I could have taken for those, but I assure you whatever the penalty, it would not have fit the crime or made me feel any better."

"Are you aware that Gian's father-in-law was the person to distribute those photographs?"

No, Cara was not.

Because Gian hadn't told her.

Fuck.

Cara handled the news with grace. "I had not known."

"I suppose you're also unaware that the man is also now dead," Seeley said quieter.

"I did know that but only because his funeral was plastered in the news. Seems to be a big thing in the city lately—organized crime, I mean. I'm not sure why the man's death should matter to me, though."

"You don't think the two are connected?"

"I—"

"You're not that stupid, are you?" the other detective interrupted. "Someone distributes racy, compromising photographs of you that effectively ruins you, and suddenly they show up dead."

"Again," Cara drawled, "I'm not sure why the man's death should matter to me. I wasn't aware he distributed the pictures. I didn't know him at all."

"Seems he knew you."

"Well, his daughter might," Cara replied carefully.

"She was the one who had been given the photographs in the first place," Seeley said as though the information were nothing. "All though, clearly she used the items for a purpose we did not intend, after pulling the files from Gian's phone."

It wasn't nothing to Gian.

It was *everything.*

He hadn't considered Elena having anything to do with the photos of Cara being distributed, because he'd *known* without question she hadn't had his phone. At least, not long enough to get inside the device. He even locked his fucking bedroom door when he was forced to sleep at the mansion.

Cara was quiet for a long while before she said, "You pulled my photos from Gian's phone."

"His first arrest included warrants for electronic devices, and we found some images. He was arrested again after the shooting at the shelter—"

"All charges dropped," Cara interjected with heat in her tone, "and for good reason."

"Nonetheless, he was taken into custody again and the phone was removed from his person. I can't help if a few image files were removed from the device at that time, too."

"That's fucking illegal! How *dare* you?"

Marcus whined at his mother's high shriek.

"It's standard procedure in a case like that for any electronics on a detainee to be searched," the detective said, "which is exactly what happened."

"But not for you to remove images, thank you very much. Not to mention, *my* images. And what business is it of yours—what effect would it have on Gian's previous arrest or the arrest after the shooting—to take my private photos and … why in the hell would you take *my* fucking photos off his phone like that?"

"We had proof he was in a relationship with you, clearly."

"But *why*? What did you need that information for and what good would it do you? It wasn't exactly a goddamn secret. Those images did nothing but hurt me, and other people. That was it—nothing more."

Gian knew exactly why.

He had never considered that it was the detectives who had removed his photos of Cara from his phone. Only because, like Cara, there was no real benefit to doing so for the police. He didn't use his phone to do any real business that would get him in trouble, and so he had never had an issue with handing the device over to cops during his arrests.

Clearly that had been a mistake.

While taking more photos off his phone after the shelter shooting had been … borderline illegal, it wouldn't matter if the detectives never intended to use those images as pieces of evidence they needed to legally obtain. It would only matter to *them* if the images could help them in some way.

Like for someone on the inside of Gian's life.

Someone they could hurt.

Someone they could use.

Perhaps, someone they were already using.

Elena had always liked her tit for tat. She gave something, she expected something back. It was always that way, no matter who she was dealing with.

Gian finally found his rat.

The fucking *cunt*.

"You need to leave," Cara said firmly, bringing Gian from his thoughts. "Now."

"We aren't finished talking quite yet, Miss Rossi. We thought this information might—"

"What, sway my opinion on Gian? You do realize I consented to those photos, I thoroughly enjoyed having my hair pulled, ass spanked, and his cum painted up and down my body in each and every one. I *liked* when he got the camera out to play. What I don't like, is that you assume telling me about his recklessness with the phone, or the way you came about the images, should affect my opinion on him. And as far as his father-in-law, may the man rot in pieces. I bet he got exactly what he deserved, and while I am sure you thought suggesting Gian did that would frighten me, it doesn't bother me a bit. Get out, now."

Gian waited in the hallway until the penthouse was quiet again, except for Cara's soothing hums to the baby in the kitchen. It was as though the meeting hadn't happened at all, but she still looked to him with sad, knowing eyes when he came out of his hiding spot.

He dropped a quick kiss to her forehead, lingering there for as long as he could, and then giving one to his son's head, too.

"I have to head out," he said.

Business like this couldn't wait.

Cara nodded, questioning in her gaze but never letting the words fly out of her mouth. "Okay. I love you, Gian."

He kissed her again. "Always, *mon ange*."

• • •

The Guzzi mansion was much quieter than Gian expected it to be for a weekday. He found there was no doorman waiting to take his coat and keys, as usual, and even the maid was nowhere to be seen. It rubbed him the wrong way, if only because he knew how much Elena liked to be attended. She liked being served as though she were a queen in her big castle. He hadn't minded indulging her nonsense, if it kept her happy and out of his hair.

Clearly, he had overlooked too much about his wife.

He had been stupid.

He should have killed her long ago.

Gian chose not to question the lack of people in the mansion, only because it benefitted him. He didn't need to demand someone get out, and no one would even know he had been there. A clean job was the best kind of job, after all.

It took Gian far too long to find Elena in the mansion, because she wasn't inside at all. He found her sitting outside, with her back turned to him, as she sat on a wicker chair and overlooked the back property. An entire empty bottle of wine rested on its side at her feet, a blanket spilling around her frame in the wicker chair that she was using to cover up with.

"Elena," Gian called quietly, already spinning the silencer into the barrel of his gun.

Easy.

Fast.

Simple.

He didn't even care about clean up, or the trouble that might come his way for this. It just needed to be done. Some things were just better *done*.

"Elena," he said again when his wife didn't respond.

Her shoulders moved slightly, and her head bobbed a bit, but that was all the response his wife gave to the call of her name. *But*, it did mean she could hear him.

"Your father warned me and I should have listened," Gian said. "He told me women like you know exactly what you're doing, even when everything says you don't know at all. You needed a short leash, he said. I thought, *why*. I give her everything she wants because she doesn't want me, so why should I worry about how far she goes? I should have *listened*, Elena."

Unsurprisingly, his wife didn't talk or move.

Gian took another couple steps across the large back deck, closer to her position. "The only thing you ever wanted was to be free, wasn't it? Something I couldn't give you, but by no fault of my own. It was your games—*your* schemes—that got us here, and you thought you could play your way out of them again. Get me locked up for good, maybe. File a divorce then, when it couldn't be contested and it wouldn't matter anyway. You would have it all and the rest wouldn't make a fucking difference."

Still, he got no response.

Elena's arm slipped off the arm of the wicker chair, falling out from beneath the blanket. Maybe it was the ashen tone of her skin, or the slackness in her opened hand, but Gian knew right then that something was very wrong.

He clicked the safety on his gun, and tucked it away, crossing the space between him and his wife in three short strides. He came around the front of the chair, already bending down to grab her by the shoulders.

Elena was conscious, but barely.

Glassy-eyed.

Slack-mouthed.

Discolored lips.

Gian's hands skipped to her face, and he tipped her head up to make her dazed gaze lock on his. Still, her eyes wavered, flickering between whatever she was seeing and whatever was just beyond her reach. She was cold to the touch, but not quite a dead-cold. Her breathing turned shallower with each inhale and no matter how high Gian tipped her head, he couldn't seem to clear her passageways.

"What did you do?" he demanded.

She smiled, chilling and fleeting. "This is even better, you get to be here. It doesn't hurt me at all, but it will for you."

What?

On her lap, two opened prescription bottles lay empty.

Gian's gaze darted back to the ashy face of his wife. "Elena, what did you do?"

"He'd have f-forgiven me for everything," Elena said, her voice barely breaking a whisper, "but not for what I did to you. He wouldn't have forgiven me for hurting you—I had to make you hurt him instead. Don't you see?"

"Who?" Gian demanded, holding her face tighter. "*Who*, Elena? Your father?"

What difference would that make, now?

Gabriel was *dead*.

She shook her head, though it was weak and faint, her eyes glassier than ever. "No."

"Who?"

"And if I can't be happy, Gian, then neither can you. *Neither can you*. I'll take it all away—all of them."

He swore he watched the life drain out of her eyes in that moment—how death crept in around her pupils, and darkened them for good. She almost felt colder in his hands in that moment, if it were possible. Perhaps it should have made him relieved, as his problem was gone, and she had done it to herself, but he only felt empty.

And lost.

Because *who*.

Who had she meant?

The empty prescription bottles clanged to the deck, and Gian broke out of his daze. He picked one up, just to look at it and see what exactly Elena had used to end her life. The strong painkiller was not what caught his attention first—it was the name written on the label, to whom the prescription had actually been prescribed.

Domenic Guzzi.

Two bottles.

Both empty.

Both Dom's.

Gian couldn't move; he couldn't take in air.

His brother wouldn't ...

Couldn't ...

Gian only came out of his stupor when he heard a faint buzzing coming from somewhere beneath the blanket covering Elena's body. He found her phone tucked into her side, and was surprised to find the device unlocked. A quick check confirmed his worst fucking fears.

A constant stream of incoming messages—each getting progressively more panicked and desperate than the last—from Domenic, which had started just an hour before. Several calls, one that was picked up, and the rest had not been. Gian scrolled up through the new messages to find what Elena had started messaging to Dom just an hour before.

He's never going to let me go.

He's got her, anyway.

I'm done.

This is it, Dom.

I love you.

Don't blame yourself.
It was him.
He did this to us.

And to top it off, she had even texted a picture of the empty pill bottles. Her intent had been clear, and even right up until the bitter end, she couldn't help herself.

Elena had to manipulate.

She had to hurt someone.

Elena's final words to Gian made a hell of a lot more sense when Domenic's final text came in. *He'll never be happy, either, not after today.*

Even in her death, Elena was selfish to those who had either cared, loved, or protected her in some way. Gian wasn't surprised at all.

This also wasn't the time for him to wonder about it. Something in his brother's last message told him that he had far more pressing matters to deal with. Unfortunately, it looked like Dom might have a few minutes ahead of him.

It'd been a while since Gian prayed.

It still felt like breathing.

EIGHTEEN

Cara had just set a sleeping Marcus into his wicker moses basket when she heard the familiar ding of the penthouse elevator ringing out in the hallway. She figured it was probably just Gian coming back, considering how long he had already been gone. Setting the wicker basket on the middle of her bed, where the baby was safe, she headed for the attached bathroom, slipping out of her robe as she went.

A hot, nearly-overfilled bubble bath was waiting.

After her morning, she deserved it.

"Cara?"

Shit.

Apparently, the bath was going to have to wait.

She had wrongly assumed the person coming into the penthouse was Gian. It sounded like Domenic. She quickly shrugged her robe back on and left the bedroom, tying the sash securely at her waist as she rounded the first corner leading out of the hallway.

"Cara, are you home?"

The buzzing of her cell phone echoed from the bedroom—she always put the ringer on silent when Marcus was sleeping. Surely, Dom could wait a second.

Cara nearly spun back around to go to the buzzing phone, but it stopped. Then, it started right back up again.

What the fuck?

"Yeah, just give me a second," Cara called back.

"Gian here?"

"No, he had something come up this morning." Cara was one step away from reentering her bedroom when Dom appeared at the end of the hallway. "I'll be right out. Did something happen?"

Dom shrugged. "Nothing you need to worry about."

Her heart stopped for a split second. "But something did?"

He didn't answer. In the bedroom, her phone continued buzzing away. Persistent and wanting her attention, clearly.

"Let me grab my phone," Cara said to Dom, "before it wakes up the baby."

Dom's strange, cold expression didn't change a bit, but he waved her off anyway. Cara didn't think it was entirely odd, considering Gian's brother was one of the few people she hadn't gotten close enough to that she considered him a friend of sorts. The man was always respectful and polite, but he didn't go out of his way to be friendly with her at all.

She hadn't minded. She understood some people—some of Gian's men or family—wouldn't be comfortable with her or her relationship.

Cara turned her back to Dom and headed into the bedroom, only to realize that was probably the biggest mistake of her life. She hadn't even taken a single step inside the room, before Dom was suddenly behind her. For such a big man, Cara barely heard him make a sound.

He had a fistful of her hair and was dragging her to the floor in an instant. The pain that radiated through her scalp and down her spine shot through her nervous system like a thousand needles. Dom didn't seem to mind her first struggle, easily overpowering Cara with his size, forcing her to her back, and then smashing her head into the floor.

Her tears were already starting to form in her pain and confusion. Those emotions were nothing compared to her *fear*. She had done nothing to Dom, nothing to justify his fists raining down on her body, or his mocking laughter as she begged for him to stop.

"Why are you doing this?"

"Don't talk," he snarled.

Why?

What?

While Cara had never felt close to Dom, or even friendly with him, the man above her now was not one she had ever seen before. It was like his entire face had changed, his expression—nearly dead looking—was one of a monster.

It was as though he wasn't seeing *her* at all. It was as though his eyes weren't looking at the mother of his nephew, or a woman who had never spoken badly about him or any of his family. He didn't care who she was, because she was just *something* to deal with.

Something to dispose of.

Her initial shock was quickly overcome by the scream she released. A scream that woke her sleeping baby.

Marcus's wail filled the bedroom. Cara's heart dropped into her stomach as Dom's next hit hesitated, and he glanced up at the bed, like he was just realizing then that the baby was in the room, too. And like with her, he didn't look at the small wicker basket with the familiarity of a man looking at something he *should* have cared for, on some level.

Cara's panic ran into overdrive just like that. She had been far too shocked and unsure before to really react, though she had tried stupidly to get out of the way of the slaps and punches. Now, with a single look at a man who she thought might kill her son for a reason she didn't understand, desperation really kicked in.

It kicked in fucking *hard*.

The taste of blood bloomed in her mouth, and pain radiated from her face to her chest, but Cara didn't care about any of it. All she heard was her crying son, and the racing beat of her heart. Her struggle under the weight of Dom increased and she struck out at him. All she had to fight with was her hands, her fingernails. But she used them the best she could, punching Dom as hard as she could and feeling her knuckles crack from the impact of busting his mouth. Her fingernails dug deep into his face, scoring lines from his eyes to his lips as she bucked and kicked out her legs in an attempt to gain some kind of traction.

"Don't fucking fight," she heard him snarl above her.

Cara didn't listen.

She wasn't sure how she possibly could.

"He couldn't just *let her be*," Dom howled as his hands enclosed Cara's throat. He squeezed hard, taking away her air and making her lungs burn. "He'd never let her be happy, not like *he* wanted to be. Fuck him, and fuck you."

Blood rushed Cara's ears. Her vision blurred. Her lips tingled with numbness, like the rest of her extremities. She swore she felt her heart slow.

She wasn't sure how it was possible, but it was as though the world slowed down all around her in those moments. It made her far more painfully aware of the fact she was about to lose her life, and there was nothing she could do about it.

"Please don't hurt the baby," Cara managed to get out with what last bit of breath she had left. "Please—"

"Shut the fuck up! Shut up, shut up, *shut up!*"

Somewhere in the back of Cara's hazy consciousness, she was sure that she heard a ding echo through the penthouse. Not that it mattered, because Cara didn't even have the energy to keep her eyes open any longer, never mind pick up her fists to keep fighting.

Please don't hurt my Marcus.

Please don't hurt my baby.

I'm sorry for whatever I did, but don't hurt him.

She wasn't sure if she said those words out loud, but she thought them. Her mind screamed them until her throat felt raw and bloody, but that could have just been from the choking, too.

The happiest memory Cara could think of in that moment was waking up in the hospital the first night after Marcus was born, to find Gian singing a French lullaby to their son. She didn't know he could sing at all, and he hadn't noticed her awake. It was the sweetest sight—proof in an instant that no matter what, he was going to love his child.

And perhaps if one of them could make it out of this alive, she would want it to be Marcus.

He would always have his father.

Crack.

The loud sound accompanied a sudden intake of air into Cara's lungs.

401

Her eyes widened at the absolute agony it caused for her to breathe in, but all she saw above her was the falling form of Dom coming at her. She couldn't even find the strength to move out of the damn way.

"Shit, Cara, just a second, baby. I got you."

That voice … it was so beautifully, wonderfully familiar.

She barely moved at all as Dom's dead weight was shoved off her. She clutched at her throat, taking in gulps of air. It didn't really help.

"Look at me," she heard the man demand. "Let me see your eyes. Don't take in such big breaths."

She couldn't focus on the blurry image above her, her pupils struggling to form the shapes it needed. Careful hands touched her face, and that hurt, too.

"Christ, *mon ange*, look at your face. Try to calm down and focus."

Cara did, but it didn't help. "My baby … get my baby, please."

"Shh. Marcus is fine, just angry."

"*Get my baby!*"

"Okay, okay."

In the time it took for Cara to smell the sweet scent of her child and have him in her weak arms, her vision had cleared enough for her to see again.

Gian.

He sat across from her, his gaze wary, and his hands outstretched to take her into his embrace when she was ready to move. She only shook her head, not wanting anything to touch her or her child in that moment. He checked her over from afar as she soothed Marcus in a daze.

"Don't look at it," Gian said when Cara glanced to the side at Dom's body.

The back of his head was blown apart.

Blood was pooling across her bedroom floor.

"I don't know what just happened," Cara whispered.

"He was going to take you away from me."

"But why?"

"Because he thought I took Elena," Gian said.

Cara didn't entirely understand.

She didn't think it was all that important.

Once again, the familiar ding of the elevator rang through the penthouse. Cara's frantic gaze darted to Gian, but he looked a hell of a lot calmer about an unknown *someone* coming into their place than she did.

"Calm down, it's probably just—"

"Boss!"

"Stephan," Gian finished with a sigh.

"*Boss!*"

"In the fucking bedroom, Stephan." Gian held his arms out to Cara once more. "I know you're scared and hurting, but I would really like to hold you right now, *mon ange*. Please."

Her skittish nod sent him moving fast across the floor. She felt better the second she didn't feel anything but him. His gentle fingers skimmed over her face, and through the tangles of her hair. He looked at the marks on her neck, muttered about a busted vessel in her eye, and mentioned a doctor that would come in and look her and the baby over once they had the mess cleaned up.

Cara didn't care, as long as Marcus was still happy in her arms and Gian was there.

"Holy shit," Stephan said from the doorway. "How did you make it here before me? I was closer by fifteen minutes, at least."

Gian shrugged, but didn't let go of Cara. "I drive fast."

"Chris always said you drove like a bat out of hell, boss."

"He understated it," Gian said deadpan. "This needs to go away, Stephan. This mess—the body. It needs to be gone, it can't be found."

Cara chose not to ask about that, either.

"I can do that," Stephan answered.

That was that.

• • •

Cara found Gian sitting on the middle of their bedroom floor, his suit jacket discarded, and his tie hanging loosely around his neck. He sat in the same spot Domenic had damn near killed her, and then subsequently lost his own life. Gian fiddled with his finger, and as Cara came closer, she realized he was spinning the wedding band around and around the digit. She rarely saw him wear the piece of jewelry—he said he didn't like it, and only put it on when necessary.

She supposed today would have been one of those necessary days.

Elena's funeral.

The last two weeks had been especially trying for Gian, she knew. Perhaps had it been any other man he'd killed, and not his brother, the heavy weight he carried around wouldn't be so present and obvious. She had gone along with him when he chose to tell his mother and father that Domenic would not be coming home ever again. Gian hadn't needed to do that, because as far as Cara knew, by Gian's request, Stephan had taken care of the body so that it wouldn't be found. As sad as it would have been for Gian's parents to realize something had happened and not have answers, Gian was not required to give one.

Yet, he had.

And the *sound*.

Oh, God.

The sound of Celeste Guzzi's heartache still resounded in Cara's mind. It was as though the woman's whole world had just fallen apart entirely. It had been a tug of war in the mother's eyes as she listened to Gian explain and apologize. Cara did not think she was as good of a woman as Celeste seemed to be in the moments that followed. A woman who faced the reasons *why*, and forgave all the same. A woman who loved a murdered child, and the child who had done the killing.

Gian's father, on the other hand, had not been so understanding. *Coward. Fool. Your fault. You did this. And for what, Gian, for a whore?*

Cara would never forget those words.

She suspected that neither would Gian.

"Gian?" Cara asked quietly.

He didn't look up at her, but his fidgeting stopped. "Hey, *mon ange*."

"I didn't see where you went when you came in the penthouse."

"I needed a second."

"For what?"

Gian let out a heavy breath. "To think. Alone, for a while."

"I can let you—"

"No, don't go." He caught her wrist in a snug grip, and tugged her down. She sat opposite to him on the floor as his ring spinning started up again. "Last time to take it off."

Gian said that with a soft smile and a shrug.

"Then why haven't you?"

"A part of me thinks it's not real. As much as I hate this ring, I don't hate what it means, Cara. I just hated who it tied me to and how it chained me. It felt like it was choking me every time I had to put it on. I'm worried, that's all."

"About what, Gian?"

"That maybe the way this one has always felt will taint the way the next one feels."

Oh.

"We don't need to be worrying about that right now," Cara whispered, reaching out to stroke Gian's tense lines away on his face. "You know that, right?"

"I'm a boss. A boss needs—"

"To be happy. To take some time. To manage a family and his organization. To be a dad. To be my lover. To be a son. Have you ever taken the time *just to be*, Gian?"

"I don't have that kind of time, Cara, not in my position."

"And who the fuck is going to tell you what you should and shouldn't do for you at the moment, Gian? Who is going to tell you *anything*? You got one thing right—you're the boss, not anyone else."

It took Gian nearly an entire silent minute before he said, "But I do want to marry you. I have wanted to marry you since the moment I knew I loved you, *mon ange*."

"And someday, you can ask. Today doesn't have to be that day and neither does tomorrow."

He laughed. "That's quite a way to leave me hanging."

"You have to ask someday, Gian, that's all."

Gian's gaze dropped. "I found out some things today—coroner's report came in, and I went down after the funeral to go over it."

"All right."

"Elena was pregnant, maybe with Dom's kid, I'm not sure. I suspect it was. They had some tissue to test against my DNA, if I wanted—they suspect me of being the father. Not possible, but I didn't correct them. They don't need it on record that I wasn't the father of the child because it'll just give them something to look into, so I didn't ask for testing to be done. As it was, I deleted the messages, calls, and Dom's contact off her phone before I left the mansion that day. I took the pill bottles with his name on it. I knew I was going to kill him, and I was still trying to protect him. I did it again today. I realized I wasn't even mad at Dom for what he did with her, or for falling into her trap. I was him once, too. I'm pissed because of what came of it, because of what he did, but not for her. I miss my brother, but not the thing she turned him into."

"Anything else in the report?"

Gian shrugged. "Toxicology said there was a significant amount of prescription opiate use going back at least two years. It explained why they found bottles of painkillers with her name on it, and the ones I found and took with Dom's name on them. Doctor shopping, likely. She hid that well."

"Addicts sometimes do. High-functioning ones, anyway."

"She was at least four months along in the pregnancy, Cara, so she had to know."

Cara sighed. "I would think so."

"That day I found her, I thought she was selfish," he admitted, "because of what she did to Dom, something that was only meant to hurt me. She couldn't help herself, clearly, she had to manipulate and play her games even at the end."

"So?"

"So, then I learn she's pregnant, too, and it just verified those thoughts. I don't feel so awful for thinking them, now. I don't feel as bad for what she did, because I don't think it was ever about me. It was always about her, that's just who she was."

"It's done now, Gian," Cara said.

He nodded. "I was wrong when I told you freedom was always weightless. Do you remember that?"

"Of course. I remember everything you've ever told me."

"Sometimes freedom feels heavy, too. Like when you don't know what to do with it."

Cara pushed up from her backside to rest on her knees. She leaned forward and kissed Gian softly on his mouth, feeling his lips grow into a sensual smile the longer she held him there. "You've got all the time in the world to figure this out, Gian."

"With you."

"With me," she echoed.

"Because I don't care much about the rest," he said, holding her gaze, "as long as you're going to be there with me, Cara."

"I'm always going to be here."

Where could she possibly go?

Life and love had entangled her heart and soul with Gian Guzzi.

He was hers.

She wasn't going anywhere.

"He was wrong. All those years, what he kept repeating to me; he was wrong."

"Who?" Cara asked.

"My grandfather. Duty. Legacy. And only then, love. Always in that order. That's what he told me but he was wrong. At least for me. He used to say that if a man failed at his duty, his legacy would be nameless, and his love, hopeless. But that only works if a man loves his duty more than anything else in his life and I never did. I love you far more—I love my son far more. I would have no legacy without love, and then what would be the point of my duty at the end of it all? There would be no point, I suppose. I would have nothing worthy to pass on, nothing to watch grow. Or worse, I would have no one to pass it on to, no one to give all of my legacy. Yet, I do, and it was only because I refused to put duty first. I'm not sure if that counts as failing, or not."

"Oh, Gian."

"Yeah, I know." Gian slipped the wedding band off his finger one last time, and handed it up as though it was an offering for her to take. "A gift I didn't think I was going to be able to give you."

Cara pinched the tiny piece of jewelry between her fingers, staring at it for a long while before she said, "One woman to one man, Gian."

"For the rest of my fucking life, Cara. I promise."

EPILOGUE

"Marcus!" Gian whispered loudly down the hall.

Nothing answered him back.

"Marcus, you better not be waking up your brothers, you little monster."

Or his mother …

Marcus could be a handful for a nearly two-year-old child. Gian turned his back on his oldest son for two seconds, and the kid was gone. Like fucking lightning.

The further down the hall Gian got, the quieter he whispered for his son to come out of his hiding spot. "Marcus, Daddy has one of your cookies."

Muffled behind the twins' nursery door, Gian heard the sounds of Marcus making car noises. He quickly opened the door to find his boy playing on the floor between the two bassinets, his favorite toy car in hand. Marcus didn't even look up at his father, instead continuing to play as though he hadn't done anything wrong. Thankfully, it seemed the plush carpet was mostly muting the noise of the toy car.

"Marcus," Gian murmured, carefully sidestepping a particular spot on the floor that creaked loud enough to wake the devil. "You know not to come into your baby brothers' room when they're napping. Come to Daddy, please."

The boy rolled over to his back, and smiled up at Gian.

"Hi, Daddy," Marcus said, barely above a whisper.

Serene.

Innocent.

Sweet as could be.

Terrible.

Good God, the boy was *terrible*. He knew exactly how to wrap his mother or father right around his tiny little finger with nothing more than a smile and twinkling brown eyes. Gian fully expected that out of his three children—whether or not more kids came in the future was up to Cara—Marcus was going to be the one Gian had to watch out for.

"Let me check on your brothers, and then we're going," Gian told the still-smiling toddler.

Gian leaned over the wicker bassinets, his gaze drifting over the swaddled, sleeping twin two-month old boys. Even small, brand new, and beautiful, he could see his features reflected in the babies. The shape of their noses, their dark hair, and the curve of their lips. Marcus had been

407

perfect, too, but Gian had forgotten how strange and wonderful it felt to simply stare at his children and *feel*.

When they slept, when they were quiet, and when they couldn't possibly know he was watching them … it was amazing. *They* were amazing.

And they had come from *him*.

Corrado preferred his thumb to a soother.

Christopher could only be soothed on the breast.

Gian vividly recalled the moment Cara had slid a positive pregnancy test into his hand with one of her sly smiles. He had never guessed that one baby would actually be *two*. Identical twins—boys, *again*.

Suddenly, their little family had become very big in a short amount of time.

He barely blinked, and he had three children. Three boys to raise. Three pieces of him to love. Others might have been scared at the changes in their life, but Gian was not one of those people. He had wanted a family of his own for longer than he cared to remember, but he had settled on the idea that he might not see those wishes through.

Yet, there he was, a father.

And there his babies were, all his.

"Daddy."

Little Marcus pushed up from the floor and tugged on his father's pant legs. Quickly, to keep him quiet and prevent him from waking up his baby brothers *and* mother, Gian scooped Marcus into his arms. The toddler peered into the wicker bassinets, curiosity lighting up his gaze.

For the most part, Marcus had no interest in his brothers. They were still too new, Gian thought. They didn't play like he did, they cried when Marcus wanted quiet time, and they took up a lot of his mother and father's attention.

He was a good big brother, though.

Or he tried to be.

That was all Gian asked of his oldest boy.

"Mook," Marcus said, clearly done with looking at his brothers. He patted his father on the cheek with a slightly wet hand. Likely drool. Gian ignored the ickiness of it. "Mook, Daddy."

"Yeah, we'll get you some milk, *bambino*."

It was better Gian did leave the nursery, anyway, as the twins hadn't been down for very long, and Cara had only fallen asleep in the next room shortly after. If he woke them up, but especially Christopher, then Cara would have to get up, too. She needed her rest; she deserved to sleep.

She had wanted a shower while she had the chance to take one, but shit, Gian didn't even think she was able to do that before she hit the bed. Out like a light.

Motherhood was tiring.

Tandem breastfeeding twins was exhausting.

Cara barely breathed a complaint.

Gian had always thought his lover was amazing, because how could he not think that when she had never proved him otherwise? Watching her navigate their twins simply reminded him of just how truly amazing she was. For him *and* their children.

Someday, he was going to be the luckiest man in the world—more so than he already was—and he would be able to tell their sons why they too were so lucky. Because they had a mother like Cara, who had loved them and given them every part of her that was good and beautiful from the moment she knew they existed.

Gian was just a sinner in nice clothes.

Cara was the angel.

Marcus hugged tighter to his father as Gian closed the nursery door as quietly as he possibly could. Downstairs in the kitchen, he found his mother wiping down the countertops. The room smelled like Lysol, and the dishwasher was running.

"Ma," Gian said, putting Marcus down to the clean floor. "You don't have to come over here to clean all the damn time."

"Nonsense," Celeste replied blithely. "This is how we *help*."

Their house wasn't dirty, anyway. They had a three-day-a-week maid. Cara was a bit anal on cleaning, too, and Gian picked up after himself and Marcus. Apparently, just the two of them made more messes than the twins.

That was a complete exaggeration …

Gian smelled the air as Marcus toddled toward the fridge, still voicing his desire for milk. Repeatedly. "And you're cooking something, too."

"A casserole. Cara doesn't need to be cooking all the time with the new babies."

"I *do* help, Ma."

Celeste eyed him over her shoulder, smiling slightly. "I know you do. You're a good man in that way, Gian. Of course you are, I raised you, silly boy. But other than your maid—who, by the way, needs a lesson on dusting higher than eye-level—who is here helping you and Cara?"

No one.

Gian had wanted to hire a nanny to help Cara, especially when he had to go into the city for most of the day, and didn't get back until late. Cara would hear *none* of it. A nanny was not going to raise their children, and if Gian brought one home, he wouldn't like what happened after. Or, that's what Cara told him. He chose not to test the theory out.

"We appreciate it."

Celeste's smile grew wider. "That's all I want to hear."

He wished it was that simple, though.

Unfortunately, his father was not of the same mindset that his mother was. Frederic and Gian had not quite made amends for the choices that had needed to be made years ago. His father had yet to meet the twins, and he hadn't even seen Marcus since the boy's last birthday. Gian suspected when Frederic did come to see them, it would not be when his only living son was in the house, too.

Gian wanted to feel guilt for his actions that pushed his father away, but he couldn't.

Had he made a different choice …

Had he been just a few minutes later …

"Mook, Daddy!"

Gian looked to Marcus. The toddler pointed firmly at the fridge, wanting what he wanted, and he didn't want to wait one more minute. His oldest son was like his father in that way.

Had Gian second guessed himself back then, he would not have what he had now.

Gian didn't regret any of it at all.

He quickly got his boy's drink set up in a sippy cup, and set Marcus into his high chair so he could watch one of his favorite cartoons. Satisfied that his boy and his mother were thoroughly distracted, Gian headed back upstairs.

He should let Cara sleep.

He *should* …

Gian had other plans. Now that his twins were born, he could finally get Cara down the aisle, as she had promised him all those months ago. The problem was, he had been overthinking this for too long. When to ask, how to ask, and all of that nonsense.

He realized one morning, while Marcus cuddled into his chest, and Cara fed the twins, that it was all rather obvious. Their best moments, and their best conversations, always happened in bed. He didn't know *why,* but it was true.

Gian didn't think this would be any different.

At some point, Gian stopped caring about what others thought—and their fucking opinions—regarding his unmarried state, his children born out of wedlock, and how it made him appear as a boss to other families.

Fuck those families.

Gian was too busy raising his own family to play into other people's politics. Besides, his ability to run a criminal organization was only dependent on his capability to keep control of the men, *not* which woman wore a ring and had his last name.

Although, he *was* working on that, too.

Just not to please anyone else but himself.

And Cara.

Slipping into their master bedroom, Gian found his wife was still sleeping happily. On the bedside table, the baby monitor lit up with the rhythmic sound of the twins' breaths.

Seeing Cara curled into the blankets on his side of the bed, holding tight to one of his pillows, made Gian pause. Instead of waking her up like he had planned, he sat down in one of the rockers in the corner, and simply watched his lover.

Marcus was fine with his grandmother.

The twins were okay.

He had time.

They so rarely had time lately.

As he watched Cara, her dreams flickering behind her closed lids, Gian found his peace. Too often, his days and duties and stresses got away with him, and he forgot about the important pieces in his life that brought him happiness. Beautiful things like Cara.

Gian hadn't realized it, but he'd pulled the small velvet box from his slacks pocket, and was flicking the lid open and closed. Why he was fidgeting, he wasn't sure. He wasn't nervous, but *anxious*.

The two-carat ruby, set atop a crown of diamonds on a white-gold band, rested inside the box, nestled amongst a velvet bed. He thought, when he had found the piece, that it fit Cara better than any other ring could. Certainly, better than normal diamonds, or something else of equal flashy appeal.

Red, like her hair and her lips.

Red, like the color of her passion and her love.

Red, like the hurricane they were together and apart.

Red was the color of all extremes, both good and bad. It was the color best described by the strongest human emotions—love and anger. Red was the color of blood, of a man's heart, and he thought if it were possible to see inside his soul, it would be a crimson shade, too.

Just like Cara and her love and soul.

A ruby was perfect.

He slipped it back into his pocket for the time being.

"Gian?"

At the sound of Cara's sleepy call of his name, Gian was up off the chair and crossing the room. He slipped into bed with Cara easily, his arms snaking around her body to pull her in close. There, he could hold her still, feel her warmth, and hide away from the world for a short time.

"Afternoon," he murmured into her hair. "Chris and Corrado are still asleep, so you can rest some more, if you need to."

Cara sighed. "I swear, I have an internal alarm now. I wake up *before* the twins do, in preparation for them."

Gian kissed the top of her head. "That might be very true."

"There's no 'might be' about it, Gian. The boobs know."

His laughter rocked them both in the bed. Cara's lips curved into a sweet smile against the column of his throat. "They do have a job to do, now."

"Apparently." Cara tipped her head back so she could look up at him, her wild red curls splaying over the pillow. "Gian?"

"Hmm?"

"Will you marry me?"

He stiffened in the bed, his gaze darting down to meet hers. "You couldn't even let me ask, could you?"

Cara shrugged, her sly smile teasing him. "I saw you looking at the ring. I figured … well, I should save you the trouble."

"You're supposed to let me ask, Cara. I've waited a long time for this."

"It *is* a beautiful ring."

"*Cara.*"

"Ask," she whispered before pressing a quick kiss to his lips.

Gian let his fingertips dance over Cara's side, tickling her. Her giggles rang out at the same time a quiet set of matching, perfectly-timed cries started from the baby monitor.

"Shit," he muttered.

Cara winked as she pushed up from the bed. "I may be queen of the house, but I still answer to the little ones. Fun is over. The princes call, Gian."

And they would keep calling, he knew.

Marcus, too.

Plus, every other person that interrupted their daily life time and time again.

Gian grabbed Cara's wrist at the last second, stopping her from climbing off the bed. He could deal with getting the ring on her at another time. He only needed to *ask*.

"Marry me, Cara," Gian said. "Please, marry me?"

Cara crawled back over the bed, kissed him hard once, and replied, "Do you expect any other answer but yes?"

"Not really, but I'm worried that if I don't ask *right now*, I will never get the chance to ask. So please, Cara, will you let me love you like this, too? I'm already happy, whole, and lucky because of you, but will you marry me, too?"

"Yes, Gian."

He pulled her back for another lingering kiss, and then swatted her ass as she clamored off the bed and headed for the nursery. It wasn't long before he was following after her, too, scooping one of the two twins from their beds to help Cara in whatever way he could. He headed for the changing table with a slightly happier Corrado, while Cara sat down into one of her rocking chairs to feed the less than pleased Christopher.

Less than a minute after the twins had woken up, a loud, chocolate-stained Marcus made his way into the room, too. He made a beeline for his mother.

Their life was busy and messy. Time was already a rare commodity. He got his yes, though. That was all that mattered.

Time could be made.

He figured that was a lesson worth learning early in their family; time could always be made.

• • •

Seventeen Years Later

Gian stared up at one of the many paintings that hung in his home. He had far more expensive pieces than this particular one; art was a good way to hide vast wealth in material things that could be easily liquidated, after all.

But this painting?

This one he could never sell.

To him, it was priceless.

Sitting on a gold chair that looked almost like a throne, in the middle of a forest that was just beginning to change to autumn, the woman stared straight ahead, as though she owned the whole world. She seemed unaware of the fact time had stopped around her—the artist catching colorful leaves as they fell, and a bird looking down from one of the trees behind her. Blue eyes, red hair. Dressed in a royal purple, knee-length gown with the heels to match.

And damn, didn't she look good acting a Queen.

Then again, Cara always looked amazing.

Surrounding their mother in the portrait were her boys—five of them. Gian had commissioned the piece when their last boys were only nine. Those same boys were fourteen now, and he still looked at the painting every single day.

Nearly nineteen-year-old Marcus shuffled past his father in the hallway with a cigarette tucked up behind his ear, a sly smile as he glanced down at whatever was on his phone, and swinging a set of Mercedes keys in his hand all the while. Gian let his oldest son pass him by, but only because this was nothing abnormal for Marcus.

Or any of their boys, really.

Gian was not the most important person in the room, not when his children were just coming home after being gone for days, or even a few hours to school. Marcus no longer lived with them—he hadn't since he turned eighteen—but he knew better than to stay away from the Guzzi home for too long. Three days, four at the max, was enough.

Then, Cara started to miss her son.

Marcus didn't like those phone calls from his father when Cara started complaining. To be fair, Gian didn't like her complaining.

Gian headed after his son, ready to eat.

No, Marcus didn't greet his father first. He moved across the dining room floor quickly, dropped his phone into his pocket, and then bent down to kiss his mother's waiting cheek. She sat at the head of the table—a spot that *should* have been reserved for Gian only.

It wasn't his spot to have.

It had never been.

It was Cara's spot in their home.

Head of the house.

She always had the floor.

The only Queen of his family.

Gian made sure not a single fucking soul ever forgot it, either. Including their *five* sons.

To be a Guzzi *principe*, those boys were never allowed to see their mother as anything *but* the queen that had birthed them. They worshipped Cara, the ground she walked on, and the very air that came out of her body. In their eyes, their mother did no wrong. Each one of their sons would defend their mother to the fucking death, and they wouldn't think twice about it. They didn't let anybody say a bad word about her, not without some kind of apology that usually included blood.

When they walked into the house, Cara was who they looked for. Cara was who they greeted first in every situation—their father second. Cara was served before them, him, and guests alike. She never had to ask a second time for anything, not when she had five sets of ears listening the first damn time. She wanted for *nothing* in their home.

His sons' greatest fears?

Failing their mom.

They didn't know it, but they could never fail Cara. She loved them too much to see their faults. Gian saw their flaws, occasionally, because he was their father and he had a different role to play, at times, with his boys. But no matter what, he was damn proud of his sons.

Gian liked to think he had a big hand in how his sons treated, loved, and respected their mother. Fact was, his boys just loved Cara. And all he needed to do was occasionally remind them *why* as they'd grown up. They did the rest themselves, honestly.

"Hey, Ma."

Cara preened up at her oldest son, happy as could be. "How was your week?"

"Busy."

"Not too busy, though," his wife said, shooting Gian a look.

Marcus shrugged. "It's good, Ma. I like being busy. Keeps me out of trouble."

Cara pursed her lips. "Mmhmm. I'm sure. Sit, your brothers are almost home from school."

She wasn't wrong.

Gian had only taken his seat at the other end of the table when four pairs of footsteps echoed down the main hall. Two sets were closer than the others. Loud, raucous laughter followed his four other boys. Nearly seventeen-year-old Christopher and Corrado moved through the dining room first, going straight for their mother. Seniors in high school, the two boys were often more different than they were alike. Which was strange, considering they were identical twins. One was more daring, the other reserved. One was louder, the other quiet.

Perhaps it was just how his first set of twin boys fed off one another. One helped the other to stay calm, the other pushed his brother to take risks.

Gian wasn't entirely sure.

He let his boys figure out this life thing all on their own.

"So, wait, she tried to—" Fourteen-year old Beni—short for Benito—quieted when he realized the entire dining room was looking in his direction. He shrugged off the dirty look his twin brother—Benedetto—gave him, especially considering Cara was now interested in whatever she had heard.

"You're an ass," Bene grumbled. "Told you to drop it."

"She?" Cara asked quietly. "Who is this *she*, Bene?"

"Ah, Ma. It's nothing."

Bene—said with an 'ay' sound at the end—and Beni—said with a hard "e" sound—were the complete opposite of their older twin brothers. Where Chris and Corrado made a great effort to be different from one another, Bene and Beni did not.

From a young age, the younger twins had stuck to one another like glue. They spoke alike, dressed similar, and rarely allowed people close enough to understand their strange bonds. Gian could bring forth a dozen memories of his youngest twins having conversations with one another in a babbling language as babies and toddlers that no one could understand. Or how one would *always* know the other was sick or hurt before anyone else did. It took Cara and Gian years—until the twins could speak properly and communicate—to understand why one would wake up in the middle of the night in a terror, only to figure out the next morning, the other twin was sick with some bug or other.

Cara had quietly mentioned once that she had shared a similar—albeit less intense—kind of bond with her dead twin. It scared the shit out of

Gian, not *because* his boys shared something so strange and wonderful, but because *what if.* Cara had never thought her twin would be taken away, and he didn't want to consider that might happen to one of his boys, too.

Because what if it did?

He did not think Bene or Beni were like their mother. He did not believe one could survive without the other, not like they currently were. They were too close, too dependent, and their lives were too intertwined. Cara told Gian all the time not to think about it. Live and let live, she would tell him. Love and let love.

Some thought the boys were a little odd or strange, but Gian didn't. Then again, he had watched his boys grow from the day they were taken from their mother's body and put into his arms. Of course, he didn't find anything odd or strange about them.

There were some who could not tell the two apart, although their parents had never had that trouble.

Gian would *never* forget Cara's tired laugh when the ultrasound technician very quietly informed them that their pregnancy was once again a multiple. Not one baby, but two, and identical.

Cara had turned to him and muttered, "You got your baseball team, Gian."

They hadn't even known the genders.

Cara always seemed to know.

She also got her tubes tied after that pregnancy.

Cara smiled, took her kisses from her youngest boys, and waved them off to their respective seats. "I will be asking about this *she* later, Bene."

Gian chuckled, his attention going to the maid as food was brought in.

"It's just some girl that he—"

"Beni, shut up," Bene barked, tossing a piece of garlic bread and hitting his twin straight in the forehead.

Beni answered back by throwing a handful of croutons, peppering his twin.

Chris and Corrado laughed, already stuffing their faces, despite grace not having been said. Marcus, on the other hand, rolled his eyes like it was any other day. The only singleton Guzzi brother, with no twin to share, Gian sometimes thought Marcus felt left out in times like these. He certainly couldn't have grown up lonely with so many siblings, but did he sometimes wonder why *he* had been the only singleton?

Gian didn't wonder at all.

Marcus was still a *principe* working his way into being a king, sometimes stumbling a bit on his way to the top. He never could have shared that kind of spotlight with someone else. He was too focused, too driven, and way too goddamn competitive.

But that was good, too.

Gian thought to correct his sons before they got out of hand, but he found himself distracted by the amused, soft smile Cara shot across the table at him. He couldn't very well correct his boys when their mother enjoyed their antics.

Head of the house.

She always had the floor.

Queen of his family.

Sitting right where she belonged.

Always.

ABOUT THE AUTHOR

Bethany-Kris is a Canadian author, lover of much, and mother to four sons, two cats, and three dogs. A small town in Eastern Canada where she was born and raised is where she has always called home. With her boys under her feet, a snuggling cat, barking dogs, and a spouse calling over his shoulder, she is nearly always writing something ... when she can find the time.

Find Bethany-Kris at:
Her website www.bethanykris.com,
or on Facebook at www.facebook.com/bethanykriswrites,
on her blog at www.bethanykris.blogspot.ca,
or on Twitter - @BethanyKris.

Sign up to Bethany-Kris's New Release Newsletter here:
http://eepurl.com/bf9lzD

www.ingramcontent.com/pod-product-compliance
Lightning Source LLC
Chambersburg PA
CBHW072020020726
47501CB00006B/1878